While You Were Reading

Ali Berg and Michelle Kalus have been best friends for life and share a burning passion for books and writing. Together they began Books on the Rail in Melbourne and their network is now Australia-wide. Ali is Creative Director and Co-founder of Hedgehog Agency, Melbourne, and Michelle is a primary school teacher. *While You Were Reading* is their second novel.

Visit www.aliandmichelle.com and
www.booksontherail.com

By the same authors
The Book Ninja

While You Were Reading

ALI BERG & MICHELLE KALUS

SIMON &
SCHUSTER

London · New York · Sydney · Toronto · New Delhi

First published in Australia by
Simon and Schuster (Australia) Pty Limited in 2019

First published in Great Britain by Simon & Schuster UK Ltd, 2019

This paperback edition published 2020

1 3 5 7 9 10 8 6 4 2

Simon & Schuster UK Ltd
1st Floor
222 Gray's Inn Road
London WC1X 8HB

Simon & Schuster Australia, Sydney

Simon & Schuster India, New Delhi

www.simonandschuster.co.uk
www.simonandschuster.com.au
www.simonandschuster.co.in

A CIP catalogue record for this book is available from the British Library

Paperback ISBN: 978-1-4711-7800-9
eBook ISBN: 978-1-4711-7801-6

Printed and bound by CPI Group (UK) Ltd, Croydon, CR0 4YY

To all the teachers who helped ignite our

love of reading and writing, and to book

lovers everywhere

'If one cannot enjoy reading a book over and over again, there is no use in reading it at all.'

— Oscar Wilde

1

Bea Babbage would have killed to be any of the ladies sitting neatly in a row in front of her. Eliza Doolittle, Elizabeth Bennet, Rachel Chu, Nancy Drew, Aibileen Clark. Each of these women lived boldly between the pages of the books nestled in the towering oak bookshelves she had come to know so well. Bea still remembered the first time she laid eyes on Cassandra's family's library. Her heart had panged with jealousy, then desire. She'd been desperate to explore its grand oak bookshelves, which spread across every wall and reached up to the high ceiling. And after she and Cassandra became best friends, that's exactly what she did most weekends, until they left their hometown of Dunsborough for university in Perth. It was something else being back in this room after all these years, as Cassandra's maid of honour.

Bea's reminiscing was interrupted by a hand on her shoulder.

'What are you doing up here?' Matt asked, eyes a little glazed. His bowtie was untied and hung loosely around his neck. His brown hair was a little scruffy, but he still looked indescribably happy.

'Me? What are you doing here?' Bea stumbled a step forward, slightly tipsy. 'You're the groom!'

He smiled, placing his hands in his pockets. Then they stood in silence for a moment, taking in the impressive room that held so many memories for them both.

'I just needed a little breather, Beatrix Potter,' he said. Matt had been calling her that ever since discovering she was named after the author. 'It gets overwhelming, everyone staring and smiling at you.'

Bea nodded, as if she'd been married tons of times and could totally relate.

'You look great, by the way,' Matt commented. Bea smoothed her sleek black ponytail and awkwardly played with the straps of her too-tight suede dress.

'Doesn't Cassandra look beautiful today?' Bea drifted to the other side of the bookshelf, fingers skimming the colourful spines. 'You're a lucky guy, Matt. Truly.'

'I know. She's perfect. But she always looks perfect.' Matt smiled. 'Except after her hen's weekend. Then she was an absolute wreck. And, Bea, she was mortified. I don't know how you let that happen!' Matt laughed.

'Oh, so she told you?'

'Of course she told me.'

'Yeah, of course.' Bea hiccupped inelegantly and covered her mouth. 'She told me she would.'

'It's just one of those things, you know? It's your last hurrah, after all! It's really no big deal, Bea. I did the same thing at my bachelor party.' Matt winked.

'You also slept with the topless waiter?' Bea gasped, dropping the copy of *Little Women* she had just plucked from the shelf.

Matt froze. 'What? No! I vomited at my bachelor party!' He took a step forward. 'Wait – Cassandra slept with the topless waiter?'

Bea shuffled uneasily. 'Oh, did I say slept with the topless waiter? I meant, um, she *was* a topless waiter. No, I meant she *danced with* the topless waiter.' Bea knew that her lame attempts at covering for Cassandra weren't working. Her head began to whirl, her chest tightening – she couldn't breathe.

'No.'

'Matt.' Bea stumbled towards him and grabbed his arm, but it was too late. He pulled away and sprinted from the library. Bea hobbled after him, struggling to walk straight in her stilettos.

'Cassandra!' Matt bellowed, storming down the flower-adorned marble staircase. Women dressed in silk gowns and pearls froze on the dance floor. Men wearing crisp shirts and sharp bowties turned their heads in surprise.

'Cassandra!' Matt roared again. He flew by beribboned chairs and tables decorated with soaring floral arrangements and sweet-smelling candles, past beaming guests and beneath fairy lights. Bea chased him. Then Matt spotted Cassandra. Standing gracefully beside the chocolate fountain, a champagne flute in one hand, the other resting on the railing of the outdoor decking, his wife was the epitome of beauty. She wore a low-backed, white lace dress that enhanced her height and her tan. Her lips were stained a cherry pink and her thick blonde hair was held in a loose braid that draped down her back. She was the stark opposite of pale, dark-haired, barely-taller-than-five-foot Bea.

'My loves,' Cassandra said in her whispery voice as she caught sight of her new husband and her best friend.

'Is it true?' Matt asked.

'Is what true?' Cassandra asked, glancing nervously at Bea, who shook her head.

3

The photographer and videographer homed in on the couple, capturing their conversation as diligently as they'd captured every minute of the ceremony.

'Did you or did you not cheat on me at your hen's party?' Matt demanded.

Cassandra blanched. She looked at Matt and then at Bea, accusation forming in her eyes. *'You told him?'* Cassandra's usual whisper was now a violent spit. The photographer snapped ferociously and the videographer fiddled with his lens. Bea hoped he wasn't zooming in.

'Cass, I'm sorry. I just blurted it out. I thought he knew. He implied that he knew,' Bea pleaded, trying her hardest not to slur her words, and not to dissolve into a heap of tears.

Cassandra ignored Bea and turned to her husband. 'Matt, it was a mistake. A terrible, horrible mistake. I was out-of-my-mind drunk. It obviously meant nothing. I love you, you *know* how much I love you.' Her hand trembled as she reached for him. Guests surreptitiously gathered around the three of them, their hushed, intrigued whispers rising like hot air.

Matt pulled away from Cassandra. 'A terrible, horrible mistake you'll have to live with for the rest of your life, Cass,' he said, his voice dark. 'I can't even look at you. How could you do this to me? To *us?*' He looked devastated. Defeated. Taking one last look at his now less than blushing bride, he spun around, pushing his way through the cluster of guests. The videographer and photographer looked at each other as if to say *Do we stay with the bride or follow the groom?*

Cassandra went to race after Matt.

Oh Bea, you terrible person, you have to fix this. She knew Matt well enough to know he needed space. So she enveloped Cassandra in the biggest hug she could muster.

'It's going to be okay, Cass. I promise you, I'll make it all okay,' she said.

Snap, snap, snap. The photographer had decided to stay.

'Get off me!' Cassandra yelped, shoving Bea away.

Bea struggled against her, holding onto Cassandra for dear life, hoping that, eventually, she would collapse into her arms. The harder Cassandra pushed, the tighter Bea held on. Then Cassandra punched and kicked, and Bea relented and fell away. Unfortunately, that was the exact moment when Cassandra gave one last heave, pushing herself and her couture dress straight into the chocolate fountain.

2

Dear Justine,

Thanks for coming on such short notice. Please do a thorough clean today, including wiping down all the cupboards and cleaning the windows. This will be my last clean as I'm moving to Melbourne tomorrow. I know what you're thinking, that's pretty short notice to uproot everything and jet off to a new city where I have no friends, job leads or accommodation – save for my sister, who lives fifty minutes out of the city. But desperate times call for desperate measures and I'm off to start afresh in Melbourne – the city of literature, coffee art and smashed avocado. I've always wanted a more exciting life, and if not now, then when? Maybe I'll even 'live large' and get balayage? Oh, Justine, I'm so excited (while still filled with the usual dread, remorse and humiliation).

Sincerely,

Bea x

PS. I know that the year's worth of cleaning services that I won from Spick & Span doesn't include end-of-lease cleaning, so I've left $50 extra for you. I hope that's enough.

3

Bea squeezed the bottom of the toothpaste tube and smeared a blob onto her finger. She put the tip of her finger on her tongue and tasted the minty freshness. Furrowing her brow, she picked up her pen and scribbled some notes: *Mildly minty, crunchy, crisp. Crisp crunch???*

This was not what Bea had envisioned her first month in Melbourne would be like. While books and reading were her lifeblood, working in the fast-paced, creative world of marketing was what got her out of bed in the morning. She thought of her work like a book cover – an opportunity to create something that drew consumers in. At her old job, she'd felt fearless – in fact, it was just about the only time she felt confident and in charge. But after securing what she thought was her dream job at a marketing agency not long after arriving in Melbourne ('They have the Melbourne Writers Festival as a client!' she had squealed down the phone to her sister, Lizzie), Bea had been positioned solely on the CoolFresh Oral Hygiene account. This involved coming up with new names and slogans for toothpastes, whitening products and, on a good day, dental floss.

Bea looked up from her desk and peered over at her cubicle neighbour, Bill, who was typing so slowly Bea thought he might actually be dying. Balding on top and bulging on the sides, Bill had barely said boo to Bea since her first day at the office. In fact, almost nobody had. Up until this point, Bea had never really had to put herself out there in the friend department. Somehow, she always ended up with the friends, boyfriends, work wives who chose her – she never had to think about choosing anyone else. Even when it came to Cassandra, the cards had never been in her hands. As a very assured eight-year-old, Cass had plopped herself down next to Bea during fruit break, declared, 'now we're best friends!' and well, they just were.

She glanced over at the Melbourne Writers Festival section of the office. In comparison to her sparse, white surroundings, colourful book posters adorned the cubicles. A giant plush penguin sat in the corner, and the Melbourne Writers people sat on blow-up bosu balls. Dressed in polka dots, Doc Martens and velvet scrunchies, they reeked of quirky fun. Bea adjusted her own drab silk shirt and beige capri pants. *No wonder they wouldn't let me swap onto their account.*

'What're you looking at, Bea?' It was Anika from Melbourne Writers. She passed Bea approximately three times a day on her way to the tea room, and was one of the few people to acknowledge her existence (possibly out of guilt, but Bea would take whatever she could get!). Dark-skinned with long brown hair, Anika was wearing her signature glasses with their thick purple frames, which took up most of her dainty face.

'Just looking at the fun you're all having,' Bea said with a twinge of longing. *Good one, Bea. Could you sound any more desperate?*

'Oh. You can come over and join us for a chat any time!' Anika said sweetly, with only a tinge of pity.

'Oh, thanks. You can come over to me too.' *Because I'm such a hoot? I am literally talking to no one at all times.*

Anika smiled at Bea cautiously. Bea needed to break the awkward silence, and fast.

'So, books.'

Anika looked confused. 'Books?'

'Do you ... like them?'

'Yes, of course.'

'Oh. Me too.'

'That's great.' Anika looked uneasily towards the big glass doors that would take her far away from Bea.

'Okay, you can leave now,' Bea said in an octave she had never heard her voice reach.

Anika laughed nervously and walked away at a speed that almost looked like running.

Bea cringed, and checked her phone hoping that she might find some less cringe-worthy human interaction there. *Nothing.* After three months of radio silence, Bea still hadn't given up her repentant daily messages, hoping to make amends with her best friend. Her cheeks still flushed red with horror whenever she thought about the wedding day. The agony of it all had taken up firm residence in her heart – the pain she caused her best friend, and the fact that she wasn't her best friend anymore, after all.

When the clock ticked over to 11am, Bea rushed downstairs to The Nook, the little café that sat under her office building, to get her second caffeine fix for the day.

It was a new, three-times-a-day ritual that she couldn't quite afford, but which almost made work bearable. Especially because of Grover Dinopoli, AKA Dino, AKA her barista-slash-knight-in-caffeinated-armour. Fond of paperbacks, poetry and soy piccolos, he was the closest thing she had to a friend. *And he only spends time with me in exchange for money,* Bea thought with despair.

She walked through the bright blue door and into her salvation. A cosy café hidden away amongst the hustle and bustle of Commercial Road in South Yarra, only six wooden tables filled the compact coffee shop. The light autumn sun shone through the large window panes, almost beckoning Bea to make the most of the warmer days while they lasted, and the soothing smell of freshly baked danishes and rich coffee made Bea feel instantly at ease.

She waltzed up to the counter and smiled, waiting patiently for Dino to recognise her. He stood in his usual pose: hunched over a Moleskine notebook, ballpoint in hand. He was scribbling away at what she assumed was his latest poem. Dino didn't seem like the poetry type. Six feet tall, with one tanned arm covered in tattoos, shaggy brown hair, perpetually clad in a dusty green apron and oversized op shop purchases, he hated talking about 'his feelings'. He was the opposite of what she imagined E. E. Cummings, T. S. Eliot and Edgar Allan Poe had been like. In fact, it didn't take long for Bea to discover that there was nothing typical about Dino at all.

When she realised Dino wasn't going to notice her any time soon, Bea cleared her throat ever so delicately. He curved around instantly, trance broken. When he spotted her, he simply raised an eyebrow.

'I should've known. Right on time, Beatrix Babbage,' he said, nodding at the clock that hung precariously on the wall behind him. Bea was never sure whether he was playing at being pissed off.

'I couldn't go another second without seeing you, dear Grover Dinopoli.' Bea feigned a faint, draping her arm across her forehead.

'We've talked about this – don't call me Grover. The very syllables of that name grate like nails on a chalkboard. If it weren't for that nasty caffeine habit of yours keeping my business afloat, I'd have thrown you to the kerb,' Dino said, already going to work on her strong skinny latte: one large hand steadily grinding the beans, while the other steamed the milk.

'Ah, you're welcome.' Bea rubbed her thumb and fingers together in the universal symbol for money. She watched his coffee-making skills with admiration, before getting distracted by a gentle lapping at her hand. She looked down to find Agatha Christie, the apricot-coloured toy poodle Dino had inherited from his late grandmother, sitting in her canvas basket on the bar stool next to the counter. 'Why, hello to you too, Agatha,' Bea chirped, scratching the tiny poodle behind the ears. The dog groaned in delight and continued stamping wet kisses along her arm.

'She's a serial licker.' Dino winked, handing over a steaming cup of frothed coffee. Bea gave him a grateful look and pressed the caffeinated goodness to her lips, savouring her first taste.

'You're an addict.'

Mouth still resting on the lip of her coffee cup, Bea shrugged, as if to say, *tell me something I don't know.*

A brief commotion from the kitchen drew Bea's attention. A flash of fairy floss–pink hair poked from a hole in the back wall.

'Bea! Is that you?' called Sunday, Dino's silent business partner, pastry chef, customer service manager and wannabe fashion stylist. 'Get your arse over here. I've got spoons that won't lick themselves!'

Bea went to the serving hatch, leaving her coffee to cool on the counter. 'What's cookin', good lookin'?'

'Peanut butter, jelly and honeycomb slice.' Sunday placed a burnt orange–coloured nugget into Bea's open palm.

Popping it straight into her mouth, Bea let the dessert sit on her tongue, allowing the flavour to slowly soak into her taste buds. She sighed, closing her eyes. 'You're an artist, Sunday!'

'Wait till you taste what I have in store for you next week. Spoiler alert: it has three different kinds of chocolate in it.'

Bea licked her lips.

'So, how's work going? Still spending your days coming up with names for toothpaste?' Sunday asked.

Bea nodded, wiping the corners of her mouth with the back of her hand. 'And to make matters worse, I'm horrible at it. I haven't thought of one approved name since I started. But work is work and I guess my bills won't pay themselves!' She forced a smile. 'Speaking of, I better get back to it.'

Sunday placed another of her peanut butter creations into Bea's hand and waved her off. On her way to the front door, Bea grabbed her coffee and bid goodbye to Dino, who was wiping croissant crumbs off the bench. At the door, she paused and turned around. 'I was in such a rush to get my hit I didn't even read your quote! Now, let's see.'

Bea walked back to the front counter and angled her takeaway cup to reveal a scratchy note written around the circumference of the cup: *Enough fuss about sleeping together. I'd rather go to the dentist.*

Dino, she had come to learn, did nothing half-arsed, nor conventionally. Rather than her name, Dino wrote a more or less accurate book quote on each of her takeaway cups. He had done so on her very first skinny latte, while her head was buried in a copy of *Normal People* by Sally Rooney, and it had become routine. A routine Bea chose to believe was shared only by the two of them.

'Inspiration for your next toothpaste commercial. It's from *Vile Bodies*, Evelyn Waugh.'

Before Bea could put her smug barista in his place, a blonde woman wearing a smear of bright red lipstick appeared next to her and coughed dramatically. 'I'd like a tall, nonfat, soy flat white with whipped cream and a caramel drizzle.'

'Coming right up,' Dino said with a scowl, already beginning on her order.

As Bea was about to leave, Dino held his finger up and mouthed, *Just give me a second.* Bea shrugged and stepped to the side. She took out her phone, hoping again she might have received an email, a Facebook message, a text, or even a Words with Friends instant message from Cassandra.

Hey Cass,
I'm thinking of you. I heard from Mum that you're back at work. That's so great! I'm still in Melbourne and you'll be happy to know that things aren't going too well for me here – I hate my job and I have no friends. Karma's a bitch, hey?
Anyway, once again, I'm so immensely sorry. I love you and miss you more than I miss summer fruit in winter. Please, please get in touch when you're ready.
Bea xo

'So, what do you think?' Dino asked as she pressed send on her one hundred and seventeenth unacknowledged message to Cassandra.

'About what?' Bea looked up, confused. The five-adjectives-too-long-coffee-orderer guzzled her drink in the corner, a dab of cream hanging from the tip of her nose.

'Jesus, Bea. You never pay attention to anything but the screen in front of you,' Dino remarked.

Bea stared at him. Dino and Bea were friendly, but not quite friendly enough for his sudden abruptness.

'I'm performing at some slam poetry gig tomorrow night,' Dino began, looking down at Agatha Christie. 'I have a spare ticket – my mum pulled out last minute, which probably says something about the quality of my art. But anyway, I thought you might like to come? Broaden your Melbourne horizons?'

Slam poetry? Bea wasn't sure it was exactly her thing, but then again, she was hardly swimming in invitations. Besides, a chance to see Dino recite poetry on stage? Priceless.

'Wunderbar, barista.' Bea smiled encouragingly and made a note of the details in her phone. Dino nodded decisively and began cleaning his coffee machine.

'Oh by the way, is it okay if I get a couple of prizes delivered here? I would get them sent to my house but I'm never home to sign for them. And we aren't allowed personal packages sent to the office,' Bea moaned.

'Ah, sure, I guess. What sort of "prizes"?' Dino narrowed his eyes, confused.

'Oh, well, you know 25 words or less competitions?'

'Mmm...'

'I've sort of, got a knack for them.' Bea shrugged.

Dino smiled, amused. 'A knack?'

'Yeah, I enter a couple a week, and I often win. The secret is to be super honest in your answers. No fluffing around, sucking up to the company who's giving away the prize. Just tell it like it is, you know?' Bea leaned over the counter, as if letting Dino in on some long held conspiracy theory.

'I think the secret is that you enter a few a week! Who has time for that?' Dino laughed.

'I don't have any friends here – remember? I've got loads of free time!'

'Okay, sure, you can get your prizes sent here, you weirdo.'

'Broaden your Melbourne horizons.' Dino's words had stuck in Bea's head all afternoon, so after work, Bea found herself strolling down bustling Brunswick Street, eyeing off young couples making the most of the last of the longer days, drinking glasses of wine on outdoor terraces, and glaring at best friends grabbing each other's arms while laughing hysterically. She so desperately wanted what they had. To think, just a matter of weeks ago, she and Cassandra had mirrored these women, meeting for their weekly 'book club for two', trading novels, gossip and pop culture titbits. A custom which they had practised just about all their lives. Only instead of hot chocolates, they now drank wine, and rather than rehashing MSN Messenger faux pas, they discussed, in minute detail, Bea's latest failed Tinder date.

She had come to Brunswick Street because her copy of *Lonely Planet: Melbourne & Victoria* had told her to. It promised a vibrant and friendly atmosphere boasting a youthful and eclectic crowd. It had also guaranteed a lovely bookstore with knowledgeable staff and an excellent selection of novels. And, after leaving most of her books behind in Perth (she had put a pile of some of her favourites on Cassandra's front porch as some kind of symbolic peace offering, but later learned that Cassandra had set the whole thing alight), Bea desperately needed to add to her dismal Melbourne collection, as well as force herself to go beyond the familiar five block radius in which she resided. Bea loved her new neighbourhood, Windsor. Leafy winding streets, and quaint Victorian terraces with brightly coloured doors, made exploring the area a treat.

But she couldn't truly call herself a Melburnian before venturing north of the Yarra River.

Arriving at The Little Brunswick Street Bookstore, she pushed open its glass door and heard a small bell chime. Inside, the familiar smell of fresh paperbacks beckoned her like an old friend. Books of all shapes and sizes lined the shelves that snaked around the store, and Bea immediately felt at home.

Two women, one with brown hair and the other with fiery red, greeted her from behind the counter. The redhead was wearing a strange knitted hat and a black knitted T-shirt, and cradled a small baby. The brunette had her feet propped on top of the counter, a copy of *The Fault in Our Stars* open in her hand. She took one look at Bea and shouted, 'Rom-com!', and then went back to reading. Bea rolled her eyes, assuming they were guessing what book she was intending to buy. She had heard that booksellers sometimes played games like that. She walked slowly through the aisles, eyeing off the classics, then Young Adult, followed by thrillers.

So, what's your plan, Bea? You came here to make a fresh start, but aren't you really just running away? You hate your job, you have no friends and your new balayage highlights look ridiculous with your black hair. She self-consciously tied her long, now slightly blonde hair in a ponytail. *What are you going to do to make things better, Bea? How are you going to shake things up?*

She absentmindedly picked up a copy of *The Huntress*, flicked through the first few pages, and racked her brain. How could she get out of this new rut she had created for herself? She could feel the eyes of the women at the front counter watching her and looked up. They smiled at her. The store was empty apart from the four of them, and she felt a sort of silent connection, a paperback-loving comradery, with these two nameless bookworms.

'Try our second-hand section, it's new.' The brunette woman pointed towards the back of the store. Bea nodded and followed the direction of the woman's outstretched hand. There, she found a stout antique armoire filled with beautiful old covers. Some hardbacks, some clothbound and some paper, but all with the worn look of a book much loved. She had always had a soft spot for second-hand books. There was something about reading the same book somebody else had already lived through. Excitedly, Bea flicked through the first few books and then paused. One was peeking up a little taller than its neighbours, as if it had been bookmarked just for her. She lifted it cautiously, grazing her fingers across its frayed edges and over the embossed title. *Meeting Oliver Bennett* by Emma Delcour. The cover blushed a dark shade of green, and was adorned with gold letters, flecks and imperfections, it instantly exuded intrigue. Bea hadn't heard of the book before, but the front matter revealed that it had been published in 1994, after being translated from French to English.

Glancing around, she checked if the women were still watching her, but saw that their heads were again buried in their own books. The redhead had hers propped in a cookbook stand, and was rocking her baby gently.

Turning the book over, Bea squinted at the slightly faded blurb.

Meeting Oliver Bennett is nothing short of magic. With broad shoulders, dark features, and a mind that ticks faster than an Imperial Model 58 typewriter, he makes Amelia's heart blossom with a love she had never dreamed possible. After a brief but impassioned courtship, Oliver gets down on one knee and proposes to cherish her forever.

And then the first bomb drops.

A daring World War Two story of bravery, the injustice of war and the unshakable determination of two star-crossed lovers amid the chaos and devastation of London. Once you meet Oliver Bennett, nothing will ever be the same again.

Bea practically swooned on the spot. A historical fiction romance was just what the doctor ordered! She opened the cover. Chapter One. She ran her fingers down the page, imagining the new friends waiting to be discovered. No character is one dimensional (even Miss Trunchbull had her charm), and they often have ways of surprising you. In fact, on the days when she would row with her sister Lizzie, or on the odd occasion when she couldn't seem to put a foot right with Cassandra, Bea wished she could be surrounded only by fictional characters, rather than those who inhabited the real world. How fun it would be to have dinner with Don Tillman, to ride a rollercoaster with Jo March or to gossip the night away with Emma Woodhouse.

She turned the page and her eyes caught on a scribble punctuating the bottom left corner. She squinted and pulled the book closer to her face.

your name is my favourite word

Each letter curled neatly into the next, without a single capital or space breaking its flow. The flawless cursive script gave off a primary school teacher vibe.

Bea frowned and flipped forward a few pages. This time, a sentence was underlined in thick, black ink. Three pages on, yellow highlighter dotted the paper, illuminating random words: *fell, alarmed, disjointed, weathered, thick fog, him.* Again, she shifted through the pages, moving chunks of paper at a time, until she arrived in the middle of the book. And there, wedged in the margin, she found another note.

ready or not?

Three little words. A question.

4

Helloisthisyourbook

Hi everyone!
I never thought I'd make an Instagram account (I don't live the kind of life that's worth snapping), but alas here I am. And here's why:

I'm looking for the owner of something. And apparently hashtags are the new mind map.

Today I bought this book because it seemed to be calling my name. And boy am I glad that I did. You see, when I cracked its spine (figuratively – I'm not an animal!) I discovered a rather extraordinary thing: scribbles. Pages and pages of personal annotations and underlines. All lowercase letters and old-school Bs and Zs. And the meaning – what meaning! What kind of person comes up with notes like 'scowls won't cover that big heart of yours' and 'a renewed brightness shifting shadows in your wake'? Could these be the scribbles of my dreams?

DM me if you've seen anything like this before, or if you're interested in discovering what other gems this story holds, stay tuned. #ilovereading #bookish

11 likes

Comments (1):

lostinthepages41: Welcome to #Bookstagram. You'll never leave ♥

5

💬 Cass, I turn 30 next week! I never thought
this was where I would be. And I certainly never
dreamed that you would be anywhere but by my
side. If a trip to Melbourne is on the cards, please
come to my drinks on Saturday. We'll be at The
Woods of Windsor from 8.30pm. I have to show
you this second-hand book I bought at The Little
Brunswick Street Bookstore (the Boffins Books
of Melbourne). *Meeting Oliver Bennett*. It's filled
with the most startling and raw annotations. You
would go crazy for it! I miss you more than I miss
Dumbledore. Love you xxx

Bea had been up all night reading the beautiful scribbles that adorned the dog-eared pages of *Meeting Oliver
Bennett*. She was so consumed by the handwritten annotations that she had barely taken in the story. In fact, she
couldn't stop thinking about the heartfelt notes, and who
they were describing, as she made her way to work. The
person on the other end of the ballpoint was like another
complex, intricate character in the book. And the best
part? This character existed in the real world! *And maybe I
could find them?* She desperately needed to fill the vacancy
left behind in her 'book club for two', Bea thought before
shaking the feeling. She patted the hardcover novel in her

canvas bag to ensure it was still there, and smoothed the front of the pink polka-dot shirt she was wearing. She had bought it the other day, thinking it was the epitome of Melbourne Writers Fest chic.

Bea stepped inside The Nook and spotted Dino instantly, wearing a shirt at least two sizes too big. Bea rolled her eyes. He had admitted to her once that he shopped exclusively at op shops; something about not wanting to spend money on things he could get for half the price. But despite his best intentions (or maybe it was intentional, knowing Dino), he tended to look a little misshapen. He was tapping a cinnamon shaker over a reusable coffee cup, as a tiny woman dressed head to toe in black stared longingly at the drink. The woman was patting Agatha Christie aggressively on the head, while her other hand held onto her phone for dear life. As soon as Dino handed the drink to the woman, she scurried away, lips pressed to the cup, eyes now ogling her phone.

Back straight, hand on hip, Bea stood at the counter before Dino, beaming.

'Bea? You've got a spring in your step. Still juiced from a big night of clubbing?' Dino chuckled.

'Reading, more like it,' she said, the excitement of her literary discovery practically oozing off her. 'I found the most extraordinary book yes—'

Dino held a finger up. 'I think I hear the oven. Sunday called in sick today and I'm like a headless chook trying to keep this ship sailing. Give me a tick.' He hurried to the kitchen.

She felt the gentle lick of Agatha Christie on her wrist. Taking a step back, she whipped out her phone, opened the camera, and crouched on the ground in an attempt to get the best angle. She was trying to get the perfect combination of cute dog and pastries, which was no easy feat – she resorted to lying on the floor. Satisfied with her work, Bea picked herself up and dusted herself off. She took the cup Dino, who had returned with a tray of scones, held out to her, twirling it around to reveal the quote.

'*Lives a mimicry, passions a quotation,*' she read aloud.

'It's Oscar Wilde.'

'I know it's Oscar Wilde,' Bea said pertly, even though she didn't. Despite her Year 9 English teacher Miss Lew's best efforts, *The Picture of Dorian Gray* had only ever been that: grey.

'So I suppose you know what I'm trying to say.' He leaned across the counter, scooped Agatha Christie into his arms and held half a piece of fruit toast to her mouth, which she nibbled at intensely.

'Of course I do.' Bea took a long swig of her latte to cover the fact that she did not, in fact, know.

'It means that today, for some reason, you're being like everyone else. Please don't tell me you're one of those Instagram influencers.' He looked at Agatha Christie as he talked, as if she totally knew where he was coming from, then gestured to the small sign hanging next to shelves of coffee beans and takeaway cups, which read: #NoFoodPorn. 'You're too good for that, Beatrix Babbage.'

Bea frowned. 'You're such an old man, Dino.'

Dino shrugged. 'Ever thought how pertinent the saying, "If a tree falls in a forest, but there's nobody to hear it fall, does it make a sound?" is today? I mean, nobody has fun these days without the validation of somebody else liking it!'

'I don't know what you're on about.' Bea didn't need his holier-than-thou attitude dampening her spirit. Perhaps today wasn't the day to reveal her discovery and social media venture. She picked up a sugar packet sitting in a jar next to her and waved it assertively in Dino's direction.

'What are you doing now?'

'I'm putting a spell on you, to stop you from being so judgmental.' She continued to wave the sugar stick at him, for once not caring how ridiculous she looked.

Dino nodded as if he understood perfectly well, and then placed his hand softly on top of hers, putting an end to her incessant waving. 'So, will I see you at the poetry slam tonight?' he said nonchalantly.

'Of course you will,' Bea said, then thought of the Mystery Writer, somewhere out there in the world, and, bolstered by this thought added, 'Can I bring a friend though?'

'A friend?'

'Yes. There's a chance I may make my first one today, and if I do I will simply have to bring him or her along.'

'Okay then. Sure.'

Bea sat on the toilet, black jeans scrunched around her ankles, *Meeting Oliver Bennett* balanced precariously on her knees. She had been relishing in the annotations and when she heard the pitter-patter of heels and the door of the cubicle next to her open and close, she lifted her eyes from the page. Bea angled her head so that she could get a good look at the woman's shoes: a pair of glittery, navy blue Jimmy Choos with a thin strap, kitten heel and diamanté pendant at the front.

'Martha?' Bea whispered.

Bea had first met Martha when she was sitting in this exact position – and had dropped her bookmark. The two had gotten talking about reading in unusual places, and the rest was history. But when Martha had flushed, Bea felt a sudden embarrassment, not wanting to say something stupid to this well-read, smart woman, face-to-face. So she stayed on her toilet seat, and had done so every time since.

Never having actually seen each other face-to-face in real life, Bea recognised Martha by her parade of fabulous shoes.

'I rewatched the finale again last night,' Martha said in her posh English accent. She was talking about the 1995 *Pride and Prejudice* series, which they had recently discovered they were both infatuated with.

'That double wedding. I still dream about it,' Bea sighed, folding a piece of toilet paper into a neat square.

'Who do you prefer, Jane and Bingley or Elizabeth and Darcy?' Martha asked.

'Is that even a question? Definitely Elizabeth and Darcy,' Bea said. Her conversations with Martha had thus far been limited to Classics specific banter, but today Bea was someone different. Today she had the mysterious annotations – written by her literary soulmate – to encourage her to be a little more open. She cleared her throat. 'So, do you have plans tonight? I'm going to this little poetry slam if you want to join?'

Bea waited for a response, listening agonisingly to the discreet rustles coming from the next cubicle.

'Oh, that's so sweet,' Martha finally responded. 'I can't tonight though. Maybe another time.'

Flush. The sound of a tap running and a final tapping of heels leaving the bathroom signalled that Bea was, once again, on her own.

'Oh,' said Bea, chewing on her lip, trying not be stung by the rejection. She took out her phone, not quite ready to leave the sanctuary of the toilet, and started to type her thrice daily apology to Cassandra when another message popped up on her screen.

🗩 Dino: See you tonight – 8pm at The Sea Bar. – D

🗩 Bea: SEA you then, D – B x

🗩 Dino: Ugh! You're terrible.

She smiled, getting a kick out of annoying Dino with a good pun.

Dressed in a tight black faux leather skirt and a low-cut olive green singlet, Bea was ready to be somebody else. Her hair was freshly curled and she had swapped her

canvas sneakers for nude wedges. She tried to ooze conviction and coolness – even if she didn't entirely feel that
way – as she walked into the hip Hawthorn bar. On an
ordinary day, walking into a bar alone would mean all
sorts of social angst for Bea. Plus, she wasn't used to
having to be alone at all. She'd always had Cassandra.
And Cassandra being Cassandra, all extroverted giggles
and brazen banter, knew how to command an audience.
To her credit, Cassandra would diligently find a way to
work Bea into any conversation, setting her up for jokes
or daring her to flirt with the bartender. But, sometimes,
it was just easier listening to the punchline than having
to devise one yourself. Now, as the increasing 'new town'
isolation threatened to consume her, Bea was desperate
for companionship. And as much as she wanted to avoid
it forever, making new friends meant making the effort
to go out.

Small tables cluttered the tiny, beer-stained bar which
was lit almost solely by candlelight. A hearty mixture of
laughter and chatter filled the room. Bea felt elated by
the buzz of the bar, so different from the quiet and slow-
paced Perth nightlife. Holding onto the glass of wine she
just ordered, she spotted a seat at a table with two women
already sitting at it, and made a beeline towards it.

'This chair free?' she said, sitting down. *So forward, Bea!
Bravo!*

'Sure,' a woman with purple hair and piercings running
along the ridge of her left ear replied.

'Come here often?' her companion asked.

'No, my first time. You?'

29

The two women smiled condescendingly and turned their heads away to chat among themselves. Bea took out her phone and snapped a photo, uploading it to Instagram.

Helloisthisyourbook

📍William ShakespHERE

Feeling #cultured waiting for my friend to slam some poetry #talknerdytome #hewouldhatethatpun

She was excited to see Dino perform. She hoped his poetry would be the funny, slightly self-deprecating kind and not the tragic, I-feel-sorry-for-you-and-must-not-make-direct-eye-contact kind.

Laughter slowly morphed into murmurs as the first poet crept on stage: a small man with a long, bushy beard, who rhymed 'dog' with 'log' approximately four times and hiccupped once in the middle of his poem. Bea bit her lip, wincing her way through the performance. Three judges sitting in the front row of the bar held up scrap paper emblazoned with the numbers 3, 2 and 5. The man was clapped politely off stage and an elegant woman wearing a high-necked, floor-length golden dress appeared. She sung her poem in an airy, high-pitched voice that was beautiful, yet completely indecipherable. She curtsied after her performance and the same judges held up new pieces of paper reading 5, 6 and 5.

Tough crowd, Bea thought. Next to her, the two women giggled, pointing at a blinding iPhone screen. Just as Bea was about to take out her own phone, Dino appeared on stage. He was dressed differently from his usual The Nook attire. He wore black Converse, black chinos and a big black tee; his hair was slicked back and a passionate expression adorned his face. Bea caught his eye and the corner of his mouth curled up ever so slightly.

He walked towards the microphone, careful not to trip on its snaking cord, and spoke into it in a deep, penetrating voice Bea had never heard before.

'Ah, this poem is a little something I whipped up a week ago.' A burst of static echoed from the speakers, forcing Dino back a step. 'It's still a little raw. It's called "The Grind".' Clearing his throat, he began.

Made of small, oval beans
Turning quick glances and brash requests
Of warm smiles and glazed eyes
Of light feet, wanting hands on frosted glass.

Bea was surprised. She had expected Dino to be bitter or trivial with his poems. She had not been prepared for – well, this.

Dino continued.

Light tug. Small whine. Bell chime.

Bea joined the chorus of claps and whoops. She tried to catch Dino's eye again, but he disappeared from stage all too quickly. Pushing her seat back, Bea stood up at exactly the same time as the purple-haired woman returned to her seat carrying two glasses of shiraz. They collided and the red liquid splashed onto Bea's silk top. She squealed as the woman muttered brash apologies and, somewhat unhelpfully, patted her down with her hand then quickly vanished leaving Bea's spirit stained.

After a few more poetry readings (and the 15 minutes Bea haphazardly spent soaping her top in the bathroom, before clumsily drying it under the hand dryer) the formalities ended and the judges announced a winner. Dino! The audience whooped and cheered, got up from their tables and gathered at the bar – ready to order their next drink. Bea walked towards the cluster of people, where she spotted Dino standing with the other poets. He was nodding along seriously to something the operatic rhymer in the golden dress was saying. He leaned in, as if to hear her better. Bea tapped him on the shoulder.

'Congratulations, you superstar!' She pulled him into a hug. He remained stiff and straight.

'Thanks,' Dino replied.

'To be honest, I didn't know quite what to expect.'

Dino smiled and took a long sip of his drink.

'But seriously, will your mum please not come in the future so I can take her ticket again? I really enjoyed myself tonight!'

'Yeah, well, I can almost guarantee that. She's missed more of my events than she's come to. So you can take her ticket any time.' Dino shrugged.

'Does she live around here?' Bea asked.

'No. Anyway, I better get back to the party. They're celebrating yours truly, after all.' Dino winked. 'Thanks for coming, Babbage. Now you can get back to your real friends!'

'Shall do.' Bea smiled, thinking of the only friend in Melbourne she had to get back to. *Meeting Oliver Bennett.*

6

Helloisthisyourbook

Scribble of the day: *Love completely. Trust wholly. Question constantly. What a farce.*

I just can't tear my eyes away from the inscriptions in this book. You know when you overhear someone's conversation at a café and you can't help but listen and wonder about their backstory, their life? About where they work and who they love, and who loves them? That's what these scribbles are like for me. I've had a glimpse into Mystery Writer's world – and I can't stop imagining who they might be. And for the first time in a long time, I suddenly feel connected to someone or something.

---

45 Likes

Comments (7)

StephenPrince: @NoOffenceBut Have you seen this Instagram account? I think you'll like it. Reminds me of the book blog where we met. 😍

Holliefraser: Thanks for following! I love people watching!

NoOffenceBut: @StephenPrince Ha, it's pretty cute. But not as cute as you.

7

Back in Perth, Bea would always host drinks at the Wines of While bar for her birthday. Every year Cassandra would come over to her apartment early, bring a spectacular present (Cass was the best at presents) and Bea's favourite bottle of pinot noir, and the two of them would have a glass before joining the rest of their friends at the bar.

Bea had tried to recreate a similar birthday in Melbourne this year. And since then had scolded herself for thinking that she could. *You have no friends and no Cassandra – how could it possibly be the same?* She paced up and down in her poky apartment, sipping on the same pinot noir, which no longer tasted as sweet. Bea was dressed and ready for her thirtieth birthday drinks with another two hours to go until anyone would arrive at the bar, which was only a ten-minute walk away. Not really knowing what to do, or where to go, she took out her phone and dialled her sister Lizzie's number.

Named after Elizabeth Montgomery, AKA Samantha Stephens from *Bewitched* (because she put a spell on her parents as soon as she entered the world), Lizzie seemed to blaze through life, collecting acquaintances, tales of romance and piercings as she went. Her most notable escapade? Being the third runner-up on the second season of *The Bachelor* (for Bea, there was nothing more mortifying than having a reality TV star for a sister). Now the mother of two-year-old identical twin girls, Lola and Willow, and a professional social media influencer, Lizzie lived her newly piercing-free life loudly through Instagram filters and Snapchat stories. Today would be only the third time Bea had seen her sister since moving to Melbourne. Lizzie lived almost an hour away in the beautiful seaside town of Mount Eliza, and Bea had moved to Melbourne knowing that she was just close enough to her sister in case the shit hit the fan (like if she became a penniless nomad), but still far enough away that she wouldn't get roped into becoming Lizzie's personal Instagram photographer. Or on-call babysitter.

'Hi Liz,' Bea chimed into the phone, holding it in between her shoulder and neck so she could pour herself some more wine.

'Bea! Aren't I seeing you in a couple of hours?'

'Yeah. Just thought I'd call to pump myself up for tonight. I used to spend my birthday pre-drinks with Cass. And now, well, I'm feeling a little lost.' Bea sipped at her wine, hating how desperate she sounded to her cool, older sister.

'Oh, Bea. Like I told you, you need to put yourself out there a little more. When I signed up for *The Bachelor* it opened so many doors for me. How many times have I told you to reactivate your Tinder account?' Lizzie shrilled.

'I don't need a boyfriend, Liz. I need friends. People who can keep me company. Right now the only thing I've got close to that is this book I found.'

'A book? Well, that's pathetic. I'm signing you up to

Tinder right now. One second. It'll only take a tick!' Lizzie interrupted.

'Liz, no! Please stop!'

'I'm almost done.'

'Liz, listen to me! I'm sick of online dating.'

'Okay, all done. Your profile photo is that hot one of me and you from my wedding. More guys will click into it if they see your sister is from *The Bachelor*. Trust me. Your username is your email, your password is my birthday. Anyway, I've got to run. Nick is starting up the car. We'll all see you soon!' Liz hung up the phone before Bea could utter another word.

Bea groaned, opened her phone, downloaded the Tinder app, logged in, and then deleted her account.

God, how I miss Cass.

Sick of aimlessly fidgeting in her apartment, Bea arrived at Woods of Windsor, a small wine bar tucked away on Chapel Street, half an hour early. Still new to town, and to the art of making friends, Bea had an embarrassingly small invite list. Apart from her family, it consisted of Anika from the Melbourne Writers Festival team at work (who Bea was convinced had agreed to come out of sympathy) and her partner Ruby, Sunday, Dino and, of course, Cassandra. Driven by blind hope and desperation, Bea had texted her not once, but three times to beg her to be there, if only via FaceTime.

Sidling up to the bar, she ordered an espresso martini – according to Lonely Planet, every local Melburnian's drink of choice – and pulled out her copy of *Meeting Oliver Bennett*. It was becoming a cherished companion with whom she felt most at ease. The notes scribbled inside it were the sort of things that she had always wished someone would say to her, but never had. In fact, each and every annotation made her feel more and more like someone was missing in her life. That person who saw deep inside your soul, and despite what they found there, still liked you. Someone who said words you still thought about long after they'd been spoken. And someone who, for once, Bea had finally chosen – even if they had yet to choose her back.

She glanced at a pair of men wearing short-sleeved checked shirts and chinos cradling pints near a dartboard. She made awkward eye-contact with one, and then quickly turned back to her book.

Twenty pages and half a martini later, she noticed what appeared to be a phone number crammed in the corner of page 32, beside which was written the letter 'e' (cursive, and lower case, of course). Bea frowned. *Who could it be? A lover? A friend? The person all these beautiful notes are directed to?* She took out her mobile to dial the number, pressing each digit resolutely. *What are you even going to say, Bea?* Inwardly rolling her eyes at her own impulsivity, she held the phone to her ear. The call went straight to voicemail, and a light, airy voice said, 'Sorry, I can't get to the phone right now, leave a message at the beep and I'll get back to you. Probably.'

'Darling!' Arms fell around Bea's shoulders, pulling her into a warm, bosomy embrace.

'Mum!' Bea disconnected the call and swivelled on the bar stool. She wrapped her arms around her mother, a petite woman with a dark, cropped bob and a warm-hearted smile.

Bea felt her mum's arms frantically patting up and down her ribs. Suddenly, she thrust Bea back, clutching her by the shoulders. 'Beatrix, you're wasting away. Have you been eating enough?' Maggie, Bea's totally 'non'-overprotective, 'non'-doting, 'non'-force-feeding mother, showered her two daughters with affection through lasagne, apple pie and barely concealed maternal angst.

'Happy birthday, love.' Bea's dad ambled out from behind his wife, bending down to plant a sloppy kiss on Bea's cheek. Martin, a recently retired GP who had, since then, developed an obsession with drones, looked pleased. 'Don't mind your mother, she's just intent on cramming as many worries into our short trip to Melbourne as possible.' He winked. 'This city agrees with you. And Lizzie tells us she's been taking extra good care of you. We're so proud of what a doting big sister she is. And of you, for making this move all on your own.'

Maggie and Martin, or the M&Ms as they were affectionately known, had only just touched down from Perth after booking a last-minute ticket to celebrate Bea's momentous birthday. Not wanting to 'cramp her style', as her mother had said (Maggie, having recently discovered Twitter and emojis, relished any opportunity to 'text and Twitter like the kids these days'), they had checked into a little Airbnb studio apartment a couple of blocks from the bar.

'Where's Lizzie?' Bea scanned the bar in search of her impossibly tall, beautiful and only slightly self-obsessed older sister.

And, just like that, Lizzie shot out from behind a pillar and raced towards her. Her husband Nick, a slightly reserved former West Coast AFL player, followed closely behind, holding a squirming twin under each arm. Lizzie sang an operatic rendition of 'Happy Birthday' (not in tune) as she went and waved vigorously with one hand, the other aiming her phone towards Bea.

'Bea! Happy Birthday! I know, I know, the twins are here. At a bar! The sitter cancelled on us last minute.' Lizzie shoved her arm around Bea's shoulders, pulling her towards her so that their cheeks were smooshed together. 'Smile!' she squealed, snapping a selfie, the flash glaring. Bea gently brushed her sister away. She had forgotten what it was like to be out with Lizzie.

'Liz, how are you?' Bea asked, fondly kissing each of the twins' curly-haired heads. The M&Ms gazed adoringly at their brood.

'Exhausted, three kilos heavier than my goal weight, and annoyed at you for deleting the Tinder account I spent so long making! Don't think I would have switched notifications off on my phone,' Lizzie thrust her chest out and popped her hip.

Bea tried to dismiss her sister with a wave of her hand. One of the twins, having freed herself from her father's firm grasp, had sat down on the floor and was now running her gooey hands up and down Bea's left leg.

Maggie chimed in. 'You really should listen to your sister. Apparently, the apps are the only way to meet new people nowadays.' Bea's face paled, wanting anything but to be speaking about her non-existent love life with her family.

'Anyway, enough about this, let's get celebrating!' Lizzie, quickly tiring of the conversation, surveyed the bar with its mostly empty round tables and handful of wonky bar stools. 'Where is everybody?'

'I wanted to keep it intimate this year,' Bea said, to cover for her dismal invite list. 'You know, not make a big fuss of the whole descending-closer-to-my-own-demise thing.' Bea whispered the last part, leaning in conspiratorially as if she were revealing the secret to staying young.

Lizzie laughed, which sounded more like a high-pitched yelp, and snapped a couple of candid photos of her gorgeous girls.

Bea looked around anxiously, then tapped at her phone, which she realised she was clutching a little too firmly. No messages. Then Maggie swooped in, engaging her family with talk of drink orders and proudly showing off Martin's latest aerial footage of Cottesloe Beach. Bea took a step back, surveying the animated group, and smiled to herself. She hadn't realised how much she had missed being immersed in the regular rhythm of familial chaos.

Laden with drinks and sippy cups, Bea's family set up camp among the tables and chairs by the window. The sound of laughter and chatter mingled with soft jazz. Her remaining guests filed in slowly, bringing with them well wishes and an immediate readiness to head to the bar to order drinks. Everybody except for Dino. Bea checked the time on her phone again, shuffling her feet as she tried to concentrate on the conversation taking place between her dad and sister. They were banging on about something to do with hashtags and the power of viral movements. If Lizzie took anything seriously, it was reclaiming the label 'mummy blogger'. Bea glanced around the room, checking that her other guests were having fun. Sunday was chatting to a random woman in the corner, and Melbourne Writers Festival Anika and Ruby were drinking quietly on the couch.

Then Bea felt a soft squeeze on her shoulder. She jumped, turning around abruptly to greet the owner of the hand.

'Bea, sorry! I shouldn't have crept up on you like that,' Dino said. He was wearing a shirt with someone else's initials etched into the front pocket: *AIK*.

'Dino, you made it!' Bea stood, planting a quick kiss on his cheek.

Dino took an awkward step back.

'Happy birthday!' He handed her a small box.

She opened it before exclaiming 'My Tamagotchi!' remembering the competition she had entered for it while watching *Les Miserables* late one night.

'I received it in the mail this morning and assumed it was one of your "prizes". Wait, did you say Tamagotchi?' Dino asked.

'Yep, haven't you heard? They're making a comeback.'

Dino laughed and surveyed Bea's empty glass. 'Come, let me grab you another. Consider it your birthday present.'

At the bar, Dino ordered a pinot for Bea and a craft beer for himself. The barman slipped the drinks in front of them as Dino dug around in each of his pockets. 'Shit, I must have left my wallet in the car,' he sighed, dismissing Bea's insistence that he could get the next round. 'I'll be right back. Don't go anywhere.'

He raced out the front door leaving Bea to make herself comfortable on the bar stool, relieved to have some reprieve from the constant conversation hiccups she found herself making. Taking a quick swig of her wine, she spotted her book, absently left behind on the counter. Guiltily, she pulled it towards her, flipped it open and pored over the words. *Just one page,* she told herself. Three lines in, a new annotation caught her eye:

keeper and maker of memories – i love you for both.

Bea tried to imagine who this Mystery Writer could be describing. She pictured a woman who had one of those faces that was instantly recognisable, even if you'd only met her once, in a fleeting second. Her favourite book would be *The Jane Austen Book Club.* But she'd probably tell people her favourite books were Jane Austen's. Bea sighed, lost in thought, before continuing to read.

'Bars and books? You might just be the woman of my dreams,' a deep voice remarked.

Bea reluctantly pulled herself away from the page and looked up. It was one of the pint-holding men she had spotted earlier in the night. Up close, he was all hazel eyes and broad shoulders, with faint stubble trailing along his jawline. He towered over Bea. Bea shrunk into herself, wishing so desperately she had the unabashed confidence of Lizzie or Cass.

'What are you reading?' He managed to nod towards her book and simultaneously order another beer with a flick of his finger.

Bea closed the cover, pushing the book towards the man. He peered at it, grazing his arms against hers.

'*Meeting Oliver Bennett*?' he exclaimed, becoming less smooth and more bubbly in an instant. 'Get out! I just gave my copy away to this cute little store over in the north. God, what was it called?'

Bea peered curiously at this seemingly well-read man with his crinkly smile and tousled, wavy hair. 'It wouldn't have been The Little Brunswick Street Bookstore?'

He clicked his fingers, his face lighting up. 'That's the one! They have that cool little second-hand section.'

'I found this very book there just last week,' she said cautiously. There's no way he could be the person behind the scratchy ballpoint jottings, the scribbles she had come to relish more than the plot.

He looked back at her, stunned. A faint smile tugged at his lower lip. He moved the book towards him, flipping through the first few pages. He gaped at the book and back at Bea.

'This is my book.'

Bea couldn't believe what she was hearing. What were the chances of her bumping into the owner of the very book she had stumbled across just days ago? The stars were going berserk, falling into place around her.

'I'm Zach, by the way.'

She shook his outstretched hand. 'Bea.'

8

Bea downed another mouthful of wine. Her third for the night. 'I just need to know *what* you were thinking when you first wrote all those annotations. I mean, they're everywhere – all over the book! I've never seen anything like it. And how could you give something so personal away?' Bea's questions seemed to tumble out one after the other. 'And the phone number, who does it belong to?'

Zach smiled, glancing over his shoulder. 'Hey, I should get back to my buddy. Looks like things are falling apart without me.' He gestured to his friend, who sat alone, skewering peanuts with darts and stuffing them into his mouth. 'More book talk a little later on?' he said, blushing slightly. Perhaps he was feeling a little exposed.

Bea jumped up and stumbled slightly. It was official, the last drink had gone straight to her head. Ignoring the clear social cues Zach was giving her, she asked needily, 'Do you do it to all of your books?' He had this easy way about him, almost as if he had been cut straight from the pages of a Maldives travel brochure. She could not let this sunny, tropical island man slip through her fingers. Not when they had only just found each other.

'Only when the mood strikes. I haven't done it in a little while now,' Zach said as he started to back away.

'How will I get your book back to you?'

'It's your book now.' Zach replied with a wink.

'Mmm hmm, yeah,' Bea said, taking a step forward. 'But like, if I were to desperately need to contact you ASAP about said book, like I had a burning question about—'

'What if I accidentally spoiled the ending? I couldn't live with myself!'

'Um, yeah. That would obviously be a travesty. But I've become a very forgiving person of late. You know, on account of being older and wiser.' Bea strung out the final R, trying to be seductive, but instead sounding more intoxicated.

Zach smiled. 'You make a solid point. And I've always enjoyed a good book club for two.' He glanced back at his friend, who was now attempting to stack as many peanut shells on his outstretched tongue as he could. 'You're right. Let's make it official. Not take any more chances with fate.' He pulled out his phone and extended it towards Bea. Gratified, she typed her number into the device, double-checking for typos while congratulating herself on her brazen move. Maybe she didn't need Cassandra to act as her wing woman after all. 'You enjoy your night, bookworm,' he said, pushing his phone back into his pocket before turning to rejoin his game of darts.

'Take that Tinder,' Bea was mid-fist pump when Dino returned, flushed and just a touch out of breath.

'Looks like you've found yourself a new drinking buddy.' He nodded over to Zach, giving him the once over.

'You made it,' Bea slurred slightly, slapping her arm against Dino's chest.

'Mmm,' was all Dino had to say.

'Thirty isn't looking so bad after all,' Bea whooped. 'I have more than just a new drinking buddy. I've got a date!'

'Congratulations,' Dino said. 'You're a regular charmer, Bea.'

'You know, Dino, sometimes you just have to take life by the horns. Forge your own density.'

'You mean destiny?'

'Nobody likes a know-it-all, Dino.'

'Come on, professor,' Dino said, placing his cash on the counter and spinning Bea around. 'Time to get back to your party.'

During their absence, the party had descended into slight mayhem. Lizzie was straddling one of the chairs taking selfies while Nick chased Lola, trying to grab her arm before she spilt the entire contents of her sippy cup onto her sister.

'Bea.' Maggie materialised before her eyes. 'Where did you get to, love? We have been itching to hear all about the Melbourne Writers Festival. I read the other day that storybooks on Instagram are the new marketing frontier. Is that true?'

Bea giggled, then hiccuped, the force of it sending her staggering back a step. Dino broke her fall with a quick palm on her back, but Bea brushed him away and regained her composure. *Keep it together, Babbage.*

'Actually, it's been a little more Colgate than Capote,' Bea began. 'But they say Rome wasn't built in a day! It's just a matter of time until that fat cat boss of mine realises my potential and fondness for all things paperback. Isn't that right, Anika?' Bea yelled to her coworker, who was wrapped up in what looked like a heated conversation with Martin. Anika cocked her head and raised her glass (and eyebrows) towards Bea in reply.

'I'm just so proud of you for taking a chance on change. Aren't you proud of her?' Maggie turned to Dino, who had been sipping his drink, ready to catch the slowly swaying Bea. 'Who are you again?'

'My barista. Dino is my saintly barista!' Bea gushed, lacing her arm around a rigid Dino.

'That's right, strong skinny latte over here works in the offices above my café.'

'Oh, how sweet! Now tell me, how does one do "coffee art"?' Maggie made air quotes.

'I couldn't tell you. I'm more of your basic rosetta kind of guy.'

'Oh, Mum, Dino's art is all in his quotes. He pops a new one on my takeaway coffee cup every day!'

Dino swatted her away. 'Really, I've just been hoping that holding your daughter up with coffee cup graffiti might convince her to finally get a KeepCup.'

Maggie nodded along, impressed. 'Sustainability is so woke right now.'

At close to 9.30pm, Bea found herself on the couch crammed between Anika and Ruby, a hand on each of their knees.

'But how? How do you do it all? And all the while radiating such fiery passion for each other?' Bea had been talking for the past twenty-five minutes about the miracle of love and landing your (or her) dream job all at the same time.

Dino appeared in front of her. 'I should get going,' he said. 'Those coffee beans won't grind themselves.'

Bea laughed, almost hysterically, as Anika and Ruby scooped up their bags and coats and called their goodbyes as they raced out the door.

'You going to be okay on your own?' Dino asked.

Lizzie and her little entourage had departed just before Bea had hijacked Anika and Ruby, and her parents had left not long after. Sunday's appearance had been fleeting; she had left not much longer after Dino had arrived.

'I'm not on my own,' Bea said, reclining on the couch, a small cocktail umbrella wedged behind her ear, and nodding over to the bartender. 'Go, get out of here! You've got an early start.'

Dino bent down and kissed her quickly on the cheek. 'Get home safe,' he called over his shoulder. 'And happy dirty thirty!'

Bea rested her head against the wall, debating getting another drink. Having moved back to espresso martinis she was too wired to go to bed. Eyes closed, she grabbed her bag from beside her and rummaged around for her wallet. *One more drink, and then I'm out,* she told herself, her head spinning.

'Okay Bea,' she said, eyes still shut. 'Last round's on me!'

'That's hardly fair,' a deep voice replied. 'I'm pretty sure it's my turn.'

Bea squinted one eye open and stared up at a blurry silhouette. *Dino?*

'You all right?'

Bea felt the couch sag, her head swimming from the movement. *Maybe another drink isn't such a good idea after all.* Bea peeled open her other eye.

'It's Zach. Second-hand book, Zach.'

Bea must have been frowning.

'How about I get you an Uber? Might be time to call it a night.'

'You're pretty,' Bea mumbled. She stretched out her hand and patted Zach's face. 'And you like to read.'

Zach pulled away with a laugh. 'Come on, Gone with the Gin. Up and at 'em!' He laced a hand under her arm and heaved her to her feet.

Bea laughed. 'Dino would hate that pun.'

Zach smiled, obviously not understanding. 'You had quite the eclectic clan here tonight.'

'Have you been spying on me?'

'If by "spying" you meant "checking you out", then yes, I guess I was spying just a little.'

Zach steered Bea out the door and onto the street. He pulled out his phone and swiped at the screen until he found his Uber app. Once Bea remembered where she lived, after going blank for a full five minutes, a car was ordered. All the while, Bea stood stock-still, leaning into Zach's solid embrace while she squinted at this unexpected and rather appealing man: a man of effortless charm, no-fuss good looks and a mighty good handle on his prose.

After an eight-minute wait (bless the Uber gods), Zach bundled Bea into the back of a grey SUV and slid in next to her.

'Zach?'

'Yes, Bea?'

'How old are you?'

'Twenty-eight.'

'Twenty-eight? I turned thirty today! Does that make me a MILF?'

'I don't know, how many children do you have?'

'Oh, well, now you sound just like my mother!' Bea pulled away in disgust.

'No, sorry.' Zach scooted towards Bea, his seatbelt tugging against his shoulder. 'I think the term you're after is "cougar".'

Bea looked at him suspiciously. 'You're too young for me.'

'Did I say twenty-eight? I meant twenty-eight and three quarters. Plus, I own at least one sweater vest *and* I just finished reading *A Man Called Ove* so I regularly find myself cursing at "hooligans" and ranting about the good old days before Kindles were invented.' Then Zach leaned in, put his lips to her ears and whispered, 'Age is just a number, baby.'

Goosebumps, on goosebumps, on goosebumps.

Who is this guy?

And then his lips were on hers. He tasted of lemon and cola and felt like new beginnings.

9

Dear Ramona,

Nice to 'meet' you!

Hope you found the key okay. Thanks again for this weekly clean for the year. This is such a luxury for me, you have no idea. I'm so relieved I could transfer this prize from Perth to Melbourne!

Oh, and sorry about the mess. I stumbled home last night, intoxicated by wine and a sneaky kiss with this guy Zach. He's all ruffled hair, hazel eyes, cute dimples. A total hunk of spunk. And I, perpetually awkward Bea Babbage, kissed the living daylight out of him. And he loved it! I think. Everything's a little bit hazy right now. Anyway, what I was saying was, after I got home I opened up a cold roast chicken I had in the fridge, and I annihilated it. I tried to clean up as much as possible, but there may be a few bones and grease stains lying around.

Yours truly,
Bea Boozy Babbage

Oh, PS My friend Sunday is going to swing by today to pick up an Ottolenghi recipe book I said she could borrow. You don't mind letting her in, do you? Thanks!

10

Bea,

All cleaning is done. I let your friend in and she picked up the book.

Congratulations on the man. He sound handsome. Also, competition only have nine months left, not year.

I be back next week.

Ramona

11

Bea could only manage to read one page of *Meeting Oliver Bennett* on her tram ride to work. Even on the short journey from her apartment in Windsor to South Yarra, every bump and bend made her feel like she was about to throw up. *Thump. Jump. Rattle.* But the one page she did manage to read made her mind tick. She liked imagining 1940s Britain through the eyes of the strapping Oliver Bennett and learning how he navigated young love with a fiery passion. Yet it was the words hastily scribbled on the page that sat open like an offering on her knees, that Bea couldn't drag her thoughts away from.

Nor could she drag them from the author of each note. *Zach.*

His name rolled off her tongue. Ever since coming close to flunking her Year 9 philosophy class, Bea had stopped believing in the fanciful notion of *fate* (especially after Cassandra vehemently insisted that such nonsense was 'kids' stuff' when they were only eleven years old). But there was something about her chance encounter with the beautiful bronzed man who had written the inscriptions she was obsessing over. And, well, fate seemed to be the first and only word to make any sense.

Bea ran the tips of her fingers across her lips, fantasising about the impromptu and slightly out-of-character kiss they had shared. Bea wasn't one to kiss strangers.

She liked to be particular about with whom she shared her saliva ('You never know who you can contract herpes from,' her dad used to say before she left the house). But it felt like she already knew him. The spontaneous annotations dotted among the pages of the book had gotten to her. The frivolous way they were written and the carefreeness of the curves, slopes and ink had trickled right under her skin.

She loved kissing the man behind the pen, and she wanted to do it again. Soon.

But will he want to? Bea leaned her head against the train window and closed her eyes. She could feel the grumble of the carriage vibrate up her heels, through her jeans and white linen shirt. *Please don't let him be like the rest of them,* she silently prayed. Flashes of disappointing dates, unreturned phone calls and Sleazy Shane – her on-again, off-again friend with benefits – flooded her mind. *Please let Zach be different, please let him live up to the annotations!* She picked up her battered copy of *Meeting Oliver Bennett* and held it close to her face, inhaling its scent. The woody smell of the pages briefly lifted her from her hangover, and she smiled, pressing the pages closer to her face. She let herself dream of apt thoughts and floods of words and scribbles and dimples and broad shoulders, and lemon and cola and Zach, Zach, *Zach*.

'Get a room!' the school boy beside her huffed, flicking the book with his finger.

Bea opened her eyes, stared at him and laughed. 'Oh, I will.' She brought out her phone, wanting to message Cassandra about the man she had just met. She sent her a quick text, and then added a post to her Instagram account, using a photo she had taken a couple of days ago.

Helloisthisyourbook

Scribble of the day: *desert your inhibitions*.

GUYS, I MET MYSTERY WRITER! THE Mystery Writer! I was out at a bar and he recognised the book. And he's just as dreamy as we dreamt he would be and has a facial structure to rival that of Joshua Templeman.

'*Drinking makes people more interesting.*' Bea read the messy writing on her coffee cup.

'It's by—'

'I know. Hemingway. Ha. Ha. Very funny,' she said. Bea had stumbled into The Nook looking worse for wear and begging for her caffeine fix. Her usually loose waves were pulled into a messy bun which sat unevenly atop her head, and her shirt was creased in every direction. Dino had scowled at her and served up her coffee without uttering a word until after she'd read the quote.

Bea gulped down her coffee. 'What?'

Dino shrugged and turned to serve the next customer. Bea rolled her eyes and played with Agatha Christie's fur, kneading it between her fingers. She watched Dino as he dusted chocolate on his latest creation, then swiftly placed a takeaway lid on top.

'So, anything happen with you and that ridiculously conventional guy last night?' he asked finally. She enjoyed how Dino reverted to talking like a gossipy teenage girl when under pressure.

She laughed. '"Ridiculously conventional"? What on earth are you on about? By the way, is Agatha looking a little chunkier than usual?'

'Don't change the subject,' Dino said as he rearranged the croissants on the front counter so that they sat in a perfectly symmetrical pyramid. He placed a miniature statue of the Eiffel Tower beside them. 'Come on, he looked like he was straight off the set of *Gossip Girl.*'

Bea felt a flush race up her neck simply thinking about the *Gossip Girl*-like character she had recently smooched. She dismissed Dino with a wave of her hand. 'I just got his number, that's all. He seemed sweet.' Apparently she had become one of those women who didn't kiss and tell. 'And he's hardly conventional. He reads! And writes!'

Dino stared at her. 'Am I supposed to be impressed that he's literate?'

'He's not just literate. He's a fucking poet!'

Dino simply raised one eyebrow.

'Well, not a poet like you,' Bea said. 'But, I happened to find a copy of a book he donated to The Little Brunswick Street Bookstore – you should so go there, by the way – which he had written all over! Almost from top to bottom! He's jotted down these incredible insights into the themes of the book and these worldly observations and parallels he draws to his own life.' At this point Bea was gesticulating so wildly, even Agatha Christie seemed to look up at her in surprise. She could no longer keep her discovery to herself. 'Anyway, he seems really interesting.'

'Sounds like quite the catch. Well done you.'

'Mmm, the book – well, Zach – he seems pretty amazing.'

'Just don't go counting your chickens before they hatch.'

'Ever the optimist, aren't we? Is it so terrible to dream a little?' Bea huffed, tossing a serviette at Dino, which he swiftly dodged. 'Now please hand me a chocolate muffin before I die of hunger,' she said.

Dino cautiously handed over the pastry. 'So, I know I'm no jotter of marginalia poetry, but will you come to *my* poetry slam again tonight?'

'Sure. Any poetry's good poetry!' Bea said, her mouth full of muffin.

Bea shuffled her chair to the very corner of her desk and opened her copy of *Meeting Oliver Bennett*. She was waiting for the painkiller she had just taken to kick in, and for her parents to arrive. They had insisted on an office tour and lunch date. Unable to ignore the scribbles, she ran her eyes slowly over each one, absorbing them.

how can something so small fill my whole world?

Now that she knew that Zach was behind the inscriptions, they all felt so much more personal. So real. What was running through his mind? She imagined his big hands curved around a ballpoint pen, his mind ticking, as he poured his thoughts onto the paper. She had never in her life seen so many annotations, each imbued with such meaning. They spread across the pages as if marking their territory. Her fingers traced down the page of the book, hovering over the detail of the tightly bound lowercase letters.

'Bea, my darling,' a warm voice cooed, dragging Bea back to the surface. 'I can't believe this is your desk!'

Quickly shoving *Meeting Oliver Bennett* under some loose briefs, Bea pushed her chair back, enveloping her mum in her arms. She thanked Anika for showing her parents where she was stationed, and then kissed her dad hello on the cheek.

'So tell me love,' Maggie leaned in, wrapping her arm behind Bea's back, 'Show me where you have your big meetings.'

Bea led her parents to the boardroom, smiling meekly at those she passed, hoping she could feign being a valued part of the professional and social make-up of the place. Maggie and Martin were thrilled, stopping every few steps to wonder at a whiteboard with a clumsy brainstorm splashed across it or ask to be introduced to a colleague – the requests were delicately ignored by Bea. As they neared the glass windowed office, Bea felt her phone vibrate in her back pocket. Leaving her parents to take in the wonders of the corridor, she pulled out her phone.

💬 Zach: Lovely meeting you last night, Bea.

'Oh my God,' Bea whispered under her breath.

'What is it darling?' Martin asked.

'Oh just a work email, congratulating me on my last submission. They're very impressed.'

Maggie clapped her hands in delight, 'Oh let us see!' She sung, grabbing Bea's phone and reading what was on the screen. She frowned, 'Who's Zach?'

Bea visibly shuddered, dreading the conversation she knew she was about to have. 'Just a friend, Mum.'

'With benefits?'

'Mum! Ach.' Bea's mum had officially taken being a Gen X wannabe too far.

'Darling, this is wonderful. You must respond immediately!'

Bea took the phone from her glowing mother and replaced it in her pocket, 'Thanks Mum, I will.'

'Now.'

'You heard your mother.' Her parents stared at her expectantly.

Without breaking eye contact, Bea slowly retrieved her phone and pulled up a new message.

💬 Bea: You too, Zach. I'm just sorry you had to meet blind-drunk-off-her-face Bea so soon.

Before she could put her phone away, it vibrated again. Bea's parents nodded at her encouragingly.

💬 Zach: Not at all. It was a pleasure to meet her. I'd love to meet sober Bea too, though.

🗨 Bea: She'd like that.

🗨 Zach: How about tonight? I've got two tickets to Alice Underground, and one has your name on it.

Bea sighed, *tonight?*

'So?' The M&Ms said in unison.

'He wants to see me tonight.'

Both Bea's parents cheered, collected Bea in their arms and jumped up and down in a circle. Bea jerked away, reminding her parents that they were at her place of business.

'I'm supposed to be going to Dino's poetry slam tonight.'

'Your barista friend who doesn't do coffee art?' Maggie asked. 'I'm sure he'll understand. When's the last time you went on a date, honey?'

'We are not discussing this right now, Mum,' Bea smiled half-heartedly as two of her colleagues brushed past them on their way to a meeting.

'Darling,' Martin held Bea's hands in his. 'Give it a go. You need to put yourself out there. Just think what your sister would do.'

It had, in fact, been ages since Bea's last date. Not long before Cassandra's wedding, she had been casually dating a particularly elusive gentleman, Paul – dubbed 'Why Did I Swipe Right?' – who had made a run for the hills when an invitation to said event was extended. The rejection coupled with the trauma of the wedding fallout had Bea sworn off men. Until she met Zach.

'Come on darling, YOLO,' Maggie muttered softly.

> 🖤 **Bea:** The immersive theatre show? I've been dying to go!

> 🖤 **Zach:** Fantastic! Meet me under the Melbourne Central clock at 8?

> 🖤 **Bea:** See you then x

'There, are you happy now?' Bea held out her phone for her parents to see, her head hung low as she realised that her social life had so deteriorated that she was now taking dating advice from her parents.

'Ecstatic!' Martin chirped. 'Now who's up for a bite to eat?' Martin draped his arm around Bea and Maggie's shoulders and guided them to the elevator while Bea took out her phone.

> 🖤 **Bea:** Need to take a rain check on tonight. Sorry, Dino! I'll come to the next one. Promise!

12

'Open wide.'

Bea did as Zach requested and he placed a tiny pink marshmallow bearing the phrase 'Eat me' on her tongue. They were standing in a room festooned with chandeliers, dusty books, an old piano and a handful of actors dressed as characters from the Lewis Carroll novel. A man in a pink faux-fur Cheshire cat costume tapped Bea on the shoulder. They were officially immersed in this alternative reenactment of Alice in Wonderland.

'We're all mad here,' he said, and cackled in her face.

Zach took her hand. 'Are you glad you came down the rabbit hole with me? Or do you think I'm bonkers?'

'You're entirely bonkers!' Bea exclaimed. 'But I'll tell you a secret.'

'All the best people are.' Zach grinned, finishing off the quote and making Bea's insides smile.

A tall man with a grizzly beard dressed in Alice drag brushed past them, pushing Bea up against a wall of yellowing book pages. Zach stood over her, his arm resting against her hip casually. He swept a piece of hair from her eyes.

Bea tilted her head sideways. 'You know I'm going to bring up that book of yours. I can't stop thinking about all the insightful notes. I can barely focus on the words written by the actual author anymore.'

'I guess I don't like to take things at face value,' Zach said smoothly.

'What did you mean when you wrote "I know the fastest way to travel"?' Bea asked, blurting out the first question of many she had for him.

'Why, books, of course!' he laughed.

The Mad Hatter, complete with a tall purple hat and striped yellow and black stockings, offered them a cocktail in a teacup. They each took one gratefully.

Zach clinked his cup against hers. 'I feel like you've had an unfair head start. You've read all of my deepest thoughts. You're getting curiouser and curiouser, and I know not a thing about you.'

Bea tipped the sweet pink liquid into her mouth and swirled it around before swallowing it. She was desperate to know about Zach's annotations, but was cautious of coming on too strong. So, somewhat reluctantly, she let him change the topic. 'What do you want to know?'

'What's your favourite book?' he asked.

A man after my own heart. 'Easy. *The Secret History.*'

'I love that book.' He smiled, shuffling a fraction closer. 'Really?'

'Wasn't it Donna Tartt who said something along the lines of: "to know a book intimately is better than understanding a thousand superficially"?'

'Show-off.' Bea pushed him away, giggling. Referencing Bea's author idol made her swoon on the spot.

A Queen of Hearts strolled past them, carrying jam tarts on a silver tray. Zach picked one up, ate a mouthful and then held the rest of it to Bea's mouth. She took a bite, then licked her lips.

'How do you know so much about books, anyway? Are you an author, editor, publisher – or just a book nerd like me?'

'Zach Harris. Editor at Thelma & Clarke. Nice to meet you.' Zach held out his hand and she took it in hers.

'Oh, that's sexy.'

'And you are?' he asked.

'Bea Babbage, Marketing Manager at AKDB, working next door to the Melbourne Writers Festival.'

'Next door?'

'It's a long story.' Bea guzzled the rest of her drink. Zach watched her with a thoughtful gaze, like he was making mental scribbles of her.

'I never thought I'd ever meet anyone who loves books as much as I do,' Zach said, in – *was that awe?*

'Me neither,' Bea replied. 'Speaking of, I have more questions! Firstly, when did you start leaving these scribbles in your books?' she asked, eager to steer the conversation towards the topic of that book again.

Zach fidgeted with his jacket for a moment, perhaps searching for the right words. 'I guess it's always been a habit of mine. Believe it or not, reading never came easily to me. Thankfully I was a stubborn little kid. And I really, desperately, wanted to read *The Famous Five*. Thank God for Blyton, hey?' He put a hand against his teacup in silent prayer. 'I would stay up late every night reading under the covers with a torch strapped to my head.'

Bea couldn't help but picture a curly-haired little boy, squinting at the pages of the book with that little crease in his forehead she saw now.

'And I would underline every word I didn't recognise or couldn't understand. Then the next day I would pester my mum with questions and shove the scribbled-on book in her face while she tried to make breakfast.'

'And now look at you! Writing your own stories on the margins of your favourite books! I swear, when you wrote that thing about how if you're one in a million, there's still over seven thousand people like you, or something—'

'I guess it just made me think how we're always so afraid to be alone, but even for the most lonely people, well, there's always someone out there, who's just the same as you.'

Bea nodded. This couldn't have rung more true for her at this very moment. She still had more questions, though. And she felt like she couldn't ask them quickly enough.

They ended the evening covered in a light glitter mist and smelling just faintly of alcohol. On their journey they had experienced Alice's adventures and Bea and Zach sipped drinks (it turned out that the Cheshire Cat was an actor-cum-magician-cum-bartender, and spent the evening making vodka shots miraculously materialise out of thin air), shared stories and savoured each other's company. Bea had learnt that Zach grew up in the leafy suburb of Camberwell, was famous for being the class clown, had loved and lost three golden retrievers, developed an aversion to dumplings after being dared to eat one hundred in one sitting (he did, but suffered the consequences) and was a serious Netflix documentary fiend ('Did you hear the existence of aliens is a mathematical and statistical certainty?' he had said earnestly).

After they had both yawned a few times, they pushed past the small pockets of guests who still remained and made their way back through Melbourne Central until they reached the entrance to the train station. Checking the various timetables flashing across screens, they searched for the fastest route home.

'Which line are you?' Bea inquired, trying to act casual.

'Alamein. You?'

'Sandringham.' She faltered, slowly searching for her train card.

Bea had such a great night. In fact, it had been one of few good evenings since moving to Melbourne. And she was afraid for it to end. So, she took a deep breath, and for the first time in a while, did something brave.

'Want to come back to mine for a drink or something? I make a mean cosmopolitan,' Bea blurted.

Zach smiled. He pulled out his train card and followed her to the turnstiles, 'That does sound very appealing, but it's been a long day. I should probably call it a night.'

'Oh yeah, of course,' Bea replied, a little dejected. *So stupid, Bea! Way too soon!*

'I'll catch you around, Bea.' Zach waved goodbye. Bea waved back, *not even a goodbye kiss?* she bemoaned to herself. She shifted awkwardly, feeling foolish, and as she made her way to her platform in the opposite direction from Zach, she couldn't help but feel more alone than ever.

13

Dear Ramona,

Just the usual clean sweep for today (or whatever's included in my prize)! Heads up – tech guy swinging by between 10–11am to check my router. My wifi crashed mid-stalk last night. Do you think it's weird or refreshing that Zach's not on Facebook?

Thanks a bundle!

Bea xx

14

Bea,
> *I let the tech man in. He said, turn switch on.*
> *Ramona*

> *PS No one on Facebook anymore. You not hear about Russian spies?*

15

'Coffee. I need coffee.'

It was just before closing time when Bea stumbled through the doorway of The Nook and flung herself dramatically across the counter. It had been a trying couple of days. She had endured back to back meetings upstairs, during which she was forced to take minutes, coffee orders and her colleagues' creative bullshit. This was only exacerbated by her late nights. In an attempt to deal with two days of no communication from Zach after she had stupidly asked him back to her place, Bea had been staying up reading until the wee hours of the morning, trying to home in on Zach through his jottings.

'Long time, no see,' Dino said, just a bit too cavalierly for her current state.

'I've got half an hour before I enter my very own living nightmare. Coffee. Please,' Bea replied.

'Do tell.'

'In thirty minutes I'll be driving a hired, impractically large people mover, *on the freeway* during the worst roadwork period Melbourne has ever seen, apparently, to drop off my parents and my sister's husband, Nick, and their twin daughters – at the airport. Nick and the twins are visiting his parents, and the catch is, my sister has "sponsorship meetings" for her Instagram page, so has to be in Melbourne, and will be staying with me, in my cramped, one bedroom, shoebox of an apartment! For an entire week!' Bea exclaimed.

Dino laughed. 'Why can't she stay at her own house while her hubby and kids are away?'

'Because she's, quote, "too little to stay in such a big house all alone."' Bea rolled her eyes. 'So, like I said, coffee. Please!'

Dino went about grinding, steaming and frothing Bea's latte. He grabbed a pen and drafted a fresh quote across a takeaway cup, then poured the hot liquid into it. He slid the drink towards Bea, who was still face down on the counter, the comforting smell eventually drawing her from her stupor. She straightened and took a long, greedy sip.

'You're the master,' Bea sighed, clasping the cup in both hands and holding it close to her chest.

Dino cleared his throat.

'How could I forget?' Bea held it up to her eyes, turning it as she read the paraphrased quote. 'After a strong coffee one can forgive anybody, even one's own relations,' she read aloud, and chuckled softly before taking an exaggerated gulp.

'But next payday you're buying a KeepCup,' Dino said, before turning his back on Bea to wipe down the milk splatter left behind by her coffee. 'Heard from Zach yet?'

'Nope, but at least I have *his* annotations to keep me company. Listen to this quote: "A life spent longing for tomorrow". Isn't it so true?' Bea adjusted herself on the bar stool and without asking, grabbed an apple and cinnamon muffin from the basket display and bit into it immediately.

Dino nodded noncommittally. 'Gorgeous. Are you sure you need a sugar rush at this time of the day?' he asked, looking up briefly from his work.

'It's got fruit in it, so it doesn't count,' Bea said, her mouth full, crumbs flying. 'Besides, I'm going to need all the pastries I can get to survive this afternoon!'

Dino, taking advantage of the pre-close quiet, snuck out to the back room and returned holding a large frame. Bea swivelled on her bar stool, leaning up against the wooden bench. She watched as Dino hopped atop the low bench that ran along the back of the café; he kicked a couple of cushions to the side as he flipped the frame and held it against the wall.

'So, what do you think?'

The frame held a simple print: a long black line. On first inspection it appeared to be a random squiggle, but as Bea continued to stare, a spattering of words appeared: *I filter coffee. Not people.*

Bea hid her smile behind her cup. *Mental note, in addition to puns, new clothing and PDJ (public displays of joy), Dino really does not like Instagram.* 'So what you mean to say is that I can't take photos in your café?'

'You betcha bottom dollar that's what I mean. This is a strictly No Instagram Influencer zone.'

'You are so full of yourself, Dino,' Bea said. 'Can exceptions be made for a humble Bookstagrammer?'

'Don't tell me you've crossed over to the dark side?' Dino said, languishing against the wall theatrically. 'Just when I thought we could be friends.'

'I couldn't help myself,' Bea replied.

Dino shook his head, tisking audibly. 'I can't believe you.'

'It's nothing pretentious, I'm just sharing my thoughts on Zach's book.'

'So you're his manager now? Sexy.'

Bea rolled her eyes. 'If you really must know, I started the page before I met him, but – well, I've come to quite like the online community of readers, so I ran with it. They're loving Zach's scribbles almost as much as I am. Listen to this one: "In a room full of art, I only see you."'

Dino didn't reply so Bea continued, feeling a strange urgency to make Dino appreciate how special the notes were. 'That's not even one of his best. I'm so obsessed with these scribbles, Dino. I honestly feel like a teenage girl, crushing hard on Homer in *Tomorrow, When the War Began*.'

'I'm so happy for you, Bea,' Dino said indifferently, giving the glass in the frame a quick wipe. Satisfied, he jumped off the bench and made his way back to his post. 'Hey, shouldn't you get going?'

Bea checked her watch, leaped off her stool and grabbed her bag, suddenly wide awake. 'Shit! Thanks for the coffee, Picasso!' she called over her shoulder as she sprinted out the door.

White knuckling the steering wheel, Bea leaned forward and tried her best to focus on the road. With the traffic piling up, the twins crying bloody murder in the back and her mum silently sobbing in the corner (Maggie was not big on goodbyes), she was regretting everything.

'Honey, just a little to the left. That's a girl,' Lizzie cajoled, snapping a couple of dozen photos of her precious, emotionally distraught girls, because nothing screamed 'I'm so real' like some bona fide tears on your Instagram feed on Hump Day. Lizzie was all about curating the perfectly balanced aspirational and relatable online profile. Willow, however, was not in a very cooperative mood this morning. She slapped the phone out of Lizzie's hand, which provoked a measured, but firm telling off from her mother.

'Lizzie, don't be so hard on Willow,' Nick interjected. 'You know we're trying to use more positive reinforcement with the girls. They need to feel safe so that they know it's okay to f-a-i-l.' Nick spelt out the word lest the twins catch onto a sliver of his negative energy.

'Don't be ridiculous, Nick, they need to understand boundaries,' Lizzie bit back.

Maggie, who had stopped crying for long enough to nod encouragingly at Lizzie, sang her praises at what a patient and positive mum she was, while Martin took the opportunity to grill Bea further on her life in Melbourne.

'Sweetheart, I've been thinking about it, and if you're not being stimulated in your current job, why not look for another?' he said, tapping his fingers along the propeller of his drone, which he refused to pack in his check-in luggage. 'Why don't you use Lizzie's CV as a template? Or better yet, go down the reality TV route. You know Celeste and Barry's daughter was on *MasterChef*, and now she gets paid just to take pictures of herself eating brunch!'

Bea nodded along, thinking that she would rather dance naked in the street than audition for a reality TV show. 'That's a great idea, Dad. I'll think about it.'

'Enough with all the thinking, you just need to take a chance,' Lizzie insisted. 'Look what *The Bachelor* has done for my career. And I've never been happier!'

Bea looked at Lizzie in the rearview mirror. She appeared unfazed as she dabbed at the clump of apple compote which Lola had just thrown into her cleavage. She continued to drone on about how to maximise job opportunities through networking events while her mother chimed in with helpful tips on how to wield LinkedIn to your advantage.

'Please tell me you've at least got a Bumble Bizz account? Bea, really.' Lizzie shook her head dismissively as the M&Ms muttered nervously. 'Bea, I'll sort it all out for you. I'm an entrepreneur after all!'

'Shhh,' Bea hummed quietly.

'What was that, Beatrix?' Bea's dad inquired gently.

'Everybody needs to shhh,' Bea whispered, teeth gritted.

'Huh?' her family mouthed in unison.

'Shut up! You all need to shut up so I can get us through this nightmare of a traffic jam and get you to the bloody airport without me *accidentally* murdering you all!' Bea yelled.

They fell into shocked silence, not used to Bea being so abrupt. She was usually the calm and placating force in the family. Even Willow and Lola shut their tiny little mouths.

The rest of the drive was spent in silence, the low hum of evening radio chatter simmering beneath the surface of their bruised spirits. Bea loved her family, adored them and had missed them terribly since relocating to Melbourne. But, crammed between the noise and the chaos and the suffocating affection and concerned glances, she now felt a certain estrangement from them.

After twenty-seven excruciatingly long minutes, Bea finally pulled up in front of the Qantas terminal with gritted teeth. She helped lug the suitcases out of the boot and hugged her teary mother and father goodbye.

'I'll miss you, Liz.' Nick kissed Lizzie on the lips before picking up a twin with each arm.

'I'll miss you so much, my beautiful babies. Mummy loves you. Have fun with Grandma and Grandpa and I'll see you soon.' Lizzie's eyes began to tear, as she hugged each of her children fiercely. As Nick, Lola, Willow and the M&Ms trailed through the big glass doors, Lizzie turned to Bea, mascara staining her cheeks.

'It'll go quickly, Liz. It's only a week,' Bea said encouragingly. She knew this was hard for her sister, who had only ever been away from her kids for a couple of nights.

Lizzie nodded, regaining her composure. 'We are going to have so much fun! *Hashtag* girls' week!'

16

💬 Zach: Hey. Sorry for not getting in touch earlier. I had to go on a last minute work trip and hardly had the chance to stop!

💬 Bea: No drama. My sister is staying with me at the moment and I've barely had a second to breathe either.

💬 Zach: Can I get you out of the house tonight then? I know of a literary pub crawl happening that I think you might love.

💬 Bea: A literary pub crawl? Count me in!

💬 Zach: Great. Pick you up at 8 x

Bea sat on the closed seat of her toilet as Lizzie applied a discreet winged eyeliner to her lids. She played with her shirt buttons. When Bea had received Zach's message earlier that day, she let out the biggest sigh of relief. One she didn't realise she had been holding, as she waited for Zach to dump her before anything really began. Knowing that she had a second shot made her stomach flutter. She then immediately googled the event for that evening on

77

her phone. She found the Facebook page for the event, and discovered that it was dress up, and the theme was A Protagonist That's Changed Your Life. *Could this guy be my soulmate?*

Bea had decided she would go dressed as Atticus Finch, the closest thing to climbing into his skin and walking around in it. Lizzie wasn't sure it was such a good idea that Bea was going on a date dressed as a man, but Bea wasn't the type of person to lie about her most life-changing literary role model. Wasn't there a saying – *books before good looks?* In the end, they had settled on 'sexy Atticus', complete with a hot pantsuit and a solemn promise to keep at least three to four shirt buttons undone at all times. Makeup and absolutely no fake stubble were obviously non-negotiables, as well.

Bea sighed, letting the sound of her sister's babble wash over her. Now a married woman and reality TV star, Lizzie felt it was her right, no, responsibility, to pass on her dating wisdom to her baby sister. Which she managed to do while name dropping everyone she could possibly think of.

'Osher would always say before a rose ceremony, "just breathe and be you",' she was saying, 'but that's the biggest crock of shit! Excuse my French. Just be you? Sure, sure, roll out of bed in the morning and slick your hair back in a pony and yabber on about the only accomplishment of your week – avoiding the forty-minute wait at that new hip café and getting seated straight away. Please, Osher. What hogwash!'

Bea 'mmmed' and 'ummed' at all the right intervals, letting herself be soothed by the light tickle of the make-up brush Lizzie was now moving rhythmically across her cheeks. Bea loved her sister, but Lizzie had always been larger than life and now she was being larger than life in Bea's cramped apartment. But after all the years of being dragged to opening nights so that she could hold Lizzie's purse, or acting as Lizzie's alibi while she snuck out to fool around in the back of her high school boyfriend's ute, Bea had realised that it was just easier to go along with Lizzie's harebrained plans, rather than fighting them.

Only one week, Bea tried to comfort herself and then let her mind wander to Zach. Golden hearted, golden eyed Zach. Bea willed the doorbell to ring. She just wanted to see him again. To talk about the annotations and get to know this man of many dimensions more. Not usually one to get her hopes up before a date, Bea had decided to throw caution to the wind and let herself be all in. *What's the worst thing that could happen?* She was no stranger to heartbreak, after all.

Makeup ready and hair slicked back into a low bun, Bea squeezed herself into Lizzie's too short, too tight black shorts and finished the outfit off with a blazer and tie, which, at Lizzie's insistence, hung loosely around her neck so as not to obscure her cleavage ('AKA the money maker', Lizzie had said. *The Bachelor* had changed her). Thankfully her buzzer rang before Lizzie could insist on Bea swapping her discreet cream bra for the black silky one that left an alluring shadow beneath her top.

Bea grabbed her hot orange clutch (because we all know Atticus Finch was a man of good taste) and left with a final 'Don't rearrange my furniture again!' to Lizzie. She jogged down to the first floor and practically flew out the security gate, where she was greeted by Zach with a long, slow kiss.

'Hey you,' he whispered into her ear in his low, gravelly voice. Bea went weak at the knees.

Reluctantly, Bea pulled back and took in his costume. Zach wore beige chinos, and his bomber jacket was inside out, so that the chocolate-coloured fur lining was on display. He had painted a dark round oval on his nose and wore a pair of floppy ears attached to a headband.

'And you are?'

'Enzo,' Zach paused, expectantly. 'The labrador cross from *The Art of Racing in the Rain*,' he said, when Bea didn't immediately reply.

Bea looked at Zach quizzically. 'You dressed up as a dog?'

'Um, I dressed up as the sassiest, most insightful, cancer-sniffing, loyal, not to mention unique, narrative voice on the market.'

Bea couldn't help but smile.

'And who are you supposed to be?'

'Guess.'

'Corporate Wonder Woman?'

'I'm flattered,' Bea said, standing a little taller. 'But no.'

'Give me a clue.'

'Mockingbird.'

'Katniss?'

'Ach, not Mockingjay! I'm Atticus Finch. Duh!' Bea protested, suitably mortified as she gestured wildly at her barely-there costume.

Bea watched as the little dimple beside Zach's lips creased in delight. 'I've never met anybody quite like you, Beatrix Babbage,' he said before opening the Uber door and ushering her into the car.

'How was the rest of your week of family bonding?' he asked, casually placing his hand on Bea's bare knee.

'It's been extended. Lizzie's crashing at mine while her husband and kids are in Perth,' Bea grumbled.

'Trouble in paradise?' Zach asked, eyebrows raised.

Bea filled him in on Lizzie's well intentioned, but total disrespect for people's personal space, barely able to stay focused because Zach's hand was inconspicuously traveling further up her leg, until his fingers traced the hem of her shorts. Suddenly, Bea wasn't so mad about having Lizzie stay.

Eventually they pulled up in front of the iconic city bookstore, Novel Place, on Bourke Street. Its tall, glass window greeted the pair, displaying a colourful array of children's picture books like *All the Ways to be Smart* and hot off the press fiction. Tim Winton, Lisa Genova, Celeste Ng, Jane Harper seemed to wave at her in welcome. *Hello old friends*. Outside, small pockets of people milled about, cradling cocktail glasses and beers. Bea spotted wizards, detectives, women dressed in long, black dresses à la Holly Golightly and even a man covered in navy blue paint, with a huge dorsal fin strapped to his back. *Moby Dick?* Bea was enthralled by the sight unfolding before her.

'I think this might just be the classiest pub crawl I've ever been on!' Bea exclaimed.

Zach grinned and guided her through the bookstore's cavernous doorway. They wove through shelves, passing two women, one who appeared to be dressed as Lisbeth Salander and, the other, as Daenerys Targaryen, kissing in the travel section, and made their way to the makeshift bar.

Bea and Zach grabbed a drink each and huddled between the Brontës and the Austens in the Classics aisle. Bea leaned against the overflowing shelves, drawing courage from the strong female leads hidden between the pages behind her. Zach propped himself casually against a shelf that sat at a right angle, sipping his cocktail.

'Melbourne. Why?' Zach dove straight in, jarring Bea ever so slightly.

'Where do I even begin?'

So she began at the start, well, almost. She politely sidestepped the whole destroying her best friend's wedding in one fell swoop, sugar-coated (*ironic, huh?*) the working on dental hygiene thing and got stuck straight into the café culture, the festivals on every other week (which she didn't admit to visiting purely online) and the bookstores.

'I'm just starting to extend my bookstore horizon, but from what I've seen so far, I love them all. The pokey second-hand ones, the secret treasure troves of discarded paperbacks tucked away in op shops, the stores that host a labyrinth of shelves, of whose contents the sales assistants know as well as the creases on their own hands. And then there's that gorgeous bookstore not far from my work which always has a stand of rainbow garden windmills sitting out the front,' Bea said all in one breath, feeling herself rambling and only a little embarrassed by her longwinded declaration of love to Melbourne's literature scene. But Zach had been listening in wonder.

Just when Bea was about to turn the tables and ask the first of the many questions she had for her date, Zach nudged her. 'Bea, isn't that your friend?' Zach jutted his chin forward. Bea swivelled around to see none other than Dino, his arm looped loosely around Sunday's shoulders. His head was tilted back, mid laugh, eyes closed in satisfaction.

'Dino? Sunday?' she called out, beckoning them over.

'Bea?' Dino looked up, surprised. Sunday waved, still laughing, as she came over to pull Bea into a warm hug.

'What are you two doing here?' Bea asked.

Dino shrugged. 'Same thing you are it seems.'

Sunday winked and took a swig from Dino's beer.

Of course they're together. They make a cute couple, Bea thought, before introducing Zach. The three of them shook hands.

Dino stalled a moment. 'You know, if you hadn't said anything, I might not have recognised you. You look different when you're not clinging to a latte for dear life,' he joked.

'You're one to talk. Who are you even dressed as?' Bea said only just noticing that Dino was draped in a thick, brown coat, with duct tape wrapped around his waist and chest.

'He's a bookworm,' Sunday interjected. 'And only the cutest bookworm I've ever seen,' she said, bumping him playfully on the arm.

'You do know what the theme is, right?' Zach asked.

Dino rolled his eyes and took another sip of his drink. 'I know, I know. It was all very last minute, and Sunday over here talked me into it.'

Sunday raised her left hand. 'Guilty!' she smiled, mischievously.

And then a bell rang. The call for them to move to their next literary destination: Basement Books, the mecca for rare and antique novels. Bea propped her empty glass next to a clothbound copy of *Doctor Zhivago* and took Zach's hand.

Bea hadn't laughed so much in what felt like months. Maybe it was the free-flowing drinks, or maybe it was being cocooned in a maze of bookshelves that left Bea so uninhibited, but she had a feeling it had a lot to do with the ever so charming Zach. The conversation had flowed easily and merrily. Bea even managed to extricate more information about his inscriptions, proving Zach's depth. Like how he chose to write his thoughts in a book rather than a notepad because he would never be able to write down all that he wanted to say, so hoped that the story could do some of the talking.

For some reason, Dino and Sunday seemed to avoid the pair, save for Dino's *subtle* glimpses in their direction. Glimpses of Zach's hand on the small of Bea's back, glimpses of her giggling into Zach's chest, glimpses of Zach grinning and sloppily wiping up the trickle of booze that fell down Bea's cheek.

Arriving back at her apartment after Zach had insisted on dropping her off first, Bea and Zach stood outside her building, just close enough that Bea's knees rested against Zach's strong shins.

'So, what did you think?' Zach asked.

'Of the pub crawl? I think I've reached peak coolness.' Bea sighed. 'But don't go getting any ideas about my coolness level. This is as good as it gets for me.'

'I happen to think you're extremely cool.'

Bea dismissed him, blushing. 'Please.'

'You're so cool, Babbage,' Zach said, 'because you are completely and truly yourself.'

'I think that's the cocktails talking,' Bea said, feeling embarrassed and ecstatic all at once.

'It's definitely not,' Zach said. 'I see you. I really do.'

'You don't even know me!' Bea laughed.

'I know. But boy, do I hope to.' He inched towards her, his hands landing on her hips.

Bea's breath quickened. And then Zach's lips were on hers. He wrapped his arm tightly around her waist, pulling her gently towards him. He felt warm and firm against her body and for a moment, Bea forgot where she was and who she was and that staggering feeling of despondency which had become as familiar as her own shadow. She let him kiss her neck and across her collarbone, tracing her skin like she imagined his pen traced the pages of *Meeting Oliver Bennett*.

'Want to come upstairs?' Bea breathed, fumbling for her keys.

'Like you wouldn't believe,' Zach said, calling out to the patiently waiting Uber driver that it would just be the one stop after all, before following her up to her apartment door, through which they practically fell.

Bea shushed Zach as they crept past Lizzie, sleeping soundly on the couch, then pulled him to her bedroom and onto her bed. Their hands raced to explore each other's bodies. With each kiss and touch, Bea was filled to the brim with desire and an even firmer conviction in the power of a good book to unite two lost souls. Lips still locked, Bea's hand travelled down Zach's chest until she found his belt buckle. But before she could unclasp it, Zach's hand was on hers. Bea pulled away.

'Everything okay?' she asked.

'So okay. So much more than okay,' Zach said, shuffling closer to Bea and kissing her lightly on the nose. 'I just want to take things slow.'

Bea, trying to push the disappointment and confusion away, fell back against the pillows and took a deep breath. 'Yeah, of course. Probably wise.'

'I should get going.' Zach's face had transformed. He was no longer breathy, dishevelled and yearning – now he was … *all business?*

'Yeah, of course.' Bea lay still, confused.

'Cool. I'll let myself out.' Zach leaned in to kiss her on the cheek.

Bea wrapped her arms around herself, listening to the door shut crisply. *What the hell did I do wrong?*

17

Win a free cut and colour by telling us in 25 words or less who your hairstyle icon is.

Definitely Krusty the Clown. His hair is naturally green (I've literally never seen his roots) and his three tufts are always perfectly in place.

18

Bea slumped into a chair in the meeting room, lost in memories of the night before. The passion, the fun, and how Zach left her with blue – boobs? She tucked a strand of hair behind her ears and tried to sit as inconspicuously as possible behind her open laptop. Clicking into a blank Word document, she dated it and then looked around at her coworkers, all of whom were sitting to attention behind realms of notepads and A3 vision boards, ready to dive headfirst into today's brainstorming session. *That used to be me*, Bea languished, recalling the good old days when brainstorming meetings used to get her juices flowing. She was so over this account.

Just as the meeting was about to commence, a message popped up on Bea's screen. It was from strappy-heeled Martha. They had recently graduated from cubicle chats to instant message.

> ⊙ Martha: Toilet break? Need to discuss latest episode of *Little Women*. Jo is so sassy and I need to be her.

> ⊙ Bea: Stuck in a meeting. FML. Wish I had Jo's 'I'm too independent and ridiculously committed to my craft for this shit' attitude to get me out of this godforsaken meeting. Also, client wants

us to promote new floss line dubbed 'Fairy
Floss'. Is it just me, or are they complete
oxy-MORONS?!

Bea closed the pop-up and sighed audibly, forcing herself
to tune back into the meeting. Joel was talking about
how to capture the 'ladies' in the market. It wasn't exactly
clear why he kept using air quotes when referring to the
female market, but everybody seemed to be going with it.
Misogynists, Bea thought derisively, then immediately casti-
gated herself for being so judgemental. That was something
Cassandra had always accused her of: 'Do you really have
the luxury of being so picky?' or 'Of course he's staring at
your chest, that's what boys do!' she would say.

'Why couldn't you just have my back?' Bea mumbled
under her breath.

'What was that?' Joel turned to her. 'Something to add,
Babbage?' He smirked, and looked at Scott, who stifled a
laugh behind his mug.

Bea froze, her hands suspended above her keyboard.
Think, Bea, think! 'Only that, I …' she began hesitantly.
'Only that I think promoting dental floss in the same way
as candy sends a confusing message to consumers.'

'And?'

'And don't we have a responsibility to educate buyers
on healthy dental care?' Bea became suddenly bolstered by
her own ethical code. 'I think this campaign stands for the
wrong ideal.'

'That might be so, but it's what the client wants, so it's
what the client gets.'

'Well, that's not good enough for me.' Before she knew it, Bea was standing, her chair thrust behind her.

'Thin ice, Bea,' Scott warned, folding his arms tightly across his chest.

Bea looked around at her bewildered colleagues and took a deep breath. *Think about the rent you can't afford and calm the fuck down.* She sat back in her chair quietly. 'Okay, sorry, you're right. Please, go on.'

'Why thank you,' Joel said sarcastically and resumed outlining his idea for a bikini-clad tooth fairy mascot.

Bea swallowed her anger, checked the time on her monitor and whiled away the minutes until she could escape back down to The Nook and grab herself another coffee.

The meeting ran thirty-five minutes over. As soon as it wrapped up, Bea bolted from the boardroom.

'Back so soon?' Dino laughed from behind the coffee machine.

'You have no idea what I'm dealing with up there,' Bea grumbled and resumed her position at the counter, which was dangerously close to a fresh plate of pastries. In a bid to distract her taste buds, she pulled Agatha Christie onto her lap, hugging her warm, thick body close to her chest.

'Bea?' Dino repeated.

'Huh? Sorry, in puppy coma. Come again?'

'So what's the deal with you and Zach? You guys seemed pretty chummy last night.'

'Mmm he seems almost too good to be true. Unlike the men I work with,' Bea said. 'I mean it's the 21st century, objectifying women for sales just cannot be an option anymore!'

'Why don't you just quit then?'

'Quit? That's a cute little idea! Who will pay for my coffees when I'm penniless?' Bea dismissed Dino's suggestion quickly.

'I'm serious, Bea. You're so unhappy working for those bigwigs upstairs. You hate your job! And you only say so every other day.' Dino stopped lecturing her to serve an elderly gentleman who had a walking stick and a hearty chuckle, giving Bea a moment to fantasise about how her life could be different. Maybe she should have just stayed in Perth, friendless and completely overshadowed by her Insta-famous sister? At least there her career had been going somewhere. The only difference in her life in Melbourne was that her mother no longer shoved bags of fresh fruit and vegetables into her arms every Thursday night after family dinner. And, while Bea was cautiously optimistic about the new romantic interest in her life, she didn't want – nor expect – her happiness to come from being in a relationship. Plus Bea had a habit of going after the wrong guy. Or rather, the wrong guys had a habit of going after her.

'What would you do if you could have any job in the world?' Dino quickly held up his hand, palm facing Bea, in an attempt to halt her protests. 'Wait a minute. Ignore all of the practicalities involved and forget about your expenses! Just take a moment to imagine a different reality.'

Bea tapped her fingers on the counter. *Anything?* 'I have no idea,' she said, as an image of a deserted tropical island and a small bookstore made out of coconut husks and palm leaves flitted across her mind.

'Come on, Babbage, surely you've thought about it? Haven't you ever allowed yourself to imagine some utopian workplace while you eat your lunch in the toilet and rack your brain for the next big thing in dental hygiene?'

Bea sighed and ran her fingers through Agatha Christie's dense, curly fur. What more did she want for herself? What more did she think she deserved? She had always done everything by the book: studied hard at school, followed in her sister's footsteps and gone straight to university to study marketing, towed along with Cassandra and had a couple of fantastic, but time-sensitive, dalliances with Europe, volunteered when she could, graduated, discovered LinkedIn and eventually got a job in the field in which she had studied. In fact, the most radical thing she had done in the eight years between finishing school and landing a nine-to-five was accidentally ordering escargot in a Paris café, expecting it to be a raisin pastry. And it's not like she hadn't been happy, it was just that, in the last few months, it had started to feel like her life had chosen her, and not the other way around.

'Oh, I don't know, it's silly really,' Bea said, taking a sip of her coffee. 'But maybe I don't need some major career overhaul. Maybe I'm just tired of following somebody else's narrative. Or some other narrative I think I should be following. I just want to be able to call the shots a little more, and, I guess, work according to a better moral code. I want to have more meaning in my life, more purpose. And moving here, uprooting my life, was supposed to be the start of all that. Of a braver Bea!'

Dino nodded along reassuringly. 'Okay, great. Well, that's a good start!'

'Don't mock me, Dino.'

'Who, me? I'm as sincere as they come,' Dino said, holding his right hand to his heart. 'Tell me more, please.'

'A very tiny part of me has always wondered what it would be like to go out on my own. What it would be like to be in a situation where I had more control over the companies I worked for. Pick and choose between the boring, the unethical and the wildly enthralling!'

'So, do it, already! What have you got to lose?'

'Stability? A roof over my head? Money to buy books?'

'Babbage, you're so practical. Fine then, start somewhere small. Try your hand at organising something little, experimenting with what's out there, and see how you like it.'

Bea laughed. 'You make it all sound so easy.'

Dino leaned opposite her, elbows on the counter, and came so close she could smell the scent of coffee beans on his fingertips. 'Perhaps it could be – in the beginning in any case.'

'So, what? I just quit my job and open up my own advertising agency? Just like that?' Bea said with a click of her fingers.

'Well, yeah.' Dino shrugged. 'You should do that. And soon. Even I can see that this job is killing you.' He tilted in even closer. 'But maybe start with something small if that's too daunting a thought. A stunt, an event, something you feel passionate about. That's what I did when I was thinking about leaving the corporate world and opening up The Nook.'

'You were in the corporate world? Somehow, I can't quite picture that,' Bea laughed.

'I worked in finance for my uncle's business a few years back. He owned an accounting firm, so you can just imagine how thrilling the gig was. I needed to get out of there. But before I overhauled my whole life, I started small. On the weekends I volunteered at a soup kitchen, making coffee and helping manage the books. And I loved it. That's when I realised I had to quit my job and open The Nook, do something that allowed me to be more creative and be in the thick of things. A few months later, I approached Sunday to start this place up with me, and the rest is history.'

'Dino, that's amazing. But I wouldn't even know where to begin. Plus, you had Sunday to take that leap of faith with. I don't really have anyone here, except for Zach, and I think it's a bit too soon to start discussing starting a business together.'

'Well, why don't we start brainstorming?'

By the time Bea had devoured two almond croissants they had a plan. With a new sense of purpose, Bea waved Agatha Christie and Dino goodbye, scooped up her coffee and practically skipped out the door. As she made her way back to her desk upstairs, she peered down at the takeaway cup in her hands on which was scribbled: *Try now, try now, it isn't too late.*

19

To: tracey@broadsheet.com
From: beababbage@gmail.com
Subject: Re: Re: Books and speed dating – need I say more?

Dear Tracey,

In two weeks' time, **Next Chapter: Speed Dating for Books**, will be launching at The Nook in South Yarra, Melbourne. The evening is all about bringing together a room full of book fanatics desperate for their next great read.

Guests will be invited to come bearing an adored book, and speed-dating style, move around, interviewing one another in the hopes of discovering their next favourite read. The event will be the perfect opportunity to inter-act with new bookish friends (because life isn't all about finding the romantic 'one') while sourcing hot new reads and swooning over the many literary loves of a reader's life.

For more information, don't hesitate to call or email.

Sincerely,

Bea Babbage

20

Bea sat at her small kitchen table. She was trying to respond to another email about the first Next Chapter event but her mind kept going back to Zach. *Does he even like me? Is taking it slow really a thing? Why did he take off the other night? Why hasn't he called me?* It was times like these that she wished she was still in Perth. She would have headed down to Scarborough Beach, her favourite place to think, stared at the ocean and analysed, in detail, Zach's actions. Bea pushed away her laptop and took out her phone. She scrolled to Zach's name, her thumb hovering over his number. *What would you even say?* But before she knew what she was doing, she had pressed the green phone icon next to his name.

'Shit, shit, shit! I'm not mentally prepared for this!' Bea frantically looked around her kitchen, as if the answer was hidden among the pile of dirty dishes that awaited her in the sink. Jumping up, she pranced awkwardly on the spot, waving her phone around. She contemplated hanging up, but then thought better of it – he'd know she'd called anyway. As the fourth ring tolled, she rammed the phone in her jeans pocket so that the speaker was just poking out.

'Hello?' she heard Zach answer.

'Oh, you are so hilarious, Bea,' Bea improvised in a fake English accent.

'Oh, stop it, you are!' Bea replied to herself, speaking loudly so that Zach could hear the conversation.

'Bea?' Zach called, no more than a muffled murmur.

'Do you hear that? I think it's coming out of your pocket,' Bea said in the fake English accent.

'Oh, you're right.' She took her phone out and held it to her ear. 'Hello?'

'Bea?'

'Zach? Is that you?'

'Er, you just called me,' Zach said, clearly confused.

'Oh, did I? Must've been a butt dial. It's been happening to me all day. Stupid phone. I'm just hanging out with my friend Martha,' Bea said in a totally blasé voice.

'Oh, cool. Now that I have you I was going to suggest hanging out, but if you're busy …' Zach said, trailing off before Bea interrupted.

'No, no. Martha was just leaving. Feel free to swing by my place in about half an hour or so, if you want to hang. Or, whatever.' Bea sprinted to the bathroom mirror and began smearing concealer underneath her eyes.

'Okay, yeah, cool. I can come round then.'

'Great. Fantastic. Anyway, I better run,' Bea said, now powdering her cheeks with blush.

'See you soon then.'

'Catch ya.'

Bea hung up the phone and exhaled. 'You loser, Bea,' she said in her terrible British accent.

'Speed dating? For books?'

'Doesn't it sound fun?'

Bea sat on the couch in her living room, one leg curled underneath her while her other bare foot grazed against the cream jute rug. Zach sat beside her. He had arrived at her house promptly, as promised, and they had spent the last hour watching reruns of *The Office* on her couch, and scoffing down caramel popcorn. Everything seemed nice. Maybe she had simply imagined him rejecting her. Maybe he really did want to take things slow. Zach was looking at her curiously as he tried to take in her surprise new venture.

'What's not to like? I mean, look at us! We're the perfect example of finding the great literary and literal leads in your life through books.' She caught herself. *Was that too much?*

She couldn't help but wish Cassandra could be here to enjoy this new idea with her. She would be all 'Is six books too many? It's like forcing me to choose my favourite child!' and 'Can it be *The Great Gatsby* themed?' Bea had texted Cassandra immediately after her light-bulb moment with Dino, but of course, she was met with an echoing silence.

And for all his bookish wisdom, Zach just didn't seem to be getting it. 'And you're doing this with Dino? You two seem pretty close,' he said, relaxing back against a forest green decorative pillow.

'He's been a good friend. Well, one of my only friends, really. In Melbourne, that is.'

'What about me?' Zach gave her one of his rich, sunshine-beaming smiles and placed his hand on her leg.

'I was hoping we were a little more than friends?' Bea inched just the slightest bit closer to him. Zach matched

Bea's cautious insistence, leaning towards her, his hand travelling up her thigh.

'Yoo-hoo! Anybody here?'

Lizzie. Bea was both utterly delighted and utterly exhausted by her sister's non-stop enthusiasm for Melbourne life and for how to live it properly. All week she hadn't stopped telling Bea how to dress, what to cook, how to speak. Bea knew Lizzie was coming from a good place, but she was tired of being told what to do all the time.

'You're back so soon,' Bea muttered to her sister, who was dressed to the nines in a billowy red chiffon dress. She shuffled away from Zach. She was not one for overt displays of public affection. Especially not when her family was involved.

'And you have company,' Lizzie said, hand on heart. 'Charmed, I'm sure.' She extended her hand towards Zach, which he half-shook and then, looking bewildered, kissed.

'I'm Lizzie Babbage, you may recognise me from—'

'*The Bachelor*, Season Two? Oh, I know. I can't believe Jake chose that devil Courtney over you!' Zach guffawed.

'Tell me about it. But it turned out for the best. I now have a wonderful husband and twin daughters and Jake has, well, a divorce, bad publicity and an intervention order.' Lizzie shrugged, almost successfully masking any hint of spite in her voice.

'You watch *The Bachelor*? You're full of surprises, Zach,' Bea whispered to him.

'You don't know the half of it,' he winked.

'Well, I won't keep you two *lovebirds*,' Lizzie trilled, 'but I just wanted to let you know that the Facebook event for

Next Chapter is live and I've been in touch with my Bachie gals.' She turned to Zach conspiratorially. 'I'm hoping they'll bring a bit of buzz to the evening!'

'Gosh, you move quick, Liz. I would have loved to have had a chance to see the event first though,' Bea said, clasping her hands tightly around her knees.

'Trust me, Bea. It all looks *fabulous*. And, like they say, you gotta be in it to win it. No time to mess around!' She subconsciously touched the giant rock on her left finger. 'Thank God I'm in Melbourne. There's far too much to organise and I can't do it all the way from Mount Eliza!'

'You know, I've really got most of it under control, Liz.'

'Sure, sure, darling,' Lizzie cooed as she sauntered away to Bea's bedroom.

Looks like I'll be the one on the couch tonight. Bea tried to feel grateful for her sister's energy and help.

'It's next Thursday, by the way,' Bea said shyly when they were alone again.

Zach picked up his glass of red wine and gulped what was left of it down. 'What is?'

'The book event. If you're free and feel like coming?' Bea said, looking away. 'You could bring an Atwood, perhaps? You mention her in one of your notes.'

'Nothing screams "it's time to party!" like a totalitarian world and sexual servitude,' Zach laughed.

'There's no pressure though, only come if, you know, you're not busy already.'

Zach fell back against the couch pillows and propped his hands behind his head, a half-smile dancing on his lips. 'I wouldn't miss it for the world. Maybe I can even work out some promotion deal with the boss?' he said. And then he kissed her.

When Zach kissed Bea it was like she was hooked on a great series and craving the next instalment to arrive in stores – she already wanted to kiss him again and again and again. But before she knew it, he was standing by the front door, his hand caressing her face, saying goodbye.

'I'm worried he's just not attracted to me,' Bea whined as she grabbed a clump of toilet paper. 'One second he's all over me, the next he's half way out the door. I mean, what sort of guy wants to take things slow, if you get what I mean?' She peered under the divider and gazed longingly at Martha's leopard-print lace-ups. Her co-worker even managed to make sneakers look uber chic.

'Honey, that gender stereotype is so 2007,' Martha replied. 'Did it occur to you that he's being honest when he says he wants to take this slow? And that doesn't make him any less of a man, or you, any less of an attractive woman. Oh bother! Love, you don't happen to have a tampon handy?'

Bea rustled around in her handbag, found one and passed it under the stall to Martha. She was right, of course. Bea was being close-minded, weighing Zach down with societal expectations. Why did she always assume the worst?

'Ugh, I hate dating! So many unknowns. So many insecurities! I like to think I am a totally sane, put-together person until some guy comes along and I immediately feel like a total whack job! Maybe I should just pull the pin while I still have my dignity intact?'

'Don't be ridiculous.' The toilet flushed. 'Wasn't it Austen who once wrote something along the lines of "my feelings won't be repressed"? Don't be afraid to get hurt. It's the only way to know you've truly lived.'

'I guess he did seem excited for my book speed dating event. Well … eventually, anyway.'

'See! He sounds great. And keen. Don't let this tall, dark and handsome book-loving guy pass you by,' Martha said before letting the cubicle door close with a muted thump behind her.

Long after Martha had left, Bea stayed in the cubicle. She pulled out her copy of *Meeting Oliver Bennett* and inhaled a few paragraphs. Then she traced her finger along the outline of Zach's annotations. Words like "elixir", "freedom" and "ecstasy" floated up off the page. In a moment of frustration, she grabbed the pen she had jammed into her messy bun and scribbled her own thought along the already clogged margin: *What the hell do you want with me?!* Then she slammed the book shut, flushed, washed her hands and, begrudgingly, made her way back to her desk.

21

Bea wound a final strand of hair around her curling wand and appraised her reflection in the mirror, her head tilted at an awkward angle. She was fresh-faced, save for a stain of red gloss on her lips and a discreet winged eyeliner. She shook out her hair and slid on a pair of sparkly silver sneakers – Martha's suggestion. Tonight was the night, her break-out moment! A chance to see if there was more to her than coordinating social media copy for the latest cordless electric toothbrush. To see if she could be brave enough to be the leading lady in her own story.

Bea had pulled out the big guns for the event, haggling down the price of champagne, and ordering some super-sophisticated, and more importantly, super-discounted flower arrangements. She'd even managed to talk The Little Brunswick Street Bookstore into offering discount coupons for guests on their next purchase. Lizzie had only been slightly controlling – *ahem* – helpful, too. The only problem was, her sister refused to believe that this was a totally platonic dating experience so she had ordered four large bouquets of heart-shaped balloons (which she at least offered to pay for) and organised sponsorship from Hello Cupid Dating. Bea had tried desperately to talk her out of it, but there was no getting through to her. Lizzie insisted that this 'wasn't her first rodeo' and that her intuition was never off when it came to matters of the heart.

She was on a mission, and no matter how many times Bea un-cc'd her sister from emails, Lizzie managed to claw her way back in. So, Bea had relented and hoped to God that her sister would at least keep herself in check on the night.

Thankfully, Dino had continued to be supportive and, more importantly, involved. He had spent the week madly decorating coffee cups with an array of quotes from some of Bea's favourite authors. And, at Bea's insistence, had patiently rearranged the tables, only to put them back exactly where they had been to begin with due to space constraints (the café was called The Nook for a reason). Not to mention the pièce de résistance – the bespoke poem he had prepared to open the festivities, which would be a surprise for Bea as well. All Bea had to concern herself with now was not falling apart at the seams or letting her visceral fear of failure, which had dogged her for days, get the better of her.

The doorbell buzzed. *Zach.*

Since he was last at her house a week ago, Zach had seemed to be overcompensating for his initial scepticism about the event with messages of encouragement and a large, totally embarrassing bouquet of tulips that had arrived at her work the previous afternoon. It was sweet, really. And it was certainly working. Bea felt a flutter deep within as she grabbed her bag and flew down the stairs to greet him.

'Hey there, little bookworm,' he said, giving her that smile of his that seemed to light up his whole face and which was impossible not to return.

Bea folded herself into his arms and kissed him with fervour.

'Ready?'

She nodded and tugged at the corner of his blue-green shirt, demanding one last kiss before settling into his car.

They were barely inside The Nook when Lizzie, who had driven down from Mount Eliza early to welcome her fellow *Bachelor* contestants, came barrelling towards them. She was dressed in a hot pink bodycon dress and nine-inch stilettos. A small bejewelled earpiece, complete with mini microphone, poked out between her luscious locks.

'Finally! You're here!' she exclaimed, grabbing Bea tightly by the shoulders. 'The florist is running thirty minutes late, all three of my Bachie gal pals have pulled out at the last minute – apparently Channel Ten is throwing some big blowout at Crown that they just *had* to attend – you're making me sleep on the couch for the night, and the cupcakes are a disaster. A disaster! It's been a total communication meltdown. Look!' she shrieked and dragged Bea over to the counter where Dino stood, shining glassware, with a barely concealed smirk on his face. She thrust open the first of four large, white boxes. Bea peered into the box.

'They must have misread the brief. I told you we wouldn't get good service if you just won them from some stupid competition! What the hell are we going to do?' cried Lizzie, clutching onto Bea for dear life.

'Misread the brief' was an understatement. Plastered on every cupcake were two bulging pink breasts, complete with liquorice nipples, and the word 'BOOBS' in black icing.

Zach placed his hand on Bea's lower back. He took one look at the cupcakes and burst out laughing.

Lizzie and Bea were not amused.

'Why not try and make the most of an iffy situation?' Dino said calmly.

'What?' Bea and Lizzie barked in unison.

'Make it a fundraiser. Pop a jar out and collect donations for—' he paused, thinking. 'The Breast Cancer Foundation.'

Bea exhaled and let her shoulders drop, visibly relaxing.

Lizzie, only somewhat placated, placed her fingers to her earpiece and chirped away a host of new instructions to God knows who. 'Do you copy?' she yelled as she stormed off.

'You're the tits, mate,' Zach said, putting his fist out for Dino to bump.

'I'm not really into puns,' Dino replied, leaving him hanging.

Bea rolled her eyes and put her hand in her bag, flicking her thumb over the pages of her copy of *Pachinko* – her other hot date for the evening. Looking to Dino and then to Zach, who were holding firm eye contact with each other, Bea suddenly felt ill at ease.

'The poem, how's it looking?' she said to Dino.

Dino placed the final champagne glass down next to its buddies on the counter. 'Let's just say, it's no Dickinson.'

Would anything go smoothly tonight?

Bea left Dino to his half-hearted small talk with Zach about football – which she was almost certain Dino did not watch – and went to survey the rest of the room. The flowers had finally arrived and Lizzie was fussing over them. Bunches of white, long-stemmed roses lined two rows of tables. Bea had wanted sunflowers, her favourite; a flower that shouted warmth and happiness without a shred of cliché typical of the very flowers that now clogged the café. She didn't want there to be anything typical about this event, but it seemed *somebody* had intercepted the order.

'Liz, did you call the florist without asking me?' Bea whispered into Lizzie's ear, picking at her nails.

'Yes, I thought I told you. Sunflowers are way too rustic. They would've clashed with the romantic theme of the evening.' Lizzie glanced around the room, distracted.

'The theme of the night is not romance, Lizzie!' Bea snapped.

'Jesus, Bea. Way to thank me for doing you a favour,' Lizzie snapped.

Funny that your 'favours' always seem to be the opposite of what I want, Bea pondered to herself before pushing away the rest of her toxic thoughts.

Bea was nervous. Butterflies-in-her-throat, need-to-devour-weight-in-chocolate and not-even-the-words-of-Liane-Moriarty-would-put-a-smile-on-her-dial nervous. It was twenty-three minutes past the event's official start time and still nobody had arrived. Bea had fluffed the flowers, tucked and untucked chairs to neaten the place up and consumed one – okay, two – glasses of wine, in an attempt to assuage her mounting panic, but she was officially on the brink. Lizzie was a mess too. She had been madly shouting into her sparkly headset for the last half an hour, calling on every favour and media influencer she could get her dainty, manicured hands on. Zach was no help; he stayed in the corner devouring the baked bosomy goodness with just a hint too much excitement.

And then there was Dino. Feet up on the table, notebook in hand and Agatha Christie standing to attention by his chair after scoffing down half a cupcake before Dino could stop her. Instead of helping, he sat flipping through the pages of his Moleskine, his pen moving from his mouth to the page, as if he didn't have a care in the world. *Well, I guess he doesn't,* thought Bea, suddenly consumed with every negative emotion known to man. *It's not like his whole sense of self rests on not looking like a fool tonight.*

Enough was enough. Bea re-lit the last of the tea lights and stormed over to the far-too-complacent barista.

'Comfortable?' she asked as she stopped in front of him, arms crossed, foot tapping.

'Huh?' Dino popped his pen behind his right ear and squinted up at Bea. 'You right there?'

'No, I'm not right here! The event is a bust! Not a single person has shown up, Lizzie is on the cusp of a social media meltdown and the fruit platter I ordered has no grapes. This is worse than Fyre Festival! Why did you talk me into doing this?'

'Bea, calm down.' Dino dropped his feet to the floor and pulled her onto the seat next to him. He placed a glass of water in her hands and instructed her to take three deep breaths. 'It's the first event. It's bound to take a while to create hype. Plus, haven't you heard the expression "fashionably late"? It's not even eight-thirty.'

Bea drank some water, putting the empty glass down on the wooden table with a jarring thump. 'You're right, I'm sorry. And I shouldn't be taking it out on you.' She sighed. 'I just so wanted this to work. I *needed* this to work.' She forced a small smile and picked up Agatha Christie, hugging her tightly against her chest.

'Just give it time.'

'You know, I really am grateful.' Bea nuzzled her face into the dog's fur. 'You've been so nice to me since I got to Melbourne.'

'No, I haven't.'

'Okay, maybe you haven't been *so* nice. But you've been present, and consistent. And you've let me just about move into your coffee shop. And I think I'm this close to convincing you to give me Agatha.'

'Dream on, Babbage.' Dino ruffled the curly fur atop Agatha Christie's head.

They sat there for a while, the poodle forming a warm wedge between them.

'Hey, I thought Sunday would be here? She isn't joining us tonight?'

Dino shrugged. 'Nah. She had a friend's gig to go to.'

It looked as though Dino was about to say something else, but he was cut off by a commotion erupting from the back of the café. She watched as Zach power-walked briskly towards her. He was gesturing wildly with his eyebrows. Bea raised her own eyebrows in a question.

'You've got one!' Zach hissed, gliding in next to Bea, not so subtly cutting between her and Dino. 'Somebody's here!'

22

Suddenly alert, Bea, Zach and Dino turned around to see a middle-aged woman enter The Nook wearing a long denim pencil skirt and a very loud, very ruffled silk shirt buttoned all the way up to her neck. She clutched a copy of *Harry: Life, Loss, and Love* in one hand, and carried a plate of biscuits in the other. She moved slowly and deliberately towards Bea, who stayed glued to her seat, transfixed, momentarily forgetting that she was in fact the host. The lady continued to move towards her, her right arm now completely rigid and rising slowly. When she was roughly a metre from Bea, she stood there with what looked like a smile plastered across her face. Bea stared at the smudge of baby pink lipstick on her front teeth.

'Ruth: royalist, historical romance and family saga reader and recent listener of the podcast *By George: A Royal Family Appreciation*. It's a pleasure to be here,' the woman said, with a slight softness to her Rs.

After a fractionally too-long pause, Bea jumped up, shook Ruth's hand vigorously and took the plate of biscuits she had pushed towards her as an offering. 'Ruth, welcome!' Bea squealed and, on impulse, pulled the unsuspecting woman into a warm embrace. 'You didn't have to bring food. That is so kind of you!'

A little embarrassed, Ruth peeled herself away, adjusting her skirt, which had ridden up. 'Oh, I thoroughly enjoy baking. They are muesli cookies. Diana's Muesli. The company I started up back in the eighties, in my kitchen. Named after the princess herself.' Ruth crossed her heart, looking solemn.

'Diana's Muesli?' Bea said, shocked. 'You mean the multimillion-dollar business? The top muesli brand in Australia? *That* Diana's Muesli?' Bea took in the slightly dowdy-looking woman standing before her.

'Yes, that one. There couldn't be two Diana's Mueslis. Trademarking, right?' Ruth said rigidly, before laughing. 'I sold the company to Heinz two years ago. So now I have quite a bit of time to myself to attend events such as these.' She gestured to the room.

Bea nodded, surprised, before pulling Ruth into the middle of the cafe and shoving a glass of champagne and a cupcake into her hands. Ruth attempted to juggle Bea's offerings and her book.

'So, how did you find out about Next Chapter?' Bea asked.

'The Next Chapter Facebook page was recommended to me,' Ruth replied. 'I don't usually enjoy Facebook, too many photos of food. Or babies. The photos of dogs I like, especially if they're in the corgi family, but otherwise I cannot abide it. All that desire to share every insipid thought and minor life accomplishment. I mean, yes, you made homemade Portuguese tarts – big whoop!'

Bea nodded along frantically, hanging onto Ruth's every word. A guest! She had *a guest*! An incredibly successful, business-savvy (somewhat odd) guest she was neither previously acquainted with, nor related to, nor dating. She was thrilled. Ecstatic! *Maybe I can make this work?*

111

'Usually my pet ferret would accompany me to such events, but midweek socialising after 8pm interrupts his cycle, if you know what I mean.' She nudged Bea with surprising force. 'But an opportunity to discuss books seemed like a worthy excuse for me to divert from the regular.'

'Yes, oh, I'm so glad you could make it. Beyond glad,' Bea gushed, taking a bite from a Diana's Muesli cookie. *Delicious!*

Zach sauntered over and slid his arm around Bea's waist. Ruth squinted at the gesture. Zach returned her look with one of his signature smiles, then introduced himself.

'Republican?' Ruth inquired, looking Zach up and down suspiciously.

'Can't say I've given it much thought,' Zach replied. 'Bea, it might be time to get the formalities underway.'

Bea nodded decisively and looped her arm through Ruth's, ushering her towards a table. She slid in opposite her, took a deep breath and watched as Dino climbed onto a chair at the front of the café.

Dino cracked his knuckles. Suddenly, he looked almost nervous, his eyes more alert than usual. Lizzie Instagrammed him at a mile a minute.

'Uh … thanks everyone for coming,' Dino mumbled.

The motley crew before him clapped. Lizzie gestured for him to smile more.

Dino pushed his fingers through his hair. 'So, this is something that's pretty exciting for Bea,' he said, pointing at her. Bea blushed a deep red as eyes fell on her. 'She's wanted to do something a little different for a while now –

and well, this seems just about perfect. I mean, books and coffee – there aren't many greater pleasures in life.'

A stunted laugh from Zach. One low 'whoop whoop' from Ruth.

'Anyway, I'm not much of a talker. More of a poet. So, uh, I'll jump right into something I wrote for tonight.' He pulled a crumpled piece of paper from his pocket and looked at it for a second too long. It was strange how edgy he seemed, Bea thought. Dino didn't get nervous at the best of times.

Between the aisles, between the shelves,
We see an image of ourselves.
Not one that sits and stands and waits,
But one that moves and finds, relates.
You can't be sure, it must be said,
What transformation lies ahead.
But with an open mind, we're told,
A new beginning will unfold.

He paused, cleared his throat and continued. 'And now, I'd like to invite the woman who made all of this happen up on stage to explain the rules. The woman whose three great loves in life are Donna Tartt, 25 words or less competitions and a strong skinny latte. Introducing Bea Babbage.'

Bea bit her lip and waved awkwardly as she scurried to stand next to Dino. 'Oh gosh, thanks Dino, that was beautiful.' She squeezed his shoulder. 'So, have you ever wanted to find the perfect book? Are you sick of trawling through books that look good on paper but aren't right for you in person?' Bea glanced at Ruth. Her hands were clasped together in front of her chest and she was nodding along to Bea's words. 'Well, I know I am. That's why we've launched Next Chapter. Simply bring your favourite book, and spend five minutes selling it to the person who appears at your table. If they like it, they take it. If they don't, you move on to the next table. Are you guys ready?'

Ruth cheered.

'And don't forget to donate to the Breast Cancer Foundation on your way out!' squealed Lizzie from the corner of the room, before twirling her phone around to take a selfie.

'On your marks, get set, recommend!' Bea called, setting a timer on her phone. She jumped off the chair and returned to the one opposite Ruth. She spied Zach pulling up a seat in front of Lizzie, who had brought along the only book she had ever read: *Textbook Romance*, by Zoë Foster and Hamish Blake.

'Marrying commoners, I can't abide it,' Ruth began. 'These young princes have no respect for tradition. It's quite astonishing really, don't you agree?'

Bea frowned, looking down at Ruth's book. Prince Harry and Meghan Markle, heads slightly tilted towards each other, grinned up at her. She listened intently as Ruth spouted about the despicable dramatic licence of the writers of *The Crown* and how Harry, a once wayward prince, had managed, to her great disbelief and disapproval, to charm the pants off a nation. And then her five minutes were up. Ruth exhaled. She smiled briefly and then nodded for Bea to take her turn.

About thirty seconds into Bea drooling over the masterpiece that is Min Jin Lee's *Pachinko*, she felt a light tap on the shoulder. Bea turned around as Ruth's resounding huff signalled her frustration at this disruption. A short, awkwardly dressed man clutching a single, red rose stood before Bea. Her heart leapt in her chest. Another guest! *This is happening!*

'I'm looking for Lizzie Babbage?'

'You're what?' Bea asked, slowly rising from her chair.

'Lizzie from *The Bachelor*. I'm here to see her.'

Bea stared at the slightly sweating man before her. *Typical, just typical.*

He leaned in closer, assaulting her with his far too liberal application of cologne. 'You don't happen to know if she's single, do you?' he asked, grasping the rose to his chest in anticipation.

Bea rolled her eyes, informed him that Lizzie was married with twins, and watched him scurry out the door as fast as he'd come in. She apologised to Ruth profusely, then finished off her declaration of love to *Pachinko*, before her alarm announced time was up. Ruth got up and settled down in front of Lizzie, and began her monologue, while Bea stayed put.

'Well, if it isn't Bea Babbage herself.' Dino sat in the seat opposite her, carrying a copy of *The Dark Between Stars*. His hair was tousled and hung loosely over his eyes.

'I know you've already read *Pachinko*,' Bea replied.

'History has failed us… Something, something.' His attempt at quoting the novel warmed Bea.

'Show-off.' Bea could see Ruth wildly gesticulating, holding the book in front of her and shaking it. Bea was sure she'd just barked, 'Long live the Queen.'

'You're right, I have read *this one*.' Dino pointed to the book, getting Bea's attention again. 'Sell your own story to me instead.'

'What?'

'The Bea Babbage story. Sell it to me,' he said, leaning back in his chair with his hands behind his head.

'There's nothing to tell,' she shrugged, playing with the pages of her book.

'There's everything to tell.'

'I'm monotonous, clumsy and ridiculous.'

'You're mildly hilarious, passionate and pretty damn brave.'

'Yeah, right,' Bea said dismissively.

Dino gave her a look which seemed to say, *You don't fool me, Babbage.*

Bea glanced down at her book, embarrassed.

'Your eyes light up when you do that, you know?'

'Do what?' Bea asked.

'When you look at a book you love. They get bigger than they already are, which you would think is impossible, and then it's like they're dancing. I've never seen anyone so happy. It's infectious.'

'I didn't realise you were watching me so closely, creep.' Bea tried to laugh off Dino's sudden candidness, but he didn't laugh back. In fact, he looked more serious than ever. He opened his mouth to say something when Lizzie approached behind Bea.

'Bea,' she hissed.

'Yes, Lizzie?'

'It's Zach,' she mumbled.

Bea looked up, searching the room for him, but he was nowhere in sight.

'He just, well, he just hit on me,' Lizzie said seriously.

'What?' Bea felt cold. She suddenly had an intense urge to be under her covers reading *The Guernsey Literary and Potato Peel Pie Society*.

The timer Bea had set on her phone chimed again. She frantically tapped at the screen to quieten it. Finally, it turned off, but both Bea and Dino stayed seated. Bea noticed that Dino's hands were now balled up in white fists. Bea simply shook her head. *This is just Lizzie. She always thinks everyone is hitting on her.*

'I'm telling you, Bea. He's been flirting with me all night and just now, he leaned in so close his stubble practically grazed my cheek!' Lizzie's voice went up an octave.

Bea glanced at Dino, who was clenching his jaw. She sighed. She did not want to make a scene. Lizzie stared at Bea, waiting for a response.

Bea sighed. 'Lizzie, I'm sure you misread the situation. He's just a friendly guy and probably wanted to make a good impression because you're my sister.'

'Bea, I'm telling you, I didn't misread it. This happens all the time, because I'm famous. But I never thought it would happen with—'

'With who, Lizzie? You never thought it would happen with the guy I'm seeing? Just like you thought my boyfriend Luke was hitting on you in my first year of university, just like you were *positive* that Jake was going to pick you as his Bachelorette – not everyone is in love with you, Lizzie! I'm sick and tired of you making everything about you!

This was supposed to be my night!' Bea's voice was just a little too loud. This was the last straw. Bea couldn't push away her frustration at Lizzie manipulating everything to suit her own agenda. 'I'm sorry, Lizzie, but tonight, you don't get a rose.'

23

Morning Ramona!

Bedsheets are all washed and ready for a good old iron. No need to put sheets back on Lizzie's fold-out. She'll be pulling up in Mount Eliza right about now and thank God for that!

Peace!

B xx

24

Bea,

   I re-washed sheets twice because they had big fake tan marks on them. I could not remove. Sorry.

   Also, your friend Sunday came back to return book. I let her in. She presented me with a salad which was very tasty. I hope okay.

   Ramona

25

As soon as the sun rose the morning after the event, Lizzie stormed out of Bea's house faster than Winston Groom had said Forrest Gump could run. Zach had straight-up shut down Lizzie's allegations after Bea questioned him. He claimed he was leaning in to show her his favourite passage from *Catch-22* when all of a sudden she started screaming. This whole situation was just classic Lizzie. In Bea's sister's mind, everyone was obsessed, infatuated and totally head over heels in love with her.

Besides, Bea couldn't bring herself to believe that Zach would ever flirt with another woman, let alone her sister. He had started looking at Bea with such ardour, it felt as if she were a character in a book and he was scribbling notes all over her. What would he write about her, she often wondered. She imagined it would be something like: *a little odd, crazy, poppy seed in teeth, why did she just say that?* And what would she write about him? *Thoughtful, witty, I wonder what he looked like as a baby? Does he like me more than I like him? Why does he never blink? Gorgeous, insightful, that goddamn face.*

Merely thinking of Zach made Bea smile. She just wanted to race from door to door, showing off this new man in her life, pointing to him and saying, 'People, I'm dating this guy! *This* guy, with the perfect mop of brown curls, a smile as bright as the Milky Way and a mind as complex and intriguing as Zadie Smith's.'

This was a new feeling for Bea. Her past relationships had been more fleeting dalliances than anything else and tended to end as quickly as they began. *'The only thing you're good at picking is a good book,'* Cassandra had always laughed. Take Lachy, for example. He had approached her last year at a café, where she was celebrating Lizzie's birthday over brunch. He had asked for her number, and Liz had *highly encouraged* her to hand it over. Two months later, she had found herself in a relationship she wasn't quite sure she wanted to be in (he was nice and all, but only ever talked about the cricket). But he had chosen Bea, amongst all the fish. So Bea went along with it, and tried to ride out the mediocrity until it transformed into your basic Nicholas Sparks novel. She needn't have worried, though. A week later he dumped her at a test match. Said *she* was too boring! And just when she had started to like cricket.

She snuggled up under her blanket, wishing Zach was lying next to her in the empty space she hoped he would one day fill. Sighing, she flicked her snooze button again and turned a page of *Meeting Oliver Bennett*, soaking up Zach's words.

'It didn't quite go exactly to plan, Martha.' Bea had been reading *Meeting Oliver Bennett* on the toilet again when a pair of slightly more muted than usual, but still effortlessly elegant pair of navy ankle boots had stalked into the neighbouring cubicle. Bea hadn't let her get a word in before she dished all the details from Next Chapter, except the part where her sister thought her boyfriend had hit on her.

'I'm telling you, Martha, I just need to keep getting the word out and somehow turn these events into a bona fide money maker. And as soon as I do, I'm going to quit this godforsaken hellhole and start up my own thing. I'm serious. I cannot stand another second here. Who grows up wanting to sell toothpaste with a bunch of idiots and sexist pigs? I've started to throw out the worst possible toothpaste names I can think of – and my bosses lap it up. Yesterday they were swooning over my Mint to Be idea. I mean, come on!'

Flush.

Flush.

Simultaneous flushes. This had never happened before. In the couple of months Bea had been working in Melbourne, she had always waited until Martha had left the bathroom – in fact, they still hadn't met face-to-face. She liked the anonymity of their relationship. She was free to be whoever she wanted, without judgement. She considered stalling in the cubicle. But then she thought the better of it. *Come on Bea.* She heard Martha open her cubicle door and went to do the same.

Bea took a deep breath, her hand hovering over the lock. She had pictured this moment for months. What would beautifully-shoed Martha look like? Would she wear a tight black bun, equally fabulous earrings and bright red lips like Bea had always pictured, or would she be plainer from the bottom up and timid – completely throwing her expectations?

Leaving the cubicle, Bea paused in the doorway. Martha was already washing her hands at the sink.

Bea's breath caught again. Martha was nothing short of exceptional.

Older than she had expected, Martha had a peppering of sophisticated grey in her honey blonde hair. Dainty wrinkles feathered her brow and her lips were pursed as if she was about to say the word *Tuesday*. Her nails were painted immaculately in a shimmering pale pink, and she wore a West Highland Terrier-printed dress that screamed 'quirky, yet incredibly expensive'.

'Martha? I can't believe it's you.' Bea turned the faucet on in the adjacent sink, regretting wearing her frumpy yellow lacy top. 'I've been dreaming of this moment since—'

'Let me stop you right there, Beatrix Babbage,' the woman snapped in the very opposite of a British accent, spitting out her name like it was poison.

Bea took a step back, aghast.

'Do you know who I am?' she said.

Bea shrunk into herself. 'Um, you're Martha from Finance?'

The woman sneered – a malevolent sneer. The sort of sneer that could burn down George Orwell's house.

'Oh, my dear, my poor, poor dear. I'm not Martha. I'm Catherine Bradley, the CEO of this "godforsaken hellhole".'

Bea's heart stopped.

'And you, my darling, are fired.'

Shit. Fuck. Shit. Fuck. Shit!

124

Bea wiped muffin crumbs from her chin while simultaneously scoffing down a chocolate croissant. Her eyes were bloodshot from crying, her mouth burning from the string of profanities she hadn't stopped mumbling.

'Fucking hell, I'm such a fucking fuck!' Bea slurred incoherently.

'Bea, if you say the F word one more time, I'm going to have to ask you to leave,' whispered Dino, glancing at the group of school-age children drinking hot chocolates in the corner with their dad. Dino was dressed in his usual dark green apron, under which he wore an out-of-character tight white T-shirt that showed off his tattoos. He had just gotten a haircut; his hair was less shaggy and more spick and span, yet it still hung over his brow.

As soon as Bea had been fired by Catherine Bradley, she had come running to The Nook, begging Dino for as many chocolate-filled pastries as he could offer. Thankfully, Sunday had been in that morning and baked up an absolute storm. Too embarrassed to face Zach, or be alone, redemption in the shape of a choc-chip muffin was the only thing that could fill the mortified hole in Bea's heart. She had been sitting on a bar stool for the past two hours and was currently on her third baked good and second caffeinated beverage, but still she didn't feel any better. Although she was as buzzed as a bloody honey bee. *Cass would know what to do,* Bea couldn't stop thinking. She would've said, 'They don't deserve you anyway. You'll find a better job.'

'Missed a spot.' Dino tapped his right cheek with his finger, while nodding towards Bea to do the same.

Bea's hands shot to her face as she brushed away the stray crumbs.

'Bea, I'm telling you, this is a godsend. You hated your job, and now you have time to pursue what's really important to you.'

'Yeah, and with what money am I going to do that?' Bea scoffed.

Dino paused to make an extra strong cappuccino for a woman dressed in lycra then placed another croissant in the microwave for Bea. Bea took the moment to finally text Zach. If she wanted to give this thing between them a go, she figured honesty and relying on each other was a good place to start.

> 🟤 Bea: Just got the sack. Drowning sorrows with coffee and sugar. May need to switch to harder stuff. Available to be my drinking buddy/patient companion while I line up at Centrelink later? x

'J.K. Rowling,' Dino said, placing the warm croissant in front of her, which drew her attention away from her phone.

'What?' Bea asked, biting into the chocolatey goodness.

'She got fired. She was working as a secretary when she got the boot for secretly writing stories on her computer. Now she's a multi-billionaire and one of the most famous authors of all time.'

Bea shrugged. 'I'm no J.K. Rowling, Dino.' She took a sip of her coffee.

Agatha Christie nestled herself underneath Bea's arm, and she stroked her therapeutically. The poodle responded by nuzzling up to Bea's croissant.

'Don't even think about it,' Dino said, eyeing the piece of croissant Bea had just torn off for the dog.

Frowning, Bea popped the croissant piece in her mouth. The memory of the afternoon washed over her again, causing her to shudder. What was she doing with her life? It was like catastrophe followed her wherever she went. Bea's eye caught on a drawing of a tornado, etched on Dino's elbow. *So very apt.* She let her eyes wander down his arms, desperate for something to take her mind off the events of the day. Dino's tattoos were like pieces of art, and she couldn't draw her attention away from them. She took in the intricate sketches of paw prints, soaring mountain tops, croissants and coffee cups, melting timepieces and words that she couldn't quite decipher. It was as if she was reading a book in another language; each section of his arm told a story that she couldn't quite understand.

'Who's Delilah?' she asked, pointing at the name printed faintly in small cursive on his wrist, and needing any excuse to change the topic from the disaster that was her career.

Dino froze, shook his head, and muttered croakily, 'Maybe another time. I'm working here!' He handed a chai tea to a waiting customer. Seeing Bea's disappointed expression, he relented a little. 'Fine, pick another.'

Bea nodded. 'What about the marbles?' She gestured to the colourful drawing of an upended bag of marbles near his elbow, which stood out among the other tattoos thanks to its fresher appearance.

He touched the spot on his arm where the tattoo was etched, and then spoke. 'Miss Marbles,' he said.

'Excuse me?'

'Miss Marbles. It's what I used to call Miss Marple when I was little. My grandmother was obsessed with Agatha Christie.'

'Go figure,' Bea said, holding up Agatha Christie the toy poodle.

'Yeah, well, maybe it was a little more than an obsession. She was fixated on Christie's stories. It was as if real life to her was inside the book, and the real world was fiction.'

'I know how that feels,' mumbled Bea, so softly it was almost to herself.

'She had copies of all her books: *The Murder at the Vicarage*, *The Moving Finger*, *A Caribbean Mystery*, *They Do It with Mirrors* ... They filled the house like her children. Maybe it had something to do with her real child, my mum, sort of not being that present in her life. Or mine, really, for that matter.' Dino leaned across the benchtop to scrunch Agatha Christie's fur, then propped his hands on the counter.

'Where is your mum?'

'She's around. When she wants to be. But when there's a festival in Byron Bay, or a guy in Daylesford, or Mornington, or Sydney, she'll be there instead. Her life motto is "fend for yourself". Dino shrugged.

'That must be tough,' Bea said. Dino's usual unwillingness to let people in, suddenly making more sense.

'Anyway, so I never met my dad, not that I remember anyway, and my mum was otherwise occupied. I mostly lived with my grandma growing up. And every night, every morning, every second, she would read me chapters from Agatha Christie's books. I would always beg for more "Miss

Marbles" stories, and Grandma laughed so hard every time I called her that.' He smiled. 'When she died last year, it hit me pretty hard. I inherited her dog, each and every one of those tattered crime books and got this tattoo in her honour.' Dino looked away.

Bea placed her hand over his on the counter. She wished she knew what to say right now. Cass would know. She always said the right thing in every situation. 'I'm so sorry about your parents, and about your gran.' She smiled at him. 'And here I am looking all sorts of ridiculous, crying over some stupid job.'

Dino's brow furrowed and he turned his back to her, his hand sliding from her grasp, and started making a coffee that no one had ordered. He took out a pen from the pocket of his apron and quickly scribbled across the cup, brow still creased. He then slid the drink towards Bea, and she picked it up, reading the words written on the cup. *The saddest thing in life, is what one remembers.*

'It's Agatha Christie,' Dino remarked, busying himself with rummaging through the cabinet behind him.

Then Bea felt someone's arms wrap around her from behind.

'I came as soon as I heard,' Zach said.

Bea leaned into his embrace.

'This is bullshit. They can't fire you on a whim like that. It's complete and utter bullshit! Tell me word for word what happened. We are going to sue their arses.' His face was flushed red, as though he had run all the way to her. Bea watched as a bead of sweat dripped down his perfectly smooth forehead and onto his cheek.

'Well?' Zach repeated. 'Bea, it's important you recount the incident as soon as it happened so you don't forget anything. I'm going to write it down.' He took out his phone and opened up the notes app, thumbs ready.

'Well, I, uh,' Bea stuttered, starting to well up again. *Stop being a baby, Bea.*

'Jesus, man. I don't think she wants to talk about it right now,' Dino said a little too tersely. His face was steelier than it had been a moment ago, like he was suddenly a cold, brand new book instead of a dog-eared, weathered, well-loved one.

'Is that so? I think I know what's best for my girlfriend,' Zach snapped.

A shiver travelled down Bea's spine, caught off guard by Zach's brashness. She wasn't used to him speaking to anyone like that. And *girlfriend*? That was the first time he had ever called her that. She had pictured them becoming boyfriend and girlfriend in a more romantic setting. *Oh well, I guess that's that.*

'Whatever. No need to be cruel,' Dino said.

'The world made me cruel,' Zach said, looking at Bea for approval.

'If you're trying to quote Emily Brontë, it's "My heart made me cruel",' Dino replied.

'No, it is not.'

'It is too. I think I would know. I actually read more than just comic books,' Dino said, stone-faced.

'I work at a publishing house, you twat.' Zach slammed his hand on the bench a little too hard.

Bea looked back and forth at the two men – boys – having this childish argument before her very eyes.

'Terror,' Bea said.

'What?' Zach and Dino said in unison.

'"Terror made me cruel". That's the quote from *Wuthering Heights*. You're both wrong, you idiots.' She laughed, allowing a small piece of tension to fall away.

'Oh.'

'Oh.'

Bea glanced at Dino slightly apologetically before turning to Zach. She took his hand and stood up shakily. Filled with caffeine and pastries, she was worried she wouldn't be able to walk in a straight line.

'Zach, can you take me home?'

'Of course,' Zach said, not just taking her hand, but picking her up and throwing her over his shoulder. She gave a squeal as Zach carried her out of the store, Dino's farewell grunt echoing in their wake.

After walking a block, Bea laughing and kicking playfully all the way, Zach placed her down delicately next to him. She grabbed his hand and they walked past bustling bars full of people who still had their jobs, sipping on after-work drinks. The sky was a misty pink; it was that special time in the day when the sun hadn't quite set but the moon was already starting to rise.

'Thanks for coming,' Bea said a little bashfully. 'And thank you for managing to make me laugh.'

'You feeling okay?'

'Well, today has been pretty shitty,' Bea sighed.

They walked in silence for a while. Bea was relieved that Zach wasn't throwing a ton of platitudes or solutions at her, but rather stayed quiet, letting her have this moment to feel low, realising that perhaps Dino was right, that she needed the space to feel and process the day.

He paused, turning so that he was facing Bea. 'You know I really care for you, Bea.' They were standing in the middle of the footpath, hand in hand, a gesture that would usually make Bea nervous, in case she accidentally blocked a stranger's path or drew too much attention. But Zach was looking down at her with such earnestness that she couldn't help but melt into this moment. Still, all Bea could muster in return was a discreet nod, suddenly feeling a bit out of her depth.

'I know it hasn't been long, but I don't know what it is about you that makes me feel as if I've always known you.' Zach laughed, seemingly embarrassed by his own candour. 'What a line, hey?'

'I like you too, Zach. I've really enjoyed getting to know you.'

'That's the thing though, it's more than that, I think.' He dropped his head slightly, giving her a look she couldn't quite put her finger on. A woman lugging a bursting green supermarket bag in each hand side-stepped around them.

'These hands.' Zach pulled her hands a little closer to him, rubbing his thumb across her knuckles. 'They are the most beautiful hands I've ever seen.' He kissed each one lightly. Then he looked at Bea again and squeezed her hands three times, gently.

Bea smiled, at a loss for what to say. Nobody in all her thirty years had ever looked at her that way before, or given her butterflies like this before.

Again, Zach gave Bea's hands three squeezes, this time with a renewed eagerness. 'Bea, you've done a real number on me.'

'What's gotten into you today, Zach?'

'You – you've gotten to me. You've crawled under my skin in a way I've never experienced before. When I met you, I never expected that you would be … you.' He squeezed her hands three more times and kissed her slowly.

Bea kissed him back, sighing into him, her skin erupting in goosebumps. She gave Zach's hands one long squeeze back.

'You're not doing it right,' Zach said, pulling away only the slightest bit. 'Let me show you. I,' he said, and squeezed once. 'Love.' He squeezed again. 'You.' And he squeezed once more.

A rush of, Bea didn't know what, flooded her body – the three little words triggering a visceral reaction. Not quite believing what she thought she'd heard, she stood there, mouth slightly agape, stunned. *I'm loveable?*

'I know, I know, it's crazy. We've only been together a few weeks,' Zach said sheepishly. 'It's not like me to move so quickly. Seriously, if only you knew. But I couldn't keep it in.'

Bea, realising that this was, in fact, not a daydream, tugged Zach forward, looking him in the eyes and willing herself to give in to this moment. *You can do it. Be brave!* 'It's not too soon,' she said and squeezed his hands three times.

Zach's face lit up, his eyes creasing in that way that made Bea's stomach flip. 'Really?'

'Really.'

A small ginger dog ran up to them, tugging on its owner's lead and scratching and jumping at their legs. Laughing, Bea and Zach freed their hands to pat the insistent pup. The dog lapped up the attention and then, satisfied, followed after its owner.

'You know, my mind is consumed by thoughts of you, Bea Babbage,' Zach said as, hands once more entwined, they resumed their walk. 'And I thought you should know right here, right now.' He smiled at her and Bea smiled back. 'There's nowhere else I'd rather be because, let's face it, I'm pretty crazy about you, Bea.'

Bea stood on her tiptoes and grabbed at his neck, pulling his face down so she could kiss him with everything she had.

26

To: cassandralucas@live.com.au
From: beababbage@gmail.com
Subject: I miss you more than I miss Richard Mercer's Love Song Dedications.

Hey Cass,

I just lost my job for being a complete idiot – typical Bea, right? I'm currently drowning my sorrows in our favourite ice-cream while crying hysterically over the ending of *Me Before You*. Why did it have to end that way, Cass? Why? She was so happy the way he was – couldn't he be happy too? COULDN'T HE?

I know you're probably sick to death of hearing from me, but I really wish you would reply just this once.

I need you.

Bawling Bea xo

P.S. I know I don't deserve to find love after everything that's happened, but I've been seeing somebody and he seems really fantastic and it felt weird not to tell you about it. Fingers crossed I don't screw it up this time.

27

Bea didn't sleep that night. Zach had left her heart full, but that beautiful and pure sensation of floating on cupid's cloud had dissipated in the wee morning hours. Alone and racked with guilt and regret over how things had fallen apart at work, she couldn't help but stare into the darkness of her bedroom and agonise over every terrible mistake and micro-tragedy (as she and Cassandra preferred to call first-world problems) Bea had caused in the last few months. She lay awake, in a cold sweat, listing them in her head over and over again.

Humiliated best friend in front of nearest and dearest and destroyed her future happiness with man of dreams. Landed dud job with little future prospects at dud agency in a new (thankfully, at least, less dud) city. Put foot in it majorly and got fired from suddenly not-so-dud-seeming agency. Spilt freshly made latte on innocent bystander three days ago. Felt worse about lost coffee than person. Never have cash to buy The Big Issue *magazine. Have zero patience for sister and gave her lacklustre goodbye hug. Don't call mother enough. Binge-watches true crime like it's entertainment when really it's about real people who were murdered! Only had four people attend stupid book club event. Definitely not an innovator. All in all, most likely, a very unlikeable human.*

At 4.10 in the morning, utterly fed up, Bea dragged herself out of bed, pulled on sneakers and a hoodie and went out to the little balcony that poked off her living room. She sat down, cross-legged, on her rickety blue seat and attempted to ground herself in the moment. The cool early morning air washed over her, cleansing her of guilt and concern over her lack of concrete direction. She tried to think of the good things – the lady who'd held the lift doors open for her the other day and the latest drone footage of the roof of her family home sent by her father. And Zach. Zach, Zach, Zach. But then the weight of her worries and fears bore down on her again. Somehow life seemed easier when she was just playing it safe and following in the footsteps of the charismatic, but mildly controlling, women in her life.

With her head resting against the brick wall, Bea stared up at the sky. She searched for extraterrestrial life and shooting stars, just like she and Cassandra used to do as kids, their heads poking out of a tent erected in her backyard. If the latter was spotted, Cassandra made Bea swear she'd wish that they would each meet somebody as charming as Laurie Laurence, get married and buy houses next door to one another, each with a purple picket fence. Bea gazed up at the sky and sighed as if she shared a secret with the stars.

'A little to the left. Yep, okay, tilt it down a fraction. Now, up a smidge,' Bea directed, sitting atop the counter in The Nook. Arms extended in front of her, she squinted through the rectangle made between her thumbs and index fingers, attempting to measure the wall opposite her.

'I don't think "smidge" is an official measurement.' Dino threw his head back in frustration while still holding on firmly to the floating shelf.

After waking up, close to frozen, on the balcony, Bea had defrosted in the shower, dressed and dragged herself to The Nook. By 9.15 she was seated at a table with a double-shot latte, one of Sunday's signature breakfast muffins, which housed a whole boiled egg, and her open laptop. It was almost as if she hadn't just been fired! *How do you like this for professionalism and work ethic, Catherine Bradley?* But after an hour and a half of frantically responding to every single job advert that fell loosely within her field of exper-tise – and a couple that didn't but sounded like good fun (*Hello, Bingo Manager or Emoji Creator!*) – she was officially over it. She had even Facebook messaged Ruth from the Next Chapter event to ask whether she still had contacts at Diana's Muesli and if she knew if they were looking to hire (after she and Dino had googled her to verify that yes, she in fact was the founder). But apparently, after Ruth had tried to tamper with the ingredients – 'I don't care about the antioxidants, acai is not a royal fruit!' – she was no longer on speaking terms with management.

Rather than face reality (it was too early for that nonsense), Bea had traipsed to IKEA, purchased three wooden shelves, a pineapple-shaped bookend and a small framed print that read 'Don't Let the Muggles Get You Down'. On her way back to the café, she detoured past her new favourite second-hand bookstore, Another's Treasure, and purchased thirteen of her most highly recommended books, including, among others: *The Bronze Horseman, Kiss Kiss, Today Will Be Different, The Mars Room, Love Letters of the Great War, Say Hello, The Jade Lily* and *The Hate Race*, plus a couple she had been salivating over on some of the many Bookstagrammer accounts she followed, like *I Am Sasha* and *The Last Man*.

The perfect smattering, she thought, congratulating herself on her choices and for haggling down the price by $5.65. With her bounty tucked under each arm, she returned triumphantly to The Nook. She was a woman on a mission and wouldn't be taking no for an answer.

And now, here they were, two small shelves, with one more to go, hung on the wall near the entrance of The Nook. Dino had been surprisingly compliant. He even raved about her book choices. '*Kiss Kiss*? That's my all-time favourite Roald Dahl!' he had cooed. Bea had laughed at him, saying of course his favourite book would be so obscure. In her mind, nothing could live up to *Matilda*. Maybe Dino felt sorry for Bea, or maybe he sensed that if he did, in fact, say no, he might not live to see another day.

'What are your thoughts on job applications that ask for a headshot?' Bea asked as she returned to her laptop and the dreaded job ads, and left Dino to hammer in the final nail.

'Pigs! Absolute pigs!' Sunday called from the little kitchen out the back. The woman had superhuman hearing. 'I wouldn't trust them as far as I could throw them.'

'Mmm, patriarchy and all that,' Bea agreed. 'Now that's what you should write a poem about, Dino.'

'I've got just the thing.' Dino cleared his throat, turning to face her. 'Mirror, mirror on the wall, who's the fairest of them all? Nobody with scarring, blemishes, deformities, or chubby cheeks, and don't even mention the wrong shade of baby pink,' he recited, hand on heart.

Bea threw her head back in a hearty laugh, clapping and demanding an encore. And then she kept on laughing. Hysterically. In fact, she couldn't stop. Tears streamed down her face as she struggled for air. Bea could feel her chest caving in and heat prickling up her neck. And then she let out a guttural sob that came from deep within.

'Bea, you right over there?' Dino asked nervously, stepping down from the chair.

Bea nodded, then shook her head, then shrugged.

'Sunday, we need you out front!' Dino yelled.

Sunday walked from the kitchen, drying her hands on a tea towel hooked into the belt loop of her jeans. She took one look at Bea and pulled her into a hug, rubbing her back rhythmically. 'You're going to be okay. This is part of your life journey. You'll be a stronger, smarter woman for it.'

Bea pulled away, grabbing a serviette from behind her and blowing her nose. 'But will I? I've been on a downward spiral for months now. Months!' She threw her hands in the air, defeated. 'I just had such different expectations of what my life would be. I'm nowhere near where I wanted to be at thirty. What do I have to show for all these years of slaving away at my desk, staying back late to impress the boss, sucking up to clients to win a new job?' She caught her breath. 'And I just can't seem to block out everybody who's doing better than me. I mean, look at my sister. She quits

140

her amazing job in media buying to go on *The Bachelor* – *The Bachelor*! – and manages to turn national humiliation into a blossoming social media career! For which she just has to take cute photos!'

'Hon, firstly, you gotta chill! Thirty is the new twenty-five,' Sunday said, sitting on the bar stool and pulling Bea towards her. 'You have to cut yourself some slack! Don't hate on yourself for dreaming big. You should shoot for the stars, and so what if on your way up you get smashed into a million pieces by an incoming comet that didn't get picked up on your fancy rocket ship's radar? At least you tried!'

Bea looked at Sunday, dumbstruck.

Sunday frowned, rubbing Bea's knees. 'Okay, forget the metaphor. But it's true, Bea. You just haven't found that thing that makes you tick.'

'But I'm a damn legend when it comes to finding the things that tick me off!' Bea exclaimed, grabbing at her half-eaten muffin. She picked off a sundried tomato from the top and popped it in her mouth. She exhaled a breath that seemed to come all the way from her toes. 'Thanks, Sunday, really,' she said, trying to sit up a bit straighter. 'I should get back to these applications. They won't write themselves!'

'That's a sport,' Dino called.

Bea scowled and hauled herself and her muffin back to her laptop. Clicking aimlessly through job ad after job ad, sighing dramatically after each one, she grabbed her phone and flicked into her text messages. Maybe she needed to get creative?

🗩 Bea: Crazy notion, but hear me out. Your bosses over at Thelma & Clarke don't happen to be on the look out for a totally bookish marketing lady? Would bend over backwards (including working through Christmas) and would consider having children so that I could name one Thelma and the other Clarke (regardless of gender) just so that I could work with books! Sincerely, one very crazed, on-the-cusp-of-a-mental-breakdown Bea.

🗩 Zach: I'll see what I can do. In the meantime, can I see you in an hour? Might have just the cure for that mental breakdown xx

🗩 Bea: 'Life is more thrilling when you just say yes.'

🗩 Zach: What a fangirl. It's nice to know I'm quotable. Meet me at Toorak Cellars and bring your happy pants xx

Happy pants? What the hell does that mean? Bea closed her laptop and discreetly pulled out *Meeting Oliver Bennett*, running her fingers along its spine. She leaned against the exposed brick wall behind her and looked at Dino, who was crouched over, dustpan in hand, sweeping up the debris from where he had drilled screws into the wall. She tried to think back to that quote Zach had underlined in the book, something about how time pursues the frightened.

28

Bea appraised her appearance in the reflection of the bar's window. She tugged at the cashmere scarf that curled up under her chin, keeping the cool wind at bay (God, how she missed endless Perth summers), then heard her name being called in a high-pitched voice.

'Bea! It's me, Ruth from your little Next Chapter event.' Ruth shuffled towards Bea, holding a bulging green shopping bag in one hand and a leash attached to what was either a very small dog or a very large rat in the other.

'Ruth, of course! Thanks for getting back to my message earlier today about the job. How are you? And who's this little guy?' Bea crouched down to get a closer look at the brown and white clump of fur scurrying madly at Ruth's feet.

'Philip, he's a chocolate mitt ferret,' Ruth said. 'But I wouldn't get too close, he hates being touched – needs a large personal space bubble at all times. He's a little like his namesake, Prince Philip, Duke of Edinburgh. Those Brits and their aversion to affection! Gets me every time.' Ruth chortled quietly but Bea didn't quite get the joke.

Bea stood. 'I've never seen a ferret on a leash before. Does he get out often?'

'Oh yes, he keeps me nice and trim. Accompanies me on most outings.' Ruth nodded emotionlessly, grabbed a small piece of carrot from her bag and tossed it down to the suddenly ecstatic animal.

Bea felt a warm pressure on her back. She turned around to see Zach standing beside her. He hung his arm around her shoulder, kissing her on the cheek.

'Ruth, isn't it?'

'Hello,' Ruth said, shaking Zach's outstretched hand.

'What's on for your afternoon? Looks like you've got a big one in store.' He gestured to her shopping bag, in which a packet of flour, sugar, eggs and a large jar of jam was crammed.

'Ingredients for a Victoria sponge cake—'

'Rewatching Harry and Meghan's wedding? It's their anniversary today, isn't it? I heard it on the radio this morning,' Zach interrupted.

'No.' Ruth stared at Zach as if he had just asked what colour underwear she was wearing. 'I protested that wedding. I can't abide Harry and Meghan's flagrant disrespect for customs and tradition. She won't even wear pantyhose, for goodness' sake!' Ruth huffed. 'Philip and I will be watching Queen Elizabeth's coronation. Won't we, pet?'

'We should join you!'

'What?' Ruth and Bea said in unison. Even Philip seemed to stop and look at Zach in surprise.

'I've never seen a coronation, and sponge cake is one of my favourite desserts,' Zach said, holding on to Bea's hand. His expression was open and sincere, and Bea couldn't help but feel that she had, in fact, won the dating lottery.

Ruth considered the oversized, overzealous man standing before her. 'Well. I usually watch by myself and take notes. I like scribbling my thoughts down.' She paused. 'Yes, you may come to my house to eat Victoria sponge cake and watch Queen Elizabeth's coronation.'

Ruth placed two pastel teacups and saucers on top of the doilies in front of Zach and Bea. They were sitting on the floor in Ruth's Toorak penthouse next to a large oak coffee table, which was positioned in front of what had to be at least a 65-inch LCD TV. Bea knew Ruth was successful, but still, she was shocked at the sheer opulence of this apartment. Each room was filled with chandeliers, lavish furniture, glossy timber surfaces and was littered floor to ceiling with British royal family memorabilia: 'It's a boy!' baby mugs lined cabinets; 'I heart the Royal Family' tapestries hung on the walls; corgi bobbleheads nodded on the mantelpiece. To top it all off, an imposing feature mural of key family members was painted in each bedroom.

But the best part of Ruth's home was the floor-length window that offered a striking view of Melbourne's CBD, narrow skyscrapers and evergreen trees dotting the horizon. Bea couldn't help but feel like this was the next best thing to Buckingham Palace.

She glanced back at the scratchy black and white footage of Queen Elizabeth's coronation, which was blaring so loudly that they had to scream to hear one another. Zach had whispered to Bea on the walk over that it would be fun, that Ruth seemed like she could do with the company and they could go and have a drink any time. That small act of kindness made Bea fall for Zach even more. *Or is he just avoiding intimacy again?* Bea quickly pushed the thought away.

Now, here they were, sitting in a stranger's house, watching a film from 1953 (converted to DVD) and – after Bea had assured Ruth that she was great with pets – Ruth had allowed Philip the ferret to nestle atop Bea's lap, nibbling on her blue jeans.

'THAT'S WHAT YOU CALL ROYALTY! NOT THAT FRIVOLOUS TV ACTRESS CLAIMING TO BE MAJESTIC!' Ruth shouted, pointing at a young Queen Elizabeth kneeling regally in a satin cloak and jewelled crown.

Bea watched Zach as he smeared a scone with jam and added a dollop of cream before taking a bite; an appetiser while they waited for the Victoria sponge to bake. His legs were stretched out clumsily in front of him – he looked cute yet awkward, like all tall men sitting on the floor do.

'SO, RUTH, DO YOU, AH, WATCH THIS OFTEN?' Zach called over the deafening singing of *God Save the Queen*.

'OF COURSE. EVERY YEAR ON THE SECOND OF JUNE. SOMETIMES I DOUBLE UP THOUGH, LIKE TODAY. TWICE IN ONE YEAR.' Ruth was sitting upright on an armchair, holding a cushion in the shape of Queen Elizabeth.

'RUTH. COULD WE TURN THE TV VOLUME DOWN? JUST A TAD?' Bea bellowed.

'WHAT?'

'THE VOLUME! COULD WE TURN IT DOWN?'

'OH, OKAY.' Ruth grabbed the remote and turned the volume down until it was almost muted.

'Thanks so much,' Bea whispered, her ears ringing just the slightest bit.

'So, who's your favourite member of the royal family?' Ruth leaned in too closely to Zach.

'What?'

'I am making conversation. Small talk. You know?'

'Oh yeah, of course. It would have to be Harry. He seems like he'd be a bit of fun.'

Bea flinched at what she was sure would come next.

'Harry? I detest him. Such a wild child. He gives a bad name to the Mountbatten-Windsor family. And you know exactly how I feel about his wife,' Ruth huffed, crossing her arms.

Zach nodded slowly, and leaned over to take Philip from Bea. 'Can I hold him?' He picked the ferret up by the neck and placed him on his lap. 'Come here, little fella.' He held onto the writhing ferret, trying to secure him.

'I think he wants to get free,' Bea murmured.

Zach smiled, holding the brown ferret down. 'He'll be fine. Animals love me.'

Ruth, no longer watching the coronation, looked at Zach firmly clasping her beloved, and obviously very distressed, ferret.

'DON'T HURT PHILIP!' She shot up from her chair and yanked at her pet.

Philip squealed and sank his razor-sharp teeth into Zach's hand.

Zach yelped and jumped up. 'Motherfucker!' he howled, dropping the ferret to the floor.

'Zach! Are you okay?' Bea stood up and took Zach's hand at the same time as Ruth crouched down to tend to her ferret.

Bea inspected Zach's hand. *Boy, ferrets have sharp teeth*, she thought as she tried to stop the bleeding with her doily.

'OUT!' Ruth shouted. 'GET OUT OF MY HOUSE! I DON'T WANT YOU NEAR MY PRINCE PHILIP!'

Zach glared at Ruth, hand in mouth, as Bea yanked at his arm, dragging him out of the apartment and apologising profusely on the way.

'Just hold still.' Bea wiped the deep gash on Zach's palm with an alcohol wipe as he tried not to wince. After fleeing Ruth's home, they had come back to her apartment to tend to his wounds, which, according to the dejected expression on his face, were more than just physical. She gently laid a plaster over the cut before bringing his hand to her lips and kissing it better.

'You're amazing. You know that right?' Zach smiled his very sexy half-smile. 'So, are you going to tell me why the hell you have the biggest first-aid kit of all time?' He gestured towards her giant, almost overflowing medical box, which was emblazoned with a white cross.

'You're not the only one who's full of surprises, Mr Harris,' Bea said in her most seductive voice, not mentioning the fact that her mother had bought her the first aid kit when she was last in town, in case Bea accidentally stapled her thumb again.

'I know I'm not, Miss Babbage,' Zach said, and kissed her.

Bea kissed him back with an intense hunger and swung her leg around so that she was sitting on top of him. Could this be the moment? Up until now, every time they'd come close to sleeping together, Zach had pulled away, insistent about not rushing into things. But Bea was sick of waiting. If there was one thing she was certain about in her life, it was Zach. No more waiting around, no more kiss and stop. Her body yearned for it.

But with impeccable timing, her phone rang. Bea winced.

'Just ignore it,' Bea whispered.

Zach kissed her feverishly, running his hand down her leg. Bea pulled him towards her, unable to get close enough. Her phone rang again.

'You should probably get that,' Zach said, breathless. 'What if it's an emergency?'

Bea groaned, but picked up her phone. 'Hello?'

'Bea! It's Dino. Guess who I just lined up for our Next Chapter event next week?'

'Dino, can this wai—'

'Sophie. Pearson.'

'What!' Bea sat up, alert. Sophie Pearson was her idol. Author, Instagram influencer, blogger, entrepreneur, wife to famous radio personality Luke Bold – she was the epitome of 'have it all'.

'I know, right? She came into The Nook for a coffee and we got talking. She *loved* the idea, Bea. I just know the next event is going to be a success.' Dino spoke quickly, clearly excited.

'Oh my God, Dino, I love you!' Bea exclaimed before she could stop herself.

Zach coughed uncomfortably and there was silence on the other end of the phone.

Bea tried to grab at Zach's shirt, but he had taken one shuffle too many away from her. 'I better go. I'm with Zach,' Bea murmured, grasping Zach's hand. 'Let's talk more tomorrow. I'm so excited!'

'Okay. Bye, Bea,' Dino said before hanging up.

Bea turned to face Zach, who was now also sitting upright.

'So, you love Dino?' he remarked huffily. He wasn't looking at her.

'Don't be silly, Zach. It's not like that. Dino's with Sunday. I love Dino as a friend. That's all.' Bea squeezed Zach's hand. Three squeezes. He paused, before whispering 'I love you, Bea,' slightly bashfully, as he traced his finger along her jawline.

And just like that, the rest of the world melted away. A tingling washed over her body. She still couldn't believe that he loved her. That Bea, whose choices of late had been somewhat questionable, who carried a bit of extra weight around her hips, who always managed to get left and right wing political parties mixed up and whose previous great loves had only ever been fictional, was loveable? And better yet, was she a little bit in love too? Bea looked deeply into Zach's eyes. Caring, witty, playful Zach. She willed herself to be courageous, to let her walls come down. To finally say the words, rather than just squeeze them.

'I love you too, Zachary Harris,' she declared, and she meant it.

Zach's face transformed. His eyes shone with a new sparkle and he kissed Bea with a desire she had never felt from him before. A kiss fuelled by desperation and need – there was no hesitation, no 'let's go slow'. In one movement, Zach collected Bea in his arms and carried her into her bedroom, throwing her onto the bed. It was like she had just opened a good book, a new sense of life consuming her. He kissed her again passionately before pulling off his top. It was like saying 'I love you' had been a trigger for him. He no longer wanted to wait. Bea mirrored Zach's actions and removed her silk blouse.

But then, all of a sudden, Zach stopped and stared longingly into her eyes. His breathing was ragged, as if he wasn't quite sure what to do next. So, Bea kissed him again, first slowly, and then more urgently. And it was when she made a husky, exhaling sound that Zach's whole body relaxed. He ran his hands up and down her body chaotically, taking her in greedily. She leaned into him, wanting nothing more than to absorb his touch. Kissing her neck, a low groan escaped from his mouth. He pulled her on top of him and she wrapped her legs around him, running her fingers through his hair. They couldn't get close enough. He unclasped her bra at the same time as she unbuckled his belt, limbs moving too quickly for their thoughts to keep up.

'I want you. Every part of you,' he whispered through his kisses, and she exhaled louder than she had intended to.

'I want you too.'

29

Helloisthisyourbook

📍 The Nook in my new fancy shoes

Scribble of the day: *Let me in. I promise not to let you go.*

I asked him about this one. He said it was about him opening up to the world, letting himself and his true desires in. Oh, how I love him and his mind. (Yes, I went there. I LOVE HIM!)

---

95 likes

Comments (11):

NoOffenceBut: After a few weeks? Please.

elephantintheroom: Follow for follow? 🙏

butfirstletmetakeashelfie: *heart melting* 💙 💙 💙

StephenPrince: @NoOffenceBut, can I move back in yet?

NoOffenceBut: @StephenPrince, definitely not. We're on a break.

Fitnesstrainer111: Wanna lose weight? Like my page.

30

> 🗨 Dino: Look what I just found in my Twitter inbox: @SophPearson: Hey @CuppaDino. So sorry I can't make your book speed dating tonight after all. Last minute deadline emergency – you know how it is! Anyway, enjoy it – hopefully I'll make the next one.

> 🗨 Bea: Well, that sucks. PS You're on Twitter?!

> 🗨 Dino: I'm only there for Trump's hilarious tweets. But, don't worry, Bea. We've got this!

Bea locked her phone and tossed it across the bed a little harder than she meant to. She knew Sophie Pearson rocking up to her random little book event was too good to be true. *Oh well, tonight will still be great,* Bea told herself about the Next Chapter event she was hosting that evening, not quite believing it. It was only six in the morning, and Bea wasn't planning on dragging herself out of bed until at least nine. But the disappointment of Dino's message had throttled her awake, and she suddenly felt antsy.

She turned to face a sleeping Zach. He was wearing nothing but loose boxer shorts, his bare chest gently rising with each breath. Bea lightly traced his jaw with her fingertips, careful not to wake him. Something seemed to have shifted in Zach of late. He seemed transformed. Present. He had stayed over almost every night since they had first slept together two weeks ago. Possibly only because he knew how in need of human contact Bea was now that she spent her long, jobless days mostly alone at home, preparing for Next Chapter and scrounging around for freelance gigs, but still, it made Bea indescribably happy having Zach around. He even left a peppermint tea by her bed before he left for work each morning, gave her massages before bed and, on one occasion, picked up a chocolate meringue from the 24/7 bakery down the road, when he knew she had been craving one.

Plus, the sex. Oh, the sex. It was the best, the very best, she had ever had. But there was something about how Zach touched her, the way he made her skin tingle and her hips arch, that was nothing short of phenomenal. She was almost embarrassed by the fact that every time they were alone, she found a way to initiate getting back into bed. Bea rolled over and nestled into the crook of his arm, slipping her leg over his.

'Good morning,' she whispered, unable to resist kissing his chest.

Zach's head lolled to the side, his eyes crunching tightly closed. 'Is it morning already?' he said in a just-woken-up voice.

She rolled onto him and they embraced, him tickling her back with his fingertips.

'So, babe, what're we doing today?' Zach asked, eyes still closed.

'Don't you need to start getting ready for work?' Bea cringed at 'babe', brushed it off (nobody's perfect) and then curled her legs tighter around his, already preparing for her morning in bed, alone.

'Not today. I called in sick last night.' He faked a cough, sounding only slightly more alert.

Bea looked at him quizzically even though she knew he couldn't see her.

'Today's a really important day for you.' Zach cupped her face between his hands, finally peeling his eyes open. 'It's your big Next Chapter event tonight. I can't have you stressing about it all by yourself.' He kissed her lightly on the forehead.

Bea smiled. 'How did I get so lucky?' she said and smothered him with kisses.

Bea tried to focus on what the lanky, middle-aged man sitting across from her was saying. He was holding a hard-cover book the size of a hamster, and had been, for the past four and a half minutes, prattling on about Sir John Monash. In spite of her best efforts, Bea had only managed to catch fragmented phrases, such as 'civil engineer', 'equip yourself for life' and 'a great and distinguished military legacy'. She shifted in her seat, nodding and smiling politely, all the while thinking, *I'm a failure, a complete and utter, useless failure.*

She looked around the room. Apart from the usual suspects – Zach, Ruth and Dino – there had only been five and a half additional attendees. The biography-loving gentleman who sat opposite her, the two women from the Little Brunswick Street Bookstore, one of whom kept doing squats between book talks, both clutching copies of Jane Austen classics (*Emma* and *Sense and Sensibility*), a young girl who couldn't have been much older than sixteen who wielded a thick stack of Virginia Woolf's novels, and Sunday. The 'half' accounted for the guy in his twenties who walked past the café, spied a stack of cupcakes sitting behind the 'Next Chapter: Free Food and Books' sign, did a double-take, entered and not so subtly swiped two red velvets before backing away slowly. Lizzie hadn't even been able to make it. She was in Perth for some West Coast Eagles event Nick was speaking at. To make up for it though, and perhaps in an attempt to put the whole 'your boyfriend is a massive flirt' debacle behind her, she had been tweeting about the event like crazy.

Quality, not quantity, Bea told herself again as she stood to shake Mr Biog's hand and wandered over to the little taco-shaped biscuits she had ordered in the hopes of making the event feel more festive. Grabbing one of the delicacies and a serviette, she took a bite, swallowing her feelings along with the sugary goodness. She had been so full of hope for tonight's event, sure it would be different this time, more bustling, more vibrant, less ... pathetic. Between the Sophie Pearson coup and her sister's relentless tweets, Bea had built the evening up so much in her head that she hadn't even allowed herself to consider that it would be anything less than a raging success.

Finishing off the biscuit, she locked eyes with Dino, who smiled reassuringly, giving her the thumbs up before returning to his conversation with Sunday. Just then, a figure sidled up behind her and, before Bea could say *To Kill a Mockingbird,* arms were laced around her waist.

'Zach?' Bea said, some of the tension falling away as she turned around, extricating herself from the arms.

Bea froze. She blinked twice, squeezing her eyes shut each time, certain she was looking at the face of a ghost.

'Bea, I caught you!' Cassandra, dressed head to toe in black, said with a half-smile.

Cassandra, Bea's long lost best friend. The very same best friend whose wedding she had ruined. The very same best friend Bea had been trying to contact, to no avail, for the past few months. Cassandra stood there looking dazzling as always, as time fell away. Even though it had been so long, it felt like only yesterday that the pair were living in each other's back pockets. Like nothing had changed. *Does she finally forgive me?* Bea thought, hopefully.

'Cass? You're here?' Bea stumbled over her words. 'How are you here?' She subconsciously inched closer to Cassandra, her face feeling hot.

'I follow Lizzie on Twitter and, fifty tweets later, I couldn't keep ignoring you, or this, ah, *event*,' Cassandra said in an apathetic tone, giving the room the once over. 'I was in Melbourne for work, so I thought, why the hell not swing by?'

'Does this mean you forgive me? That we can start over?' Bea asked, unable to hide the glee in her voice. Suddenly it all felt worthwhile – the heartache, the disappointment, the busting her chops for the chance at a fresh start – because it had brought Cassandra back into her life.

'How about I let the book do the talking? That's what this *little* event is all about, after all, right?' Cassandra said, narrowing her eyes just slightly, judgement dripping from her voice.

Bea backed away slightly, remembering the infrequent, but flippant manner in which Cassandra could make her feel intolerably small. 'Oh yeah, of course.' Bea felt a rush of heat wash down her back. Tentatively, she looked down at Cassandra's outstretched hands and picked up the literary offering. Turning it over, she read the title aloud '*Great Expectations*?' The words 'you are in every line I have ever read' flashed across her mind.

'Thanks so much for bringing a book. You really didn't have to! It was enough for you just to be here.' Bea tried to grab at Cassandra's hand, but she pulled away.

Instead, Cassandra lazily pointed at the book with one slender finger. Obliging, Bea peeled open the worn cover and flipped through the first few pages, running her finger down its empty margins. Like magic, a folded sheet of paper fluttered to the floor. Crouching to retrieve it, Bea opened it up. Tucked away in the top left corner of the page sat a passport-sized photo of Zach. Bea stood up, the suddenness of the movement causing her to feel momentarily woozy, and looked at Cassandra quizzically, before devouring the words on the pages.

That's when her heart truly sank. Even further than the book which fell from her open hands.

31

Bea took one last look at the Airtasker profile in her hands before storming across the room and pushing the piece of paper towards Zach, her heart pounding. She felt light-headed. 'What is this, Zach?'

Tentatively, Zach took the piece of paper from Bea's hand, his eyebrows creased in confusion, or perhaps concern. Unfolding it, he ran his eyes down the page, shaking his head. 'Shit, Bea, I can explain.'

'Airtasker? What the hell is Airtasker and why on earth does your profile say "I'll do just about anything, winky face"?' Bea asked, hands on hips.

'Should I tell her or would you prefer to?' Cassandra said, appearing beside Bea.

Bea looked from Zach to Cassandra, taken aback. 'You two know each other?'

'You could say that.' Cassandra gave a cold laugh.

Bea could feel eyes prickling along her back. Hushed whispers and lingering looks followed the group. Bea grabbed Zach by the elbow and pulled him into the kitchen, away from prying eyes and ears.

Squashed between the narrow bench and industrial dishwasher, Zach stared at his feet. He looked genuinely terrified. Then he stepped towards Bea. 'Bea, before I say anything, you need to remember how much I care about you. How much I love you and how special getting to know you has been. Please, please, just hear me out.' Zach ran his hands through his hair, which suddenly looked limp and lacklustre. Taking another step towards her, he tried to take her hand, but Bea recoiled. A touch that just minutes before had filled her with hope and light now stung like a freshly scabbed wound.

'Zach, you're scaring me.' Bea trembled, glancing at Cassandra. Her mind was in overdrive. She tried furiously to figure out how Zach could know Cassandra. Had Cassandra ever mentioned a tall glass of water named Zach from Melbourne? Could they be long lost relatives? Was Cassandra here to kiss and make up? Or was Zach her attempt to kiss and make up? But Bea kept coming back to a lingering sensation of doom. And the fact that she needed answers before her head imploded.

Zach took a deep breath. 'A couple of months ago, Cassandra got in touch with me through my Airtasker profile.'

Bea shook her head. 'What the hell is Airtasker?' she repeated.

'It's an online community of people offering various trades and skills on the cheap. I've been a little tight on cash and was looking for a way to squeeze in some odd jobs here and there. I'm trying to save up to open my business. I've always dreamed about opening my own PT studio.'

'A PT studio? What are you talking about? You're an editor, why would you want to open a personal training business? You're not making any sense.' Bea was on the verge of hysterical laughter. But something told her this was no joke.

'Cut to the chase, Zach.' Cassandra pushed forward. 'I hired him to woo you and then, once you were smitten, break your heart. But it seems he was unable to follow through, so I've had to take matters into my own hands. And don't think you're getting that bonus.' She glared at Zach.

Bea felt nauseous. Everything she'd believed in, all the goodness she'd seen in Zach and the intensity of feelings she'd felt between them shattered before her eyes. 'You did what?' she yelped, unable to make sense of what her so-called friend had just said.

'You didn't think you'd get away with it, did you?' Cassandra said, arms crossed. 'Humiliating me? Destroying my relationship? Stealing my every happiness? Bea, you ruined me. *Ruined me!* My family has just about ostracised me, they're so embarrassed. And Matt refuses to forgive me, refuses to even talk to me. No matter what I say, he won't see my indiscretion for what it was – a stupid, drunken mistake that meant nothing.' Cheeks flushed and eyes wet with grief, Cassandra's shoulders heaved with every word. 'I've been assaulted by email after email from his lawyers. He's determined to get the marriage annulled. And while my life was falling to pieces, what do you do? Slink away as if nothing happened! You were meant to be my friend, my *best friend*, but you abandoned me after taking a huge dump on my life!' She yelled as a single tear traced down her cheek.

Bea was dumbfounded. She'd always known Cassandra had a predisposition for drama and a tendency to be passive aggressive. Like when she stopped speaking to Bea for weeks when she felt that she wasn't making enough effort to 'nurture their relationship'. But Bea never saw this betrayal coming.

'So, this was all a lie?' Bea mustered after several seconds of silence, turning back to Zach. 'We were a lie?' Zach opened his mouth, but before he could say anything, Bea faced Cassandra again and continued, 'Cassandra, I know what I did was terrible. Unforgivable, maybe. But it was an honest mistake. And I haven't stopped begging you to forgive me, for you to let me help make this better. I moved to Melbourne to give you the space you asked for! You know I could never be so callous intentionally. That I would never do anything to hurt you on purpose.' Bea paused, still unable to comprehend how her oldest, supposedly dearest friend could take such hideous revenge on her. 'But what you've done, this premeditated betrayal … I can't believe that you could despise me so much.' Zach's duplicity was one thing, but such an attack on her by a friend, a friend she had idolised for almost her entire life, was too much to fathom. Too much to bear.

Cassandra stared back at Bea, her features sharper, colder than Bea had remembered. Suddenly, she was almost completely unrecognisable. Where were the delicate laugh lines that usually creased her eyes? The lines that traced their shared history, all of their happy memories of reading *Charlotte's Web* and *The Lion, the Witch and the Wardrobe* and *A Little Princess* by torchlight, hidden under bed covers during countless slumber parties. Of exchanging emails during university lectures, salivating over the love stories in the pages of *Outlander* and *The Time Traveler's Wife*. Of each time Cassandra was there to read between the lines of every text message and unpick Bea's failed dates. Of the time Cassandra asked Bea to be her maid of honour. Of watching Cassandra walk down the aisle, her heart bursting with pride and love. And now, those memories dissolved before her very eyes. *Or had I remembered it all wrong?* Bea thought. Either way, none of it meant anything now.

'You know what, Cassandra. I've been beating myself up about what I did, about my stupid slip of the tongue, when, in fact, I wasn't the one who slept with the damn topless waiter! No, that was you!' Bea suddenly snapped. She'd moved from shock, to denial, to outright rage. 'And what poetic justice for you. Hiring some kind of … some kind of *escort*! You must be very proud of yourself.'

Cassandra huffed in reply, not used to Bea being so defiant.

Taking advantage of the moment of silence, Zach stepped in. 'I'm not an escort! Bea, you've got it all wrong.'

'Have I? Have I really? A rose by any other name would smell as sweet.' Bea couldn't believe the soap opera that was suddenly her life. If she hadn't been so shocked, so hurt, she might actually have found this laughable. *I mean, betrayal, escorts, salacious affairs – you can't make this stuff up. This is worse than an episode of* The Bold and the Beautiful.

'Okay, yes, Cassandra paid me to spend time with you.'

'Paid you? I did more than that. I spent all of our honeymoon money on you.'

Bea ignored Cassandra and turned to Zach. 'Spend time with me? We've been dating for over a *month*! You told me you loved me. We've—' She stepped closer, lowering her voice. 'We've been intimate with each other, for God's sake.'

'Bea, I'm so sorry,' Zach said, spinning a spatula left on the bench, unable to look Bea in the eye. 'I don't know what to say. I didn't want you to find out like this.'

'Were you ever planning on telling me? Or were you just going to up and leave, just like Cassandra asked you to? Break my heart in some tragic act of vengeance?' Bea couldn't believe what she was hearing from this man with whom, just hours ago, she had shared a bed – shared her body and innermost thoughts and feelings. 'How many more are there?'

'More?' Zach asked, genuinely bemused.

'Don't play dumb with me. How many more women are you stringing along?'

'None! You're the only person I'm seeing.'

'Ha! Lucky me!' Bea cackled, feeling slightly deranged.

The group fell into stunned silence. It was hopeless. Was there really anything either Cassandra or Zach could say to make any of this okay?

Zach was the first to speak. 'I didn't sleep with you until I knew how I felt about you. That was why I waited. I never meant to hurt you. And I was going to come clean, I promise. I was just so afraid that you'd hate me, that I would never see you again. The fear of losing you has been eating me up. You have no idea how conflicted I've been. But I know I've cheapened what we have. I can't tell you how sorry I am.'

'What we *have*? Please. Next, you'll be telling me that I was more than just a job. Is that right?' Bea spat.

Zach stepped forward, unsuccessfully trying to take Bea's hand in his once more. 'Yes! Well, it was only a job at the start,' he spluttered. 'You have to believe me when I say that everything we've shared was real. Truly.'

Bea shook her head. *Does he think I'm an idiot?* 'Bullshit! I call bullshit! I'm not falling for that. Not for one second. Zach, you've been lying to me. And you've been bloody profiting from spending time with me! How could you possibly think that I could believe anything you say now?'

'Because – because I'm in love with you, Bea,' Zach whispered.

Bea saw Cassandra's jaw drop. Cassandra pushed forward, trying to interject, but Zach powered on. 'Bea, you have to know how much I've come to care for you. How enlightening your presence has been. You're so bold, so full of wonder. I know you've felt so alone these past months, so lost, yet look what you're trying to create, what you *are* creating. And how you connect with people. You are amazing.'

Bea rolled her eyes. 'Oh, you're good, Zach. Oh, you're really good. Forget escorting, that was an Oscar-winning performance!' Unexpectedly, Bea felt almost entirely disconnected from her surroundings, as if she were having a total out-of-body experience. She could see Zach's mouth moving, but she only managed to catch fragments of what he was saying. Something about funds and starting his own personal training business, about not being an editor, the word sorry crushed between each excuse. But all she really heard was: *Poor creatures. What did we do to you? With all our schemes and plans?* which pulsated through her head on loop. Ishiguro's *Never Let Me Go*, which had kept her company this week, seemed to be speaking to her on a whole new level.

And then, one last heartbreaking thought pushed to the front of Bea's mind.

'And what about the book?' Bea asked. 'Was that at least real? Or did Cassandra tell you about it? Get you to say that it belonged to you?'

Zach froze, eyebrows raised, his mouth forming a response. But he didn't need to say anything. At that moment, Bea knew. She knew that the man who stood before her wasn't even close to the man she thought he was. She understood now how deep his deception ran, how cunning Cassandra's plan had been. It was all a lie. One big, ugly, gaping lie.

Bea had heard enough. No longer able to be in the same room as them, she snatched her bag from the staff cupboard and made for the door.

At the last moment, she paused, a question dancing on the tip of her tongue. But rather than ask it, she started riffling through her bag. Eventually, she found her wallet and extracted it. Unzipping it, she began frantically grabbing at the receipts and notes crammed inside. She swivelled around and thrust the clump of money and paper at a shocked Zach.

'For the overtime,' Bea said, her voice wobbling, before turning on her heel and bolting out of The Nook.

And then when she was finally alone, wrapped up in the cool night air, Bea let the tears fall.

32

Dear Ramona,

Please don't bother vacuuming up the crumbs or mopping the floors. Just tidy up the chocolate wrappers and empty pizza boxes on the floor and maybe make my bed, if there's time. Sorry there's so much mess. I just found out I'm living in a real-life *Taming of the Shrew*, *and*, *well*, *my empty Mars Bar wrappers will tell the anger of my heart.*

Yours,

Bea Katherina Babbage

33

Bea,

    The place is very messy. I stay 45 minutes longer. This time is not included in prize small print. Please pay extra next time.

    Also, I hope everything okay.

    Ramona

34

don't speak when your mouth is full of lies.

Bea aggressively highlighted the annotation in *Meeting Oliver Bennett* with a bright yellow marker. Her hair, which she hadn't washed in days, was pulled into a messy bun and she was sitting cross-legged on her couch, wearing nothing but a sweater and a pair of lacy black undies. Bea had spent the past four days consumed with trying to digest the madness that had unravelled in her life. Walking home from The Nook that terrible night, she'd felt a mixture of hurt, betrayal and overwhelming disappointment. *This is how Julia must've felt when Winston gave her up to the rats,* she had thought bitterly to herself, appreciating *1984* in a whole new, very dramatic light. But this morning when she woke in her quiet, cold, empty apartment, she'd felt a different sort of emotion.

Apathy.

She was *over it.* Over Cassandra, over Zach leading her on, being some kind of freaking escort, and she was absolutely and truly over her ridiculous life and everything that came with it. Sick of shedding tears over people she knew would probably never shed tears over her, Bea had a new sense of purpose. Instead of moping, she was going to focus her energy on connecting with the one person in her life who didn't judge, who didn't swindle or misguide or disappoint. The person whose heartfelt insights lingered in Bea's mind. The person who had comforted her when Bea felt entirely alone.

The *real* Mystery Writer.

Bea was going to find out who the true person behind the annotations was if it was the last thing she did. And she was going to do it without letting out one more wail, cry or scream.

At three in the morning, she was halfway through *Meeting Oliver Bennett* for the second time. Again, she wasn't paying attention to the storyline at all. Instead, she sat on the couch hunched over the book, analysing each comment, mark and note with new scrutiny. She poured herself another glass of vodka on the rocks – *Hey, if I can't cry, at least I can drink*, she told herself – and then downed it, smacking her lips at the violent taste.

melbourne never liked me, anyway.

Bea quickly highlighted and then took out her note-book, scribbling into it:

Possibly from out of town? Possibly doesn't live in Melbourne anymore?

She sighed, cracked her knuckles and furrowed her brow. She was determined to find something, anything, that would lead her in a direction that was far from her ex-boyfriend, the con-artist. She rolled onto her back, lifting the book above her head. She stroked its hard corners and caressed the battered pages lightly with her fingers, flicking through them aimlessly.

sympathy looks good on you.
you were full of rare smiles.
hold on pretty enigma.
your farts smell like honey.

Bea burst out laughing. 'Oh beautiful writer, who are you? If you can make me laugh at a time like this, what can't you do?' she mumbled to herself. Was she officially going mad? She held the book closer to her face, tracing the cursive letters with the tip of her finger. While she was lost in thoughts about what sort of person had such delicate handwriting, the novel slipped through her hands, landing with a smack on her face. She yelped, sat upright and threw the hardback down by her phone. She let it sit there for a moment, its pages peeled open to one side, brushing against the edges of her phone. The phone that she refused to answer as she disappeared within herself. Then she remembered. *The phone number. Maybe they will be able to tell me about the owner of the book?*

She retrieved the book and scrambled through the pages, before landing on the number scrawled hastily into the margin. She pointed her index finger at it, picking up her phone from the floor. She switched it on, eyes screwed shut. She knew what was coming.

6:02pm <Missed call from Zach>

7:36pm <Missed call from Zach>
8:34pm <Missed call from Zach>
8:55pm <Missed call from Zach>
9:44pm <Missed call from Zach>
10:08pm <Missed call from Zach>

💬 Zach: Bea, please. I'm sorry. I love you. Please can we just talk this through?

A lump started to form in Bea's throat, but before she could stop herself, she was dialling a number she hadn't planned to dial at all.

'Bea, are you okay?' Dino was standing at her door. He was wearing loose track pants and a white singlet that revealed the tattoo sleeve travelling down his arm. His hair was more ruffled than usual and his eyes were unfocused and glazed. It was too early in the morning for him to have walls up, and this was the first time Bea had seen him look so vulnerable. It was unexpected – suggestive.

'I'm sorry, I shouldn't have told you to come,' she said, playing with the drawstrings of the pyjama shorts she had just thrown on.

Dino pushed past her, making his way to the couch. In a last minute attempt to clean up, she had shoved a glass of vodka, five chocolate wrappers and a bra (which she had ripped off earlier in a fit of feminist rage) into a box under her coffee table. She had forgotten about the

Absolut Vodka bottle, which Dino was now holding up accusingly.

'You drank all of this?'

Bea looked at the floor, sheepishly.

'No wonder you look like shit.'

Bea rolled her eyes, before walking over to sit next to him. 'Thank you for coming. I didn't know who else to call.' She looked into his eyes.

He nodded back. 'Do you want to explain what exactly happened that night? And why you haven't answered any of my calls since racing out of my café?'

So, for the first time, Bea recounted the story.

Dino paced up and down Bea's living room, fists clenched, pupils dilated and angry. 'I can't believe him,' he spat.

As she let it all pour out of her, Cassandra's deceit, Zach's Airtasker profile and that Zach wasn't the Mystery Writer after all, she felt a certain peace wash over her, as if she was letting go of all the ruthlessness, all of the deceit and betrayal with every word. She lay flat on the couch, head upside down, soaking up her new, surprising indifference. She watched Dino pacing. His eyes flickered with wrath, his lips pursed as if he'd just bitten into a lemon.

'That bastard.'

Bea sat up. 'What?'

'I'll kill him.' Dino punched his open palm with his fist. Bea had never seen him like this. So livid, so protective.

'Dino, don't be ridiculous.' Bea stood up, but he looked straight through her. He was breathing so heavily it made Bea's breath deepen too. 'Dino,' she whispered, placing her hand on his. Dino looked up, finally making eye contact.

His stance eased just slightly. 'I'm sorry. I'm just so angry at him for doing this to you.'

Bea could feel his hand relax under hers. She half-smiled, wanting him to know it was okay, and that she was grateful for his concern.

He glanced around the room, staring at her disorganised, sad pile of scattered books and magazines. 'If a book title could sum up your mood – what would it be?' Dino asked.

'What?'

'It's what my grandma always used to ask me. I used to get into these fits of rage when I was younger, and I could never explain why. My grandma would tell me to try explaining it with a book title, and somehow it helped. I was usually *The Very Hungry Caterpillar*,' Dino joked, trying to lighten the atmosphere.

Bea smiled. 'Your grandma sounds like a wise woman.'

'She was.' Dino nodded solemnly.

'*You Should Have Known*,' Bea replied. 'It's by Jean Hanff Korelitz.'

Dino gripped her hand, such an intimate act surprising Bea, and then replied, '*The Amber Fury*.'

She was glad he didn't correct her, tell her she couldn't have known. She wasn't in the mood for sympathy. '*Hopeless*,' she replied.

Dino stared at her intently, before responding, '*Persuasion*,' in an uncharacteristically hoarse voice.

A shiver ran down Bea's spine. She bit her lip.

Dino gripped her hand harder. '*Everything I Never Told You*.'

Bea inhaled before murmuring, '*Hunger.*'

'Oh my God, Bea.'

'That's not a book.'

'*The Life-Changing Magic of Not Giving a F**k,*' he replied before pulling her face towards his and kissing her with everything he had.

Her breath caught, taken aback by what was happening, then she kissed him back. She could still taste vodka in her mouth, but his intense minty flavour overcame it. Her mind felt like it was floating as he kissed her with such desire, it seemed he had been waiting his whole life to do so. He wrapped his arm around her waist, pulling her closer to him, still not taking his lips away from hers, lost in a haze of lust and perfect touches. Dino slid his hand slowly under her loose jumper, trailing his fingertips lightly along her stomach. Her breath caught.

Bea couldn't believe how good this felt, how right it was to be held tightly in his arms. *No – how* wrong *it was to be held tightly in his arms.*

'Wait. Stop.'

Dino dropped his arms and leaned back. 'Are you okay?'

'This isn't right. We shouldn't be doing this,' Bea said, eyes averted.

Dino wiped the back of his hand across his mouth as if trying to wash her away. 'Yeah, yeah, you're right. Too messy. Way too messy,' he muttered, stepping backwards, placing as much distance between them as possible.

'Let's just pretend this never happened,' Bea said quickly.

Dino simply nodded in reply.

'We're both not in our right mind. Drunk on anger, and in my case, lots of vodka.' She let out a weak laugh.

They stood there for a moment, staring at the chasm that had torn open between them. Bea felt terrible. Worse than terrible – like absolute shit. No, worse than shit. Like the lowest creature to ever roam the world. She was the dung beetle that shovelled shit. How could she do this to her friend? To Sunday? In this moment, she was no better than Cassandra.

'I should go.' Dino turned on his heel and made his way to the door, collecting his jacket on the way.

'Wait,' Bea called quietly.

Dino turned, eyebrows raised expectantly.

Her heart rattled in her chest. She opened her mouth, but nothing came out. Shaking her head, she managed, 'Nothing, nothing. I'll see you on my next coffee run.'

With a final and resounding grunt, Dino half-smiled, half-frowned, then left Bea breathless and standing regretful, in her living room.

35

Helloisthisyourbook

In a fit of rage I tore a page from *Meeting Oliver Bennett*. Before you block me for defacing a book, hear me out. I recently found out that Mystery Writer is not Mystery Writer after all. I was, of course, distraught, and did things that I regret (like tearing pages from books). But then I realised, it's not the scribbles that I'm angry at. In fact, the person behind them has been nothing but consistent and comforting since I moved to a new city. So, I'm going to stop relying on everyone else, be the leading lady in my own story – and make it my sole mission in life to find the *real* Mystery Writer. Will you come on this journey with me?

---

312 likes

Comments (72):

bookishflavour: Don't worry, hon. Men suck. 👎

Misterhottie: You're ugly.

Caughtreadhanded: I can't believe you tore a page out of your book. This hurts my soul!

StephenPrince: Oh, I'm so sorry to hear 🙁 I agree @bookishflavour, men do often suck.

NoOffenceBut: @StephenPrince, you're telling me! I just saw you on Tinder.
StephenPrince: @NoOffenceBut: We're on a break!

36

'Just do something different.' Bea stared at herself in the mirror, a scratchy cape wrapped tightly around her neck, her long hair hanging past her shoulders. The past month had been a blur of working so hard and burying herself in *Meeting Oliver Bennett* that she didn't have time to eat, sleep or most importantly, think about Zach. Which was proving especially difficult, as Zach would not let up. She had received countless text messages, phone calls and even one very sad postcard featuring a basket of tiny golden retriever puppies that read: 'I'm lost without you. Please can we put this behind us?' He was desperate to win her back.

In an attempt to get that horrible Next Chapter out of her head, she and Dino had dedicated themselves to planning their next event, which would be so fantastic and extravagant no one would remember the last one. Dino had proven to be indispensable, regularly surprising her with his ability to think outside the box.

They had also spent the last month avoiding discussing *that* kiss. 'I feel weird not acknowledging what happened,' she had cryptically messaged Dino one late night. 'There's nothing to say. It didn't mean anything,' he had written back. After that, Bea forced herself to forget, to convince herself that it *did* mean nothing and that it could obviously never happen again (she wouldn't do that to Sunday, although she'd avoided her as best she could, in case her guilty eyes revealed her nasty secret). So Bea and Dino returned to being friends who awkwardly hugged, discussed books and, in Bea's case, got hot flushes whenever the other was around.

While secret fantasies of Dino and planning the Next Chapter extravaganza were unnerving distractions, Bea still felt a messy void in her heart where Zach used to be. Trying to fill the abyss, and pay the bills, she had started freelancing for a few small clients. She had even toyed with the idea of starting up her own agency.

And now, in an attempt to further 're-launch', Bea did what Eleanor Oliphant did when she wanted to feel better – she headed straight to the hairdresser. In her case, a small, hairspray-smelling one around the corner from her apartment, for which she had won a coupon for a free cut and colour. She was putting herself at the mercy of scissors that belonged to a hairdresser she didn't know.

'Oh, darling. You've got to give me more than that. Are we talking "I just got a new job" different or "I just went through the worst break-up of my life" different?' Vaughn the hairdresser asked animatedly. His long silver hair was tied in a sleek ponytail and his manicured eyebrows were raised eagerly.

'Definitely the latter. You don't know the half it,' Bea replied.

'Oh, darling.' Vaughn put his hand on Bea's shoulder. 'Did you fall down the rabbit hole?'

Bea smiled. *Isn't it funny how ingrained some stories are in our lives?* And then it reminded her of her first date with Zach. 'Oh boy, did I fall down the hole. I bumped my head,

I bruised my soul.' She paraphrased the quote, wishing that, like Alice, she had come to and realised it had all been a dream.

Vaughn nodded knowingly. 'I have just the look for you.'

With a thick layer of white goo caked all over her hair and half an hour to sit and wait, Bea picked up her copy of *Meeting Oliver Bennett*, resuming her search for whoever lay behind the pen. She had called the phone number scribbled in the book countless times, but it kept going straight to the same woman's voicemail. She now knew the message by heart: *'Sorry, I can't get to the phone right now, leave a message at the beep and I'll get back to you. Probably.'* She had also read and then re-read every single inscription, hoping that once she transported this character from the page to real life, everything in her world would suddenly make sense again.

Learning that Zach wasn't who he'd said he was had been painful. And discovering that Cassandra was behind it all hurt even more. But for some reason, finding out that she could no longer put a face to the scribbles was what wounded her the most. It was like she had fallen deeply for the words, given each letter, each mark, each dot, its own meaning. And now that she no longer knew who wrote them, well, it was like she had to start reading them all over again. *Why do you even care so much about finding the owner of this damn book?* she asked herself repeatedly. But deep down, she knew why. Discovering the annotations and meeting this enigmatic figure had given her the sense of being tethered to something, of feeling a certain connectedness to someone, even as anonymous as the Mystery Writer, when so much of her life felt so empty. It made her want to think differently, to question more and dare to dream just a little.

Bea flicked *Meeting Oliver Bennett* open to a dog-eared page and whipped out a pink highlighter. She scanned the pages, reading the words that had become dear friends, crafting an Instagram post in her head at the same time. Her Bookstagram following had grown significantly since she had revealed that the man behind the book wasn't the man behind the book after all. She had received an outpouring of comments empathising with her, and, most intriguing, offering to help her track down the real owner of the book. She highlighted a sentence.

you are entirely whole as you are.

She took out her phone, snapped a photo of the page and typed a quick caption.

Mystery Writer thought provocation for the day! How to be loved like this, am I right?

Instantly, a few comments appeared underneath her picture.

Hear, hear. Hope you're doing okay, babe xx
Sah poetic.

Bea smiled. She scrolled through her feed, liking and commenting on different photos of novels, coffees and bookshelves.

'Ready to wash, darling?' Vaughn grabbed her shoulders, waking her from her reverie.

After a blow-dry and copious amounts of fluffing and styling products, Bea stared at her reflection in the hairspray-misted mirror, not recognising the woman looking back at her. It was perfect. An almost white-blonde pixie cut now framed her face, the opposite of her usual black mane. Her skin looked even paler next to her new hair, her black mascara even darker. She looked like a Scandinavian exchange student who had come to Melbourne to study literature, drink wine and meet boys.

'You're fabulous! Fabulous!' Vaughn cooed, running his fingers through her newly peroxided hair. 'But it needs something else. Kristy!' he yelled towards the back of the salon. 'Come here, and bring your bag!'

Seconds later, a small, mousy girl dashed towards them, hairdryer in one hand, purple makeup bag in the other. Vaughn took the bag from her and rummaged through it. 'Voila!' he said, taking out a half-used hot-pink lipstick. He turned Bea's chair around to face him and, before she could speak, swiped the lipstick across her lips.

'Perfection,' he whispered with pride, swivelling her chair back to the mirror.

'Perfection,' Bea whispered, grinning.

'So, who is this for?' Vaughn asked, stroking her hair, admiring his work.

'For? It's for me.' Bea shrugged, still not able to take her eyes off her new source of confidence.

'Oh, I know that, honey. But nobody comes in to get their hair did without a place to be after. Where are you going? Wedding? Party? Girls' drinks? Hot date?'

'Oh, nowhere special,' Bea admitted. 'Just a visit to my local coffee shop.'

Bea was wearing an emerald green knit that made her eyes shine, skinny jeans and her sparkly silver Converse. She had just applied a fresh layer of her new hot-pink lipstick (which Kristy had insisted she keep – 'It looks better on you,' she'd declared) and her ice blonde hair was tucked effortlessly behind her ears. For the first time in a month, she felt strong, empowered and – dare she say it – beautiful.

As soon as she walked through the blue door of The Nook the scents of baking muffins, roasting coffee beans and cinnamon filled her nose. A young man sitting at the furthest table from the door looked up from his phone to trail his eyes over her. She stared him down as she made her way to the counter. She spotted Dino, and before she could stop it, her heart did a somersault.

'One strong skinny latte please, extra hot. It's freezing out there,' Bea said in a husky voice that wasn't her own, staring at Dino's sturdy arms. He was wearing a burgundy jumper and scribbling in his Moleskine, probably liberating sonnets from his mind.

'Coming right up,' he replied, turning around.

'Busy day?' she asked, enjoying the fact that he hadn't recognised her.

'Mmm ...' he replied and Bea let out a laugh.

'What's so funny?' He turned to face her for the first time. 'Bea?'

'Yes?'

'Your hair! It's blonde!' he exclaimed, staring at her. 'And short.'

'I know. Do you like it?' she replied, butterflies dancing in her stomach.

'Yeah. It's different,' he said, still not taking his eyes off her.

Bea nodded, holding his gaze. 'Did you like it better before?' she asked, nervously tucking some loose bits back behind her ear.

'I like it both ways,' he replied. He blinked twice before turning his back to her to prepare her latte. 'Oh, by the way, fifteen giant jars of jelly babies arrived for you this morning. I mean, what the hell are you going to do with 5,000 jelly babies?'

She'd almost forgotten about the Allen's competition she had entered two weeks ago, writing: 'I'm 30 and recently single, this might be my only chance of having a family.'

'Don't worry, I'm a changed woman. I'm going cold turkey on the material competitions. I live a minimalist lifestyle now.'

'Uh huh, I'll believe it when I see it,' Dino replied, his back still to her.

Bea, after watching *Tidying with Marie Kondo* on Netflix, had decided to embrace the old adage of less is more and thrown just about everything that didn't 'spark joy' into six large garbage bags. She had needed to rid herself of everything that came close to reminding her of Zach and Cassandra, including many of her – she hated to admit – unnecessary competition winnings. She'd then moved on to folding her underwear in the prescriptive way that would allow it to stand up in a drawer.

Bea whipped out her phone and scrolled through her Instagram feed mindlessly, trying to steady her heartbeat. The shop was unusually quiet for a Tuesday afternoon. The song 'Here Comes the Sun' played softly from the speaker that hung in a corner of the ceiling. The bell on the front door rang.

'Dino!' Sunday yelled, making her way to the counter. Her eyes were red and her usually tanned skin pink and blotchy. She jutted her chin upwards in acknowledgement of Bea, who smiled meekly back at her. 'Bea, is that you? Sexy hair.' She winked, the simple nicety making Bea feel even worse about what had happened with Dino than she had before. Sunday's own pink hair was thrown up in a high ponytail and she wore a blue button-down shirt paired with black boyfriend jeans and Doc Martens. She looked chic, edgy and carefree all at the same time. Bea started to feel stupid about her own blonde hair and pink lips.

'What's going on, Sunday?' Dino stopped making Bea's coffee and came around to the front of the counter, placing his hand on Sunday's arm. 'I've never seen you like this.' Bea's coffee was left, half-made, on the bench. Bea averted her eyes.

'Oh, it's stupid, you know,' Sunday sniffed, sitting on a bar stool. 'It's just, I was chilling at ARK café, watching some documentaries about animal welfare on my phone. And one really got to me. *Cowspiracy*. It's just horrible, what we're doing to these animals, to our planet! I can't stop thinking about it. That's why I want to work with vegan clothing. I just want to do something to help, you know? But at the moment, I feel like I'm not doing enough, and every time I close my eyes, turn a corner, I can't stop seeing those horrible images. I just walked past a McDonald's and burst into tears. I've gone crazy!' Sunday said, welling up again.

'Sunday, that's not stupid. It means you care. Plus, you *are* doing something. You're looking for a job in ethical fashion as we speak, and you're constantly haranguing customers to donate to a new charity.' Dino sat on the bar stool next to her. 'Look, I'll tell you something I do to make myself feel better. It's something my grandmother taught me. Tell me a book title that explains your feelings,' he said.

Bea looked at the ground, remembering when he had distracted her with the same riddle.

'What?' Sunday said.

'Look, I'll start. *So Sad Today*. Because I saw you cry for the first time,' he said with a gentleness that was unfamiliar to Bea.

'Okay,' Sunday sniffed. '*Ferris Bueller's Day Off* – because I desperately need a holiday.' She put her arm on Dino's and nudged him.

Bea withheld an eye roll at the movie, not book, title. Dino said nothing.

'You're right, this does make me a feel a little better,' Sunday said, more chirpily this time.

Bea held in a cough, not wanting to spoil the moment between the pair. She took one last longing look at her half-made coffee before slowly backing away towards the front door. Her eyes trained on the floor, she bumped into a man who had just walked in.

'Bea?'

'Zach?'

37

'Zach?' Bea stammered, regaining her composure. Shakily, she stepped backwards to where Agatha Christie was sleeping in her dog bed and scooped her into her arms for emotional support. Or to provide some kind of animal shield. She sat down, not trusting her legs to keep her upright. 'What are you doing here?'

Zach looked terrible: his hair was ruffled, his shirt was half-untucked, and dark circles accented his eyes. But his face, his body, *that sexy, beautiful body*, still made Bea tingle and she hated herself for it.

He took a tentative step towards her, then paused. 'I had to see you,' he said, running his hands through his limp hair. 'You look amazing, by the way.'

She ignored the compliment. 'How'd you know I'd be here?'

'Of course you would, Bea. When you refused to answer any of my calls, I had to come straight to the source.' He glowered at Dino, who scowled right back. 'Can we go somewhere? Please? Even just for a few minutes.'

This was typical. Just as Bea was getting closer to some semblance of calm, Zach reared his betraying, lying head. She had hoped that she could declutter him from her heart and peroxide him out of her life, strand by strand. But now, here he was, all doe-eyed and apologetic, begging her to forgive him. This was not the kind of romantic gesture she could stomach right now.

She held Agatha Christie more firmly against her chest, breathing in her sleepy poodle scent. 'I don't think that's a good idea,' she said.

'Please, Bea. I'm begging you, just give me a chance to make things better. To explain myself properly,' Zach said.

'Didn't you hear her, mate? She said no,' Dino interjected, taking a step closer to him. Sunday eyed Zach, but said nothing, her expression and power pose doing the talking for her.

'Stay out of it for once, *mate*,' Zach said. 'This is between Bea and me.'

'And Cassandra, apparently,' Dino said. 'How *is* the Airtasker business going? It has some serious benefits, I hear.' As soon as he said it, though, he seemed to regret it.

Bea frowned, then sighed. 'Zach, what could there possibly be to say? The whole situation is unforgivable. I just can't get into it again. I'm trying to move on. Finally. From you, from Cass, from this whole damn fantasy that happily ever after exists in real life.'

'You have to believe me when I say it really wasn't all a lie, Bea. When I told you I loved you, I meant it. Truly,' Zach said, sneaking an awkward glance at Dino. 'Yes, the way we met was terrible, a huge betrayal and totally thoughtless. But I can't let myself regret it fully because it brought you to me.'

Bea heard Sunday sigh and Dino huff. She was sure if Zach stayed any longer, Dino might actually end up huffing and puffing and blowing this coffee shop down.

'When I agreed to Cassandra's plan, I was desperate. I needed the coin and it all seemed so temporary, so petty. But I was obviously deluded.' Zach hung his head.

'Understatement of the year!' Dino burst out. Bea, momentarily forgetting herself, couldn't help but snort.

Zach frowned at Dino, then sat down on the bar stool next to Bea. 'When I got into this ridiculous business, I could never have imagined that you would be you.'

Bea felt her heart race and her palms become sweaty as she grasped the dog even tighter. She exhaled, not realising she had been holding her breath. Looking into the eyes of the man of whom she had become so fond – who she'd thought she *loved* – a tight twinge caught in her chest. 'It's too little, too late, Zach,' she said. 'There have been too many lies exchanged. How could I ever trust you again? I don't even know who you are!'

'Let me show you,' Zach begged, pulling one of her hands to his chest.

For a moment, they sat there, transfixed, and Bea fell just a little deeper into his gaze.

Dino cleared his throat, startling them back to reality. 'Bea, you're not going to fall for that shit, are you?'

Bea, pulling away from Zach, placed Agatha Christie on the floor. She took a look at her wayward barista, thinking about the last month. The awkward double-takes, the half-hearted hugs, the total denial of feelings or honest admissions about any saliva ever being exchanged. And then she thought about the month she had shared with Zach. His spontaneity, his wit, the way he would hold her hand with his thumb always gently caressing her index finger. The three squeezes. She thought about that time they visited The Avenue bookstore on the hunt for as many books with the names Zach and Bea in them as they could find, and how he'd charmed a group of young girls reading the latest illustrated Harry Potter book by reenacting, with accents and imaginary wand flourishes, the fight scene from *Harry Potter and the Deathly Hallows*.

'Zach, I just don't know,' Bea said. 'I need time.'

Shooting up from the stool, Zach grinned widely. 'I can wait. You take all the time in the world.' Zach squeezed her shoulder, smiling that blasted sunflowers-blooming-in-the-meadow smile. With a final reassuring nod, and one last menacing look at Dino, he strode out of the coffee shop, at least understanding one thing: how to quit when he was ahead.

Ruffling her blonde locks, Bea dared not make eye contact with Dino. 'I need to get some air. I'll catch you later.'

'Wait,' Dino called, and Bea's heart skipped a beat. 'Your coffee.' Pushing the takeaway cup towards her, he spoke slowly and deliberately. 'Just be careful, okay?'

Eyes still averted, Bea picked up her bag and the coffee, promising to come back for the lolly jars. She walked out of the shop, pulling her jacket tightly around her neck. Before taking a sip of her drink, she looked at the cup. Snaking around it were the words: *Never argue with an idiot. They'll always beat you with experience.*

Bloody Twain.

Bea felt unhinged. The kind of deranged, on-the-verge-of-several-mental-breakdowns kind of unhinged that not even a good book – or even a great book – could take her mind off. Not *The Light Between Oceans*, not *The Invention of Wings*, not *The Nowhere Child*. And not even the annotations in *Meeting Oliver Bennett*. So, in a bid to get her mind off her earlier encounter with Zach – *just when I had started to forget that chiselled jaw and that smile and the way his shoulders shake when he laughs. Damn that man!* – she called the only person she knew would take her mind off things. The person who would consume Bea with her own world, allowing her some reprieve from worrying about her own.

Her sister.

Lizzie picked up on the third ring, screamed with glee, then hung up and called her straight back on FaceTime. Bea sighed, answered the phone, and couldn't help but smile as her sister's face (camera aimed down at her most flattering angle) grinned back at her.

'Bea!' Lizzie squealed. 'Long time no speak. I promise I'll drive up to Melbourne soon. I miss your face. And – oh my God – your hair!'

Bea smoothed her bright blonde hair self-consciously. 'I needed a change.'

'I can see that. You look so much better.'

Bea shuddered at the backhanded compliment.

'Tell me, what's the latest with Next Chapter? I have some thoughts for you.'

Bea was filling her sister in when, without warning, she burst into tears.

'Bea, what's wrong? Talk to me,' Lizzie said.

Tiny tears dribbled down her cheeks as she tried to get a handle on herself. She knew she was overwhelmed, miserable even, but it wasn't until this moment that she realised just how overcome she really was. Despite her best efforts, forgetting Zach wasn't going to be as simple as she would have hoped. She hadn't told Lizzie about the real, completely mortifying reason that she and Zach had split. 'It was a mutual decision' had been her go-to line, without going into more details. But now, between sniffs and desperate gulps for air, Bea let it all out. The love, the hurt, the betrayal, and now, the confusion.

Lizzie nodded along and then, when Bea was finally done, she looked Bea straight in the eyes and said, 'I called it.'

Dumbfounded, Bea struggled to find the words to match what she was feeling. 'What?'

'Bea, I told you I thought he was suss. He practically pinched my arse mid-book club. Remember? I know a rat when I see one.'

Bea furrowed her brow. Of course this was how Lizzie would respond. In Bea's vulnerable state, Lizzie had to make it all about her. A vivid memory of getting fired from her first job at McDonald's when she was fifteen because she was too shy to talk to customers flashed before her eyes. 'What am I going to tell my friends? I promised I could get them all free soft serve this weekend. Bea, you are so selfish!' Lizzie had cried.

'Lizzie, you're crazy,' she said, surprised to find herself defending Zach all over again. 'He's just an overly friendly person. And you do, after all, have a very pinchable arse.' *Did I really just defend the guy who has proven to be nothing but duplicitous?*

'Cute. But don't you dare go making excuses for him.'

'But what if he means it when he says he actually loves me? What if he did fall for me in spite of everything?'

'Honey, that may be so, but call me crazy if I find it hard to believe that somebody who is willing to purposely trick another person into a relationship – *and love* – all for a few bucks, can be trusted.'

'No, you're right. Of course, you're right.' God, how she hated when Lizzie was right.

'Thatta girl! Now, tell me, what's your take on super-moons and mood swings? Because I've been a total bitch lately.'

Bea tried to focus on what her sister was saying, but her thoughts kept going back to something Zach had said the night before everything fell apart. He had looked at her with such intensity and asked her if she believed in parallel universes and, if so, did she think they would've still found a way into each other's lives? Could they have met under different circumstances and still have hit it off? At the time she had put the comment down to sappy musings, but in hindsight she was remembering it in a different light.

The logical section of her brain knew he was trouble, knew that Lizzie and Dino were right not to trust him. But then why, when Bea finally hung up the phone, did a part of her feel like giving him one last chance?

38

Helloisthisyourbook

Scribble of the day: *Messina, 7pm*

I've started to list all the real-life places that Mystery Writer mentions in *Meeting Oliver Bennett* – there aren't many of them, but it's a start. It seems as though Mystery Writer used the book as a bit of a calendar because there are a few places scrawled in the margins next to times of day or addresses. I'm going to try and visit most of them, and put up a Wanted sign in each – with a photo of the scribbles, in the hopes that somebody who knows something might stumble across one and get in touch.

I've already popped some up in and around the little Brunswick Street Bookstore. Next, I'll hit Gelato Messina. Our Mystery Writer, like me, seems to think that dessert is the answer to all of life's problems.

PS I should tell you, the fake Mystery Writer is back. He's apologised profusely and claims he's still in love with me. Should I take him back, even though he's not our man behind the pen?

77 likes

Comments (112):

BookishBabe: You have to try the burnt caramel and condensed milk custard flavour! 🍦

Trollylolly: You suck.

NoOffenceBut: Do not take fake Mystery Writer back! I repeat, do not take fake Mystery Writer back! Once a liar, always a liar.

gensteiner: Hon, you can do so much better than him. Do not fall for his tricks!

StephenPrince: @NoOffenceBut, but you took me back last night 😉

NoOffenceBut: @StephenPrince, it was a one-time thing!

39

What a day, Bea thought as she climbed into bed. She plugged in her phone, curled onto her side and picked up *Meeting Oliver Bennett* from her bedside table. She flicked to a random page and began to soak up the cursive inscriptions, ignoring the neatly typed words. The scrawls engrossed her just like any good book, keeping her warm and safe. She inhaled the scent of the paperback, not wanting the feeling to dissipate.

She was about to turn to the next inscription when she spotted a faint pencil-sketch of a platypus sitting at the bottom right-hand corner of page 72. It was so faded that she had missed it every other time she had read the book. Underneath the sketch, written in pencil so light it looked like it had been erased, was written, *there's no one quite like you.*

Bea smiled at the duck-billed, semi-aquatic, egg-laying Australian mammal that was so totally and utterly unique. Taking her phone off charge, she snapped a photo of the drawing. She was about to open her Instagram app when an email notification popped up on her screen. It was from Mia Molesworthy.

Bea's heart skipped a beat. Mia worked at Thelma & Clarke as a marketing assistant. They had met last month after Bea had discovered Zach's indiscretion. She had called the Thelma & Clarke offices incessantly, refusing to believe that Zach did not, in fact, work there, and one afternoon the receptionist was so sick of her calls that she transferred her to Mia. Bea blurted out her whole life story and Mia, to Bea's great surprise, was completely entranced. The two had been emailing book banter, reviews and gossip to each other ever since. Bea swiped up to read the email.

To: beababbage@gmail.com
From: molesworthym@thelmaandclarke.com
Subject: You owe me

Bea!

Remember when you told me you were dreaming of converting your freelancing work into your own advertising agency? Well, I might have just scored you your first client. Thelma & Clarke is running a campaign in a few months for Cecilia Beechworth's next crime book and I pitched your new agency to work with us. My boss is keen to meet you. Are you free to come in the next couple of days? You better not let me down. 😉

M x

To: molesworthym@thelmaandclarke.com
From: beababbage@gmail.com
Subject: Re: You owe me

WHATTTTTTTT! I AM ACTUALLY HYPERVENTILATING!

You do realise this is my dream come true?! I ADORE Cecilia Beechworth! Trust me, I will NOT let you down. I'll work day and night on this. Tell me when you want me and I'll be there.

I THINK I MIGHT ACTUALLY LOVE YOU!

B x

PS I've thought of a name for my new agency which I have just decided to create, inspired by you. It's Platypus. There's no one quite like us.

To: beababbage@gmail.com
From: molesworthym@thelmaandclarke.com
Subject: Re: Re: You owe me

Platypus. Love it! Aussie, adorable, totally distinctive – just like you.

Come past the office on Thursday at 11am. Have some promotion ideas in mind and some info about a recent campaign you've worked on. Get ready to wow us!

xx

Bea locked her screen, sat up in bed and let out a squeal. 'We did it, Mystery Writer! We did it!' she whooped, picking up *Meeting Oliver Bennett* and kissing the faint sketch of the platypus smack-bang on the bill.

'Oh my God, Lizzie – it was so intense!' Bea shouted into her phone. She had just left the Thelma & Clarke office in South Yarra and was walking briskly down the street, the cold air whipping against her face. Pedestrians pushed past her brusquely, hypnotised by the tiny screens in their hands. 'I finally met Mia Molesworthy, the marketing assistant I told you about, she was lovely. But Janine, her boss, well, she's something else. Absolutely incredible. She's been responsible for almost every single ground-breaking marketing campaign in the publishing industry. She completely changed the landscape. Oh, and Liz, she is glamorous with a capital G. She was dressed in Versace!' Bea picked up her pace, overtaking a bunch of teenagers who were sipping slushies outside a 7-Eleven.

'Jesus, Bea. I can't imagine you coping well in that situation. From experience, you're not usually very confident around well-dressed people,' Lizzie laughed. Bea could hear the twins wailing in the background. Bea ignored her and powered on, too excited about the morning's turn of events.

'Well. I don't know how I did it, but apparently I won her over! I spurted out some facts, figures and campaign ideas and she ate it all up. She said she was happy to give me a go, and Mia and I are meeting soon to go over the brief!' Bea let out a little scream of happiness.

'Well what a lovely surprise, Bea! I'll have to pick out your new wardrobe of course. Now that you're a business woman you can't be wearing flannel,' Liz giggled. 'Speaking of which, did I tell you that I might be doing a modelling campaign for The Iconic? They're looking at using some of the ex-*Bachelor* contestants – and of course they don't have many options with a lot of them pregnant or notorious party girls nowadays. They of course want someone with a good image, wholesome, keeps herself in shape,' Liz rattled on. 'I'm thinking of doing it, but I'm not sure whether I should just be focusing all my attention on my online presence now that I've hit 200k followers.'

Bea 'mmed' and 'ahhed', thinking to herself that she finally felt good about something. After all the shit that had happened to her in the past few months, things were starting to fall into place.

'Anyway, I better run – I've got work to do! I'll speak to you soon, sis.'

Bea heard Lizzie smack her lips together in a kiss and hung up.

Bea was heading to Revolver Lane, a coworking space on bustling Chapel Street. She needed a change of scenery and to feel like she was out in the real world again, contributing to something purposeful. So she sold the Dyson vacuum she'd won last month on eBay and put the cash towards the small fee for a single desk. An easy walk from her apartment, the office instantly inspired innovation. Backing onto a notorious nightclub, the coworking area was an atrium filled with plants of all shapes and sizes. A coffee shop manned by a very hipster-looking vegan called Ricki, who wore his shoulder-length sandy curls in a half-ponytail and kept his moustache neatly trimmed, flanked the front entrance. (Dino would have a field day if he met him.)

Bea walked over to her allocated workstation, took out a cup-sized cactus from her bag placed it in the corner of her tiny standing desk, and clasped her hands together in satisfaction. She tried to smile at the burly man standing in front of her wearing Beats headphones and typing manically into his computer, but he averted his eyes immediately, and Bea did the same. She shrugged, not dispirited, and opened up the new email account she had created late last night.

Mia was due to arrive at any moment to iron out the contract details and talk strategy, having had to rush off immediately after their meeting. Bea was anxious and excited. Having lost all hope at rectifying things with Cassandra, Bea was somewhat desperate to fill her giant friendship void and hoped Mia might be a suitable candidate for the position.

A cold gust of air hit her face as the front door swung open. Bea looked up to see Mia, tall, brunette and dressed in an immaculate green trench coat and black boots, enter. Mia was unusually striking, with honey-brown hair and almost-black eyes accentuated by thick winged eyeliner. She pushed the aviator sunglasses she was wearing up onto her head and waved.

'Bea!' she exclaimed, air kissing Bea on both cheeks.

'I am completely indebted to you for setting up this opportunity for me.'

'Don't be silly. I'm so happy to help. I can already see how talented you are. And anyway, what are friends for?' She laughed as she grabbed Bea's hand.

Bea blushed. 'So, should we get cracking?' she asked, checking the time on her watch in an attempt to look professional. 'I'm sorry I only have this small desk, but if you want to gather round my laptop, I can run you through some initial questions I have.' Bea shuffled over to let Mia sit on her swivel chair.

'Oh, don't be silly. This was just an excuse for us to meet and gossip!' Mia squeezed Bea lightly on the arm. 'So, should we grab a coffee?'

'I can do you one better,' Bea said.

The women walked side by side down Chapel Street, past aromatic kebab shops and buskers playing on xylophones. They discussed how Sunni Overend's book *The Dangers of Truffle Hunting* made them want to move to the Yarra Valley, how Buttercup Bookstore was one of their favourite bookshops, and what it was like for Mia to work with authors all day. Bea was exhilarated by all the book talk. But Bea's breath truly caught when she saw the Messina sign in front of her. She braced herself, knowing that in just a moment she would be walking in the same footsteps as the Mystery Writer. Shifting the handbag strap on her shoulder, she eyed the entryway for a place to stick a Wanted sign.

'Gelato Messina,' she whispered under her breath, memories of the scribbled writing in *Meeting Oliver Bennett* flooding her.

'Oh my God, I love Messina! It's time to desert our inhibitions, am I right?' Mia winked at Bea.

Isn't that what Mystery Writer said?

Bea stared at beautiful Mia. Even though they had been emailing for the past month, Bea had skipped over talking about *Meeting Oliver Bennett* with her.

'You've been here before?' Bea asked, wrapping her arms around herself.

'To Messina? Yeah, me and every other Melburnian since it opened here. Come on, let's get ice-cream, baby!' She laughed, dragging Bea through the door.

Despite the cool weather, there was a line of people waiting to be served. The shop was moody and dark, almost as if they were inside a hip club rather than an ice-cream parlour. Flavours like pannacotta with fig jam and amaretti biscuit, salted caramel and white chocolate were scrawled on a chalkboard in front of them.

'I suggest the mint choc chip. It's absolutely dreamy,' Mia purred. Bea tried to think about what flavour to choose, but she couldn't stop thinking about the marginalia in her book. Her heart began to flutter.

'Ah, I think I'll just have the hazelnut,' Bea said, struggling to get the words out.

Mia smiled and ordered two ice-creams in waffle cones.

Bea watched her silently. Mia bit her lip after she spoke. Her eyes closed for a second too long when she described something she loved. *Could she be?*

While waiting, Mia started chatting casually about how the TV show *Younger* was, unfortunately, not at all reminiscent of what the publishing world was like in real life. She laughed after every few sentences. Now that Bea thought about it, there was a certain eloquence to the way she wrote those emails. *She couldn't be, could she?*

Then Mia looped her arm in Bea's, and Bea froze. The man behind the counter handed them each a cone, and Mia paid before quickly taking a generous lick of her ice-cream.

'Delicious, hey?' Mia beamed, guiding them to a seat at the window.

Bea sat down on the stool, frantically licking her dripping cone.

'Can I try some of yours?' Mia leaned over to Bea's cone, pursing her pink lips over her hazelnut ice cream. *Did Mystery Writer just take a lick of my ice cream?* 'So good,' Mia laughed, ice cream still on her lips.

'Mia?' Bea said.

'What is it?' Mia's eyes dazzled, they were almost dripping with secrets, scribbles and annotations.

'Have you …'

'Have I what, Bea?'

'Have you read *Meeting Oliver Bennett*?'

Mia looked at her quizzically, her brow furrowed. Bea's breath caught.

Mia inhaled deeply, eyes dilated, before saying 'Nope. Never heard of it!' The two finished their ice cream quickly, before Mia announced she had to get back to work.

Bea waved Mia goodbye as she walked out the front door. She shook her head, silently berating herself for being so deluded and hopeful. She then peered at the workers diligently scooping flavours, each one a different colour of the rainbow into cones and cups. Satisfied that they were sufficiently distracted, she quickly whipped out a Wanted sign, complete with photos of the scribbles and big bold letters which read 'IS THIS YOUR BOOK?', and stuck it to the window, facing the message to the street. Quick as lightning, she barrelled from the store, muttering a silent prayer as she went.

40

Morning Ramona!

I know what you're thinking, where the hell is all of Bea's stuff?! I'm now living a Marie Kondo-inspired minimalist lifestyle and gave all my worldly possessions to the Salvos.

You should be able to make quick work of the apartment. So shall we call it even on the last clean?

Joking, joking!

But seriously, I'm close to broke.

Chat soon,

Bea xxx

41

Bea,

 Cleaning still took same time, you still owe money. Sorry.
 Also, I can't come next week. I go away with new girl I am seeing, on romantic getaway.
 Ramona

42

💬 Zach: Have you had enough time yet?

Bea rolled her eyes and turned her phone over on her desk. She had just pressed send on emails regarding the couple of freelancing gigs she had managed to finalise and was ready to begin researching crime fiction-buying habits in preparation for the Cecilia Beechworth campaign. Zach's messages was distracting her from much-needed work time. She took a deep breath, tried to block everyone else out (including the heavy-breathing man standing two feet away from her) and typed. As she did, she could sense the roots of a sharp and cohesive strategy beginning to form.

💬 Zach: What about now?

Bea let out an exasperated grunt. The heavy-breathing man glared at her. *Like you can talk,* she thought as she glared back. She typed out a quick message before she could stop herself.

💬 Bea: What do you want, Zach?

💬 Zach: To take you out for a meal. For you to give me the chance to explain. Please.

Bea pulled at her hair, frustrated. She had been trying to bury her feelings for Zach, but they were seeping out of her skin like beads of sweat on a hot summer's day. So many thoughts crept into her mind, polluting her ability to think clearly. *Would hearing him out be so terrible? But what's the point? How could we ever move past what happened? Maybe agreeing to go will finally shut him up? And doesn't everyone (except for maybe Voldemort) deserve a second chance?*

Bea bit her lip, muttered, 'Fuck it,' under her breath and gave in.

> 🟤 Bea: Fine, Zach. You win. Meet me at Journeyman Cafe in twenty minutes. You get one chance to explain yourself.

> 🔴 Zach: Done! See you then. Thank you Bea.

Bea sat at a small wooden table, staring at the pastry display in front of her. A very significant part of her (mainly the feminist part which encouraged her to 'respect yourself' and remember that 'you don't need a man to complete you') hated herself for being here. But alas, here she was, sipping nervously on her second skinny latte for the day while she waited with looming dread for the man who had lied to her with soap-opera flair.

'Thanks so much for coming.'

Bea almost jumped out of her skin at the sound of Zach's voice. Straightening herself, she smiled coolly and gestured for him to take a seat opposite her. 'You know I'm only here so you'll finally stop bugging me, right?' she said, composure regained. She internally high fived herself for acting so composed. Zach was not going to rattle her today.

Zach smiled and put his hands up in submission. 'I'm just grateful you're here.'

Then silence. He stared at her for a moment too long, and she stared back. Up close she could see the faint creases around his mouth, the golden flecks in his eyes. Her whole body yearned to touch him, which in turn made her feel utterly pathetic.

She was the first to break eye contact. Taking another sip of her drink, she wondered how things could change so quickly. How intimacy could so rapidly shred away, leaving a chilly, disarming feeling in its wake.

'So, landed any more *jobs* recently?' *Shit, there goes my cool-girl demeanour.*

Zach winced. 'Bea, it doesn't have to be like this, you know?'

Ha! Easy for him to say. Bea could feel herself getting hot, that prickly feeling in her throat returning. She suddenly felt disoriented, ashamed.

And then his hand was on hers.

'Bea, I really want to make things better, to regain your trust. For us to go back to the way things were. Would I have really spent every waking minute trying to win you back if you were just some silly "job"?' Zach said with apparent sincerity.

Zach suddenly appeared gaunt, and she noticed that more stubble than usual framed his jaw. He looked like he hadn't slept in days. Something about the expression on his face made her relent.

'But where would we even start? How could I even begin to trust you again?'

Sighing, he said, 'I guess I just have to try everything in my power to prove to you that this is all real. That I love you and want you in my life.'

211

Bea shook her head. 'It's not as simple as that. You know that.'

A waiter approached their table and they each ordered a serve of smashed avocado with an extra piece of toast and halloumi on the side. The waiter diligently took down their order, smiling. Bea fiddled with the salt and pepper shakers, pushing them up and down the table until they were alone again.

'I just don't understand how you could do it,' Bea said softly.

Zach looked down, and at first Bea thought he wasn't going to reply. But then he coughed and said, just as softly, 'I'm so sorry, Bea.' He raised his head, his eyes anxious. 'I was stupid. And so naive. I was desperate for the extra cash, and I thought it would be an easy gig. I never thought I would meet someone, anyone, as amazing as you.'

'But that's just the thing, Zach,' Bea said, raising her voice a few octaves. 'It shouldn't have mattered who I was. It's not okay to act that way with *anyone*. To treat anyone like that is, well, it's evil.'

'I know, Bea. I know. But wasn't it Nicola Yoon who once wrote something about not being able to live if all you can do is regret?'

'You read *Everything, Everything*?' Bea asked, surprised.

'I read everything you recommended, Bea. I ate at every café you suggested too.' He shrugged. 'For an out-of-towner, you sure know your smashed avocado. And I guess I also hoped I might run into you.'

The waiter returned, placing a white serviette and cutlery next to each of them. Grateful for the intrusion,

Bea took a moment to gather her thoughts, to remember all the confrontations she had had with Zach in her head, which were so damn eloquent. Too quickly, the waiter left.

'I don't know if I can get past this, Zach. I'll never know what was real, and what could be real moving forward. I mean, was that story you told me about learning to read using Enid Blyton's book even true? Did you actually watch every season of *The Bachelor*? Are you even a Libra? Or was it all just part of the facade?' Since their inglorious break-up, Bea had run each little tidbit and story through her head a million times, searching for any clue that not everything was fabricated. He had seemed so genuine.

Zach's face fell – in fact – his entire body seemed to wilt like three-day-old tulips. No matter how much Bea had resolved not to feel pity for him, to not fall for any heartbroken act he threw at her, she couldn't help but melt a little at the sight of this new, deflated version of Zach.

'All the important things were true. Everything I showed you about who I am, the core of me.' Zach shrugged.

Bea nodded, though she remained unsure. 'Did you … did you really love—' she began, then took a long sip of her coffee. 'Did you really love *me*?' Bea was relieved to have finally been able to ask the question that had haunted her since she found out Zach was not who he had said he was.

'Bea,' he breathed, and her heart sank. 'Of course, I did. I loved you. I still do.' His voice quavered. 'I would never have slept with you if I didn't. That's why I waited so long.'

Bea searched Zach's face for any hint of deceit or insincerity, but all she found was heartbreak and remorse. *Snap out of it, Babbage, don't fall for this puppy-dog-eyes act!*

'Can't we try and start from scratch?' Zach said, extending his right hand.

Bea stared at it a moment, narrowing her eyes in confusion, then took his hand in her own. Zach, relieved, shook it vigorously and Bea couldn't help but remember when he had pulled the same move on their first date.

'Zach Harris, I enjoy Netflix binges, watching hot air balloons in the morning and moon gazing, and I hate eating orange food.'

Bea nodded absently. This was all too much.

After a moment, Zach raised his eyebrows in anticipation.

'Oh, right. My turn.' She paused, thinking that this all felt so unnatural, so forced. 'Uh, I'm Bea Babbage. I like toasting marshmallows on my gas stove in winter, reading anything mildly romantic, I've just started a one-woman marketing agency called Platypus, and incense gives me a thumping headache.'

'You've started an agency?' Zach beamed, pleased for her, and Bea's heart ached for only the hundredth time that day.

'Yeah, and I've just landed my first client. You may be familiar with them – I thought you worked there for the first month we dated. Thelma & Clarke,' Bea replied, a little too venomously. *Who was I kidding when I said I was over this?*

'Wow, that's huge. I'd love to hear more, when you're ready,' Zach said without an ounce of bitterness. 'What else do you want to know?'

Taking a sip of water, Bea mentally arranged everything she wanted to – no, needed to know about Zach, in order of priority. 'So you're a personal trainer?' Bea asked. 'You even had to lie about your job?'

Zach shook his head. 'I'm sorry, I needed you to fall for me and Cassandra told me you were a die-hard bookworm. When we first got to talking, the lie just tumbled out. You have no idea how stressful it was pretending I was an editor. Why do you think I went to the toilet so regularly? I was always googling books!'

'That must have been *so* difficult for you.'

'Bea, all that stuff is inconsequential. It's just a job. I'm still me. Give me a chance to show you that.'

Bea let out a long breath and gestured for him to go on.

'I'm trying to open up my own gym. That's why I've been picking up the extra odd job here and there—' Zach stopped suddenly, an embarrassed look appearing on his face.

Bea raised her eyebrows. *Was that all I was to you? An odd job?*

Zach powered on, trying to brush past the slip-up. 'It's going to be called Zed-Fit. My gym. I want it to be all about teaching people how to look after themselves in all aspects of their life – physically, nutritionally and, most importantly, mentally, which is something that's really important to me.'

'That's great, Zach. Dream big,' Bea said only slightly derisively as she tried her best to acclimatise to this whole new brand of Zach. She wondered if they still had anything in common.

'This feels weird, Zach,' she said, rearranging her cutlery again. 'Starting from scratch, I mean.' She couldn't stop thinking about what to do about the complicated, flawed, but supposedly sensitive man sitting in front of her. Was Dumbledore right when he said something along the lines of it being easier forgiving those who are wrong than right? Or was Jane Austen correct when she wrote, 'I could easily forgive his pride, if he had not mortified mine.'

Zach sighed and flicked some imaginary crumbs off the table. He opened and closed his mouth, appearing to be searching for the right thing to say. 'I know,' he eventually admitted.

They whiled away the next fifteen minutes trying to pretend everything was normal and that Zach had never been paid to date Bea in an act of brutal revenge by her ex-best friend. *From the outside, you might have even been fooled into thinking that they were no more than just your regular brand of complicated exes*, Bea supposed. Zach laughed when she told him about how she had thrown out almost every piece of clothing and trinket she owned, which made her slightly furious, even as she found his soft chuckle endearing. Then their food arrived and Bea breathed a sigh of relief. They tucked into the overflowing avocado goodness sitting before them.

'Holy guacamole, this is good!' Bea exclaimed, a tiny speck of avocado landing on her chin.

Zach leaned forward and scooped it up with his thumb, then put it in his mouth with a cheeky grin still plastered to his face. Bea flinched ever so slightly, but hoped she could pass it off as caffeine jitters. There was something electric about his touch, but as much as her heart still longed for Zach, her mind – and gut – told her that pursuing this any further would be a terrible idea. But, for the sake of civility, and to avoid having to see Zach's forlorn expression, she let Zach drive discussion towards neutral topics and enjoyed her lunch.

43

Bea left the café full and physically content. She would even go as far as to say that she was relieved she had seen Zach. Relieved that she hadn't burst into tears, thrown plates against walls in a fit of rage or screamed hysterically. There was still so much that needed to be said, but she was happy to bury the hatchet for now.

With her head practically jammed in her shoulder bag, Bea fumbled for her keys as she moved along the corridor to her apartment door. She hadn't been home since before the sun had risen, and now, one long day of work and a date with Zach later, it had finally set.

'Babbage!' a voice yelled, prompting Bea to let out a loud shriek.

Before she had the sense to grab the portable panic alarm her mum had mailed her, she looked up to find Dino slumped up against her apartment door, wearing a worn flannel shirt two sizes too big.

She fell back against the wall, clutching her chest. 'Jesus, Dino, you startled me half to death!' She was panting, adrenaline coursing through her body. 'What are you doing here?'

Dino bounced off the floor and stumbled towards her, smelling distinctly of bourbon. She pushed him away, and he staggered backwards, catching himself on the opposite wall.

'Dino! Jesus, you absolutely reek! Where have you been?'

'I was at the pub. With a mate.'

'It's—' Bea checked her watch, 'only seven thirty. How did you manage to get so drunk in the three hours since you shut up shop?'

Dino gave a hearty chuckle, which quickly turned into a coughing fit. As Bea looked on curiously, he pounded his chest and winked at her. *Dammit, winking is your weakness. Look away, Bea! Look away!*

Bea dropped her eyes and resumed fishing for her keys. Finally locating them between the pages of *Meeting Oliver Bennett*, Bea approached her front door, jammed the keys in the lock and jiggled them until her door opened. Dino followed her into the apartment.

'Shit, Babbage. Where's all your stuff?' Dino asked, looking around Bea's sparsely furnished living room. 'Oh my God, did you get robbed?'

Bea swatted Dino away, explaining her Marie Kondo episode, and manoeuvred him to her decorative cushion-free couch. 'Now, I need to go to the bathroom. Can you sit here for two minutes?'

Dino nodded bashfully.

Bea scooted to her bathroom and locked the door behind her. Closing the seat on the toilet, she sat down, leaned her head against the cool, tiled wall, and closed her eyes. *What the hell was Dino doing here?* The last time they were in a room together alone, they had kissed. Which had been a mistake. Obviously. He was with Sunday and

Bea loved Sunday. And what about Zach now? The waters around her were all kinds of muddy.

All of a sudden, she felt completely drained and very much not in the mood for this. She wanted nothing more than to be in her fleece pyjamas, curled up on the couch with a tea and the movie adaptation of *To All The Boys I've Loved Before*. She would ask Dino to leave. It would all be fine. She flushed the toilet for authenticity, washed her hands, splashed perfume on her wrists just because, and took three deep breaths before opening the bathroom door.

Bea returned to the living room to find it empty. She looked over her shoulder, checking that the front door was still closed. 'Dino?'

'In here!'

Bea followed the sound of his voice and the opening and closing of cupboard doors into the kitchen, where she found Dino standing on the kitchen bench, the top part of his body almost completely submerged in one of the cupboards.

'I see you've taken the minimalist thing to your pantry too. Entertain much?' he slurred, and then hopped back to the ground, landing effortlessly. 'I'm starved. Want to order some pizza?'

At the mention of pizza, Bea's stomach gave a loud grumble of consent. *And it's not like I have anything better to do.* 'Okay, Dino. You're on.' But as soon as she said it, she had a feeling she would regret it.

After Bea won the argument over whether pineapple on pizza was a sin or a virtue, Bea and Dino found themselves slumped on her couch, generous slices of Hawaiian pizza in their hands.

Dino swallowed his last bite and began absentmindedly tracing his *Delilah* tattoo with his thumb. Bea watched him.

'Want to know about her?' he asked, his mouth full of cheese and pizza dough.

Bea nodded, surprised by his sudden candour. *Dino must be very drunk.* She'd never seen him so eager to share.

'There is nothing more tantalising than a thing like this which lingers just outside the borders of one's memory,' Dino quoted. 'That's from a story in my favourite Roald Dahl. *Kiss Kiss.* Remember?' Dino slurred.

'But about Delilah?' Bea prodded him, not wanting him to avoid the topic.

'She was only the love of my life.' He gave a cold laugh. Bea swallowed. 'But unfortunately, I was not hers.' He looked down at his tattoo pensively, still touching it. Bea put her hand awkwardly on his arm.

'At first I didn't want to fall in love, you know? Love seems to get people into trouble. And I didn't want any part in something that could risk turning my life upside down.'

Bea nodded, knowing that feeling all too well.

'But then I realised that the fear of falling in love, well, that's already love. Just not spoken out loud.'

Who is this talkative, emotional guy and what has he done with my introverted barista?

'Oh, how I fell, Bea. Not just for her face. She was beautiful. *Is beautiful.* But it was so much more than that.'

Bea shifted next to him. He wasn't hers, so why did it hurt to hear him talking like this about someone else?

'She was such a great storyteller. And she was nice to everyone. Literally, everyone! She even felt empathy for bruised fruit. But God she was a mess. Yet somehow, even that I loved.'

Bea caught her breath. She was falling for his falling. And she wanted it to stop. But she also needed to know how it ended. 'So, what happened?'

'She broke my heart.' Dino didn't break eye contact.

'How?'

'Ah, it's all ancient history now, isn't it?' Dino said, snapping back to his usual self all too quickly. They sat in silence for a minute. 'I wrote you a poem, you know?' Dino said, in a lighter tone.

'You did? Really?'

'Yup, I wrote it a couple of weeks ago. It mightn't be as poetic as those 'Mystery Writer' scribbles you're always going on about. But, wanna hear it?'

Bea nodded and licked her lips happily, washing away traces of tomato sauce. She sat up a little straighter, ready to listen.

'A freckle tells a story,' Dino began.

On your life it traces your inventory.

The beaches at which you've soaked,

The friends with whom you've joked.

But that freckle, that one that sits by your bottom lip, is

The one that shadows your courtship.

The one that demands your wishes be heard,

The one that keeps dreams stirred.

'Wow, Dino.' Bea was at a loss for what to say.

'It's nothing really, Babbage,' he replied, picking up another slice of pizza and shoving three-quarters of it into his mouth in one go. 'I just like you, I guess,' he said between chews. 'And I know that you're going to be okay.'

'You like me? I thought you just tolerated me?'

'Nah, girl. I like you.'

Bea frowned. 'But what about Sunday?'

'What about Sunday?'

'Wouldn't she be uncomfortable if she knew you were writing poems about other women?'

'Why would she be uncomfortable? Sunday doesn't even like poetry,' Dino said matter of factly.

'Oh,' Bea said, picking at a piece of discarded pineapple. 'I don't know, Dino.'

'What don't you know? That you have a dollop of sauce on your nose?' He chuckled.

Bea swiped at her nose with the back of her hand, blushing. 'What about Zach, then?'

'Zach? What's there to think about? He's a tool. End of story,' Dino said. He seemed to be sobering up, the carbohydrates soaking up the bourbon.

'I saw him today,' Bea muttered, averting her eyes.

'You what?' Dino dropped his pizza crust on the plate in his lap. 'Please don't tell me you said what I think you just said.'

'It was just lunch.'

'Just lunch? You're not thinking about getting back with him, are you? He's bad news, Bea.'

Bea pushed herself off the couch, suddenly frustrated. Who was Dino to gatecrash her home and give her advice?

The same Dino who'd just recited a poem about one of her freckles when he had a girlfriend. 'It's really none of your business, Dino.'

'None of my business? Was it none of my business when you spent two weeks sobbing into every one of my lattes, yelling that everything reminded you of him?'

Bea sighed. She knew Dino was right. But she wasn't in the mood to be lectured. It had been a bloody long day and she was beyond exhausted. Her bones ached and her heart felt twisted. 'I don't want to do this with you, Dino. I'm sorry, but I have to work this out on my own.'

'Fine. I'm just warning you to be really sure you want to go there again. I wouldn't trust him as far as I could throw him.'

'Mmm hmm.' Bea folded her arms firmly across her chest. 'I'm a big girl, Dino. I can look after myself.'

'Just be careful, is all I'm saying.'

They held each other's gaze and something passed between them that Bea couldn't quite name.

'I should go,' Dino finally said.

Bea nodded. 'Thanks for the pizza. I hope the hangover isn't too rough tomorrow.'

Dino went to the door with Bea following him. He pulled the door open, then turned around abruptly. He took Bea's hands in his, squeezing them tight. Bea inhaled sharply.

'You know what?' Dino said and Bea inclined towards him just the slightest bit. 'I'm taking the pizza with me.'

44

In 25 words or less, why do you want to win 6 months of unlimited visits to the zoo?

My BFF hates me. I imagine if I visited the zoo regularly, I could befriend a smart and friendly giraffe who could fill her place.

45

It was a Wednesday afternoon and Bea was procrastinating. Avoiding work, avoiding assessing her thoughts about how she left things with Dino, avoiding whether she should reply to Zach's last message asking how she was feeling. She was procrastinating so much that she had dragged herself across town to a café that she wasn't nearly cool enough to be frequenting.

The café in question was ARK. And the visit was part of her hunt to find the Mystery Writer. Earlier that day she had highlighted and then googled an address that turned out to belong to this very café. The address was scrawled next to a simple sketch of what looked like a croissant. She had her Wanted posters curled up in her handbag, and was ready to place them in the window of this uber trendy café, as soon as she'd had her caffeine fix. She had heard that the coffee was better north of the river, and, while sceptical, she was about to put it to the test.

Hidden behind her menu, Bea peered around the café, taking everything in. It was relatively packed for a mid-week afternoon: small pockets of friends and families with young children, chatted conspiratorially, catching up over lattes and slabs of sourdough toast. She jotted down a few things on the notebook she had left open next to her, deciding on the best place to stick the poster.

'Ready to order?'

Bea looked up, knocking her menu to the floor. The waiter bent down to retrieve it.

'Sorry, you caught me unawares!' Bea said apologetically, to which the waiter, sporting an impatient smile and ripped jeans, simply raised his eyebrows. 'Um, one skinny latte, please.'

When the waiter returned with her drink, Bea decided to pounce, hoping to get some information from him. 'Busy day for you guys, isn't it?' Bea asked coyly, taking a gulp of her drink. 'Ugh, too hot!' she yelped.

The waiter looked on, unperturbed. 'Will that be all for now?'

'Mmm, just one more thing,' Bea said, gulping down some cold water. 'Get many broody writers in here? I'm such a book nut! Last year I took myself on a road trip based on one of my favourite books: *Lost & Found*. Have you heard of it? I pretty much just visited bus stops all over Western Australia, but still. Book nut!' She practically yelled and took another tentative mouthful of her coffee.

'How fun for you.' The waiter was clearly not having a bar of Bea today.

'So, a lot of writers come in tap, tap, tapping away at their laptops? Scribbling notes in journals? Annotating books, by chance?'

'I don't know. I guess so. We're in Northcote, after all.'

Propping her elbows on the table and leaning in, Bea said, 'Could you be more specific?'

'We get a couple of book clubs in, every now and then. Lots of post-it notes get left behind. I don't know, maybe you could join one?' The waiter had taken two steps back.

'Oh, that's great. Great! Do you have any contact details for them?' Bea asked, pen poised.

The waiter frowned. 'I doubt it, but I'll check with my manager.' And, with a sigh of relief, he left.

Bea felt frustrated. She hadn't gotten any intel at all. She polished off her coffee, including licking the cup's rim while nobody was watching, downed two glasses of water and trotted off to find the bathroom in the rear courtyard-hoping to find a place to put her Wanted signs. Thankfully, the toilet was unoccupied, so Bea slid straight in. She stuck a poster to the back of the stall door and one to the right of the mirror. Then, sitting down, she relaxed, and began swiping away on Instagram.

A shake of the door brought her back to reality.

'Sorry! Ocupado!' Bea yelled out.

'My apologies,' a feathery voice called back.

I know that voice! Bea bent forward until she was almost folded in half, craning to look under the slit at the bottom of the door. Two cobalt blue suede skyscraper heels. *I know those shoes!* Bea frantically balled up some toilet paper, wiped, flushed and washed her hands. *I can't believe this!* Her heart was racing. She quickly dried her hands, stuck another poster above the paper towel dispenser and swung open the stall door.

'Martha!'

A short, petite woman with dark skin, shoulder-length blonde hair with a textured fringe and fabulously large resin earrings turned towards Bea.

'I'm sorry, do I know you?' the woman asked, clearly embarrassed by the fuss.

'Martha, it's me! Bea! From AKDB Agency,' Bea said, already pulling the unsuspecting woman into a hug.

'Cubicle Bea?' Martha pulled away, holding Bea by the shoulders. 'What are you doing here? I can't believe it's you!'

'I know! I've missed our toilet chats so much.'

They stepped to the side as a young girl eased her way into the toilet, throwing curious looks back at them.

'How's work going?'

'Terrible!'

Bea raised her eyebrows in concern.

'Oh, you know, just the usual staffroom politics. In fact, I'm playing hooky today. If anybody asks, I've got conjunctivitis,' Martha said, surprising Bea. She had always thought Martha would be a stickler for the rules on account of appearing so posh. 'And since you've been gone, I don't have the same Jane Austen escapism to look forward to each day! I miss the familiar sound of pages turning whenever I go to the bathroom. Although, I must say, I've been far more productive of late.'

They laughed. It was a little strange to be talking face-to-face.

'Now tell me.' Martha leaned in, the smell of her expensive perfume wafting over Bea. 'When's the next book speed dating night? I hope you're still running them. I've just finished the most extraordinary book – *The Girl with Seven Names*. It's about a woman who escapes from North Korea. True story! I'm just dying to talk about it. And my husband is sick to death of hearing about it!'

Bea was heartened by Martha's interest. 'I have one pencilled in for a few weeks' time. It's all been a bit of a juggle, there's been a lot happening with work.' Bea brought her ex-colleague up to speed about Platypus Agency.

'That sounds just fabulous, darling! Fabulous! Any way I can help?' Martha inquired, side-stepping out of the way of the waiter, who was delivering coffees to a pair gossiping in the corner of the courtyard.

'Oh! Help from you? I would love that! Accounts are absolutely not my thing!' Bea said.

'You know what, give me a call. I'll see what I can do.' Martha slipped her hand into her purse, pulling out a card on which she hastily scrawled her mobile number. 'Just don't email me at work. I can't be seen consorting with the enemy.' She winked and handed over her details before pulling Bea into a warm embrace.

'It was so good running into you,' Bea gushed.

Martha blew a kiss to Bea and strolled out of the café. Bea collected her jacket from the back of her chair and went to pay, when she glanced at the waiter one last time. He was standing behind the register. She decided that she needed to up the ante, and do more than just stick pieces of paper to random toilets.

'Hey,' she said, walking up to him. The waiter nodded apathetically, without a doubt sick to death of her by now. 'Just one last thing, I promise! Have you ever spotted this book?' She took out her copy of *Meeting Oliver Bennett* and held it in front of him, flicking through the pages, practically shoving her secret scribbles in his face.

The waiter faked interest, momentarily squinting at the page before shaking his head. 'That'll be three fifty today.'

Bea wasn't ready to back down. 'Are you sure nothing's ringing a bell?' She waved the open book even closer to the waiter.

'I see a lot of signatures and notes every day, and if I were to remember every single scribble that came through these doors,' he nodded to the entrance, 'there'd be no more room left up here for the important stuff.' He tapped his temple.

Bea conceded, and finally dropped the subject. She dug around for loose change in the bottom of her bag then handed over a hodgepodge of gold and silver coins. The waiter cupped them in his hands with a grimace.

Noting her disappointment, he said, 'You could try the fishbowl.' He gestured to a large glass bowl filled with business cards that sat on the counter. 'We used to run a competition once a month – the name we pulled out would win a week's worth of coffee, but between you and me,' he leaned in, 'we haven't done it for a couple of years now. The bowl keeps getting filled anyway. People usually write their names on the cards, so you could try your luck to see if there are any matches.'

Bea smiled gratefully at the waiter and picked up the bowl, taking it over to an empty table near the back. Humming a quick prayer, she stuck her hand in, pushing it all the way to the bottom. Flipping through each card, she took in the variety of names and numbers left behind. Large, thick handwriting, loopy handwriting, handwriting that was so messy it was impossible to decipher, but not a single word that belonged to her Mystery Writer. Repeating the process, she plunged her hand into the bowl, extracted a pile and sifted through them, meticulously checking each one. Again and again, she performed the same ritual, until more business cards and discarded receipts sat outside the bowl than in. On two occasions the waiter sashayed past her, simultaneously tutting and peering over his shoulder with curiosity.

'One more pile, and then you're taking your sorry arse back to work,' she whispered. She closed her eyes and grabbed another bundle.

No, no, definitely not, no – wait a second.

Bea paused, her hand suspended in the air almost in front of her nose. Curled between her thumb and forefinger was a movie ticket stub. Bea examined it closely. It was so faded that she could only just make out the film, but above the cinema's name, in the scribble she had come to know so well, it read: *kindness. pass it on.*

'It couldn't be.' Bea quivered. Her hands shaking.

She quickly grabbed *Meeting Oliver Bennett* from her bag and compared the handwriting, even though she knew she couldn't be mistaken. She knew the writing too well.

'Found something?' the waiter said, appearing by her side.

'You have no idea!' Bea jumped up, the force of the movement sending a small handful of business cards fluttering to the floor. 'Can I take this?' She waved the ticket stub in the waiter's face.

'Sure, go for it. It's just an old ticket stub.'

Just an old ticket stub that might help me get to the bottom of this mystery.

46

Helloisthisyourbook

📍 Finding my inner film buff

Scribble of the day: *Kindness. Pass it on.*

Guys, I just discovered an old movie ticket stub with OUR EXACT SCRIBBLES on it! I finally feel like I'm onto something. In the meantime, I'm off to @astortheatremelb to put up more posters. We're getting closer! I can feel it!

---

88 likes

Comments (32):

NoOffenceBut: I love the Astor!! One of the only sensible things you've said so far.

BookClubbing: Ohhhhhh I can't handle the suspense! I hope you find Mystery Writer! I'll keep my eyes peeled. 👀

MinkyPinky: @TheWayWeWere, have you read *Meeting Oliver Bennett*?

TheWayWeWere: @MinkyPinky Nope, sorry! But sounds interesting. 🖤

StephenPrince: @NoOffenceBut, can I take you there this weekend? (and maybe also move back in?)

NoOffenceBut: @StephenPrince Okay, fine. (And I'll think about it)

47

Bea sat at her desk in her leafy coworking space and played with the ticket stub, which she had tucked in the pocket of her jeans. She typed 'Astor Theatre' into Google and scrolled through the movies on offer. Deciding on one that sounded like the perfect combination of quirky, romantic and entertaining, she was about to take out her credit card to purchase a ticket when she stopped herself. *Invite someone to join you.* Bea had always relied on others to invite her places, but since coming to Melbourne she realised that she needed to be more proactive. She picked up her phone and clicked Zach's name. He had been texting her incessantly since their lunch date, but she had been cold and casual in her replies. Absolutely no x's at the end of her messages. She took a deep breath. She couldn't leave him hanging forever.

Bea: Hey

Zach: Hey! How are you? X

Bea: Good. You?

Zach: I'm good thanks. How's your day going?

Bea: Great.

Zach: That's good, Bea. I'm glad you messaged 😊

Bea groaned and clicked out of the messages. *Chicken!*
She opened a new text message to the other man on her
mind, Dino. She hadn't spoken to him properly since he
had recited that freckle poem to her. She didn't want to get
too close – she was afraid of what she might do. *Remember
Sunday,* she thought, and then drafted a quick message – as
a friend.

> 💬 Bea: Hey!

> 💬 Dino: Hey.

> 💬 Bea: Wanna catch a movie with me tonight at the
> Astor?

> 💬 Dino: Sorry, can't. I'm going to some gig with
> Sunday. Raincheck?

> 💬 Bea: Yep, sure. Have fun!

Just friends. Just friends.

Bea wondered who else she could invite to the movies
tonight. *Lizzie?* No, she didn't leave Mount Eliza on school
nights unless it was to get her name in the *Daily Mail.*
Martha? Mia? But she had just seen them both. *Ruth?* Bea
smiled at the idea. Ruth, although a little kooky, was lots
of fun to be around. She laughed at the thought of Philip,
Ruth's ferret, biting Zach's hand. She sent her a quick
Facebook message.

> 🔘 Bea: Hey Ruth. Fancy seeing a movie with me
> tonight at the Astor? x

Ruth: Hello Beatrix. I love the Astor. But which movie? I don't like thrillers, action or anything with Adam Sandler.

Bea: Perfect – it's a rom-com. It's called *The Book Ninja*.

Ruth: Without Adam Sandler?

Bea: Yes, no Adam Sandler.

Ruth: Great. What time?

Bea: Meet me out the front at 8pm 😊

Ruth: See you then.

'Ruth!' Bea exclaimed as soon as she spotted her outside the cinema. Ruth was wearing a heavy plaid coat paired with blue jeans and a jumper with Queen Elizabeth's unsmiling face printed on the front. She carried a large tote bag over her shoulder. Bea gave her a (seemingly unwelcome) hug, and then ushered her into the warmth of the cinema. The Astor Theatre was otherworldly. An institution, it boasted old-fashioned terrazzo floors and sweeping, decorative-plaster ceilings that made Bea feel as if she had stepped into another decade. She could almost feel the history of music, art, dance and decadence with every step she took.

'Thank you for inviting me on this impromptu outing,' Ruth said.

'Of course! I thought it would be nice to catch up.' Bea smiled, and then felt slightly guilty about her ulterior motive – the ticket stub sitting in her coat pocket.

'How much do I owe you?' Ruth asked.

'For what?'

'For the ticket of course.' Ruth took out her wallet and began to remove some notes.

Bea waved her away. 'Don't be silly. It's on me,' she said.

'No, no. I insist. I detest owing people money.'

'Well, how about you get us popcorn and I'll go pick up the tickets. It'll work out roughly the same,' Bea suggested.

Ruth nodded and waltzed over to the candy bar. Bea felt for the ticket stub in her pocket and took a deep breath. *This is it, Bea.* She waited in line behind a grey-haired man, before cheerily approaching the pimply teenage boy sitting behind the counter.

'Yes?' he asked.

'I'm just picking up two tickets to *The Book Ninja*. Under Beatrix Babbage.' She flashed her ID. He nodded and handed over the tickets – the same kind as she had in her pocket. Before he could say, 'Next,' Bea pulled out one of her Wanted posters and put it down on the counter in front of him.

'One more thing,' she said urgently.

'Yes?' the boy asked again, annoyed this time. There was a line of people behind her.

'Would you mind if I pinned a couple of these up?' She pushed the Wanted poster forward, a little embarrassed. She knew how unlikely, how utterly preposterous it was that the owner of the book would ever see it, but she had to try.

The boy picked it up, examined it. 'I'd have to check with management.'

'Now? Can you check now?' Bea insisted. She felt a bead of nervous sweat pool on her top lip.

'Why don't you leave this with me and I'll speak with management as soon as I'm on break.'

Bea thanked the boy, took her tickets and went to join Ruth. On her way, she ducked into the Ladies and slapped a sign to the back of each of the stall doors. She wasn't going to take any chances.

Bea sat next to Ruth in the small cinema, each shovelling popcorn into their mouths silently. Bea hummed quietly along to the adverts, imagining the Mystery Writer here, in this very cinema, performing the same ritual. She willed the Mystery Writer to return in time to see the posters before 'management' undoubtedly tossed them out.

'Thanks again for getting the popcorn. I'm not sure I can finish this family size all on my own though!' Bea said, popping another handful of the salty morsels into her mouth.

'Nonsense. Every time I go to the movies I finish a family size.'

The cinema was almost full with young couples or groups of girlfriends. There was a gentle hum of whispers as the adverts ran on the big screen.

'So, how's your work going?' Ruth asked.

'Good,' Bea replied. 'I've actually just gone out on my own and started a little marketing agency. It's difficult, but I'm enjoying work a lot more.'

'Remember to breathe,' Ruth said.

'What?'

'Breathe. You can get swept away when you're starting a new business. Remember to take time to step back, analyse and slow down,' Ruth said, surprising Bea with this motivational tidbit.

The lights began to dim, the chatter hushed, and Bea cooed, 'It's starting!'

'I know,' Ruth replied. She then opened her giant tote bag, which was sitting beside her, and rummaged through it noisily. The racket made Bea uncomfortable as the title of the movie appeared on the screen.

'Oh no,' Ruth gasped.

'What?' Bea whispered.

'Philip. He's gone.'

'What? Philip the ferret? Gone where?'

'He was in my bag. He must've escaped somehow.'

'He was in your bag?' Bea hissed, a little too loudly. A couple sitting in front of them turned around, to shush them.

'He was exhibiting signs of separation anxiety and I could hardly leave him home alone, now could I?'

They looked at each other in a state of panic, realising there was a ferret on the loose. Bea checked under her seat, while Ruth looked on the seat next to the one her bag was sitting on.

Then a woman squealed from the front of the cinema.

Bea and Ruth turned to each other before jumping from their seats and sprinting towards the screaming woman. She was shaking her wide-legged pants aggressively. While her friend patted her soothingly on the back. Ruth and Bea stood in front of her.

'What happened?' Bea asked.

'A giant rat ran up my leg! It was disgusting! It ran out but I feel like it's still there!' the woman shrieked, still flapping her pants and stomping her feet.

'That wasn't a rat, you rude girl. That was a ferret. *My* ferret!' Ruth snapped. Even in the darkness of the cinema, Bea could tell that her face was red.

'I'm so sorry,' Bea whispered to the distressed woman who had just had a ferret up her leg.

From the back of the cinema, a man shouted, 'Rat!' and Ruth and Bea looked over in time to see him put his legs in the air. The woman next to him screeched a second later, and followed suit. The couple beside them did the same thing, creating a 'dodge the ferret' Mexican wave.

'He's running along the rows,' hissed Bea to Ruth.

Ruth was exasperated. 'Poor Philip. He must be so terrified,' she said. Bea felt sorry for Ruth despite the fact that she had ill-advisedly brought a ferret into a crowded cinema.

'It'll be okay, Ruth. We'll catch him.'

'No, it won't be, Beatrix. Once he gets loose, he's so hard to catch. I'm afraid I'll never get him back,' Ruth whimpered.

Bea closed her eyes. She cleared her throat. 'Attention, everyone!' she shouted from the front of the cinema. People groaned and told her to sit down, but she continued. 'I'm sorry to interrupt the movie, but as you may know, there is a creature loose in the cinema. Most of you think it's a rat, but it's a ferret. My dear friend Ruth's ferret.' She touched Ruth's arm gently. Ruth nodded, holding back tears. 'His name is Philip and he is very fast. If you see him running past your feet, can you please try to pick him up? Carefully. The sooner we collect him, the sooner we can go back to watching the movie.' Bea was proud of her announcement, of swallowing her embarrassment and trying to help a friend. What she wasn't proud of was the chaos that followed.

People shrieked, jumping up from their chairs and lifting their seat cushions. Some lay on the ground, looking for Philip, while others grabbed at him, unsuccessfully, as he swished speedily past them all.

'Philip! Philip!' Ruth called, tears now streaming down her face.

Suddenly, Philip whooshed down the aisle, ignoring his owner and the people who were trying to capture him. The film played in the background, the sound blaring. Two ushers had entered the cinema and were trying to calm everyone down, but to no avail. One of them had even tried to snatch Philip as he sped past him, toppling backwards in his attempt. It was a disaster.

Then Bea remembered her dog Lulu. She was a crazy border collie with more energy than one dog should ever have. The only way she could calm her down was by being incredibly placid and still herself. Bea would sit peacefully to entice Lulu into jumping onto her lap. So, among all the pandemonium, Bea sat down at the front of the cinema, legs crossed. She took a deep breath, trying to zen out, and whispered Philip's name.

'Philip … Philip … Philip.'

But the ferret continued to speed around the cinema.

Bea persevered. She closed her eyes, exhaled deeply, and continued to gently call the ferret's name.

When she opened her eyes, she saw Philip pause for a moment just to the left of her. His ears were up, his paws clenched. Then, with everyone watching, he ran towards Bea. The crowd gasped as he sped by. Philip stopped in front of Bea and she steadied her breath. *In and out. In and out.*

In one swift move, Philip jumped into her lap and curled into a tight ball. Bea let out a giant breath, and held on to Philip the ferret with everything she had. He purred like a cat as his panting settled. The cinema erupted in applause, to which Bea responded with a bow of her head.

'Now can we please watch the bloody movie?' a gruff voice called from the back row.

48

Helloisthisyourbook

Scribble of the day: *Fawkner Park, 12.30pm (by the big tree, corner Toorak/Punt Rd).*

Perhaps this is Mystery Writer's thinking spot? I'm going to head to Fawkner Park on my lunch break to put up more Wanted posters. Is it fate that it's right around the corner from my office?

---

92 likes

Comments (44):

NoOffenceBut: Really grasping at straws here …

Kettlechipbabe72: Don't give up, hon! You'll find your man.

VictoriaParks: Thank you for enjoying Victoria's wildlife.

Sexydiva112: Love your style. Follow my page and I'll follow yours back. 🙈

StephenPrince: @NoOffenceBut Always the buzzkill.

StephenPrince: @NoOffenceBut Sorry I didn't mean that.

StephenPrince: @NoOffenceBut I love you.

49

Bea zipped her black Kathmandu puffer jacket all the way up to her neck. Having had a breakthrough on the Thelma & Clarke campaign (murder mystery launch party – could it get any better than that?), she'd decided to reward herself with a casual lunch in the park. Fawkner Park.

Armed with *Meeting Oliver Bennett,* her mobile and a handful of Wanted posters, Bea was ready to put herself in Mystery Writer's shoes and take a walk down memory lane. After her somewhat disastrous evening with Ruth (the silver lining being that the movie was laugh-out-loud-until-you-peed-your-pants-a-little-bit funny), she was well and truly ready to keep up the momentum of her hunt. Bea had to be optimistic and strong-willed. It was the only way to find the Mystery Writer.

With a little extra time to kill, Bea decided to walk the seventeen minutes to the park. Winding down the narrow back streets that snaked behind Chapel Street, she passed boutique shops sporting everything from eyewear to high-end lingerie, through bustling and aromatic Prahran Market, and past The Nook (she decided not to pop in and say hi), all the while mentally planning her tactic. It would be simple enough: she would pin her signs to as many trees and benches as time would allow. And, worst-case scenario if nothing came of this venture, at least she'd had a nice view for her lunch.

Eventually Bea found herself standing at one of the entrances to Fawkner Park, the pathway led to a large, central oval and was flanked by rows of towering oak trees. *Shit, this place is huge!* Bea thought, at a loss as to where to begin. But, not allowing herself to be overwhelmed, she took a hesitant step forward and then another and then another, until she was striding with a new vigour through the canopy of trees. On high alert, she scoured her surroundings for anything that might trigger some revelation or, at the very least, recognition. Every so often, she paused to tape a sign to a tree or the seat of a bench, ignoring the curious looks of the other park goers.

Hungry and feeling just a touch ridiculous, she pulled out one of the sushi rolls she'd purchased at the market, doused it in soy sauce and took a large bite. And then she spotted it, looking like an overgrown head of broccoli: an enormous Moreton Bay fig tree at the far edge of the park, its branches spilling out to every side. Quickly scoffing down what remained of her sushi, Bea began jogging towards it, as if some cosmic force had taken over her body.

Halting at the base of the tree, Bea peered up between its leafy arms. She walked around the circumference of its trunk, searching for the most visible place to stick a Wanted poster. Settling on a spot, she fastened the sign to about eye level and stepped back to admire her handywork.

Bea eyed the huge tree, picturing the Mystery Writer leaning against its broad trunk. Standing here, Bea couldn't help but be reminded of the summer she and Cassandra had built a treehouse – ahem slab of wood wedged in a tree – in her garden and how much she enjoyed perching herself up there and reading until sunset.

Shoving her book, phone and what remained of her lunch down the front of her jacket, she searched for a foothold. Finding one, she wedged her sneaker into it and hoisted herself up before falling back down again. Giving it another go, she added a little jump and managed to propel herself up just high enough that she was flopped over one of the lower branches. From there she was able to sit herself up and crawl, branch by branch, until she was in the centre of the tree, where the intersecting branches created a small ledge. Crouching, she ran her eyes over the branches. To her disappointment, all she spotted was a blob of green chewing gum and a crushed Diet Coke can.

'You right up there?' a voice called, startling Bea.

Poking her head out of her hiding spot, she saw a lanky man wearing bike shorts jogging on the spot. 'Yep, great. Fantastic! Just enjoying the serenity!' she yelled, putting her hands at the back of her head and half-sighing, half-yawning.

The man looked at her sceptically, as if to say, 'Aren't you too old to climb a tree, Peter Pan?' but eventually he resumed running.

Bea stood up and assessed the sturdiest branch that would allow her to get herself further up into the dense foliage. Putting her foot on various surfaces, she grabbed hold of a higher branch and pulled herself up. She then inched her way out along the branch. From up here, she had a whopper of a view of the park, which really was beautiful.

'If only I could ...' Bea took another step back, arms stretched out so that her fingertips grazed the limb above her. Out of nowhere, a magpie swooped past, causing her to lose her footing. Bea yelped and swayed back, her left foot shifting from under her and wedging itself between a couple of branches at a decidedly unnatural angle. A searing pain whizzed up her leg, making Bea twist on the spot in agony. 'Fuck! Fuck! Fuck!'

In the heat of the moment, she forgot where she was, and her last twist went a bit too far, tipping her to the edge of the branch. She felt a small pop in her ankle as she fell the short distance backwards to the ground. She landed on the gravel path with an almighty thud, winded and wounded.

She lay there unable to move, eyes wide open, struggling to catch her breath. The world spun around her.

When her breath eventually returned, she tried to sit up, but the smallest movement shot more pain up her leg. Tilting her head to the side she spotted her iPhone, which must have fallen out of her jacket during the fall, just out of arm's reach. Shifting to the left just slightly, she managed to grab the device by flicking it towards her. *Who to call?* She wished her parents were here. And, for the first time, that Lizzie wasn't all the way out in Mount Eliza. *Dino?* She dialled his number and prayed that he would answer. After several rings, the call went to his voicemail. She tried The Nook, even though she knew Dino never answered. Again, the line clicked out. *Fuck, fuckety, fuck, fuck!*

She tried to sit up again, and this time managed to prop herself up on her elbows. She knew she'd have to call Zach.

He was the only other reasonable and reliable option who would be strong enough to lift her. Flipping through her contacts, she reluctantly pressed connect on his number.

On the third ring, he picked up. 'Bea? I'm so glad you called! I was just about to—'

'Zach, I need your help,' she said and then burst out crying.

'You see what on the X-ray?' Bea asked, now less sore, and more high, thanks to the morphine. She was lying on an emergency bed in the Alfred Hospital, dressed in a white gown. There was a drip attached to her hand, pumping in good old-fashioned pain relief. By the time Zach had located her in the park, a passerby, who happened to be an ex-Scout, had found her and hastily secured her leg in a makeshift splint made out of Moreton Bay fig branches. 'How's that for irony?' she vaguely remembered wondering out loud.

Since arriving at the hospital, Bea had endured one very confronting MRI, an X-ray and three excruciatingly long hours of waiting to finally be told that she had not, in fact, broken her back, but had definitely done a number on her left ankle.

'You see that?' the doctor said, pointing to the screen. He looked too young to be a doctor. His hair was dishevelled, and he wore black-rimmed glasses that made him seem as though he was playing dress-up. Zach held her hand, squeezing tightly. In fact, he hadn't let go since they arrived.

'What is it?' Bea asked urgently.

'It's a shattered malleolus. I knew it!' The doctor practically whooped, like he was a little boy who had just found a bag of biscuits in the pantry, not a doctor conveying a diagnosis.

'What does that mean?' Zach asked, exasperated.

'Surgery,' the doctor said, smiling unnervingly.

So, my search for the Mystery Writer almost killed me. Great, Bea silently berated herself for being so reckless.

The doctor clicked off the X-ray viewer. 'You've got a break in two parts, looks pretty nasty from where I'm sitting. I'd suggest getting an operation as quickly as possible. Dr Richards seems to be free first thing tomorrow,' he said nonchalantly, running his finger down the schedule on his clipboard.

'An operation?' Zach and Bea exclaimed in unison.

'Yes, it's routine, really. Dr Richards does them all the time. Mainly on elite footballers.' He paused, looking Bea up and down. 'But you'll be fine. Nothing to worry about. You might want to consider taking a few days off work. You'll be in a moon boot for a few weeks after that, I imagine, but with some light physio you'll be right as rain. Nothing to worry about.'

'Oh,' Bea muttered, while Zach rubbed her hand soothingly. Bea hadn't had an operation since having her wisdom teeth removed when she was nineteen. In her post-operative state, she'd been convinced she was in Narnia and kept referring to the duty nurse as Aslan. Bea shuddered.

'Do you have any family you want me to call?' the doctor asked.

Bea couldn't find her voice to reply. She shook her head, an image of her frantic mother popping into her mind. Maggie would just stress, and Martin, well, he would practically demand to do the surgery himself. It would be better if she delayed that conversation for now.

'I'll be here though. I won't leave her side,' Zach said, injecting confidence and warmth into his voice.

'And you are?' the doctor asked.

'I'm her boyfriend,' Zach replied, glancing at Bea for approval.

She closed her eyes and exhaled loudly. *I guess we're back together then.*

50

'**Z**ach, I don't think I want to do this.' Bea squeezed the hand of her new-old boyfriend. She was lying on a bed in pre-op, wearing nothing but a hospital gown and thick socks. She had just gotten off the phone to her parents and sister, who were all fretting over every detail. 'It's just routine,' Bea had told them. She had also sent a quick message to Dino to let him know what was going on. Just in case he was worried when he hadn't heard from her. He hadn't replied.

'Don't be nervous, Bea. Like the doctor said, you're in great hands and it will be over before you know it! And I'll be waiting here the whole time.' Zach tried to sound cheery, flashing her one of his movie-star smiles.

She still couldn't quite believe that yesterday she was single and healthy, and now she was in hospital, about to be cut open, with an apparently doting boyfriend by her side. And the overwhelming and numbing fear (not to mention pain) of it all was enough for her to temporarily put her rage and downright scepticism on hold because she just couldn't fathom being alone right now. *Does that make me entirely pathetic and the total antithesis of a strong, independent woman?* Bea asked herself, lamenting that they had disconnected her morphine drip.

'You do realise that they're going to slice open my skin, crack my bones and jiggle them into place? Slice, crack and jiggle! Slice, crack and jiggle!' Bea said, trying to act casual.

'Stop saying slice, crack and jiggle.' Zach shuddered, tickling her stomach lightly through the blankets. 'You're going to be fine.'

A man wearing light blue scrubs entered the room. 'Miss Babbage, are you ready? I'm your anaesthetist, John,' he said kindly, shaking her hand reassuringly. 'I'll be taking you into theatre.'

'Ready as I'll ever be,' Bea said lightly, but her heart was racing.

'Is this where I leave you?' Zach asked.

Bea nodded, unable to speak. Her body was limp, she needed to catch her breath.

'I love you,' Zach said.

Bea swallowed. *Love you?* Before she could think how to respond, she was wheeled away towards the operating theatre. She stared up at the big bright lights that shone down on her as if she were in an interrogation room. *You're going to be okay. This is all routine,* she reminded herself over and over again. She then let her mind wander to thoughts of lattes and poodles and Dino and … *Doesn't he care that I'm about to have surgery?*

'Now, I'm just going to put this on you.' Dr John said, pulling a mask over her mouth and nose.

Bea closed her eyes.

'You're about to have one of the best sleeps of your life,' he said in his calming voice, as Bea felt a coolness creep through her veins as the Propofol was injected into her IV line.

'Okay. Sweet drea—'

'I'm fine. Just sore. I can't walk, but the doctor said they'll help get me up and moving tomorrow, with crutches and a moon boot,' Bea said into her phone. She was FaceTiming Lizzie from her hospital room. Bleached white walls, a tiny window and a small painting of a sailboat stared back at her. Bea had been lying there for the past four hours, and the only things keeping her sane were Zach's company (believe it or not) and a good supply of endone. She was still in her hospital gown with her leg propped up on a tower of pillows, and she didn't even want to think about what sort of state her hair was in. She felt self-conscious, allowing Zach to see her so exposed. But Zach didn't seem to care. In fact, he seemed to relish looking after her. And, she had to admit, he had been truly brilliant at it. She had woken to a room full of sunflowers and Zach had read to her, talked to her and even (mortifyingly) watched her fall into a drug-induced sleep complete, no doubt, with drool and snoring.

'Oh Bea, I wish I could be there, but both girls have chicken pox and it's an absolute animal farm over here. And of course, Nick is off in Perth for work again – I'm thinking of calling him to come home, telling him I need to be in Melbourne to help you,' Lizzie said apologetically, pressing her face so close to the camera that Bea could see the clumps of mascara that accented her lashes.

'Don't be silly, Liz. I'm fine. My *boyfriend* is here to look after me.' Bea turned her phone towards Zach, who was sitting on a chair in the corner of a room, flicking patiently through a copy of *WHO* magazine.

'Your boyfriend?' Lizzie's tone instantly changed.

'Oh Liz, don't be rude. Speak to you later. Love you!' Bea blew air kisses at the camera and then switched it off.

Zach grimaced. 'Well, she hates me.'

'She just needs time to forgive you. And possibly for also allegedly flirting with her. She'll come round.' Bea shrugged. *Have I forgiven him yet?*

Zach's face blanched. 'I would never do that to Lizzie! Oh my God, I am still mortified that she thinks I was coming on to her.'

'Yeah, yeah, yeah,' Bea said dismissively, too tired to get into that again. In fact, she felt utterly drained and the dull throb in her ankle was proving more and more difficult to ignore. 'Zach, you must be tired. You haven't slept since – when? Two nights ago?' Bea asked, taking in his sunken cheeks and the bags under his eyes.

'I'm fine, Bea.'

Bea smiled. 'So am I. Seriously. I'm going to fall asleep now for the next few hours. Why don't you head home, have a quick nap, and then pick us up some takeaway? I can't bear to eat hospital food again.' She knew the only way to get him to leave was to spin the situation to make it seem as if he was doing her a favour.

'Fine, fine, you have a point there. Are you sure you don't mind?'

'I don't mind one bit. I'm so out of it I won't even remember any of this tomorrow anyway! Go home, get some rest, and then bring me back a Nando's burger,' Bea said, rubbing her hands together and practically licking her lips in anticipation.

'Okay, if you're sure.' Zach put on his boots and stood up.

'I'm positive.'

He bent down and kissed her lightly on the lips, almost as if he was afraid she might break.

She looked up at him. 'Thank you for everything, Zach. Really.'

'Of course.'

'Oh, and don't forget the fries!' she called as he walked out the door. Then she closed her eyes, relieved to have some solitude.

A loud crash brought Bea back from the depths of a deep, drug-induced sleep. Bleary eyed, she scanned the room to find a dark shadow on the floor next to a toppled-over chair.

'Dino?' Bea asked. 'Is that you?'

Hopping up, Dino adjusted his grey hoodie and dark blue jeans, flour still scattering his clothes. He must've come straight from work. 'Sorry, I didn't mean to wake you. I was about to leave when I saw you sleeping, but I tripped over this inconveniently placed chair,' he said, righting the chair. 'What the hell happened to you, Babbage?' He lightly punched her on the arm.

She revelled in the friendly nature of the gesture, sick of all the nurses, even Zach, treating her with such delicacy. 'Oh, you know, your standard Thursday. Sushi for lunch, climbing and then falling from a tree resulting in an ankle break for dinner and impromptu operation for dessert. Just the usual.'

'What were you doing climbing a tree? Actually, let me guess. Mystery Writer again?' He awkwardly sat on the bed, his legs dangling clumsily from the side.

Bea caught her breath, feeling things she didn't want to. *We're just friends. This is fine,* she told herself.

'I was pretty worried there for a second, Babbage,' he said.

'It didn't seem like it.'

'What do you mean?'

'This is the first I've heard from you. I've been out of surgery for hours.'

'Bea, my phone died. I called the hospital as soon as I found out. Don't ever think I don't care about you.'

Bea nodded, relieved. *He didn't forget about me.*

'I can't believe you had to do this alone. Bea, just the thought of it …' His brow furrowed.

'I wasn't alone,' she admitted quietly.

Dino raised an eyebrow.

'When you didn't answer, I called Zach. He was the one who came to fetch me from the park. He didn't leave my side until I made him go home after my operation. He's been quite sweet, really. He seems different.'

Dino's face contorted. He shuffled back, leaving a cool, empty space between them. 'Why would it have even crossed your mind to call him, Bea?'

'Because I have no family here and – well, I'm thinking of giving him another chance, Dino. Like you said, it's ultimately my decision. And I'm being smart about it and seeing what he's like, and I have to say, he's trying his best to make things up to me. Heck, he got me through this whole ordeal when I had no one else,' Bea said firmly, attempting to convince herself just as much as she was trying to convince Dino.

Then Dino was up and off the bed and pacing, frustration rising from his skin. 'I thought you only liked him because you thought he wrote those stupid inscriptions in the book and, well, how do we even know he can read now?' he spat. 'So – what? You're back together now? Just like that?'

'I don't know, maybe, something like that,' Bea replied, attempting to edge her way up to a sitting position. 'Do we have to do this now?' She gestured to the hospital room.

Dino ignored her, powering on. 'I can't believe you, Bea. Jesus, I thought you were smart, but your judgement is totally off with this one.'

'Excuse me? How dare you!' Bea spat. 'You don't know me at all. I had this whole fantasy in my head that my ideal man was the Mystery Writer, and when Zach told me it wasn't really him, well, I threw the idea of him out the window. But maybe that's ridiculous. Maybe the owner of *Meeting Oliver Bennett* is just some random person who I'll never meet, and the real love of my life is Zach. I owe myself a chance at finding love, don't I?'

'Jesus, Bea. You're so gullible sometimes, so willing to trust others, even when they have proven on countless occasions that they are completely untrustworthy. You've been so caught up with living in the margins that you're totally blind to what's actually reality. You have to get out and start living for *you*.' Dino paused. His fists were balled up by his sides and he was taking heavy, shallow breaths, seemingly trying to get a handle on himself.

'I'm living in the margins? *I'm* living in the margins? Well, I'm sorry, Mr I'm-too-cool-for-everyone, don't-look-at-me-the-wrong-way-or-misquote-a-piece-of-poetry-or-I'll-bite-your-head-off. No one can live up to your ridiculous standards, Dino. And quite frankly, I'm sick of it.' Bea crossed her arms. Her mind was foggy and she couldn't quite see straight. She did, however, see Dino's face contort in – *was that hurt?*

'Well, good luck, Bea,' he said in a chilling voice. 'I'm out. I can't watch you self-destruct. If you're going to include that lunatic in your life, I want no part of it. I hope you two are very happy together.' He turned and walked out the door without looking back.

'Fuck you, Dino,' Bea muttered, unsure why she was crying so much.

51

**Tell us in 25 words or less, why you want
to win a year's supply of Kair's large
wax strips.**

Lost my razor. Haven't had time to buy
another, and now mobility restricted due to
broken ankle. Leg hair currently longer than
War and Peace.

52

It had been a few days since Bea had arrived home from the hospital and she was still groggy and out of sorts. She reclined against the couch, running her eyes around the perimeter of the ceiling. She counted one crack, two small spider webs, an unidentified bluish-green stain and a small glow-in-the-dark star. She shook her head, thinking back to her childhood bedroom, which was adorned with her very own glow-in-the-dark constellation. Cassandra had taken one look at her pride and joy, smirked and said, 'Cute.' Even as a ten-year-old, Bea had known that she wasn't trying to be flattering.

Picking up a half-empty takeaway cup, she took a sip of the cold latte. Being limited in her mobility, and on less than great terms with Dino, she had begun ordering coffees from The Nook on Uber Eats. Bea could handle distance from Dino, but her caffeine cravings were a different story: they couldn't stomach going without The Nook's strong, smooth, hit-the-spot coffee. So she had convinced herself that the $5 delivery fee was well worth it. She just wouldn't look at her bank balance.

Her buzzer blared. She frowned, checked the time again, and wondered if it might be Dino, grovelling and begging for her forgiveness. Easing off the couch, she used one of her crutches to hoist herself up and then half-hopped, half-hobbled on her moon boot to the intercom, her gait noticeably awry.

Clicking the speaker button, she yelled down the line: 'Hello?'

'Beatrix? It's me!'

'Who's "me"?' Bea called back, her heart sinking at the distinctly female voice, racking her memory for recognition.

A muffled pause, followed by a shrill, 'Ruth!' blasted up the line.

'Ruth? What are you doing here? Did we have plans I forgot about?'

'No.'

'Oh, well, how lovely and unexpected!'

'Do you think you could let me up now?' Ruth said, matter of factly. 'I have business to discuss and would rather not do it in front of the whole street.'

'Oh yes, yes, of course! Sorry!' Bea fumbled with the intercom, releasing the lock.

Looking over her shoulder, she surveyed the mess that was her living room with a sigh. Half-drunk cups of tea, tissues, a bowl of chicken soup (her mother had couriered a container of frozen chicken soup, distraught that she couldn't visit herself), dirty socks and cartons of the various drugs Bea was taking littered the room. Before she had a moment to rectify the situation, a firm knock announced Ruth and Philip's arrival.

Bea plastered a smile on her face and opened the door. 'Ruth! How did you know where I lived? How lovely to—' Bea stopped, taking in Ruth's dishevelled appearance. Her frizzy hair sat in an unruly bird's nest on top of her head and her red paisley shirt was half untucked and hanging over green cargo pants. 'Ruth, are you okay?'

Ruth took a sharp intake of breath and held some very intense eye contact before dissolving into a puddle of tears. It was only then that Bea noticed Ruth's ferret, Philip, scampering about at her feet.

'Oh, Ruth! Please, come in.' Bea ushered her surprise guest into the living room and plonked her down on the couch, surreptitiously kicking her pyjama bottoms under the couch with her good foot. Grabbing a box of tissues, she thrust a handful at Ruth, then hovered awkwardly. 'What can I get you? Tea? Chocolate? A scotch on the rocks?'

'English breakfast!' Ruth wailed. She hadn't seemed to notice Bea's own wounded appearance.

Relieved to have something to busy herself with, Bea shuffled to the kitchen, grabbing at chairs and walls to steady herself. She boiled the kettle and rummaged through her bare shelves. Finding exactly three tea bags left in her tea canister, she grabbed an English breakfast and looped it into a mug.

'Milk? Sugar?' she called through the open door. When there was no reply, she shrugged and plopped a liberal dose of both to the brew.

Thankfully, when Bea emerged from the kitchen, precariously balancing the mug, Ruth seemed to have calmed down somewhat. No longer actively crying, she sat on the couch blowing her nose with one hand while methodically patting Philip with the other. Bea cautiously put the tea on the coffee table, using all of her energy not to spill it or tumble forwards.

'I love this book.' Ruth gestured at *Meeting Oliver Bennett*. It was sitting on Bea's coffee table.

Bea was over the moon to know that someone else had read the book. 'You've read it? This one, well, it's really special. It's filled with—'

'What happened to you?' Ruth interrupted, eyeing Bea's moon boot.

'Oh, just a little accident, I'm fine. What happened to you?' Bea asked as she delicately fell onto the couch next to Ruth.

It took a moment for Ruth to respond. Her eyes were frozen on the wall opposite her, miles away. She sniffed. 'I've never been separated from Philip before.'

'Separated? What do you mean? Is everything okay with Philip?'

Ruth dabbed her eyes with a tissue. 'Yes, everything's fine. I decided to get his room repainted, including some updates on the Elizabeth and Philip mural.'

Bea nodded along, trying to keep up. A new painted room for a ferret? She thought of her own bedroom walls, cracks and all.

'The contractors came yesterday and they said we'd need to evacuate Philip from the house for at least the next week! Apparently the fumes won't be good for him or me. Can you believe it? So, naturally, I looked into staying at one of those dog stays. But they don't allow ferrets. The nerve!' Bea had never seen Ruth as frazzled as this. 'I tried to smuggle him in to The Langham but housekeeping sprung us and management threatened to kick us both out if I didn't rehome him! I didn't know what to do. Philip doesn't get along with strangers and I can't very well give him to my insipid *sister* for the week, can I? He despises her.' Ruth gave a stressed cackle. 'Then I remembered how good you were with little Philip. How he bonded with you, and ran into your arms at the cinema. I've never seen anything like it.' Ruth smiled fondly, before frowning again.

Poor Ruth. 'So, how can I help?' Bea asked.

'Well, seeing as you're so good with Phil ...'

Oh no.

'And he can't stay in the house for the week ...'

Oh dear God, no.

'The paint fumes will kill him ...'

Shit, shit, shit, shit.

'And he can't stay with me ...'

Look apathetic. Look apathetic. 'Oh?'

'Would you ... Would you perhaps consider ...'

I'll do anything but this! Anything!

'Looking after my dear Philip? Just for a few days, two weeks maximum, while I sort myself out?'

NOOOOOOOOOOO! 'Yes.'

'Yes? Really?'

'Yes?' Bea said tentatively.

Ruth let out a large whoop and pulled Bea and her recently operated-on ankle towards her. Philip wiggled uneasily between their bodies.

Bea gently extricated herself from Ruth's painful hug, easing her bottom backwards until her top half could follow.

'Well, I'm just so relieved,' Ruth gushed. 'Philip means everything to me and I can't stand being away from him. I can't even go to the loo without bringing him along! I hate to be indebted to people – makes me feel weak and burdened – but I had to put my baby first. Didn't I, Prince Philip, Duke of Edinburgh?' she cooed, tickling the now very contented ferret under his chin.

'Of course, I'm so pleased I could help,' Bea said through gritted teeth.

'Excellent, excellent!' Ruth trilled. 'I'll just pop down and get his things!'

'His things? Already?'

'Well, yes. Best he moves in right away. All this change and uncertainty hasn't been good for his mental health. Plus, I'm due to be in Sydney for some female founders function and I couldn't bear to upheave him again.'

His mental health? What about my mental health?

Ruth stood up, shoving Philip at Bea, and headed for the door. 'I'll be right back. Should only take two trips.'

Following three trips to her car, Ruth had officially overrun Bea's living room with ferret paraphernalia, including a large chicken wire enclosure, two harnesses – one for day and one that glowed in the dark for those impromptu evening walks he liked to go on – food and water bowls, litter box, cleaning products – 'he needs his enclosure swept clean twice a week' – two large boxes of toys, a fluoro tunnel to 'mentally stimulate him', a sleeping bag, a small hammock and a round wicker basket for him to sleep in. Oh, and Bea's freezer was now filled to bursting with raw chicken. 'He'll only need eight to ten small meals a day. His metabolic system really is something to envy!' Ruth told Bea. Thank goodness Bea had thrown just about everything out during her Marie Kondo cleanse, otherwise she might have been forced to move to a bigger apartment.

'I so appreciate you helping me, Beatrix. Really. Is there anything I can do to make it up to you?'

Bea thought for a moment. 'Well, yes, actually. Remember how I mentioned that I've just started a little marketing agency? It's nothing really. But I was wondering whether you might be able to help me at some stage? Just some advice, if you don't mind. Seeing as you're such a successful businesswoman and all.' Bea shrugged, embarrassed. She always felt a little uncomfortable asking favours, but seeing as she had just agreed to babysit a ferret, she thought she was probably owed one.

'Oh yes, of course, Beatrix. If you help my Philip, I'll help your business. One piece of advice for you: Grow silently. That way your competitors won't know what hit them when you're giant and brilliant.'

Bea nodded, taking in Ruth's wisdom.

'Okay then, now you be in touch,' Ruth said to the ferret.

'Um, okay. Well, let me know how the painting progresses!' Bea said desperately, propped against the wooden frame of her front door. Ruth waved, making her way down the corridor.

Sighing, Bea placed a disgruntled Philip in his enclosure, popped two more endones and lay back down on her couch. *What the hell just happened?*

Bea's eyes fluttered open. She squinted, the glare of the day penetrating to the very back of her skull. So she closed her eyes again, pulled her throw over her head and tried to fall back to sleep. A soft clanking sound coming from her kitchen forced her eyes back open. Still huddled under the blanket, she listened carefully. *Yep, that was definitely my cupboards opening and closing.* Bea stiffened. Still achy and slightly high from the last dose of painkillers, she tried to retrace her steps to where she had discarded her portable panic alarm. Her nightstand. She would never make it there in time, not in this state. *Okay, maybe if I just lie really still, they'll just leave.* She squeezed her eyes shut and clenched her jaw.

A loud crashing sound made Bea jerk. *I hope to God that ferrets are the German shepherds of the weasel family,* she thought. Footsteps. She could definitely hear footsteps getting louder. They traced around one length of the room, paused, then continued. Then they paused again. Bea felt a looming presence, heard ragged breathing. Two fingers laced themselves under the side of her blanket.

Bea tensed, bracing herself. 'Please don't kill me!' she cried.

'Bea?' a voice said. 'It's me, Zach. Relax!'

'Zach?' Bea opened one eye. 'What are you doing here? How did you get in?'

'With the key you gave me.'

'I gave you a key?'

'Yeah, you gave it to me when I dropped you home and insisted that I use it to check that you hadn't died in your sleep.'

'God, painkillers make me dramatic.' Bea let herself relax. 'Here, help me up.'

Holding her hand and elbow, Zach carefully hoisted Bea to a sitting position, an arm tucked behind his back.

'How are you feeling? And what the hell is that ferret doing in your home?'

Philip! She had hoped she'd dreamt his arrival.

'He's already tried to bite me! He and I do not get along.' Zach frowned. Bea rubbed her temples, worried about animals' intuition.

'Hey, I brought you these.' Zach extended his arm, revealling a bunch of purple and white daffodils he was holding.

'They're beautiful!'

Zach beamed, his whole face lighting up like a labrador who had just received an encouraging pat on the head. 'I couldn't find a vase. In fact, it looks like the only things left in this place are your couch and the stuff for that ferret.'

'I'm trying something new.'

'I can see that.'

'Let me see if I can find you something.' Bea shuffled to the edge of the couch, grimaced, and slid back down.

'Don't move. Let me,' Zach said, squeezing her arm.

Bea smiled in thanks and rested her head against the back of the couch. She had absolutely no recollection of handing over her keys to Zach. *Damn, those drugs have a kick!* But in the dim, ferret-filled, empty-cupboard, afternoon light, Bea was more than slightly grateful for the company.

'That should do the trick!' Zach returned triumphantly from the kitchen, holding a large, deep pot and a recycled pasta sauce jar, out of which poked the daffodils. He side-stepped the ferret's cage (which did not go unnoticed by Philip, who let out a low, menacing hiss), placed the flowers on the coffee table with a flourish and then flopped onto the couch next to her.

'Well done, you. Very resourceful.' Bea clapped theatrically. 'Are you even real?' She narrowed her eyes.

Zach frowned. 'Of course I'm real. Are you real?'

'As real as an evergreen tree.'

Zach laughed – a full, hearty sound. He pinched her cheek and snuggled in a little closer. 'You're odd. But I like odd.'

'You're the one who's odd. One minute you're being paid to date me, next minute you're bringing me flowers and cleaning my living room.'

'Hang on a second, I haven't cleaned your living room!'

'Yet.' Bea winked.

Zach laughed and kissed her delicately on the lips. Bea kissed him back with a passion that she probably shouldn't have had only a couple of days after surgery. He leaned his body over her, while being careful not to settle any weight on her. She let out a small moan.

'Zach,' she purred.

'Bea,' he whispered back huskily.

'I want to, you know …' Her face was flushed, her ankle still propped up awkwardly on a pillow.

'Oh! You want to do … it?' Zach raised an eyebrow. He was still balancing on his hands, holding himself over her. Their noses were so close they were almost touching. 'Are you – are you sure you're okay to?' Zach asked tentatively, glancing at her moon boot.

'Yes,' Bea said definitively. 'You might just have to do all the work.' She shrugged playfully.

'I can handle that.' He kissed her softly on her neck, then her collarbone, and then propelled himself down lower, half his body now dangling clumsily off the couch, to kiss her chest, her stomach. Bea's whole body was instantly covered in goosebumps, her breathing shallow. She ran her fingers through his hair, and felt him smile. He slowly but carefully slid down her tracksuit pants and underwear in one go, as Bea awkwardly shuffled back, her broken ankle not allowing her to move as quickly as she desired. Zach returned to kissing her stomach, excruciatingly and agonisingly slowly. Her back arched, her breath quickened even more as if telling him to *hurry up*. And then he was kissing her lower. And lower. Until he was kissing her exactly as low as she wanted him to go.

53

Dear Ramona,

I know, I know! The place is a pigsty. I've been recovering from surgery and barely able to function (plus you not being here last week really threw me! How was your holiday, by the way?) Do me a favour and please, please, throw out what's left of the endone. I do not need any more chemical highs in my life.

Thanks. Sorry. Lots of love.

Bea xx

PS How do you feel about cleaning ferret cages? I owe you one!

54

Bea,

 I allergic to animal hair so cannot clean today. Please tell me when animal has left.

 Sorry.

 Ramona

 PS My holiday very nice and romantic.

55

SPEED DATE A BOOK

Quit trying to find your perfect man or woman, and start seeking your perfect paperback. Founder of Melbourne-based marketing agency <u>Platypus</u>, Bea Babbage, and local barista, Grover Dinopoli, have founded a dating platform with a twist. Rather than helping you to find your soulmate, Next Chapter will assist you in finding your next great literary love. Hosted at Mr Dinopoli's <u>The Nook</u>, participants simply bring their favourite novel and have five minutes to sell it to another reader. If you like the sound of the book, you take it; if you don't, you move on.

'We're really excited. We're expecting a big turnout, and maybe a surprise celebrity guest or two,' says Ms Babbage of the upcoming Next Chapter event.

'I think the beauty of Next Chapter is we're uniting people over their passion for books. Nowadays, reading is rarely a solitary pursuit. It's about camaraderie, companionship, community. And we want to celebrate that in our own unique way,' says Mr Dinopoli.

The next event is Saturday 25 July at 7pm at The Nook, South Yarra. Entry is $10, and you'll need to register for a spot via beatrix@platypusagency.com.au

56

💬 Bea: Dino, did you see? Our article is finally up on Broadsheet. This is going to be huge for Next Chapter. Only ten days to go now! We really should meet to iron out the final details. Let me know when suits AHHH 🙀

Bea slid her phone across the kitchen table and rolled her eyes. Why did she even bother with Dino? Of course he wasn't going to reply. He was so stubborn. And besides, Bea was angry with him. *How dare he tell me who I can and cannot be in a relationship with? Who I can and cannot forgive? It's not like I have any say over Sunday!*

Today was her first day back at work and she couldn't have been more excited. After she had handed over her keys to Zach in a drug-induced state, he had been practically living at her place. The past week had been a haze of hand massages, cleaning up after Philip's indiscretions (which wasn't easy with Philip's vehement hatred of Zach), healthy food banquets, and blissful, mind-blowing sex. However, while she was enjoying Zach's company, and his commitment to keeping her fridge stocked and her body satisfied, Bea couldn't deny that she was starting to feel a little stifled.

Bea poured herself a bowl of gluten-free grains and almond milk. Having mastered the awkward moon boot shuffle/limp, she was able to get around without needing her crutches. She sat down with her bowl of health and spooned the bland concoction into her mouth.

Zach, fresh from the shower, sauntered up behind her. His hair was damp and he smelled of strawberries. 'First day back! Are you sure you're ready for this, babe?' he asked, massaging her shoulders temptingly from behind.

Ach! That nickname. I can't stomach it. 'I'm positive. You have to stop worrying about me, Zach. I'm fine,' Bea said, scraping her spoon along the rim of the bowl and distracting herself from the fight she wanted to pick with him. 'Plus, I have to get back to it. I'm so behind on everything! I have a million missed emails from Mia and don't even get me started on the freelancing work I'm not even close to finishing. And then there's Next Chapter. I really need to get Dino in a room and finalise our plans.' Bea exhaled. 'The list is never-ending!' she exclaimed, slowly getting up from her stool to put her empty bowl in the sink.

Before she could take a step, Zach took the bowl from her, kissing the back of her head as he passed. 'Just make sure you take it easy.'

Bea wasn't sure whether he was referring to her healing ankle or her interactions with Dino. While she hadn't brought up their tiff, he had found the Uber Eats delivery bags stashed in the back of the pantry cupboard. 'Stop fretting. I'll be fine. Will you be here later?' she asked, kissing him lightly.

'Do you want me to be?' He kissed her back with ardour.

She leaned in for a moment, giving in to him, before pulling away. She had to get to work, and she couldn't help feeling that he was trying to use sex as a way to trap her into staying. She turned around as abruptly as her moon boot would let her, picked up her red tote bag, then attached a lead to Philip and hobbled towards her front door.

'See you!'

'Love you!' he called back, but Bea had already closed the door behind her.

It felt good to be back at work. Even though she only had a small desk to herself, it felt like she had more space than she'd had all week. The cathartic sounds of keyboards clacking, brainstorming sessions and client phone calls from the start-up founders around her fuelled her creativity. It was a relief that, for the first time in a week, her head was now filled with strategies and flowcharts, rather than *Zach, Dino, Zach, Dino, Zach*. Philip's leash was tied to the leg of her desk (thankfully Revolver Lane was a pet-friendly space) and he was sleeping soundly, making a gentle purring noise.

Just as she was getting settled, the front door swung open. Bea heard her before she saw her – she would have recognised those heel clicks anywhere! She looked up and, sure enough, standing in front of her was fabulous Martha. Bea still wasn't used to seeing Martha in the flesh. She was wearing a bright red trenchcoat, which worked perfectly with her skin. Her hair was now shoulder-length and Cleopatra black, and Bea realised she must be wearing a wig. Bea smiled broadly, waving Martha over as she looked enviously from her ex-colleague's exquisite shoes to her own Nike sneaker and clunky moon boot.

'Martha! So good to see you. I am totally in your debt.' Bea leaned in to kiss her on the cheek, but Martha air-kissed her on each side of her face.

'The pleasure is all mine. I'm due some sick leave, and to be honest, this whole start-up vibe really gets me going. Besides, there's not much I wouldn't do for a fellow Austen fan! Now, what can I do to help you out?' Martha stepped over Philip, not even mentioning the sleeping animal, pulled up a stool and perched on it cross-legged. Her posture was immaculate and she smelled of Chanel No. 5 – the epitome of sophistication.

'Essentially, I have no idea how to create a financial forecast,' Bea admitted, pulling up a spreadsheet she had put together and pointing at some numbers.

'You're in luck, Bea. That, I can help with.' Martha smiled, pulling her laptop from her black bag and placing it neatly on her lap. 'Do you have Xero?'

'No.'

'MYOB?'

'No.'

'QuickBooks?'

'No.'

Martha looked at Bea with a touch of pity before saying, 'Don't worry, dear, I've worked with worse. I'm going to make you the best damn financial forecast you've ever seen!'

Bea laughed. 'Thank you so much, Martha. You have no idea what this means to me.'

Martha shook her head as if to say, *Don't even think twice about it,* and began typing ferociously on her rose gold laptop. Just as Bea was about to return to her own typing, Philip started squirming uncontrollably. Aside from the occasional sneering at Zach, Philip had been surprisingly well behaved, but now he was losing control. He was wriggling and hissing and writhing. Martha squealed and moved her legs to the side as Bea crouched down next to the ferret.

'Philip, are you okay?' Bea whispered to him. *Are you meant to talk to ferrets?*

'He's just excited to see me,' Ruth said, appearing as if out of nowhere. She then unhooked Philip from his leash, picked him up and held him to her chest. He curled up into a ball.

Ruth wore black capri pants and a 'Team Sarah, Duchess of York' sweater. Her hair was secured in a very tight ponytail, pulling back on her skin so forcefully that Bea thought she might pop.

'You missed Mummy, didn't you? Didn't you?' Ruth kissed Philip a little too affectionately on his belly, and pieces of fur stuck to her lipstick.

Martha coughed.

'Ruth, you're back! And now you're here?' Bea exclaimed, surprised by the unannounced visit.

'Obviously I've come to see Philip. And to help you, Bea.'

'Really? Thank you!' People were giving them looks, no doubt disapproving of the loud noise her impromptu crew was making. Ignoring them, Bea offered quick introductions.

'I notice you have a British accent. Do you know any of the royals?'

'The royals? You mean ... the Windsors?'

'Of course, who else Martha?' Ruth replied, clearly frustrated.

'Oh, no, I don't know them personally, sorry.' Martha looked confused.

Ruth held Martha's gaze for a second longer than was necessary, frowned, and then turned abruptly to face Bea again. 'Beatrix, I assume you know nothing about starting a business?' Ruth sat cross-legged on the floor letting Philip climb up her arm.

When Bea shrugged, Ruth powered on. 'Let's start by making mistakes. The sooner you do, the sooner you can fix them,' she said.

'Bea?' someone called, and Bea inhaled before turning around. *What is it with this day?*

'Sunday?'

'What are you doing here?' Sunday asked.

'I'm renting a desk here. What are *you* doing here?' Bea asked, flustered. Martha and Ruth were staring at the two of them, waiting to be introduced.

'I got a job here! As a fashion assistant at this awesome vegan, eco-friendly, anti-slavery, start-up clothing brand.'

Impatient, Ruth, still sitting on the floor, reached her ferret saliva–covered hand up to shake Sunday's. 'Ruth, Bea's mentor.'

'And I'm Martha, Bea's financial planner.' Martha stuck out her own hand.

'Uh, hi.' Sunday tapped both of their hands limply.

'So, you're not at The Nook anymore?' Bea asked, desperate to ask after Dino – in a casual, nonchalant way.

'We're still business partners – but I don't work there anymore. I had to follow my dreams, you know. Be free like a bird!' Sunday mimed flapping wings.

Bea nodded, unable to imagine The Nook without those heavenly pastry creations Sunday would whip up in flavours Bea didn't even know existed. 'Dino must hate it without you there.'

'He'll survive.'

Bea nodded, ready for her chance to swoop. 'How is he anyway? I'm not sure whether he told you, but we had a sort of disagreement. I haven't been able to get a hold of him.'

'I don't know, to be honest. I've been holidaying in Bali right up until getting this gig. Haven't seen him for a week or so now. I should go visit him actually.' Sunday said cheerfully.

'You haven't seen him? Did you guys break up?' Bea asked too quickly.

Sunday laughed. 'Break up? Lady, are you crazy? We're just friends. Don't you know I'm gay?'

Bea dropped the notebook she was holding. *Dino is single?*

'I've been seeing Ramona. Your hot cleaner. I met her at your house when I picked up that Ottolenghi book. She didn't tell you we were just in Bali together?'

'No!' Bea exclaimed, shocked. 'I mean, I knew she was away on holidays. You're the girl she's been seeing?'

Sunday nodded, smiling widely.

'So you and Dino?' Bea asked tentatively.

'God, no. We're just mates. If you ask me, I always suspected that Dino had a thing for you.' Sunday pinched

Bea's arm playfully. 'Anyway, I better run. Those recycled plastic bathing suits won't design themselves! Catch you later, sweetie! I'm so excited we're work neighbours!'

Dino has always been single?

'Bea, why do you look so pale?' Martha asked.

'Yes, are you okay?' Ruth added.

Bea shook her head. 'I think I'm going to faint.'

57

Bea couldn't concentrate for the rest of the day. *Dino is single!* she kept thinking, over and over again. But she had seen him with Sunday. Or had that been a figment of her paranoid imagination? And Sunday and Ramona? *How did I miss that?*

As Martha and Ruth bickered over computer systems and Philip ate, ate, ate, then pooped and then ate some more, Bea went into a state of shock. *You're with Zach*, Bea reminded herself, as she tried to focus on drawing up storyboards and processing the briefs sent through from Mia. And when Martha and Ruth said it was time for them to leave, Bea waved half-heartedly, hardly able to move.

She checked the time. She was afraid to go home to Zach, but she was also equally terrified of what she would do if she didn't. So, when Sunday asked her to go for an after-work drink at the Lucky Coq, Bea accepted, grateful for the excuse.

Four hours, three tequila shots, a glass of red wine and a message to Zach not to wait up later, Bea stumbled out of the pub, Sunday holding her arm, laughing.

'Are you sure you're okay, hon?' Sunday's purple lipstick was smudged and her lip ring twinkled in the light of the street lamps. She let Bea lean on her as her ankle gave out while they stumbled down the street.

'Of course, *hon*! I'm freaking fantastic!'

Sunday burst out laughing again. 'So, tell me more about Zach. I can't believe you two are back together!' she slurred.

'It all seemed to just happen. We sort of fell into it, you know? He was there when I had no one else. And he's been good to me. Plus, the sex is so bloody brilliant.' Bea hiccuped and covered her mouth.

'Oh, girl. I hear you. Good sex is everything! Too bad I let my best get away.'

'Oh? Ramona?' Bea was still not over the revelation that Sunday had been sleeping with her cleaner.

'No! That's just fun. The best I've ever had was the love of my life – Ella. She was beautiful and ridiculous at the same time. And the sex! The sex was fantastic. But I remember the first time I realised it was more than just physical. It was her laugh. I fell so hard for it.'

'What happened?'

'She ghosted me. One day I tried to call her and it just went straight to voicemail. Never heard from her again. She broke my heart into spaghetti,' Sunday said.

'Spaghetti?' Bea giggled.

'Spaghetti!' Sunday exclaimed, joining in. 'You know what we should do?'

'What?' Bea beamed at Sunday. She hadn't felt this carefree, this uninhibited, in a long time. She took Sunday's glitter-manicured hand and swung it back and forth, her mind abuzz with the carefree gesture.

'Go to The Nook!' Sunday dipped Bea in her arms and Bea giggled hysterically.

'No way, José! Dino hates my guts. I can't see him right now.' Bea took out her phone to order an Uber. Enough was enough, she should get home to Zach. Plus, she didn't like how her stomach fluttered when Sunday mentioned Dino's name.

'He does not, he *loves* you!'

Bea rolled her eyes.

'Come on,' Sunday said, snatching Bea's phone from her hand and redirecting her to The Nook, in the opposite direction from her home. 'He's finishing up some work function and I said I'd swing by to help with the clean-up.' Sunday smiled as the Uber pulled up, and Bea grudgingly fell into the car after her.

Bea's stomach was in knots as she approached the little blue door of The Nook. *This is a bad idea*, the sober part of her said, the cool winter air making her shiver. But her drunk self shoved her inside, close on Sunday's heels.

'Hello, Dino! You still here?' Sunday yelled a decibel too loud for Bea's thumping head.

Bea hung back, playing self-consciously with her hair. Agatha Christie immediately waddled up to her and licked her shoes.

'Sunday?' Dino shouted from the kitchen. 'Everyone just left.' He stepped out to greet her wearing his standard green apron. As soon as he saw Bea, he froze, his demeanour changing: his eyes narrowed and he stood up straighter, his hackles up. 'Bea. What are you doing here?'

Bea scooped up Agatha Christie and hugged her firmly, her eyes blinking quickly. *I will not cry.*

'Come on, grumpy pants. We're all mates here.' Sunday kissed Dino on the cheek. 'You know what Bea thought? You are going to find this so hilarious.'

Bea shook her head slightly. *Don't say it, Sunday.*

'That getting back together with the guy who lied to her was a good idea?' Dino snapped.

Bea rolled her eyes, fed up with Dino's persistent angst. 'Why do you even care, Dino? Besides, Zach's changed. He's wonderful.'

'A wonderful lover, more like it.' Sunday winked.

'So, that's why you're with him? The sex? I've been trying to figure it out.' Dino remarked

'That's not it at all,' Bea bit back. *But was it?*

'Anyway, as I was saying.' Sunday cleared her throat. 'Bea thought *we* were together. All this time, she thought you and I were a couple!' Sunday burst out laughing.

Dino's eyes widened. He looked to Bea as if asking if it were true. Bea gave an embarrassed shrug.

'Jesus. You thought Sunday and I were together? All this time?' he murmured.

'Of course I did, Dino. You never told me otherwise,' Bea said.

'I didn't realise I had to, given there wasn't anything to tell,' Dino said with a slight quake to his voice.

Sunday eyed Dino and Bea who were looking at each other, lost in all that hadn't been said. 'Dino,' she said, breaking the silence. 'What can we do to help?'

Dino looked around at the sparkling café. 'As always, Sunday, your timing is impeccable. I'm just about done with the place.'

Sunday clicked her fingers. 'Drats,' she said with a smile. She checked her watch. 'Looks like I'll make it to that Collingwood house party after all. Bea, want to join me?'

Bea looked at Dino, who had begun to retreat to the kitchen. Her heart skipped a beat as if physically missing a part of itself. She needed to fix whatever it was that had broken between them. And, just maybe, discuss some of the much-needed Next Chapter formalities. Turning down Sunday's offer, she kissed her goodbye. Sunday strutted out of the café, waving three fingers in the air. The bell over the door chimed ominously behind her. Turning back to Dino, she started to say something before realising he had left her standing alone in the cafe. Sighing, she placed Agatha Christie gently on her bed and walked to the kitchen.

'Dino?' she said as she leaned up against the doorframe, her head still swimming.

'You still here?' Dino said, without turning around.

Bea took a step forward, paused and shuffled back. *I can do this. I can mend us.* 'Dino, please, can we talk?'

'Shoot. What's up?' Dino said dismissively, pressing a lid down on a container of mini quiches and placing it in the fridge. Then he faced Bea, crossing his arms and looking at her with raised eyebrows.

'Dino, I just want things to go back to the way they were with us. I miss the ease we had with each other. I miss those annoying quotes on my coffee cups. I miss the banter, the chats and I miss the muffins you'd always save for me at the end of the day.' Bea forced a small smile, feeling a weight lift from her shoulders.

Dino shook his head, gazing absently out of the small serving hatch. 'I don't know if we can go back, Bea.'

'Please, Dino.' Bea pushed herself forward, determined to close the gap that kept widening between them.

'Why are you really with him, Bea?' Dino asked, his arms dropping to his sides. 'I can't understand it. I can't understand *you*.'

Bea looked Dino in the eyes, recognising a sadness and anguish and maybe also a hint of desire in them. *Why am I with Zach?* she asked herself. It was a question she couldn't quite answer. It had all happened so quickly and now it just ... was. Possible reasons clouded her mind. *I feel safe with him. I like his company. I love his cooking.* But she kept coming back to one: *Because otherwise I'd have no one.*

Dino took a step closer. 'Bea, I didn't want things to change between us. Believe it or not, I miss you too,' he said, softening.

Bea faltered for a moment, then retreated an inch. Dino's expression hardened just the slightest at her movement.

'Why can't you just tell me why you're with him, Bea?' Dino pleaded. Agatha Christie joined them in the kitchen, pushing her curly body against Dino's leg, staring up at him with a knowing look.

'Because—'

'Because, what? Circumstance? You felt too bad to reject him? Because I can't think of any other logical reason.'

'That's not fair, Dino. That's a horrible thing to say. It's different this time. I know it is.'

'I don't think even you believe that. You two have nothing in common.'

'And you and I do?' Bea almost shouted.

'Bea.' He moved towards her again, cupping her cheek in his hands, his warm, rough hands. '"Whatever our souls are made of, his and mine are the same,"' he quoted Brontë.

'What does that even mean? I never understand you, Dino. You never tell me how you actually feel. You're constantly talking in platitudes and quotes. I don't care about how Brontë feels, or Wilde, or Austen.' Bea's voice shook. Dino seemed to have mastered the art of communicating while keeping everybody at arm's length. The constant quotes and metaphors he hid behind. The incessant barriers he couldn't seem to stop himself from erecting. Was it that he didn't care? Or were they just a crutch? 'I want to know how *you* feel!'

Dino faltered, still holding on to Bea.

'Dino. Just tell me! Tell me what you really mean.'

'Don't make this about me. I don't need to justify how I feel,' he said, dropping his hand to his side.

'Why not?' Bea pressed.

'There's nothing to say.'

Bea shook her head. 'There's everything to say. You know there is.'

'It's not me. I wasn't raised to chit chat about my feelings. I don't let people in, and, so far, this has served me just fine,' Dino said all in one breath.

'Dino, for me just try. Please tell me what you meant,' Bea was standing so close to Dino she could feel him shake. The silence dragged between them.

'I meant … I meant that whether we like it or not, we are connected. We are the same. When I get good news, you're the first one I want to call. When it's raining, I wonder whether you're staying dry. And when my head hits the pillow at night, I can't stop thinking of you, and only you. Tell me it's not the same for you, Bea. Tell me you don't feel the same way.' Dino leaned his forehead against hers, appearing liberated by his openness.

They hung there, foreheads pressed together, her knees a little weaker than before. For a moment she imagined drawing him towards her, his stubble grazing against her lips. But she caught herself, remembering Zach. He may have betrayed her once, but that didn't give her the right to do wrong by him. But Dino had just opened up to her. She couldn't abandon him.

'Dino …' she managed, taking a step back.

Dino sighed, defeated, and returned to his cold, distant self.

'I still want to be friends, Dino. I miss you.'

Dino grunted in reply.

Bea wanted to say more, but taking one last look at the stiffness that had returned to Dino's stance, she forced herself from the kitchen, from the café and from her overwhelming desire.

58

Hot, sticky flashes of confusion and downright angst clung to Bea like a bad smell. Last night with Dino had been so unexpected, so deeply unnerving. She had never seen him so open, so unsure of himself. *But I have Zach*, she told herself, remembering the way he had wrapped his big arms around her as she crawled into bed beside him, as if he were protecting her from all the bad in the world. And she liked being in Zach's arms. She really did.

She pulled her bag out from under her desk, knocking her head on her way up. She let out a small yelp and rubbed the spot that had come into contact with the hard wood of the table. If she wasn't done before, she was definitely done now.

Her phone chimed, and another frantic message from Zach flashed across her screen. Zach, having no clients for the day, had offered, despite Bea's objections, to work from her apartment so that he could watch Philip. But he was not coping. Messages like 'He just tried to claw me through the wire', 'Fourth attempt at feeding ferret aborted due to excessive hissing' and 'This thing is possessed by the devil' had been streaming in all day.

As she quickly stuffed her phone, laptop, lip balm and copy of *More Than Words* into her bag, her phone buzzed again. Lizzie. She had a meeting nearby with some soda water company that wanted her to be a brand ambassador, and was due to swing by Bea's co-working space for a quick coffee any minute now. Bea checked her phone, hoping to see her sister's name, but 'Dino' flashed on her screen instead. *Shit.*

> 🔵 Dino: Bea, I think it would be best if you found somewhere else to host Next Chapter. Everything's just too complicated, so I'm moving on from Bea Babbage.

'Motherfucker!'

A couple of curious, bleary-eyed faces popped up from behind laptops.

Bea put up her hand in apology, then pointed to her phone and said, 'Clients! Am I right?'

She fell back in her chair, swivelling away from prying eyes. She knew that they had left things on a weird note. But Bea and Dino were constantly on a weird note. She didn't think he would let that get in the way of business. Of her dream. *What the hell am I going to do?* She racked her brain, a familiar tightness returning to her chest. Next Chapter was only a week and a half away, how would she find another suitable location in such a short amount of time? Not to mention what this would mean for the press the event had already received. If people rocked up to the wrong venue it would be a public relations nightmare! This was the absolute last thing she needed. Consumed by a bitter rage she had never known before, she shook her head and clicked her phone to life once more.

🗨 Bea: Thanks a lot, Dino. Thanks a heap for leaving me high and dry NINE DAYS BEFORE THE EVENT!!!!!!! If I didn't think you were impossible and selfish before, I certainly do now!

Two minutes later, her phone lit up again. Bea had begun pacing awkwardly around her small desk and was dizzy with frustration.

🗨 Dino: I'm not being selfish. I'm giving us space.

🗨 Bea: Great. I'll take all the space I can get. And you better not eat a single one of my jelly babies!!

Bea stared at her phone, willing it to stay quiet and light up all at the same time. When it remained mute, she let out a long, exaggerated sigh. *What have I done?* She shouldn't have gone to see Dino last night. Why couldn't she just let sleeping dogs lie?

Swinging her bag over her shoulder, she hobbled down the narrow corridor, cursing Dino all the way to the front door.

🗨 Bea: Liz? Tell me you're almost here.

🗨 Lizzie: I've just finished my meeting. I'm five minutes away.

🗨 Bea: Good. Meet me at Borsch, Vodka and Tears in five.

🗨 Lizzie: Vodka? At this time of day?

🗨 Bea: Trust me. I need it.

'He can't just pull out of Next Chapter like that!,' Lizzie said, sipping on her Diet Coke. They were seated in the corner of the dark empty bar that smelled like beetroots and alcohol.

'It's a disaster, Liz.' Bea took a big gulp of her vodka soda, letting the bubbles pop on her tongue before swallowing down the bitter liquid.

'Okay,' Lizzie said, eyes down, now scrolling through her phone. 'I have a plan.'

Bea nodded. She was eager to hear how Lizzie was going to solve this one.

'I'm thinking a huge event,' Lizzie said, still tapping away at her phone. 'And we'll make it more of a dating thing, you know? I went to this awesome Tinder launch party a few years back and it was epic. Hot, sexy, fun – just the sort of thing you want. No offence, but just books alone can be a bit drab, you know?'

Not this again. 'Well, hot and sexy isn't exactly our angle,' Bea replied.

'That's just the thing, honey. It's not "ours" anymore. It's *yours*! No more Dino means you can make it your own. Less conservative, and a hell of a lot more saucy. We'll dress you up really sexy too. Not slutty sexy, just elegant sexy. I've got this amazing dress in mind. Backless, black, tight. I'll email the designer to see whether we can borrow one for the night. Usually he'd want me to be seen it, but you know, you're family, so we can try. Emailing now!' Lizzie typed quickly into her phone.

Bea watched Lizzie mumble under her breath as she quickly crafted an email, her thumbs dancing across her phone with spitfire precision. She could picture exactly what Lizzie had in mind: red velvet tablecloths, shots flowing, music pumping, a photobooth! The books would become inconsequential, it would just be another excuse to be seen and to maybe get somebody's number. She knew Lizzie wanted Next Chapter to succeed, and she admired her flair, but this just wasn't Bea. And Bea couldn't let the integrity of Next Chapter be affected. She would not be a sellout! Not this time.

'No,' Bea said quietly.

'Nonsense, Bea. It'll be great.' Lizzie continued to type.

'Please, Liz. I said no.'

'What's gotten into you, Bea? I'm just trying to help.' Lizzie's brow was furrowed – well, as furrowed as you could get when your forehead was choked with Botox.

'That's exactly it, Lizzie. Maybe I don't need your help. Not like this. Our whole life, you were always claiming to be helping me get a good boyfriend, a job, a body, a life, when really it's just been you telling me what to do, not listening to who I am or what I want, and me going along with it. And Lizzie, I love you so much, I really do, but I'm not that person anymore. I have to make my own decisions now and do what I think is right,' Bea said, surprising even herself with her honesty and directness.

'I get that, honey. But I'm just looking out for you, you know that, right?'

'I know you are, Liz. I know. But I'm not who you think I am any more. I'm no longer going to be defined by my connections to other people: Lizzie's little sister, Martin's daughter, Cassandra's best friend.' Bea flinched at the name. 'So many women fall into that trap, and I don't want to be like that anymore. I'm the new Bea.' She pointed to her haircut. 'Which is basically the same as old Bea, except she's not afraid anymore.' Bea half-laughed, relieved.

Lizzie looked at Bea for a moment, saying nothing (which was new for her). Her eyes seemed to grow wider, almost as if she was finally seeing her sister for the first time.

'Okay. Okay. I like that. The new-old Bea.'

A new-old Bea that Bea felt more comfortable with. 'Nice to meet you.'

'Lovely to meet you too,' Lizzie replied. 'Has anyone ever told you that you look exactly like my sister?'

59

To: beababbage@gmail.com
From: gerardsmith@gmail.com
Subject: Our books are one of the same

Dear Bea,

I came across your Wanted sign slapped to a tree outside The Little Brunswick Street Bookstore last night. And while I can't help you find the owner, I do own one quite similar. It's covered in the same lowercase annotations and underlines. But instead of *Meeting Oliver Bennett*, my scribbles belong to *Norwegian Wood*.

Unfortunately, I can't take credit for the poignant thoughts that dot its pages, having acquired it in such a state from a little second-hand bookstore in Sassafras. Maybe enquire there?

Enjoy the power of your book and good luck finding its owner!

Regards,

Gerard

60

Helloisthisyourbook

📍 On the hunt

So here's an update for you. I'm dragging my sorry arse all the way to Sassafras because I've been sent a lead from the literary gods/a lovely gentleman who frequented a second-hand bookstore, and picked up a book WITH THE SAME SCRIBBLES AS MINE. Can you believe the odds? Please don't judge me for trekking all the way out to the mountains. I'm desperate. And, as Veronica Roth wrote, 'Desperation can make a person do surprising things.'

109 likes

Comments (32)

gossipqueen89: You go gurl! 👏

Booksontherail: Wowee!! Keep us posted. And please send through a new Mystery Writer quote, I need more worldly wisdom in my life.

StephenPrince: @NoOffenceBut I agree with Veronica Roth! PS Meet me at our favourite Thai place this Sat night at 8pm? 🖤

NoOffenceBut: @StephenPrince, please stop publicising our relationship online.

Sexyboy98: You're hot.

Botboy76: Like my page please.

61

'Excuse me, have you seen this book before?'

Bea was standing in a small bookstore in Sassafras. Situated up in the mountains, it was even icier than in the city. She was wearing her puffer jacket, a red woollen scarf and matching beanie, and her heavy moon boot, and still she found herself shivering.

The older woman standing behind the counter picked up Bea's copy of *Meeting Oliver Bennett* and began flicking through the pages. A pair of purple reading glasses sat on her head, which bobbed up and down as she skimmed various pages; she eventually put them on, allowing her to inspect the inscriptions more carefully.

Bea looked around. The store had a wholesome, antique feel to it and smelled of the rich, woody scent of second-hand books. The shelves were so tightly crammed with a mix of new and old books that they appeared concave, as though they were in a constant state of exhaling.

'I haven't seen this book in a long while,' the woman finally cooed.

Bea jumped, all ears. 'You remember it?'

'Of course. All those beautiful inscriptions, they're a masterpiece in their own right.' The woman smiled fondly. 'Where did you find it?'

'At The Little Brunswick Street Bookstore. Do you have any idea how it could have gotten there?' Bea asked urgently.

The lady shook her head, 'I wish I did, isn't it amazing where books travel to? Almost like they have a mind of their own,' she supposed, closing the book and gently placing it on the counter between them.

'Do you remember who gave the book to you originally?'

'Of course, she was a local.'

She? Bea's heart raced.

'She lived just up the road for years, used to pop by all the time. She was a ravenous reader and loved a good chat!' The woman chuckled.

'You said "lived"? She doesn't live around here anymore? Do you know where she went?'

The woman returned her glasses to the top of her head, her energy fading. 'She passed away not long ago now. It was a big loss for the community. She was a beautiful lady, somebody who really knew how to bring people together.'

Bea was crestfallen, an unexpected grief thumping heavily against her chest. The person behind all of those beautiful thoughts and curiosities couldn't be gone. 'What was her name?'

'Alena. Alena Loris. God, how she used to make me laugh! Not long before she passed, she donated a whole stack of books. There were a couple more that were filled with notes and highlights, just like this one. Exquisite commentary, each telling their own truth. Those ones didn't last long, practically ran out the door when people discovered what was inside. I'm sure I kept one though. It should be here somewhere.' The woman bent down, so all Bea could see were her glasses, balancing unsteadily on the top of her head. She rustled about under the counter. After a minute or so, she stood up, clasping a faded cover in her hand. 'Here we go.' The woman dusted off the book and handed Bea a copy of *The Children Act*.

Bea peeled it open, almost afraid to look. She shifted slightly, placing less weight on her injured ankle. When she saw what was inside, her chest tightened. Just like her copy of *Meeting Oliver Bennett*, the pages were accented by little annotations and frantic underlines in the same delicate handwriting that looped and coiled into each other. Bea's throat felt thick, and her eyes began to well up.

'What is it, dear?' The woman placed her bony hand on Bea's arm.

'Oh, it's stupid. It's just … it probably sounds strange, but I've sort of fallen in love with these scribbles. And I just so desperately wanted to meet who wrote them.' Bea realised that she probably sounded insane. 'To me, they were always the main character of the book. And for some reason, that made me feel like an important character in the world too.'

'That's not silly, dear.'

Bea smiled, grateful for her validation, but her heart was slowly sinking. All this time she had spent searching for her Mystery Writer, for The One at the end of the ball-point pen, and now she was gone? *What have I been wasting my time on?* Bea closed her eyes and tried to imagine Alena Loris. She would have been kind, oh so kind. And she would have smelled like gingerbread. Definitely. The sort of inspirational woman who couldn't care less about what other people thought. The sort of woman Bea aspired to be. *Oh, how I wish I could've met her.*

Opening her eyes and shifting through the pages of the new book again, she stared down at them blankly until realisation hit her. 'Where did she live?'

'Oh gosh, I think it was somewhere near the end of Kenneth Crescent. She once had me over for tea and baklava. If you think the quotes in these books are good, you should've tasted her cooking!'

Bea smiled, lightened by the knowledge that the Mystery Writer had charm. Not that she'd doubted they would. 'Is that far from here?'

'No, just a couple of streets away. You could probably walk it,' the woman said slowly, looking sceptically at Bea's hefty moon boot. 'But I'm pretty sure the family sold the place. There'd be new tenants in there by now.'

Bea ignored the woman's pragmatism. 'What did the place look like?'

'It was small, but something about it reminded me of a humbler version of *Tara*. You know, from—'

'*Gone with the Wind*,' Bea finished her sentence abruptly. She wasn't usually one to pass up an opportunity to discuss Margaret Mitchell's masterpiece, but she was on a mission. 'Can I take this book? I'll pay anything for it! I know it must mean a lot to you,' Bea said in a rush.

The woman appraised Bea, registering her enthusiasm. 'You know what? It's all yours. I think you need it more than I do.' When Bea tried to grab her wallet from her bag, the woman waved her off. 'Consider it a gift from one bonafide bookworm to another.' And she turned around, busying herself with the shelves behind her.

Bea smiled, repeated her thanks, and tried her best to get out of the bookstore as quickly as possible.

Bea perched herself against the trunk of an old jacaranda tree, panting heavily. She had walked as swiftly as her encumbered self could go to Kenneth Crescent, her moon boot dragging stoically behind her. Not believing her luck, she tried to compose herself, worried that any sudden movement would make it all disappear before her very eyes. She must have read Mystery Writer's scribbles over a hundred times, analysing every word, every curve and slope. Looking for hidden meanings and insights into who they were. And now, Bea was so close to finding out more about the true Mystery Writer.

Spying the humble home that sat neatly in the crook of the dead-end street, Bea peeled herself away from the tree and limped towards the fence. Running her fingers along its stout edge, she tried to picture the old lady the woman at the bookshop had described, sitting on the little patio reading her novels and pouring her heart into them as though they were her children. *If only these planks could talk!*

'Can I help you?'

Bea looked up to find an older gentleman staring at her from the property next door. He held a bulging brown paper bag and stared at her with the sort of expression that said, *Do I call the police?*

'Sorry, I was just passing by.' Bea fell over her words, feeling a little foolhardy.

The man continued to eye her suspiciously.

'But I guess, while you're here …' Bea began, trying her luck.

He didn't say anything.

'Have you lived here long?'

'Yes,' clearly a man of few words.

'Alena, the lady who lived next door to you, did you know her?'

'You an old friend or something?'

'You could say that,' Bea said, patting her handbag, which now held both *Meeting Oliver Bennett* and *The Children Act*. 'I found something that belonged to her, and I know she's not around anymore, but I wondered if I might be able to track down a relative, and try and return it to the family.'

'I knew her. But not well.' His mouth twisted, as if he was remembering something unpleasant.

'Oh? What was she like?' Bea tried to sound calm, but she was losing it on the inside.

'She mostly lived on her own. And I'm not much of a chatter. Obviously,' he trailed off, rattling his keys and eyeing his front door.

'You sure you don't remember anything else? What about old mail? Anything ever get sent here accidentally?'

The man scratched his thick whiskers. 'Even if I did have some of her mail, do you think I'd give it to you? You could be some loony for all I know,' he said without a hint of humour. 'Anyway, these beers won't chill themselves.' He gestured to the bag he was holding.

Bea smiled, trying to hide her frustration, and faked a knowing nod. *What an anticlimax.* She turned to go, then stopped. 'Hey!' she called. 'Can I leave my number? In case you remember anything else?'

The man scrutinised her again, his wariness clear as day. After a couple of beats, he shrugged. 'Fine. But don't hold your breath.'

Bea muttered her gratitude and scribbled her number down on an old receipt she found in her wallet.

He took it from her and said, 'Now get outta here, you're giving me the creeps!'

Bea laughed nervously and made her way back down the street. 'Call me, okay? If you remember anything. Anything at all!'

'Nothing. I did a thorough online search, and I couldn't find anybody called Alena Loris. Well, nobody who meets the description of the Sassafras lady,' Bea called out to Zach as he made dinner in the other room. She was nestled in the corner of her couch, legs up, *The Children Act* propped open on her lap, laptop beside her. She had spent the whole afternoon combing each and every little jotting for clues. Zach's five o'clock personal training client had cancelled, so he had taken the opportunity to get to Bea's early and whip up a romantic dinner. 'I've skimmed through the whole of *The Children Act*, and there's nothing obvious jumping out at me. This one doesn't seem to be quite as full of annotations, which surprises me.'

She opened to a page at random and inhaled the scribbles as if they were a drug she couldn't get enough of. Words like *mellifluous* and *hypnotise*, and sentences like *big ideas have small beginnings* jumped off the pages. But she was still just as clueless as ever as to the true motivation and inner workings of the Mystery Writer.

'Aren't you meant to be working on your presentation?' Zach yelled back. He was making zucchini noodles in the kitchen, banging pots and pans, pouring water and grating things. Bea was touched by the gesture, but really, all she wanted was some peace and quiet. And carbs.

'Soon.' Bea said, not tearing her eyes away from *The Children Act*.

Zach walked out of the kitchen, a tea towel slung casually over his shoulder. 'You don't want to blow this work opportunity for the sake of these silly notes. It's not worth it.'

Bea ignored him, taken aback by his abruptness, and continued to read.

'Look at you. You're obsessed. It's taking over your life! You've barely looked me in the eye since I walked through the door,' Zach pleaded

It was true, Bea had hardly acknowledged Zach. Not just tonight, but not properly since her overwhelming run-in with Dino at The Nook. She closed the book and looked up at her boyfriend. Really looked at him. She wanted to give this thing with Zach a proper go, but everything had happened so quickly. She didn't quite know how she had arrived here, with the fake Mystery Writer cooking fake noodles in her kitchen.

'I'm sorry, this is just something I need to get to the bottom of. And I would have hoped you might understand that. Especially after everything we've been through.'

Returning to her place in the book, Bea skimmed to the end of the page and then grabbed her phone, angling it so that she could take a picture of the page for Instagram.

'Jeez, enough with the photos, the Instagram this and the Instagram that,' grumbled Zach as he fell onto the couch next to Bea, grabbing at her phone.

'Zach, stop it! You're ruining the lighting,' Bea whined, less playfully than she had intended. She shuddered at how much she sounded like Lizzie.

Catching her hand in his, Zach delicately pried the phone from her grasp. Bea sighed and crossed her arms firmly across her chest. 'Please, come back to me,' he said softly.

'What are you talking about? I'm here. I'm literally right here next to you.'

'But are you? Are you really present with me? I feel like all you ever think about is work and those damn squiggles. You're consumed by them and I feel like I can't measure up.' Zach ran his hands through his hair, the loose curls springing back into place as his fingers travelled along his scalp. 'I mean, I know I work hard on training my clients and setting up the gym. We both love work, and that's great. I love how driven you are. But this is different. This is too much. I feel stupid for even saying this, but I think I'm jealous of a bloody ballpoint pen.'

Bea put her hand on Zach's knee. They watched as Philip poked his head out of the little hut that sat in the corner of his cage, spotted Zach, hissed and then retreated quickly.

Zach made a hissing noise back at him.

'Zach, I get it,' Bea began, her stomach twisting for a reason she couldn't yet identify. 'I'm sorry, I've just been so swept up in work and the events and all this—' she gestured to the book still open on her lap, '—and, well, you and me … I'm still getting my head around us. Maybe it's all just starting to get to me a little.'

Zach blinked quickly, clearly not wanting to hear her doubt. He shook his head, interrupting Bea before she could say anything more. 'You know I love you, right? I just hate having to share you all the time,' he said, leaning in to kiss her lightly on the lips.

Softening under his touch, she kissed him back, hard, until he was on top of her. Neither of them spoke, only breathing heavily and running their hands up and down each other's everywheres. The only time Bea felt like they were on the same page was when they were in this exact position. But tonight, Bea's head wasn't quite focused on the beautiful man on top of her. She was thinking about what Zach had just told her. Maybe she did have to let things go. Maybe she had to bring herself back from the depths of the pages and start living in reality. *I can't exist in the margins forever*, she told herself in an attempt to ease the blinding disappointment that rested heavily on her shoulders. Or maybe the margins were the only safe place for her to belong.

62

Bea sculled an Uber Eats–delivered strong skinny latte from The Nook, then placed the cup on the kitchen bench. Somehow the coffee didn't taste quite as good without one of Dino's signature quotes scrawled across the cup. It was early afternoon and she was yet to leave the house. Having wasted far too much time trying to decipher the annotations in *The Children Act*, and 'kissing and making up' with Zach, she was paying for it now. She had been ferociously prepping all day for her big presentation with Mia and Janine, trying to play catch-up.

She stared in the mirror as she smoothed down her hair. The deep, purplish bags that weighed down each of her eyes were now covered, somewhat indiscreetly, with a slick layer of concealer, and her lips were painted a bright red (an attempt to distract onlookers from said weary complexion). She smiled at her reflection, baring her teeth in an exaggerated expression. *You can do this,* she told herself, pushing thoughts of disagreements and make-up sex with Zach and stone-cold silence from Dino to the back of her mind. Now was not the time to focus on confusing feelings. Now was the time to nail her presentation and win over her client.

She slid on her I'm-a-professional black pea coat as she bent over Philip's cage, kissing the sleeping ferret goodbye on his furry forehead.

Bea sat in the yellow boardroom of her coworking office, tapping her moon boot impatiently. She glanced at her watch – 3.50pm. Only ten minutes until the ladies from Thelma & Clarke arrived.

'Sorry we're late,' Martha said, bursting into the boardroom with Ruth, carrying a tray of coffees. Martha wore a knee-length velvet dress (like an absolute boss), paired with a black blazer. Her face was framed by a ginger wig cropped neatly at her shoulders. Ruth wore a checked jumper with a white shirt underneath and a small corgi brooch pinned to her collar. The two of them looked at each other and laughed at some unspoken joke.

Bea watched Ruth, who had only just recovered from the disappointment of Bea not bringing Philip to work, grab a croissant from the pile on the table only to see Martha swat her hand away, reminding her they were for the clients. In this moment, Bea felt lucky to have friends who had been selflessly helping her, for free, when she felt so out of her depth. Friends who cared for her with no hidden agenda.

'Now, remember to smile. In business, there is no finish line, so enjoy this journey!' Ruth briskly tore off a piece of Danish and shoved it in her mouth, and Martha looked less than impressed.

'God, I feel a bit sick, Bea flicked the remote control that connected to the projector, testing it for the hundredth time.

'Stop fretting. You've got this, Bea,' Martha said as she removed a notebook and pen from her bag and placed them on the table in front of her. 'Oh, by the way, your speed dating event is next week, right?'

'Don't remind me,' Bea grumbled. She was yet to find a new space for her event.

'Well, I found you a bar, if you're interested. My friend owns a little place in West Melbourne called Willows & Wine. It's cute and rustic and one of the walls is lined with a bookshelf. He said he'll rent it to you free of charge for the night if you push drink sales,' Martha said, reapplying a hot pink layer of lipstick, using a pocket mirror as her guide.

'Really? Martha! You're my knight in shining armour!' Relief washed over Bea. *Everything might just work out. It had to.*

'It's nothing, really. Now, let's go over what we're saying today. Does everyone know their parts?' Martha shuffled the papers in front of her, getting down to business. Bea and Ruth nodded. But, before they could say 'content marketing strategy', Bea's phone pinged with a message from the receptionist:

> 🔘 They're here!

Bea shot up from her chair and rushed out of the boardroom, limping to the front of the building in her coolest, I've-got-this hobble.

She found Mia hovering in the poky foyer, a certain calmness to her. Standing next to her was the glamorous Janine Partridge wearing a grey power suit and a chunky emerald green necklace. She exuded authority.

'Mia, Janine, nice to see you both again,' Bea said, extending her hand. 'I'll just take you to the boardroom, where my two consultants, Ruth Lester and Martha Peters, are waiting.' Bea led the women down the narrow hallway, listening to Janine's heels click formidably behind her.

As soon as they entered the room, Ruth and Martha stood up, shaking each of the women's hands. Bea walked to the front of the room and turned on the projector.

'You can have some croissants. They're for you.' Ruth pointed towards the pastries, a smattering of crumbs on her cheek. Janine and Mia smiled kindly.

Bea flicked on her presentation, cleared her throat and took a sip of water. *Keep your shit together, Babbage!* She thanked Mia and Janine for coming, then ran through the agenda for the meeting, finding her feet and beginning to enjoy herself.

'Who's the main character from Cecilia Beechworth's newest novel?' Bea asked and looked around the room.

'Rachel Belton,' Mia and Janine both replied.

'No. It's Cecilia Beechworth.' *Pause for effect.* 'Cecilia has become the main character, the leading lady, of her own novel. People pick up a Beechworth novel to read her latest work, whatever it is, whoever it's about. Others won't read it, just because it's a Beechworth, even though it's a brilliant story. So, how do we strip all that back and let her characters – Rachel, Neville and Gloria – do the talking, while still intriguing existing crime fiction lovers, but also enticing those who might never consider reading a mystery at all?'

Janine scribbled something in her notebook and Mia gave Bea two subtle thumbs up.

'Picture this.' Bea flicked to the next slide, a book with a metallic cover and a bold green title. 'What's missing from this cover?'

'The author,' Mia replied.

'Exactly.' Bea beamed. 'Imagine if we were to sell Cecilia's books like this. The story will be as brilliant and addictive as usual, and of course there will be lots of hype about it, but we won't tell anyone who the author is,' she said, flicking to the next slide, which featured newspaper headlines.

'We'll run a press campaign: "Who is the mystery author? The biggest mystery of this book is – who wrote it?" We'll let the protagonist be the real protagonist again, the setting be prominent – but the main character? The leading ladies and men? They're every person who's brave enough to pick up a copy of this book and read it without any pre-conceptions defining what they should think, or who they should be. Those who become detectives in their own narrative – on the hunt for the person who wrote this story that changed their world. You see, by removing Cecilia's name from the book, we'll in turn, let our entire audience become part of the story.' Bea took a deep breath.

'I can see publications like *The Age*, or even *Cosmopolitan*, going crazy for this campaign.' She flicked to the next slide. 'Then, one week later, once hype is at its absolute peak and people are tearing out their hair wondering who the mystery author is, we'll reveal it's the legendary Cecilia Beechworth. It'll be a media explosion!' Bea waved her hands in the air to signify the magnitude of the idea. 'But more than that. It'll change people's attitudes. Allow them to be more courageous, more confident in their reading choices. And once we've done that, we've won them over for good.'

Bea then sat down as Ruth took the stage, taking the remote from Bea's hand.

'Now, let me talk a little bit about market research,' Ruth began.

Bea, Ruth and Martha hovered outside the boardroom door, waiting for Janine and Mia to gather their belongings. As far as Bea could tell, the presentation had gone well, but she had no idea what Janine was thinking; she'd maintained the same cold, somewhat vague and judgemental smile with which she'd arrived. *Please don't hate it*, Bea thought, nervously cracking her knuckles. Martha rubbed Bea's back and Bea looked at her appreciatively.

After an excruciating wait, Janine burst from the boardroom, Mia on her tail. Janine took Bea's hand and held it firmly.

'Thank you very much for your presentation, Bea. I am impressed. Thelma & Clarke will be using your agency for future projects.' Janine let go of her hand, shook Martha's and Ruth's swiftly, and went to leave, Mia following closely behind.

As soon as they were out of sight, Bea looked at Martha and Ruth and the three of them let out a squeal.

'They loved us!' Bea exclaimed, hands in the air.

'They loved you, darling,' Martha cooed.

'I think they loved me too. Janine couldn't stop talking about how much she adored Diana's Muesli!'

Bea clasped her hands together, beaming at the women before her. 'I really couldn't have done any of this without both of you.'

'You're a natural, Bea,' Ruth replied.

'I take it that it went well?' a deep, familiar voice asked.

'Zach? What are you doing here?' Bea asked. He had appeared next to them as if out of thin air.

'I couldn't help myself! I had to hear firsthand how the presentation went. I've been hanging around waiting for it to finish. Tell me everything.' He kissed Bea on the cheek and her heart stopped. She suddenly felt hot.

She began filling him in, rushing over the details, desperate for some air.

'Stop being modest, Bea. It went fantastically!' Martha smiled before introducing herself to Zach.

'Bea, I knew you'd smash it. We have to celebrate!' Zach said, pulling Bea towards him and hugging her around the shoulders. Ruth and Martha nodded in agreement.

'How's that for timing, I'm off to get a drink myself!' Sunday appeared in the corridor, so there were now five of them squeezed into the tight space. She looked flushed and energised as she leaned against the wall to face Bea directly. 'But what are we celebrating?' she asked.

'Oh, just us kicking goals in a big presentation!' Bea shrugged.

'Way to go, Bea!' Sunday exclaimed, practically 'whoop wooing' on the spot. 'Well, in that case, drinks are on me. And I know just the place.'

The group smiled back at Sunday, eyebrows raised in anticipation.

'The Nook!'

At the mention of the café, the group's enthusiasm noticeably wilted. Unperturbed, or unaware, Sunday carried on 'Dan Murphy's was having a killer sale on Kahlúa and vodka, so I stocked up. I stupidly left them in the pantry at our last WIP meeting and keep forgetting to pick them up. And if this isn't the time for espresso martinis, I don't know when is!'

'I'm not sure it's a good idea for me to go to The Nook just now,' Bea practically whispered, looking everywhere but at Zach.

Sunday looped her arm around Bea's arm, forcing Bea to unlace her firmly crossed ones. 'Don't worry, hon, Dino won't be there. He's at some slam poetry thing tonight. Plus, I make a killer espresso martini!'

'You didn't happen to purchase any gin, did you?' Ruth asked, giving Bea another excuse not to make eye contact with Zach. 'My drink of choice is a Dubonnet with a dash of gin, same as the Queen.' She smiled proudly. 'I always carry a flask of the fortified wine just in case the opportunity for a stiff drink should arise!'

Sunday stared at Ruth for a moment. 'I might have some strawberry liqueur handy? I can make something that looks like Dubonnet?'

'We'll take it!' Martha interjected, pulling Ruth into a side hug. 'Plus, I'm British, so how much more royal can you get?' she said, nudging Ruth with her hip.

Zach looked at Bea, rubbing his hands across his stubble. 'It's your call, Bea.'

Bea sighed, trying to get back in touch with the high she'd felt only moments ago. She looked from Zach to the three ladies she had come to call her friends all of whom stared back at her, smiles wide. 'Ah, what the hell. Let's do this!'

'Well, you heard the woman. We're going to The Nook! Ladies and gentleman, follow me!' Sunday shouted, walking ahead as she plugged in her earphones and turned the music up so loud the others could hear the Spice Girls.

63

As soon as Bea entered The Nook, she felt nauseous. The familiar scent of the place, which had once soothed her, now jarred, reminding her of the intense moment she had shared with Dino. So much had changed since then.

Zach squeezed her hand three times, drawing her to him. She didn't squeeze back, pretending, instead, to be distracted by a loose thread on her blazer. Ruth and Martha trailed happily behind Sunday. Entering the kitchen one by one, they crammed into the tight space. Thankfully, just as Sunday had promised, Dino was nowhere to be seen. Bea was both relieved and just a touch disappointed.

'Aha!' Sunday exclaimed, holding a bottle of vodka above her head triumphantly. 'Right where I left it!'

The group cheered. Zach pulled mugs from behind Bea, sliding them down the counter towards Sunday. Before Bea knew it, everybody had a mug of espresso martini and they were clinking them together. The kitchen was alight with laughter and merriment.

'You did it, babe,' Zach whispered in Bea's ear, his breath tickling her neck. 'I'm so proud.' He leaned in and kissed her on the forehead.

'This drink is missing something,' Ruth said, squinting down at her martini, which, after much cajoling, Sunday had talked her into trying.

'Don't be ridiculous,' Sunday retorted quickly. 'If there's one thing I know how to make, it's an espresso martini.'

'No, it's definitely missing something,' Ruth repeated, looking to Bea, of all people, for backup.

They all glanced down at the foamy beige liquid in their mugs and took another swig.

'Tastes damn good to me,' Zach said.

'See?' Sunday said, satisfied.

'Coffee beans! That's it! It's missing coffee beans,' Ruth cried. 'It should have at least two to three coffee beans, preferably placed in an equilateral triangle.'

Sunday let out a long sigh. 'Don't be ridiculous. It doesn't need that showy nonsense. It's fine as is.'

'I really don't think it's showy nonsense, Sunday,' Ruth replied, placing her mug firmly on the bench. 'It's simply protocol.'

'You know what, why don't I just grab a handful of coffee beans. Keep everybody happy!' Bea said, freeing herself from Zach's arms and squeezing out of the kitchen.

She eased her way behind the counter, running her fingers across its familiar timber surface. Reaching the coffee machine, she leaned over and picked out a handful of coffee beans from the large plastic container that sat on top of the grinder. It was only when she turned to join the party again that she spotted it – Dino's notebook. The same notebook that Dino would curl himself around, pouring God knows what into. Its cracked spine seemed to call to her.

She took a step to the right, dragging herself backwards without taking her eyes off its worn, bound pages. Taking a quick look at the kitchen, she stepped forward almost as if the notebook had changed the direction of the Earth's magnetic pull.

Her head knew that she shouldn't, that it would be a huge invasion of privacy and totally out of line. But her heart couldn't let her ignore this rare opportunity to discover more about the elusive, closed-off Dino. Checking again that nobody could see her, she dropped the beans on the counter and swiped up the little book. Bea flipped open to a random page, running her fingers along the indents left behind by each letter. She threw another sheepish look towards the kitchen. Bea considered putting the notebook back where she had found it, but curiosity overrode her guilt, and she dared to take another look. Turning to the next page, her eyes caught on a compact poem which had been hastily marked along the edge of the page.

I kissed her.
I yearned for her.
I chose her.
She kissed me.
She yearned for me.
She chose him.

'Dino,' she breathed, quickly turning to another page. There she found another poem, this one titled, 'Sunflowers'.

Dancing sun upon your face,
You light the world in all your grace.
Standing tall ablaze in colour,
I long for you through every hour.
Golden petals everywhere,

> *Your scent floats softly in the air.*
> *I pick you up, my spirit lifts,*
> *More precious than a thousand gifts.*

She flipped back to the start of the book, eager to take in as much as possible before being sprung. In her haste, she fumbled and the book fell open to the inside cover.

She froze. *It couldn't be.*

Closing her eyes, she willed what she hoped she was seeing to be true. Cautiously opening one eye at a time, she looked back down at the brief inscription written inside the top left corner of the cover. Hardly believing what she was seeing, her eyes raced across the words over and over again. The words made of letters that curled and looped into each other, like a horde of eager children trying to get to the front of a line. The handwritten letters that ignored capitals. The handwritten letters that she had come to know so well. That she would recognise anywhere. The handwritten letters that belonged to Alena.

> *my dearest grover,*
> *these pages will not judge. write here what you long to speak aloud.*
> *i will always love you.*
> *gran.*

Dino's grandmother is Alena Loris?

The same grandmother that Dino spoke of with such warmth. The woman who had nurtured Dino, loved Dino, encouraged Dino to realise his potential.

Bea's breath caught as she processed what she'd just unearthed. She adjusted her footing, wishing the throb in her injured leg would dissipate. The injury that she had sustained because of this mad detective journey she had been on, which had taken her all over Melbourne, only to lead her to the very place, to the very person who had always seemed to slip through her fingers like sand.

Bea racked her brain, thinking of all the times she and Dino had discussed the notes in the book. Had she ever actually shown him the writing on the page? Could he have missed a major clue that would have triggered some recognition of his grandmother? But she kept coming up blank. And then, once she had thought the book belonged to Zach, Dino had been borderline agitated whenever she brought it up. It was almost as if he refused to learn more about Zach, or ever acknowledge that there could be some goodness to him. She wished she had pushed him more, forced Dino to be more present with her, more engaged. Anger tinged with sorrow filled with bittersweet relief coursed through her.

'What the hell are you doing?'

Bea jumped, dropping the book. *Dino.* Taking a moment to compose herself, she braced herself with a deep breath before turning around.

'What are you doing here, Bea?' Dino repeated, glancing at the rectangular hole in the kitchen wall, through which he could see flashes of torsos mingling together and hear the sound of overlapping laughter.

'We're celebrating. Our pitch was a huge success,' Bea said. She couldn't look at him; she needed more time to digest all of this. 'What are *you* doing here?' Her eyes were welling up. *Not now, Bea.*

'I left Agatha's toy flamingo behind and you know how she is with that thing. She's been stress eating like crazy all afternoon. Not that I should need an excuse to swing by my own café.'

'What's taking you so long, babe?' Zach called. When he entered the room and spied Bea and Dino standing opposite each other, he paused. 'Dino,' Zach said curtly, nodding his head slightly. 'Might be time to bust a move, Bea?'

'I was just going,' Dino said, his tone changing. 'Make yourselves at home.' He bent to pick up Agatha Christie's mangled toy and pulled his keys from his pocket.

Bea watched as he took deliberate steps towards the door, the tension in his body apparent. A heaviness descended on Bea. She wanted to say something, to call after him, reveal what she had found, knowing what it would mean to him, but she couldn't. Not while Zach was there.

'I hope we can put all this to bed finally,' Zach said, out of nowhere.

Dino stopped, rolled his shoulders back before turning to face Zach. 'What are you talking about?'

'Bea and I are together now.'

'Uh huh.' Dino's vague response seemed to say everything.

'She doesn't love you. And she's sick of you pining over her,' Zach said bitterly.

Bea shot a look at him. 'Zach. Please.'

'Really? Did she tell you that herself?' Dino asked.

'She didn't have to.' Zach took a step closer to Dino. 'I know her well enough, I *love* her enough, to be able to see it for myself.'

Bea looked nervously from Zach to Dino to the three faces that stared not so discreetly through the hole in the wall. Martha's mouth was agape. Sunday's eyes were wide as she drank from her mug. Ruth bit into a muffin, a little disinterested.

'Why don't you let her speak for herself?' Dino replied tensely.

Zach looked expectantly towards Bea, almost as if he had just remembered she was standing there. Bea shifted anxiously, wishing she hadn't left her espresso martini behind.

'Let's not do this here,' said Bea, suddenly irritable. She couldn't get into this. Not now.

'Bea, just tell him. Tell him we're together and committed to each other and that won't be changing any time soon,' Zach stated almost condescendingly. His calm demeanour now a distant memory.

'Come on, man. She said she doesn't want to do this,' Dino said, sensing Bea's discomfort.

'No. You have to hear this, so you can finally back off. Is it me or him?' Zach asked, eerily blank.

'Zach, leave her alone.'

'It's him,' Bea said, so quietly she wasn't sure whether anyone had heard. *It's him,* she thought to herself again. *Of course it's him.*

'What?' Zach snapped.

'I'm so sorry, Zach. I didn't mean to feel like this. I've been trying not to. But it's Dino. I want it to be him,' Bea said, tearily.

Zach's whole body tensed. Bea glanced at his eyes, the only part of him that was not rigid, but saw only heartbreak. Her stomach twisted. She so wanted to reach out to Zach, to hug him, to tell him it would all be okay, that she was so sorry. But she knew she couldn't. She had to stay strong. To finally say what she had wanted to for so long.

'Fucking hell, Bea.' Zach stormed out of The Nook.

Bea looked at Dino, her heart completely and utterly on her sleeve. *It's you. Oh, how glad I am that it's you.* A small smile appeared on her lips, just as Dino shook his head.

'Jesus, Bea. It's too late for this,' he said, so scathingly it broke Bea's heart in two. And then he followed Zach out the door.

Leaving Bea completely and utterly alone.

64

'**D**ino, please don't go,' Bea called, about to run after him, but before she could get anywhere, she felt a strong grip holding her back.

'Let him go,' Sunday said into her ear.

'No. No. I need to tell him.' Bea tried to escape Sunday's hold, but she wouldn't surrender. Instead, Sunday pulled her into an embrace, just like Bea had done to Cassandra on her wedding day so many months ago. But rather than fighting as Cassandra had, Bea fell into Sunday's arms, burying her face into her chest, tears streaming, and struggling to breathe.

'It's alright.' Sunday rubbed Bea's back soothingly. Martha and Ruth stood awkwardly beside them. Ruth was breathing particularly loudly and Martha was cooing variations of 'It's going to be okay', over and over.

'It's not okay,' Bea gasped, embarrassed by her tears. 'Not at all. I've been such a fool. I've been so fixated on finding the perfect *something*, when really it's been right in front of me all along. *He's* been here all along. I've just been too afraid to see it,' Bea whimpered, head still pressed into Sunday's chest.

'That's normal, Bea. We're all afraid. Some of us are just better at hiding it,' Ruth said solemnly.

'I have to tell him.' Bea pulled her face from Sunday's now-damp T-shirt. Mascara ran down her cheeks.

'Maybe he needs some time, Bea,' Sunday said.

'Not about me. About her,' Bea replied, thinking of Alena Loris. 'He deserves that at least. Even if I don't deserve him.'

Sunday nodded, feigning understanding, as if to question Bea would send her over the edge. She released her arms and Bea apologised to the three of them for ruining the evening, and walked out the blue door into the crisp Melbourne air.

🗨 Bea: Dino, please. I know you don't want to talk. I know my timing is terrible. But I need to tell you something really important. Bigger than us. Bigger than all of this. I need to see you.

🗨 Bea: Dino, please.

🗨 Bea: Goddammit, Dino! You're so stubborn.

🗨 Bea: For fuck's sake, Dino.

🗨 Bea: Sorry. Just please call me back.

Despite it being close to midnight, Bea, curled on her couch, pressed send on her latest message to Dino. She so desperately needed to tell him what she knew: that his grandmother was the person she had been looking for all along. That her words were magic. And that Bea owned a portal into her soul. When he didn't answer – again – she threw her phone down and opened up *Meeting Oliver Bennett* and read a few notes. This Mystery Writer knew Dino.

She picked up a pink marker from the coffee table and highlighted a line.

please don't turn your back on me.

Bea wondered who Alena was talking about. She dogeared the page and continued reading.

how can something so small fill my whole world?

Could she be speaking about Dino? She dogeared that page too, wishing Dino was here.

scowls won't cover that big heart of yours.
the gift of life.
you were full of rare smiles.

Bea tabbed page after page. How could she have been so blind? This book wasn't filled with romantic love – it was a love letter to Alena's family. To her grandson, the most important man in her world. Suddenly, Bea was seeing Dino in a completely different light. Those black eyes were never angry, they were filled with wonder and anguish and wisdom. His lips weren't dubious, they were concealing heartbreak and a yearning to be loved. His tattered shoes, baggy denim jeans and loose shirts weren't messy, they were an ode to giving everything a second chance. And his tattoos. Oh, his tattoos. They were another way of telling his beautiful story.

She flipped a page.

She made a mental note of all the things she wanted to ask Dino about his grandmother. *But what if he didn't want to know about this? What if he never answered her calls again?*

Then a thought dawned on her. Grabbing her discarded phone, she brought up Dino's Twitter account, the closest he would ever get to entering what he thought was the inauthentic world of social media. She scrolled back in time a few years.

🐦 **CuppaDino:** Roses are red, violets are blue, Trump for president? That's some kind of sick voodoo!

🐦 **CuppaDino:** Make America great again? Bitch please.

🐦 **CuppaDino:** Come to The Dead Poet's Society @8pm to see me slam.

🐦 **CuppaDino:** Anyone know where I can buy bamboo cutlery for takeaway? Fitting out my new cafe, @TheNook, and I'll be damned if we won't use recycled goods!

🐦 **CuppaDino:** Date night with Gran!

And there was a photo of Dino, leaner with slightly longer hair, standing next to a delicate-featured lady, her skin olive toned and leathery. Her eyes were wide, brown and gleaming, as if she had seen the whole world.

'Alena,' Bea whispered. She couldn't believe it. There, standing next to the man she adored, was her Mystery Writer. And she was more exquisite than Bea could have ever imagined.

Bea felt high on the new knowledge. Greedily, she scrolled deeper into Dino's Twitter feed. Photos of him with friends, excerpts from poetry, more ironic political retweets and pithy book reviews. There were a few more photos of Dino with his grandmother, and Bea stopped at each one, taking time to analyse them, hungry for more information. Despite Alena being almost a foot shorter than her grandson, Dino seemed to look up at her.

Bea stopped at a photo of Dino, Alena and another woman, ice-creams in their hands. 'Three generations of waffle-cone lovers,' the caption read. Bea looked at the unfamiliar woman. Dino's mother? She was beautiful. And so young. Tall and thin like her son, she wore a white singlet that bared her toned midriff, and a flowing orange skirt. Dino leaned into his grandmother, while his mum's hand rested loosely on his shoulder. Alena and Dino's mother both smiled, almost wildly, while Dino was caught mid-expression, his blurred face showing the wisp of a joke just shared. Something about the carefreeness of it, the uninhibited nature of each of them, mesmerised her. She peered at the screen, looking closer, tracing the arches of each smile, glance and posture, until she drifted to sleep.

💬 Zach: Bea, I'm coming over shortly to pick up my things.

Bea woke to the sound of her phone vibrating. It was eight am. *When did I fall asleep?* Drool dotted her mouth and her hair felt rough and untamed. She read the text from Zach again and her stomach dropped at the thought of seeing him. Tapping away from it quickly, she scanned her phone for any response from Dino. Nothing. She texted him again for good measure and then dragged herself from the couch to the bathroom to brush her furry teeth.

As she spritzed perfume on her wrist, her doorbell rang. *Zach. Shit.* Bea wasn't ready for this. She felt awful about the position she'd put him in last night. It wasn't fair of her to humiliate him in front of so many people. *But then, didn't he do the same to me just months ago?* She pushed the thought away. An eye for an eye would not be her trademark move. And she knew this break-up wasn't about that. She quickly gargled some mouthwash and then ran to the door, took a deep breath, and opened it.

'Zach. I'm so sorry,' she said instantly.

Still wearing last night's clothes, Zach glared at her, then entered the apartment without saying a word. He walked into her bedroom and Bea followed. Opening cupboard doors, he grabbed blindly at his belongings, stuffing them into the duffel bag slung over his shoulder.

'Zach, please,' Bea said. 'Let's sit and talk.'

'I'm not here to talk. I'm just here to get my things,' Zach snarled. His voice was icy.

'I'm so sorry, Zach. I never meant to hurt you.'

Zach zipped up his bag. 'Well, you did, Bea. I am hurt.' He looked up at her, his eyes watery.

Bea faltered. 'I know, and I'm so sorry, Zach. I owe you an explanation. I really did love our time together. But it just wasn't the same. It wasn't like before,' Bea stammered.

'You didn't even give us a chance.'

'But I did. I gave us one hell of a chance. I just feel like we sort of fell into this without thinking of the repercussions. And I went along with it because I think I loved being loved. As terrible as that sounds.' Bea was trying so desperately hard to be honest, not just to Zach, but to herself. Now, she would not shy away from the truth.

'I did love you, Bea. With all my heart. And you trampled all over it like it was nothing. Like I was nothing.' Zach violently slung the duffel bag back over his shoulder and walked towards the front door.

'Jesus, Zach. Like you trampled all over my heart when you were paid to date me?' Bea replied, hating herself for sounding like a petulant child.

'I thought we had moved past that, Bea?'

'I don't think I'll ever be able to move past that.'

Zach looked up at her again, a tear trickling down his face. 'If only things were different, Bea. I guess we've both been hurt now.'

'I guess so.'

Zach twisted the doorknob, ready to leave her life forever. But before he did, he turned around one last time.

'Was it ever really me, or was it always him?' he asked, shuddering at the mere thought of Dino.

Bea swallowed, hard. 'I—' she began, her heart breaking.

'That's what I thought.' He slammed the door and was gone.

65

Bea closed her copy of *Meeting Oliver Bennett* and sighed. She held it to her chest, hugging it as if it were a person before placing it on her bookshelf and walking to the bathroom. She had decided that this would be the last time she would read it. It wasn't hers to keep, not now that she knew for sure that it had belonged to Alena. And now, well, it belonged to Dino.

It had been a week since Zach had left Bea's house and she had last messaged Dino. When Bea's incessant messages enticed no response from Dino, she eventually halted contact. Perhaps it was space that Dino needed. So far her silence had been met with more silence. Bea had heard nothing from Dino and it was making her crazy.

As she brushed her teeth, staring at her reflection, the cool realisation that she couldn't hang on forever struck her. *It's time to move on.*

She had thought that Dino was her person, but she was no longer his. She had lost the man who filled her days with sunlight – well, sunlight tinged with slight disinterest and black humour. The man who challenged her and encouraged her to consider things from a different perspective. But he had turned his back on her when she was finally able to open up. Remembering this detail, Bea couldn't help but feel as though he had never really liked her like that at all.

Returning her toothbrush to its holder, Bea closed her eyes. *It's time to move on*, she chanted silently. She had to. Because, quite frankly, she was sick of feeling sad. She had moved to Melbourne for a fresh start. And she had gotten it. She had new friends, a new job and a new passion project. *So what if I've totally screwed it up in the love department?* If she'd learnt anything these past few months, it was that she did not need a man to complete her – she did the completing all on her own. Yet while she tried to practice mindfulness and gratitude and all that wishy-washy positivity bullshit, she couldn't quite get her heart to listen.

It's time to move on. It's time to move on. It's time to move on.

Her phone beeped. Her Uber driver had arrived with a freshly brewed The Nook coffee. She threw on a woollen jumper, slipped on some ugg boots and rushed downstairs to greet Savinay, her caffeine saviour.

'So you really don't think he's going to show?' Lizzie asked, knife in one hand, phone in the other. Lizzie was staying (uninvited) at Bea's for the night, promising to make the Next Chapter event a huge success, after the last disaster. She had (again, unwelcomely) organised a group of ex-*Bachelor* contestants and D-grade Instagram influencers to come to the event, promising that this time they would definitely show up, despite the lack of any real chance of finding a mate.

With only a couple of hours to go, Bea and Lizzie were standing side by side in Bea's kitchen, arranging fruit and cheese platters for the evening. Bea was wearing black yoga pants and a loose grey hoodie while Lizzie was, as usual, overdressed in black leather pants, a glittery tank top, red lipstick and wedges.

'I doubt it.' Bea sliced a strawberry decisively in half.

Lizzie grabbed Bea by the shoulders, her eyes wide with excitement and anticipation. 'You can't give up. You have to make him come!' *Once a hopeless Bachelor romantic, always a hopeless Bachelor romantic.* 'Come on,' Lizzie continued, squeezing Bea's cheeks a little too firmly. 'You know what Osher always used to say: you've got to fight for the one you love! Otherwise the love of your life will pass you by and before you know it, you're a crazy cat lady with an unhealthy obsession with erotic fiction.'

'Please, Liz, haven't we evolved past the spinster stereotypes? I've just about been single my whole adult life, and I'm doing perfectly fine.' Bea brushed her sister away. 'I'm moving on. He's not going to come round. He's too stubborn and it's all just gotten too complicated. I am making myself okay with moving on from him, and I'm committed to weaning myself off his coffees eventually,' Bea said, only half-believing herself.

'You're still getting his coffees delivered? Bea, that's ridiculous!'

'Don't worry Liz, I won a week's worth of free Uber Eats deliveries.'

'I'm not worried about that, just go in and see him.'

'Lizzie, I'm moving on,' Bea replied firmly.

'Fine. Be that way. Consider this my first attempt at respecting your boundaries, or whatever,' Lizzie grumbled, and resumed carving up slices of watermelon, slamming her knife down angrily on the cutting board. 'But what about the book? Are you at least going to give that to him? He deserves to know about his grandma.'

'I know. I've decided. First thing tomorrow morning, if I still haven't heard from him, I'm just going to leave it outside The Nook for him to find.'

Lizzie raised her eyebrows.

'I know I wanted to tell him in person, but I can't hold onto this knowledge any longer. It's not fair.'

Lizzie shook her head – which was never a good sign, as she hated, *hated*, doing anything that would risk unsettling her perfectly coiffed curls – and returned to her chopping.

Bea attempted a smile. She wasn't going to let anything get her down. Tonight was the night that she had been working so hard for. She would get excited. She would be okay that Dino wasn't there.

'These Bachie friends of yours, they won't be too wild, will they? We need to keep it all above board, Liz. You did update them and tell them that this is *not* their typical speed dating night, right? Plus, I promised Martha we wouldn't make a mess of her friend's bar,' Bea said, slicing a piece of brie and shoving it in her mouth.

Martha had followed through with her offer, and Willows & Wine, which was significantly bigger than The Nook, was locked in as the venue. She had received close to thirty emails requesting tickets, and an additional twenty-five more had clicked 'interested' on the Facebook event.

'Yes, yes, don't worry. It'll be uber chilled, honey.' Lizzie winked at Bea, and Bea rolled her eyes. Lizzie would describe Miss Clavel from *Madeline* as laid-back.

'And Zach? He definitely won't be there will he?' Lizzie said, poking Bea with the end of the spoon she had been using to mix a bowl of berries.

'God, I hope not. I couldn't bear to see him again, not after seeing how defeated he was as he lugged the last of his stuff out of my apartment,' Bea said.

'Good riddance, I say. I never trusted him. Although I have taken on board what you said about the whole flirting-with-me incident and my tendency to read into things a little too much. Maybe you were right.' Lizzie said, adjusting Bea's top. Bea smiled. This was big for Lizzie. She had never once admitted that somebody wasn't completely infatuated with her.

Lizzie rubbed her sister's arm, then glanced at her diamond-encrusted watch and squealed. 'Oh my gosh, Bea. You better get a wriggle on. We need to be there in an hour. I'll finish this up.' Lizzie gestured to the half-done platters in front of her.

Maybe it wasn't so bad having her sister stay at her apartment again. She went to her room, threw off her clothes – dumping them in the corridor carelessly – and stepped into the bathroom, ready to freshen up before her big event.

66

Bea nervously pushed open the door of Willows & Wine. She surveyed the bar's interior, mentally rearranging the room. After greeting the bar's owner, who turned out to be a diehard Jodi Picoult fan and was thrilled to be hosting the event, Bea and Lizzie went about transforming the space. They rearranged the twenty-five two person tables so that they ran parallel to each other down one side of the room and placed sleek, golden stands (which Bea had won, obviously) with a note on each one, which read 'your favourite book goes here'. Near the fireplace in the corner, which crackled, warming the room, Bea trailed posters on which passages from some of her most cherished books were written in elegant cursive.

Bea was putting the last of the small jars of sunflowers in the crevices of the bar's wall-long bookshelf, when the front door opened.

'Beatrix!' Ruth and Philip, who sported a tiny polka dot bow tie, had arrived. 'You've done a remarkable job, Beatrix,' she said, waving her copy of *Victoria & Abdul* in the air. 'You should be very proud of yourself.'

Bea smiled nervously, stepping back and admiring her handiwork. 'Really?'

'Really.'

Not long after, Martha and Sunday arrived, gushing at the room and congratulating Bea on her decorative flair.

Lizzie nudged her way to the front of the group. 'You must be Bea's friends! I think I've met some of you before, at Bea's previous events. For those of you who don't know, I'm Lizzie, Bea's sister. You might recognise me as the runner-up from season two of *The Bachelor*.' Lizzie gave each of them a peck on the cheek. 'And who might this be?' Lizzie asked, bending down to get a closer look at Philip.

'This is Philip. Named after the prince,' Ruth said bluntly. She was still recovering from Lizzie's impromptu and unnecessary kiss.

'Oh. I see. Is he a weasel?'

'Technically, yes. He's a ferret.'

'So, Liz. What's happening with *The Bachelor* contestants?' Bea interrupted before a full-blown discussion of the Mustelid animal family erupted before her.

'Oh, yes. Lily and Scarlett are on their way! Instagram ready!' Lizzie chirped.

As Bea laughed, the door opened, and the trickle of guests began to enter.

Bea had never seen so many book lovers crammed into one bar before. Men and women of all shapes, sizes and ages sat across from each other, their chosen books placed in front of them on the delicate stands. Copies of everything from *Crazy Rich Asians* to *The Thing About Jane Spring* to *Normal People* filled the room. She couldn't believe how many people the event had amassed.

Lizzie and her two ex-*Bachelor* contestant friends – after recovering from their initial shock that the event was in fact exactly how Lizzie had described it – were taking a continuous stream of selfies. Bea watched Mia and Ruth, who were locked in a heated discussion. She also eyed Ramona (who Bea hadn't actually seen in person since moving to Melbourne so, by way of hello, shrieked, 'I'm sorry I'm such a slob!') holding hands with Sunday. Two waiters weaved through the crowd with trays of champagne and wine, and bread baskets and bowls of olives sat proudly in the corner, alongside Bea and Lizzie's fruit and cheese platters. Bea scanned the room for the hundredth time, squinting.

'I don't think he's coming, babe,' Sunday said from beside her, sidling up to Bea while Ramona helped herself to a piece of cheese.

'Who?' Bea replied, feigning indifference.

Sunday gave her a knowing, and only slightly pitying, look.

Breathing in deeply, Bea smoothed down her silk dress. 'Did you ever meet his grandma?' She had promised herself she wouldn't bring it up, but she couldn't help it.

'Whose? Dino's?' Sunday asked, confused.

'Yeah.'

'Only a couple of times. She passed about six months after I started working at The Nook.'

'What was she like?'

'I don't know really. She seemed friendly. I know she used to visit The Nook whenever she could. She and Dino would often grab a croissant and eat in the park.'

'Fawkner Park?' Bea held her breath.

'Yeah, that's the one.'

Of course.

'Why do you want to know all this anyway?' Sunday peered at Bea curiously.

'It's a long story.' Bea glanced at her watch. I should probably get the ball rolling.' Sunday gave Bea a final good-luck squeeze before linking hands with Ramona, who looked very happy with a face full of cheese

Bea marched to the front of the bar, stood on her tiptoes and said, in her loudest voice, 'Welcome everyone, to Next Chapter!'

Heads turned and silence fell over the room.

'Thank you so much for coming. Next Chapter started in a small alcove of a café and look how far we've come!' Brief applause resounded around the room. Bea continued. 'This whole event is about sharing stories. It's about giving us a chance to connect and to pass on our favourite tales.' She informed them of the rules before clearing her throat and picking up her phone. Holding it above her head, she said, 'May you find the book of your dreams and live happily ever after. On your marks, get set, recommend!' And set the timer on her phone.

Warm chatter filled the room as people began describing their favourite reads. The sound was the feeling of bare feet on cool grass, or a hearty, gratifying sneeze – her guests appeared utterly content.

Bea settled into her own chair and pulled out her book of choice from her bag – *Nine Perfect Strangers*. She let her hand linger in the bag, her fingers grazing the spine of the book she'd promised herself she would give to Dino tomorrow. *Meeting Oliver Bennett.*

It's time to move on, she reminded herself, again, as she placed *Nine Perfect Strangers* on the table in front of her.

A man wearing a crisp button-down shirt appeared opposite her and, after some initial introductions, Bea dived straight into detailing the masterpiece before her. Each time the timer sounded, she explained to fresh-eyed book lovers how hilarious yet poignant the book was. How she thought it was one of Liane Moriarty's best. And while all of this was true, each compliment seemed slightly hollow, because all she wanted to do was talk about *Meeting Oliver Bennett.* She wanted to hold the book high above her head like a trophy, and yell at the top of her lungs, 'If there's one book you need to read this year, it's this one. Not for the story, for the scribbles!'

But of course the only person she wanted to share it with wasn't here.

A few people seemed interested in Moriarty's latest and said they would come back to her. Others said contemporary fiction wasn't exactly their thing (and Bea tried, with all her might, not to judge). While waiting for her next suitor, Bea snuck in a quick read.

Then a man coughed in front of her. Bea slammed her book shut, embarrassed to have been caught mid-read, even among this brood of bookworms. She looked up, and froze.

Matt. Cassandra's Matt. Cassandra's Matt who had had his life turned upside down by Bea (and, well, the whole blushing-bride-sleeping-with-topless-waiter thing). But somehow the strangest thing wasn't that Matt was standing there before Bea with a slightly crazed smile plastered across his face. It was that his arm was linked protectively through the long, delicate arm of a blonde who was not Cassandra. She was short and wore heavy make-up and oversized black sunglasses despite the fact they were indoors. And it was night-time.

'Scarlett.' The blonde, who was definitely not Cassandra, extended her petite hand to shake Bea's. 'I've heard so much about you!'

'You have?' Bea stood to give Matt an awkward hug. 'Matt, what are you doing here?'

'I'm here as Scar's plus one. She heard about the event through your sister—'

'I was on season three of *The Bachelor* and your sister was somewhat of a mentor to me. It was actually Lizzie who came up with my entrance idea: arriving wearing boxing gloves and saying, "I knew you'd be a knockout!" Adrian went nuts for it, he was a massive boxing fan, even if I did get eliminated after the fifth round.'

'Scarlett!' Lizzie bellowed from across the room as she pranced towards them, arms open. 'You made it!' She pulled Scarlett into a hug.

Matt took the opportunity to lean around the pair of reunited friends. 'Bea, it really is good to see you.'

Taking a step to the side, Bea replied, 'Matt, you too. I can't quite believe you're here!'

'I know, things have been moving pretty quickly with Scar. We met on Tinder while she was holidaying in Margaret River and I guess the rest is history. Although if anybody asks, we are not a thing. She's waiting for the official reveal in next month's *Women's Weekly*. Hence the sunglasses. But for now, I'm happy.'

Bea nodded knowingly, even though she had no idea what 'official reveal' really meant. 'Well, you look happy, Matt. And I'm glad to see you happy. I can't tell you how much sleep I've missed agonising over how things went down at your wedding. Did you get my apology fruit basket, biscuit bouquet and "I have no tact, please forgive me?" balloons?'

Matt laughed. 'Yes, sorry I never thanked you. Between all the wedding gifts I had to return and then the lawyers, I just didn't get around to it.' He paused. 'I think it was all for the best, you know. A part of me always knew Cass and I weren't going to work out in the end. I mean, don't get me wrong, I miss her, but I think we outgrew each other in the end,' he paused. 'I only wish she had told me herself, let me keep what little remained of my dignity!' he said. 'Just don't beat yourself up about it all. You were a good friend. Too good a friend sometimes!'

'Thanks, Matt,' Bea said, and she meant it. She felt some of her guilt shifting. 'How is she doing, anyway?'

'Cass? According to her Facebook page she's at some lavish detox retreat right now.'

'Sounds like our Cass.' They stood there for a moment, bonded together by their shared pain, and renewed openness to change. 'I'm really glad you came, Matt. Now, why don't you two get yourselves a drink? Oh, and there's an epic cheese board too.'

Bea watched as Matt took his date's hand and led her over to the bar, smiling as he leaned down and planted a quick kiss on the nape of her neck. Without thinking, Bea put her own hand to the same spot on her neck, thinking how lovely it would be to be the beneficiary of such warm and casual intimacy.

'Mmm, totally.' Bea listened diligently as a gangly young man who couldn't have been more than seventeen years old enthusiastically described his own self-published memoir: *Orange is the New Brunette: One Boy's Life as a Ginger.*

'You might not realise this, but redheads are actually becoming extinct,' he said.

The buzzer went, signalling the next rotation. Before the boy left, he stuffed a glittery business card into Bea's hand and mumbled, 'Seb Mooney. We're reclaiming the word "ginger". Pass it on.'

Bea bent down to put the card in her handbag, which sat under the table between her moon boot and sneaker. There was only one more round of book sharing to go before the night would draw to a close. Having been an almost booked-out event, Bea was thrilled. The sight of gleaming faces and sound of exuberant chatter – over the magic of books! – filled Bea with an immense feeling of satisfaction. And, aside from the short-lived commotion that broke out after one of Lizzie's Bachie pals uploaded a photo to Instagram in which Lizzie had a double chin, everything seemed to have run smoothly. But of course, Bea couldn't ignore the flash of disappointment at Dino not turning up. Even though she knew it had been a long shot, Next Chapter had been conceived with him, launched with him and nurtured with him. And not having him here felt like sacrilege.

The final buzzer rang, and the room dissolved into frantic and excited talk as people began trading books and swapping numbers, promising more book chats to come. Bea stood to the side, absorbing the merriment.

Slowly, the room started to empty. Bea waved each of the guests goodbye, reminding them to follow the Next Chapter on Facebook for updates on the next event. After each guest had left, she joined the clean-up crew, brushing away the last of the crumbs and returning the empty glasses to the bar.

'You did good, girl,' Lizzie said. 'You even got me hooked on books! Look, I have acquired my very first psychological thriller.' She proudly held up a battered copy of *Call Me Evie*. 'I'm a changed woman!'

Bea congratulated her on her bravery.

'It's going to be okay, you know,' Lizzie said.

'I know,' Bea replied, sounding only slightly less sure of herself.

'No, you will be. You're wonderful, Bea, and wonderful things await you. You don't need him or his lukewarm lattes. You'll see.'

'Hey! Leave the coffees out of it.' Bea laughed, as she thought that maybe something wonderful had already happened.

67

The next day Bea woke early to the sound of Lizzie's less-than-ladylike snores. Groggy and disoriented, she turned to find her sister sprawled across the other side of her bed, tangled in the majority of the sheets and her own hair extensions. Vague memories of Lizzie storming into her bedroom in the middle of the night citing the injustice of having to sleep on the fold-out and jumping into bed with Bea, demanding that she spoon her, came to her mind.

Bea eased herself out of bed, careful not to wake Sleeping Beauty, grabbed a pair of jeans and her favourite orange cashmere jumper and slipped into the hallway, closing the door behind her. She swapped her pyjamas for the clothes and went to wash her face and brush her teeth while ordering her coffee on Uber Eats.

In the living room she spied the lonely copy of *Meeting Oliver Bennett* where she had left it the night before – sitting idly on her bookshelf between copies of *Educated* and *The Sunday Girl*. Retrieving it, she held it gently, running her thumb along its spine. This was it. Today she would finally give the book back to its rightful owner whether he wanted to see her or not. As soon as her coffee arrived, she would run downstairs, taste its caffeinated goodness, and then charge to The Nook, where she would leave *Meeting Oliver Bennett* for Dino to find. That was the plan, anyway.

It's time to move on.

Right on schedule, her phone beeped: Amit had arrived with her latte. Slipping on a pair of sneakers, Bea thrust the book into her bag, and threw open her front door.

The fresh morning air hit her cheeks and she inhaled, bracing herself for the journey to The Nook. She marched towards the front gate of her apartment block, where she always met her driver. Walking past the line of mailboxes, she rummaged through the various items in her bag – *What would Marie Kondo think?* – and then picked out her iPhone.

> 💬 Bea: Liz, I'm on my way to drop off *Meeting Oliver Bennett* for good. Feeling a bag of mixed emotions. Text me when you wake to make sure I've handed over the goods. I need you to keep me accountable.

'Your coffee,' Amit said as she reached the front gate.

Bea, eyes still on her phone, grunted her thanks and grabbed the latte. The delivery man cleared his throat.

She looked up.

Dino.

The cultivated confidence Bea had felt just moments before dissipated. There, standing opposite her, was pensive, broody, beautiful Dino. His stubble thick, his eyes lit with a sense of mischief. It was really him. After what had felt like a lifetime of pining after him, Bea couldn't believe that he was actually here, in the flesh. The tension in her shoulders melted just a fraction.

'Dino,' she said.

'Bea.'

'You're here.' She felt foolish for dreaming of this moment, because seeing him made her insides hurt, breaking her heart all over again.

'I'm here.'

'What are you doing here?'

'I came to deliver your coffee,' Dino said, his eye contact not faltering. A certain calmness seemed to have washed over him, making him almost unrecognisable to her.

Bea looked down at the latte she was holding, only now realising it wasn't in her usual paper cup, but instead in a plastic, reusable one. A KeepCup. Bea smiled.

'I can't believe you've been ordering them twice daily.' Dino laughed awkwardly.

Bea ignored the playful comment. 'I have something for you too,' she blurted, finding her words again, though not as eloquently as she would have liked. She extracted *Meeting Oliver Bennett* from her bag and held it in the space between them.

Dino appraised the book, confusion spreading across his features. 'Why are you giving this to me? Isn't this your thing with Zach?' he asked.

'No, it's my thing with you.'

Dino looked at her quizzically. 'Bea.' He shook his head, his patience seeming to dwindle. 'This isn't funny. I came here because—'

'Just take a look,' Bea interrupted.

Reluctantly, Dino took the book and opened it to a random page. Aside from the regular text, it was uncharacteristically lacking in scribbles. 'What am I meant to be looking for exactly? I thought you put your hunt to bed.'

'Try another page.'

Without breaking eye contact, he thumbed to another page, then glanced down at the book. He ran his eyes over the paper, doing a double take. 'The handwriting. Why does it look so familiar?'

Bea hung back, feeling a sense of closure as she watched Dino flip through the book, exploring each little jotting. She smiled as she saw Dino's stance visibly relax, his usually closed expression now exultant. She could see his mind ticking as he struggled to make sense of what he was seeing. Bea let him process, wanting him to come to the realisation on his own.

'It couldn't be,' he said. 'Oh my God, it's her.' He looked at Bea, his eyes damp. 'She's here. How did you – how on earth did you work this out? And how did I miss it?'

'You didn't know she did this sort of thing?'

'God, no. Don't you think I would have jumped at the chance to read these notes if I'd thought there could have been the smallest chance they were hers? I mean, I knew she was a reader, but this – this is a whole new level.' He ran his fingers absently along the markings in the book as if he was trying to absorb his grandmother's thoughts into his skin. 'She was always up to something, my grandmother.' He smiled fondly.

Bea felt relief wash over her. Even if it was too late for them, at least she could give him this parting gift.

'How the hell did you work it out?' Dino asked. His neck was flushed pink, the colour creeping up to his cheeks.

'It was no trip to Disneyland, I can tell you that!' Bea said, giddy with this newfound honesty. 'When I first found the book I fell in love with the beautiful, cursive words on the page.' Bea looked down at her copy of *Meeting Oliver Bennett*, and touched it lightly with her fingertips. She gazed up at the man standing in front of her, and wanted to touch him too. She quickly wrapped her free hand around the coffee cup to stop herself.

'I practically gallivanted around the whole of Melbourne on my search.' She filled him in on the last few weeks of searching. About how she tried to piece each clue together, the posters, her calamitous visit to Fawkner Park, about the Astor Theatre and ARK cafe, Sassafras – where she found *The Children Act*.

He shook his head. He looked relaxed, almost serene, a long way from the cool, collected, comfortably aloof man she so often saw.

'And yet, the final piece of the puzzle was staring me right in the eyes all along.' Bea paused, knowing that what she was about to say might push Dino over the edge, but also knowing she had no choice. 'Your notebook.'

'My notebook?'

'I read …' Bea began, before trailing off.

'What was that?' Dino said, eyebrow cocked.

'Your notebook. I may have read it just a little bit.'

Dino winced, holding his hands over his eyes.

'I'm sorry, I couldn't help myself. I wanted to try and understand you more. You're always so elusive. I needed to know what you were thinking,' Bea said, embarrassed. 'When I saw her dedication, her handwriting, I knew.'

Dino stared at her blankly. He opened his mouth, as if about to speak, then closed it again tightly. Bea and Dino stepped to the side of the pavement as two young children were shepherded expertly by their parents across the pedestrian crossing. The little girl turned towards Bea and Dino and yelled, unprompted, 'I love hummus!' before scurrying after her family.

Bea and Dino let out a strained laugh, the innocent moment thawing the ice.

'Bea, I can't quite believe all of this – how you managed to pull this off. I'm just so sorry I was so stubborn. I'm sorry I didn't let you tell me sooner.'

Bea was pleased. Not wanting to waste this opportunity, she powered on, needing Dino to see everything, to have a chance to communicate in some way with his beloved grandmother again. 'I highlighted some things I thought you might like to read,' she said, telling him to flip to the pages she had dogeared a week ago. He absorbed the notes on those pages one by one.

'I hope that's about me,' he whispered almost to himself, touching a line with his finger.

Bea leaned over to read the note.

how can something so small fill my whole world?

Bea urged him to keep reading, asking the questions to which she had so long desired an answer.

'And maybe this is about my mum?' he said, eyes red, pointing to the note that said, *i heard you love me.*

'My mum would never answer Gran's calls. She would always take it so personally. It was the only time Gran's tenacity seemed to falter, when her frustration with her daughter became too much to hide. I remember as a young boy begging her to be okay, telling her that it was just Mum's way, that she still loved us, in her own way.'

That's it! Bea thought.

'Do you know whose phone number this is?' She leaned over to grab the book and then flicked forward a few pages until she found it, the mobile number she had called so many times, written next to a single initial.

Dino read the number. 'E for Eva. My mum's. Near the end Gran was always jotting down numbers and addresses in strange places.'

'I called it so many times to get some answers, but she never picked up.'

'She's always going off the grid. It's always been that way,' he replied. Dino turned his attention back to the book and read the next page Bea had set aside for him.

After repeating the ritual again, opening to a new annotation and hypothesising over its meaning, Dino finally closed the book. 'In the last few years, she wasn't as sharp as she used to be. She became more reserved, less talkative. But maybe she was just too busy saving all the memories for after. Documenting it all,' Dino said. 'I can't tell you what this means to me, Bea.'

Bea smiled, feeling immensely grateful for having played a small role in giving Dino this posthumous gift. 'Well, I'll let you two get better acquainted. I'm glad I ran into you. Saved me the walk to The Nook.' She tried to sound lighthearted, even though the thought of the impending goodbye made her feet feel laden with bricks.

'Wait.' Dino held her wrist gently.

Bea looked at his hapless expression, noticing again how perfectly lovely he was.

'What is it?' Bea asked.

Dino's face crumpled. 'I guess, it's just that – did you read my note?'

Bea frowned. 'What note?' Then she remembered the KeepCup still in her hand. Tentatively, she took a closer look at it, turning it around in her hand. And, as she should have expected, there were words scrawled on it in black marker. *I may be a grumpy, closed-off, old man with terrible fashion sense – but I'm willing to be open for this – and from here on out.*

'Dino, what is this?'

'It's 25 words. I took your advice. I sure hope I win!'

Bea laughed. 'You wrote this for me? But wait, what was the competition for?'

Dino swallowed. 'In 25 words or less, why do you deserve for Bea to give you a second chance?'

Bea held her breath, sure she had misheard Dino.

'I've been stupid, Bea. I should've returned your calls. I definitely should've turned up to Next Chapter last night. And I shouldn't have left you there, at The Nook, that day. I know I said it was too late, but it's not, Bea. It's still not too late. Not for me anyway.' Dino's eyes pierced her. 'And, I hope, not for you either.'

Bea shook her head, hardly able to process this change of heart. She thought of what Alena had written – *little by little, you charge forward* – and she wondered whether this was a motto they could live by. Whether they could be brave and open-minded enough to try. *God, he was so lucky to have known her*, Bea mused, wishing she could ask Alena what they should do.

'Bea, it all happened so quickly, that night at the café with Zach. I was so not expecting you to say what you said. When you chose me after choosing Zach time and time again. I thought you said it because things weren't going smoothly with him. And I didn't want to play second fiddle to Zach, after everything he did. I didn't know how you could …' He let the thought trail off.

'Dino, you were never second to Zach. I mean, what Zach and I had, it was fun and exciting. But there was something missing. He chose me, and like usual, I went along with it. But that's not me anymore. I know what I want, and Dino – I do still choose you. I thought it was you who didn't choose me,' Bea said in a rush, her heart racing.

'How could you think that, Bea? While you ordered your coffee – didn't you see I chose you? While you were searching for that mystery writer, didn't you see I chose you then? While you were reading, didn't you know you were the one I chose? I chose you every day since the day I met you. I'm so sorry, Bea. Sorry that I didn't tell you sooner.'

'I'm sorry too, Dino. For making you ever think you weren't enough.'

Dino inched closer to Bea before letting his hand rest against her cheek. Bea practically melted into his palm. 'We're a couple of ships passing in the night, hey?'

Bea nodded, unsure how to respond. The sound of a bird's call and the hum of traffic flowed easily around them, the regular beat of the day powering on without regard for this moment.

They looked down at the worn edges of *Meeting Oliver Bennett*, a book that traced the landscape of different journeys, of different relationships. A book that had brought them back to something, or someone; that made them feel whole again. As if the pages had, or could, fill the cracks in their world with words of vulnerability and hope.

'I really do hope it's not too late for us, after all?' he said, taking her hands in his.

'I hope it isn't either,' Bea said.

'*In Search of Lost Time*.' Dino took a step forward.

Bea smiled, understanding. '*The Secret History*.' She pointed to her copy of *Meeting Oliver Bennett*.

'*You*.' Dino leaned forward, closer to Bea's face.

'*An Absolutely Remarkable Thing*.' Bea laughed.

'Do you remember my favourite collection of Roald Dahl's short stories?' Dino asked, eyebrow raised.

'*Kiss Kiss*?'

And they did.

68

Helloisthisyourbook

I know what you're thinking. What is that scrunched-up scrawl and what have you done with our beautiful, smart, obsessively neat Mystery Writer? Well, you caught me, ballpoint-pen handed! I've taken to writing my own annotations, writing my own destiny, so to speak, because I found her, guys. I actually found our Mystery Writer! I'm sorry for not updating you sooner, but I was too busy being *in love*. (I haven't said those three little words just yet, but I feel it. Plus, I know he wouldn't dare set foot in the land of Instagram – so this is a safe space!)

In other great news, Mystery Writer's grandson (yep, what are the chances?) and I will be hosting an event together in a couple of weeks: Write Your Own Chapter. More details to come soon. Be there or be … forever out of reach of your next great read!

Love you guys. Thanks for coming along for the ride.

Bea x

122 likes

Comments (32):

SillyMilly: You found Mystery Writer?!?!?!? Jesus! I've been waiting for this for months! Share a pic please!

RyanHotling: I'LL BE THERE! Can't wait to meet you in person!

StephenPrince: @NoOffenceBut, want to go to this event? Sounds cool.

NoOffenceBut: @StephenPrince, please stop asking me on dates via Instagram comments. It's weird.

NoOffenceBut: @StephenPrince, PS I've been 'accidentally' showing off my new sparkly diamond all day 😉

CuppaDino: I love you too.

While You Were Reading Book List

Little Women, Louisa May Alcott
The Breast, Philip Roth
Normal People, Sally Rooney
Vile Bodies, Evelyn Waugh
The Fault in Our Stars, John Green
The Huntress, Kate Quinn
The Picture of Dorian Gray, Oscar Wilde
The Jane Austen Book Club, Karen Joy Fowler
Doctor Zhivago, Boris Pasternak
Sense and Sensibility, Jane Austen
A Man Called Ove, Fredrik Backman
Alice's Adventures in Wonderland, Lewis Carroll
The Secret History, Donna Tartt
Tomorrow When the War Began, John Marsden
To Kill a Mockingbird, Harper Lee
The Art of Racing in the Rain, Garth Stein
All the Ways to be Smart, Davina Bell
Moby Dick, Herman Melville
Lost & Found, Brooke Davis
Everything I Never Told You, Celeste Ng
A Little Life, Hanya Yanagihara
The Great Gatsby, F. Scott Fitzgerald
Pachinko, Min Jin Lee
Harry: Life, Loss, and Love, Katie Nicholl
Textbook Romance, Zoë Foster and Hamish Blake
Pachinko, Min Jin Lee

The Dark Between Stars, Atticus
The Guernsey Literary and Potato Peel Pie Society, Mary
    Ann Shaffer and Annie Barrows
Forrest Gump, Winston Groom
Catch-22, Joseph Heller
The Murder at the Vicarage, Agatha Christie
The Moving Finger, Agatha Christie
A Caribbean Mystery, Agatha Christie
They Do It with Mirrors, Agatha Christie
Me Before You, Jojo Moyes
The Bronze Horseman, Paullina Simons
Kiss Kiss, Roald Dahl
Today Will Be Different, Maria Semple
Love Letters of the Great War, Mandy Kirkby
Say Hello, Carly Findlay
The Jade Lily, Kirsty Manning
The Mars Room, Rachel Kushner
The Hate Race, Maxine Beneba Clarke
I am Sasha, Anita Selzer
An Absolutely Remarkable Thing, Hank Green
Emma, Jane Austen
Great Expectations, Charles Dickens
Charlotte's Web, E.B. White
The Lion, the Witch and the Wardrobe, C.S. Lewis
A Little Princess, Frances Hodgson Burnett
Outlander, Diana Gabaldon
The Time Traveler's Wife, Audrey Niffenegger
Never Let Me Go, Kazuo Ishiguro
1984, George Orwell
The Very Hungry Caterpillar, Eric Carle
You Should Have Known, Jean Hanff Korelitz

The Amber Fury, Natalie Haynes
Hopeless, Colleen Hoover
Persuasion, Jane Austen
Hunger, Roxane Gay
The Life-Changing Magic of Not Giving a F**k, Sarah Knight
Don't Stop Now, Julie Halpern
Eleanor Oliphant is Completely Fine, Gail Honeyman
So Sad Today: Personal Essays, Melissa Broder
Harry Potter and the Deathly Hallows, J.K. Rowling
The Light Between Oceans, M.L. Stedman
The Invention of Wings, Sue Monk Kidd
The Nowhere Child, Christian White
The Little Prince, Antoine de Saint-Exupéry
The Dangers of Truffle Hunting, Sunni Overend
Everything, Everything, Nicola Yoon
To All the Boys I've Loved Before, Jenny Han
The Girl with Seven Names, Hyeonseo Lee
More Than Words, Jill Santopolo
The Children Act, Ian McEwan
Victoria & Abdul, Shrabani Basu
Gone with the Wind, Margaret Mitchell
Madeline, Ludwig Bemelmans
Crazy Rich Asians, Kevin Kwan
The Thing About Jane Spring, Sharon Krum
Nine Perfect Strangers, Liane Moriarty
Call Me Evie, J. P. Pomare
Educated, Tara Westover
The Sunday Girl, Pip Drysdale
In Search of Lost Time, Marcel Proust
You, Caroline Kepnes
An Absolutely Remarkable Thing, Hank Green

Book Club Questions

1. Bea decides to flee town after ruining her best friend's wedding to start afresh. Do you think her actions are cowardly or brave?

2. The inscriber of *Meeting Oliver Bennett* becomes a character in their own right, someone that Bea is drawn to and enamoured by. Have you ever fallen in love with a fictional character or someone you've never met?

3. Why is finding the Mystery Writer so important to Bea? Discuss.

4. Eventually Bea realises that her friendship with Cass is flawed. What makes friendship endure?

5. Bea's character develops immeasurably over the course of the story. How does she change? What are her strengths and weaknesses?

6. *While You Were Reading* has a delightful array of supporting characters. Discuss the roles of Martha, Ruth, Sunday and Philip.

7. How does her relationship with her larger than life sister Lizzie impact on Bea?

8. Initially Bea seems more comfortable with being an 'extra' rather than the 'leading lady' in her own life. Have you ever felt this way?

9. Do you think Zach's actions are unforgivable?

10. Still mourning the life she left behind in Perth, Bea forced herself to be so blindly brave in Melbourne that she toppled head-first into a fantasy based on the pages of *Meeting Oliver Bennett*. As such, she became consumed by an idealised conception of living and what love should look like. Discuss.

11. *While You Were Reading* reveals the power of books to draw people together. Does this concept resonate with you?

12. Discuss how the use of social media, in particular Instagram, drives and enriches the story.

Featured Bookstagram Accounts

When brainstorming ideas for *While You Were Reading*, we knew we had to include members of the unique, book obsessed, recommendation rich Bookstagram (readers of Instagram) community of which we are a part. Each of Bea's Instagram pictures is a real photo, taken by the owners of some of our favourite accounts. In order of appearance, these include:

Chapter 4: @Crimeofrhyme
Kim runs the photography account @crimeofrhyme on Instagram. She loves reading, agenda-less rainy days, and working hard when it counts. She owes everything to Jesus. Also, she's perpetually fueled by some sort of caffeine.

Chapter 6: @lifeandliterature
Tracey is a book lover, tea drinker, coffee addict. Most days she can be found indulging in all three.

Chapter 11: @Babblingbooks
Babbling Books is run by Melbourne local Tamsien West. She shares her love of books, travel and tea with her

followers around the world, and writes articles about life, reading, and bookish travel destinations on her blog.

Chapter 29: @Lillytales
Kate Lloyd is a Melbourne-based blogger and a queer, feminist bibliophile. Kate blogs as 'Lillytales' on Instagram, YouTube, Twitter and on her blog where she posts book reviews, as well as musings on life, food, fashion, travel and more.

Chapter 35: @Readwithkatie
Katie is a self-proclaimed bibliophile, and when she isn't reading she can be found capturing photos, creating content and perusing new online ventures. Residing in Melbourne she lives with a lifetime collection of books, a pet cat and a dog.

Chapter 38: @Crazybooklady_
Michaela is a Bookstagrammer based in Adelaide, South Australia who will happily talk books to anyone who will stand still long enough. Her perfect bookish situation involves a great read, a large coffee and brunch that preferably includes halloumi.

Chapter 46: @ab_reads
Abbie is a voracious bookworm from the North East of England passionate about reading as widely and as much as possible.

Chapter 48: @sweptawaybybooks
Alyssa is a twenty something lifelong reader who fulfilled her dreams of moving to her favourite literary setting, the U.K. She'll read anything that interests her but has a soft spot for a happily ever after.

Chapter 60: @booksontherail
This is Ali and Michelle's Instagram page and social initiative. Aussie Book Ninjas spreading a love of reading on a train, tram or bus near you. Books are there to be discovered, read and returned for the next unsuspecting commuter to find! A part of the wider @booksonthemove-global community.

Chapter 68: @Halfdesertedstreets
Danielle Carey lives in south east Queensland, where she teaches writing and English lit and tries to keep her bookshelves from gaining sentience and taking over her entire house. She blogs at deecarey.com

There are so many more accounts who we love to follow and get book advice and #shelfie envy from. For a full list, head to our Instagram accounts @booksontherail and @aliandmichelle, to see who we follow.

Acknowledgements

While You Were Reading could never have come to be without the incredible team at Simon & Schuster Australia. Your support, commitment and willingness to take a chance on two book-lovers, have been outstanding. A particularly special thanks to Publisher Bert Ivers, Publishing Director Fiona Henderson, Publicity Director Anna O'Grady, Editor Kylie Mason, Proofreader Vanessa Lanaway, Project Editor Michelle Swainson, Publicist Rachael Versace, and Managing Director Dan Ruffino.

Bert, you are the best editor that ever was and ever will be. Thank you for being so warm and for telling us gently when to kill our darlings. Anna, you started this all! That coffee will forever be in our hearts and so will you. Fiona, your emails are the ones we like opening the most. Thank you for your championing and for being the bearer of such exciting news about international (and film) deals! Kylie, your meticulous editing made our book what it is today, and we often find ourselves saying 'What would Kylie say?'

There are so many more kind souls who have helped us so generously along the way. To our first reader and wise mentor, Sharon Krum – your early morning and late night phone calls, edits and emails helped us bring Bea's story to life (and kept us sane). To Henry Kalus, our good-humoured and wise lawyer and confidante, thank you for your enthusiasm and sage advice. To our featured 'Bookstagrammers', thank you for your book recommendations, for embracing this project and for sprinkling your creative spark throughout the pages of this novel. To Josh Appelboom and Alicia Kalus, our very own, real life Dinos, thank you for your guidance and for transforming our sad attempts at writing poetry into lyrical gems! And, of course, to our Super Best Friends, for bringing so much joy into our worlds.

A gigantic, train-shaped thank you must also go out to our Book Ninjas. You are the best of the best – we are so lucky to have you out there, on the trains, trams and buses, sharing a love of reading!

And finally, to all the people who read our first book, *The Book Ninja*, all over the world. To those who discussed it in book clubs, bought it from bookstores, borrowed it from libraries, planted it on train seats and rated it on Goodreads. You have all made our dreams come true and we hope you like *While You Were Reading* just as much.

Ali's acknowledgements

Thank you to everyone who believed in me – even when I did not!

Starting with the love of my life, Alex. My biggest cheerleader. I don't know what I would do without your constant updates and alerts telling me when *The Book Ninja* receives a positive review on Goodreads, is featured in Italian *Vogue* or has a good photo on Instagram. I need you like Bea needs coffee. Thank you for being you.

To my parents, Cindy and John. Thank you for encouraging me to follow my dreams and be a writer. Thanks for buying more copies of *The Book Ninja* than you need, and for making sure you could always visibly see it in every bookstore you visited. Mum, thanks also for being my own personal editor and number one cheerleader (equal first with Alex).

To the rest of my wonderful family. My brother Josh, sister Emma, grandparents Harry, Jacqueline, Cilla, Paul and golden retriever, Lulu, thank you for your ongoing love and encouragement.

And finally, to the lady I wrote this book with. Remember that time you had an intruder in your house at 3am and I woke up at the exact same time and texted you because I telepathically sensed that you were in danger? That's what this whole experience has been like. Thank you for successfully transforming into one person with me. For all the laughs, for absolutely zero fights and for sensing when I need a character development, storyline change or just a cup of tea – even before I know myself. You're the Cat to my Frankie and I love you.

Michelle's acknowledgements

To my parents, Susie and Allan, for your support, enthusiasm and PR efforts. Your generosity and love are boundless, and I am so proud to be your daughter.

My sweet Lici, you may be my little sister, but there is nobody I look up to more! You are wise, just, witty, deeply intelligent, and the greatest source of joy and inspiration.

Sarah and Iwan, for your love, encouragement and, most importantly, for creating Oliver, our little muse! It's quite true, 'once you meet Oliver Bennett, nothing will ever be the same again'.

To my fiancé Dave, for turning my world into one big romantic comedy! You are endlessly kind, charming, wise, patient and supportive, and I am all the better for loving you.

To Ali, the most talented writer, business partner, social media aficionado and friend a gal could ever hope for! Your wit, creative spark, meticulous plotting and drive never cease to amaze me. You are the most generous, kind, hilarious lady I know, and manage to transform even our darkest writing days into one full of light and laughter (and Pad Thai)! You are such a dream to work and live life with.